ALONG CAME JONES

"Ms. Windsor's latest novel is peppered with gun-toting mobsters, a flock of well-meaning church members, and full of love—between Deanna and Shepard, as well as God's forgiving love. Their tale of triumph over heartache and evil make this one romance that will not be forgotten. *Along Came Jones* will leave readers spellbound and wanting more." —*BRIDGES* Magazine

"Linda Windsor has done it again. In *Along Came Jones,* Linda has crafted a wonderful novel that takes you on a journey out West, transporting you into its pages and carrying you along on a journey of love and adventure. *Along Came Jones* is a story you don't want to miss."—CHERYL WOLVERTON, author of *In Search of a Hero*

"Another great romantic comedy from Linda Windsor! *Along Came Jones* is full of sweet romance and humorous situations, with a touch of suspense that makes this a delightful read."—NANCY FARRIER, coauthor of the American Dream anthology

IT HAD TO BE YOU

"Windsor's style is fresh and pleasing."—PUBLISHERS WEEKLY

"Linda Windsor never fails to deliver an insightful, wonderfully funny story!" —LORI COPELAND, bestselling author of *The Island of Heavenly Daze*

"Ms. Windsor has outdone herself with *It Had to Be You,* sure to be one of the best comedic romances this season and finding itself on many a keeper shelf."—THE BEST REVIEWS

"Linda Windsor is a real find. Read one of her books and you're hooked! Her writing is an inspiration in itself."—THE BELLES AND BEAUX OF ROMANCE

"With likeable characters, comical interactions, and a story that hits you squarely in the heart, this delightful book is a winner." —KAREN BALL, author of *Wilderness* and *Three Weddings and a Giggle*

DEIRDRE

"Linda Windsor weaves this ancient Saxon and Irish love story much like the intricate tapestries of the same period. The characters are vibrant, her imagery and use of detail are transfixing, and the author's skill at combining these elements is exceptional."—CROSSHOME.COM

"Windsor provides a rollicking historical adventure fraught with intrigue and romance in a worthy addition to the series and to all collections."— LIBRARY JOURNAL

"This is a beautiful and exciting story of how wonderfully the Lord uses the imperfect to bring about His perfect and everlasting love."—READER TO READER

RIONA

"Linda Windsor deftly weaves a tapestry of Irish myth and legend with the glory of knowing Christ, creating a masterpiece of medieval fiction. *Riona* is more than a novel, it's an experience—a journey to a faraway time and place where honor and faith are lived out amid the clamor of swords. A glorious read!" LIZ CURTIS HIGGS, bestselling author of *Thorn in My Heart*

"With a lyrical voice worthy of the Isle of Erin, Linda Windsor's Riona is a wonderful novel, peopled with memorable characters who will lay claim to your heart. I believe I could see the green hills and feel the kiss of mist upon my cheeks with every page I read." ROBIN LEE HATCHER, Christy Award-winning author of *Firstborn*

MAIRE

"Linda Windsor's talent for creating a faraway land and time is flawless."— ROMANTIC TIMES magazine

"*Maire* has a host of exceedingly wonderful characters who support the exceptional story line—it shows the love and strength that comes from God for us to meet life's many challenges if we only accept His love. Excellent reading and definitely a keeper."—RENDEZVOUS ROMANCE REVIEWS

"This enthralling tale reveals God's miraculous power at work and how His love conquers all....A definite page-turner."—INSPIRATIONAL ROMANCE PAGE

Along Came Jones

LINDA WINDSOR

Multnomah®Publishers *Sisters, Oregon*

ALONG CAME JONES
published by Multnomah Publishers, Inc.

© 2003 by Windsor Enterprises, Inc.

Published in association with the literary agency of
Ethan Ellenberg Agency.

International Standard Book Number: 1-59052-032-7

Cover image by Getty Images
Image of old town by Corbis/Buddy Mays
Image of modern city by PhotoSpin

Unless otherwise indicated, Scripture quotations are from:
The Holy Bible, New King James Version (NKJV) © 1984
by Thomas Nelson, Inc.
Other Scripture quotations are from: *The Holy Bible,*
King James Version (KJV)

Multnomah is a trademark of Multnomah Publishers, Inc., and is registered in the U.S. Patent and Trademark Office.
The colophon is a trademark of Multnomah Publishers, Inc.

Printed in the United States of America

For information:
MULTNOMAH PUBLISHERS, INC.
Post Office Box 1720, Sisters, Oregon 97759

Library of Congress Cataloging-in-Publication Data
Windsor, Linda.
  Along came Jones / by Linda Windsor.
     p. cm.
  ISBN 1-59052-032-7 (pbk.)
  I. Title.
PS3573.I519 A46 2003
813'.54--dc21   2002154296

03 04 05 06 07 08 09 10 — 10 9 8 7 6 5 4 3 2 1

To my husband, Jim, and my mom,
whose help, encouragement, faith, and humble witness
are my earthly inspiration and a testament of God's
unconditional love and understanding.

NOVELS BY LINDA WINDSOR
Along Came Jones
It Had to Be You
Not Exactly Eden
Hi Honey, I'm Home

THE FIRES OF GLEANNMARA SERIES
Maire
Riona
Deirdre

One

"Easy, ma'am! Are you all right?"

Someone squeezed Deanna's shoulder, drawing her from the numb shock that suspended her somewhere between awareness and unconsciousness. *What had happened?* The question floated in her mind, calling her dazed senses into a defensive formation until she knew if the warm hand thawing the ice encasing her awareness belonged to a rescuer or a captor.

One minute she was making good time down this road to nowhere, and the next—this. Through the blur of confusion, she made out a ditch bank beyond the crinkled hood of her car. A sharp pain reported in from the side of her head. Her car had careened off the road, but why? Had she blacked out?

A large face edged into her line of vision. Deanna squinted through the glare on the dirt-spattered windshield to see a one-eyed horse staring back at her. Wait, it was white splotched with a black patch obscuring the *missing* eye. She closed her eyes, trying to separate whimsy from reality.

A memory clip of a horse dashing across the road in front of her played for her. She hadn't blacked out! The beast bolted across the road like a streak of fire against the Big Sky landscape. Not the ordinary animal staring at her through her windshield, but a magnificent red with a golden mane and tail—truly worthy of any silver screen hero.

Or were they *both* hallucinations? Had the same people who'd killed her boss caught up with her as well? Of late, reality and nightmare were impossible to separate. Deanna took a deep breath, fighting a wave of dizziness, and peeked again through the windshield. Old One Eye was still there, but dare she trust her senses yet? It had been three days since she'd had a decent meal. Maybe she had blacked out and was still dreaming. Maybe…

"Ma'am, where are you hurt?" The voice aggravated her aching head, invading her surreal world.

Deanna groaned. She hurt, and pain had no business in this hallucination…if indeed that's what it was. And hallucinations didn't talk either. She turned her head in the direction of an alarmed masculine voice. Like shaken snow in a glass dome, her senses began to settle. She wasn't alone with a one-eyed horse. There was a man as well—or a man and a half. Gradually the images of her faceless companion merged into one against the blue sky beyond him.

Straight from one of those backwoods horror films was a character as unsettling in appearance as her circumstances—scruffy beard, dusty leather and denim, even his horse was patched. Whatever happened to those clean-cut, pistol-wielding heroes in the Westerns she'd watched with her dad as a child in Brooklyn? That was what she needed now, not some backwoods nature freak in a beat-up Stetson—or someone even worse. She noted the lethal-looking knife sheathed on his thigh. Serial killer came to mind.

Get a grip, girl. You've watched one too many horror films.

"Ma'am?" Although he seemed to be a polite serial killer. The concern etched on his shaded forehead by two arched brows seemed genuine. But were those rusty-looking stains on his worn jeans and shirt blood?

Deanna's voice squeaked through the noose of anxiety constricting her throat. "I…I'm fine."

This was not what she'd come west to find. But then, nothing in the seemingly green pastures of Montana's Big Sky country had been what a city born marketing exec once dreamed of from her office. Certainly not the smooth-talking weasel in an Armani suit and flawlessly shaped Stetson who'd lured her like a sheep to the slaughter from Manhattan to his Great Falls business with promises of advancement mixed with romantic innuendo. But if C. R. Majors had been a weasel, what kind of homegrown varmint had she stumbled across now?

"Can you move?"

Deanna shook her head. She wasn't moving anywhere with him. She glanced beyond the man to where his ink-blotched horse nuzzled him from behind. Hanging from a sling on its saddle was a gun, a high-powered looking thing that... She closed her eyes to still the alarm unsettling the tentative balance in her stomach. Was he one of those gun-hoarding militia fanatics with six wives and three dozen children? Where was the ATF when a gal needed it?

At the touch of his fingers over her eyelids, Deanna bolted toward the passenger side of her small car, but her seat belt cut off her startled gasp.

"Hey, take it easy. I'm not gonna hurt you. I thought you'd passed out on me."

"Not a chance." Deanna summoned what reserve she had left and settled in the driver's seat, loosening the nylon garrote. "I'm okay, just a little stunned. You wouldn't have a cell phone, would you?"

He grinned, nodding toward his horse. "Nope, Patch here didn't come equipped with one."

Duh. Why would a guy whose transportation was a horse have a cell phone? At least he had all his teeth. And on closer look, his eyes twinkled beneath the dusty brown bush of his brow. The effect was disarming. Serial killers didn't have twinkling eyes, did they? Criminals leaned toward those wild, elevator-doesn't-go-all-the-way-to-the-top eyes. And their hair didn't lie in rakish curls around their collars.

"I'd feel a whole lot better," he said, taking advantage of her confusion and tilting her face toward him for further study, "if you'd just step out of the car. I'd like to see you stand on your own. Think you can get out? Or do you want me to unload my guns first?"

"Like in more-than-that-one-hanging-on-the-saddle guns?" she quipped before she could catch herself. The same wry wit and ready tongue that had propelled her up the corporate ladder could be a curse on occasion.

To Deanna's embarrassment, the cowboy-extremist-serial killer, or just plain ordinary Joe, roared with laughter. Her blood rushed warm and ebbed cold at the same time as he drew a pistol from beneath his vest and ejected the cartridge. With a patronizing smirk surrounded by a week's worth of stubble, he laid it on the hood of her car. White teeth flashing as he untied the leather thong of his hunting knife, he put her in mind of a young Clint Eastwood—before a bath, shave, and a much needed curbing of his swagger.

Galled into action, Deanna swung her legs around to get out. Bloodstains or not, she hadn't gotten where she was—or rather, where she'd been until three days ago—by cowering. He might strangle her, or heaven knew what, but she was not going to be laughed at. Just short of her feet reaching the ground, she was jerked back into her seat by the belt she'd forgotten in her addled state.

"It helps to unfasten this," her rescuer drawled, reaching in and releasing the restraint with annoying amusement.

Deanna endured his ministration, her abdominal muscles contracting in further retreat as the back of his work-roughened fingers pricked warm against the thin silk of her blouse. As he helped her out of the vehicle, whatever bravado she'd accumulated in her once bright career had abandoned her like everything else she once depended upon.

Even if this man had been clad in a police uniform, she had every right to be rattled. She'd just been run off the road by a runaway horse and wrecked her car in a ditch. The crumpled, blue hood of the import looked as if it had taken a giant bite out of the dirt bank that had stopped it. The fact that she still owed money on the indulgence rolled her stomach.

"This is all I need," she muttered through clenched teeth to hold back an overwhelming rise of despair. Instead, it struck her across the back of the knees, buckling them beneath her weight.

"Whoa there!"

Before she knew it, her companion swept her off her feet and eased her back against the car seat with surprising gentleness. He examined her head. "Looks like you took a nasty bump."

"So much for the air bag." As far as Deanna could tell, it was still neatly packed in the steering wheel. "If there really is one in—"

"Just relax," her rescuer said as she drew away from his tender touch. "I'm unarmed and harmless."

The muscles in his sun-bronzed forearm contradicted his claim, but Deanna ached too much to protest his tender attention to her aching head. Instead, she leaned against the leather headrest while the man wiped her brow with a red bandana he pulled from his hat.

"Just a little cut on that lump there," he murmured, all business as he tied it over the lump swelling just within her hairline. The bandana was damp from having served as a sweatband, yet she was surprised to feel nothing of her initial revulsion.

She'd reached her limit. Nothing else could faze her, not after what she'd been through. Dare she hope that her luck, if she could call it that, was changing?

"It's bleeding a little." He backed away to inspect his handiwork. "You got a name, ma'am?"

Okay, she might hope, but she wouldn't trust.

"Manetti," Deanna ventured. "Deanna Manetti." At least she still knew who she was, much as she'd like to forget it.

"Can you tell me what happened, Miss Manetti?"

The questions were getting harder already. Her head throbbed worse, now that the man had pointed out the swelling. She felt as though she were about to lose her brunch, a mini-candy bar devoured hours earlier.

"A horse raced out in front of me and ran me off the road. A red horse." Fourteen years since she got her driver's license in New York City and not once had she had an accident. Instead, she'd traveled across the United States to have a run-in with a horse. She almost laughed at the absurdity, but her throat merely squeaked.

"How about some water? I have some in my canteen."

Of course a cowboy would have a canteen, she mused, daring to nod in cautious assent. If he even was a cowboy. She was so tired and hungry that she'd grown slaphappy.

Her companion approached the spotted horse, removed a canteen from its saddle, and returned to her with long booted strides. In a wink, he uncapped it and handed it to her.

Deanna didn't go for the idea of drinking after anyone, but under the dire circumstance, the water was like nectar from the gods…and cold too! Upon closer examination, she discovered the container was insulated. Thermoses had gone west, if not cell phones.

"Best swish that about in your mouth and spit it out. Then swallow the next sip."

"You a dentist too?" Her paltry attempt at humor made her wince. She didn't understand the reasoning behind his odd request, but he was in his element—dirt, rocks, smelly horses, and leather. She was out of hers—diesel smut, skyscrapers, swerving taxis, and tailored executive fashion.

"No, but I've been up all night with a horse that took too much sand. Gives 'em a bellyache."

Uncertain as to whether or not he was pulling her leg, Deanna followed his instructions. *When in Rome...* She swished and spit as delicately as possible. To her horror, it landed on his dusty boots.

"I'm sorry!"

"S'okay. It takes practice." He scuffed them in the dirt, more intent on her than her poor aim.

Never in her life had she expectorated in front of anyone. Along with the rule about not drinking after others, her mother had drilled that lesson into her head as well. Toothbrush time at the bathroom sink summed up Deanna's entire experience with spittle aim.

What she wouldn't give to go back to those days, but they were gone. Her parents had died in a traffic accident shortly after her high school graduation. Deanna sold their modest apartment in the city when she made the big move to Montana. After all, she'd had no reason to stay, no relatives to speak of, and no one special in her life.

"What brings you to Buffalo Butte, Miss Manetti?"

Ambition was on the tip of her tongue. *Romance* flashed through her mind. That was why she'd left the city and come west. C. R. embodied both, but all he'd led her to was disaster. And now she was in no-woman's land.

"Where did you say I was?"

"Actually Buffalo Butte's the nearest town. You're on Hopewell, my ranch," he said. "You've been on it for the last four miles, since you ran out of paved road."

"I made a wrong turn." It was true. She never should have turned west on the interstate from New York, and she certainly didn't know where she'd turned in these Montana hills. She was lost. Worse, she was glad of it. If she didn't know where she was, no one else did either.

"Where were you headed?"

"Do you ever run out of questions?"

"Got a whole hat full," her rescuer shot back with a grin. It was one of those wide, lazy grins his kind had invented.

"Have you a name in it as well?"

He shoved the dusty brim off his face in a cordial manner. "Shepard Jones, but most folks call me Shep."

Shepard. Heaven knew she needed one about now.

"I was just sightseeing," she lied, before adding an element of truth to salve her guilt. "Guess I made a wrong turn. I didn't know this was private property." And technically, she had been seeing sights, all unfamiliar.

"Was it a sorrel...the horse that caused this?" Shep pointed to her buckled hood.

"No, it was red."

"Sorrel is red, Slick." At Deanna's astonished expression, he explained the nickname away. "I saw those New York license plates and figured you to be a city slicker."

"There *are* horses in New York," she reminded him, bristling at his condescension. "Even in the city."

"Wherever they are, red ones are still sorrel."

Okay, he was teasing her, but how could a girl complain when it was done with a grin, bracketed by lines that betrayed a long-time sense of humor? "So you know the horse?" she returned with a wry tip of her lips. For the first time, Deanna felt as though the uncomfortable shoe had been switched to Shepard Jones's foot.

He looked away for a moment and nodded. "'Fraid so. He's one of mine." Pulling his hat down lower, as if shifting down to business, he returned his attention to her. "Looks like I owe you. Think you can walk now?"

"Walk? Walk where?" Deanna stalled, not the least bit certain she could. Besides, she felt as if her head might fall off if she stood again.

Instead of answering, Shep pulled her to her feet with a firm grip on her upper arms. This time, it was Deanna who shouted, "Whoa!" as she grasped the front of his shirt to keep from falling.

In an instant, his long arms were under her, lifting her into the air with little effort. She fell hard against his chest with a gasp, still clinging to the loose-fitting front of the garment as if to choke him.

"What do you think you're doing?"

"Why, rescuing you. Isn't that what we cowboys do?"

So he really was a cowboy...and a bit of a smart aleck. She

refrained from complaining that he was three days too late to be of any real help to her. This little fender bender was the least of her worries. Just as she started to relax, Deanna realized they were approaching the spotted horse, which had moved a short distance away and stood patiently, awaiting its master.

"You've *got* to be kidding!" Her eyes widened with dubious alarm. "I...I can't *ride.*"

Shep's chuckle shook her. "You won't have to. All you have to do is sit still and look pretty in the saddle. *I'll* do the riding."

Before she could say another word, he placed her in the worn saddle as easily as a carnival man puts a child upon a painted carousel steed. She wasn't overweight by any means, but her five-foot-eight height made her self-conscious around most men. Now that she'd seen him stand up full height, she realized that even in heels, she wouldn't intimidate this guy. With that rumpled hat of his, he looked to be at least six-six. Most of it was man rather than topper. He wasn't the slump-shouldered Neanderthal she'd first taken him for, but strapping Montana prime.

"If you swing your leg over and ride astride, you'll be more secure, not to mention comfortable."

Glad that she wore linen-flax trousers instead of a skirt, Deanna complied. The horse acted as if it had women slung over its back every day, even ones who were so stiff with apprehension that they grazed its ears with a heel while trying to mount.

"Take it easy; I gotcha." His grasp on the belt of her slacks was as unrelenting as her fear that the animal might dash off with her.

"So does he," she managed in a shaky voice. Without taking her eye off the horse's now laid-back ears, she sought the stirrups with the toes of her kiltied pumps.

"He is a *she,* and I'll be needing that." Shep moved her left foot forward, just as she seated it in the stirrup. "Her name's Patch, for obvious reasons."

"Why not Spot?" Certain the saddle would be crowded, Deanna eased toward the pommel as her companion slipped his boot into the stirrup to swing up behind her, settling on the horse's back to the rear of the saddle. Reaching to either side of her, he picked up the reins from where they rested on the horse's neck. At the soft click of his tongue, Patch turned toward the blazing bright horizon.

"Oh, my purse." The glaring spectacle assaulted her eyes. "And my sunglasses. They may have fallen on the floor during the accident."

Shep reined the horse in and slid off its back without the formality of stirrups.

Frozen at the idea of being abandoned on what seemed to be a ton of snorting horseflesh, Deanna watched statue-still as he rummaged through the car and found her things. Her purse was intact, but the glasses were snapped in half at the bridge. He handed her the first and tossed away the latter. Then, with a running start, he vaulted up on Patch's back, Indian fashion.

The black and white horse took a step forward and Deanna's derisive, "Show off," erupted on a note of alarm.

"Easy, gal...*both* of you," he consoled in an easy drawl she'd heard movie cowpokes gentle animals with.

It worked on the horse, but Patch was in her element. Deanna wasn't.

She started again when her companion slapped his hat down on her head, shading her eyes from the sun. "Thanks," she murmured, ashamed of her skittishness. But then, how would Shep fare on the subway?

Probably just fine. He struck her as the sort of man who, while comfortable in the saddle, could take the city in stride. She sucked in a breath as he slipped his arm snugly about her waist while taking up the reins with his free hand.

"Ready, Slick?"

Ready? That was a joke. "Yes, but where are we going?"

"Home. A good meal and a bath will make a world of difference in how you feel."

And how you smell, she thought, keeping her opinion to herself. Rakish and disheveled was one thing, but Shepard Jones's horse smelled better than he did.

"In fact, I'm looking forward to both. A week in the high country'll make a man offend his own nose."

"I hadn't noticed," she lied politely, so as not to wind up abandoned in the wild by offending her rescuer. Like she could miss that mingle of horse, sweat, and leather. Stranger still, it wasn't entirely offensive but rather made her aware of his raw masculinity.

"Well, you're still dazed." He urged the horse forward with his knees.

Deanna's fingers tightened on her purse. She noticed the stains on his knees, her wariness assuaged by his easygoing charm returning. Cowboy or not, this was a total stranger who could be taking her anywhere for any reason.

"Why not take me into town?"

"Because, Slick, town is an hour's ride by car. On four feet, it's a half day's ride."

"So take me in your Jeep."

She felt his arm relax against her. "If that's what you want," he said, confirming her guess that he owned such a vehicle. It fit his image. "We can report this to the authorities. My insurance will pay for it, of course, but I can tell you, it'll take a while to order parts for that fancy rig of yours."

Deanna felt the blood leave her face. Report the accident to the authorities? But then she'd be right back where she started—in a brimming kettle of trouble that was not of her own making.

What had she done to deserve this? It wasn't as if she'd been a bad person since she stopped going to her parents' church. She'd just been busy building a career in marketing.

"If you'd like to keep this off the record, for the sake of my insurance rates as well as your own, I happen to know a good mechanic who might be able to get you back on the road with used parts and a little bodywork. He's a shade-tree genius."

"A what?" The brush of an unshaven cheek against her ear as Shep leaned forward to see her face snatched her out of her reflection.

There was that grin again. This close, it was toe-curling and smelled of mildly redeeming spearmint. Was this guy a scruffy angel or yet another trap waiting to spring on her?

"I said I have a friend who might be able to get your car back on the road. I'll pay him and put you up until he's done. That way nobody needs to be called, and my premium will remain affordable."

Nobody needs to be called. Deanna sighed. "That's fine with me," she heard herself saying, even as anxiety began to demand to know if she'd lost her mind, agreeing to stay overnight with a complete stranger.

But then, what was she going to do with no money, no car, and more important, no food? She tried hard to concentrate on her predicament rather than acknowledge the uncomfortable jarring between her temples with each step the horse took.

So far, Shepard Jones had been as gallant, if not as polished, as his movie counterparts. And he was a rancher. Somehow, she didn't think serial killers lived double lives as Montana ranchers who worried about insurance rates. Maybe his name was no coincidence. Maybe God had listened to her plea for help and sent a shepherd—even though it had been a long time since she'd been her parents' version of P.C.—practicing Christian. Politically correct had been more her lifestyle since their deaths. Was this guy the kind of shepherd she needed, or God's way of getting even for her neglect?

Deanna clenched her purse against the pommel of the saddle as if her life depended on them both. The pepper spray in the purse gave her small comfort. For now, she had a place to stay, which was more than she'd had before she wound up in the gully by the side of the dirt road. There was nothing left to do but ride off into the sunset with her rumpled Montana cowboy and trust—not him but God.

Even if he looked like a movie star when he was freshly scrubbed and in clean clothes, she'd keep her eyes wide open. Deanna had been taken in by a man just once, but it was one time too many. This time she intended to live up to her new nickname—*Slick*.

Two

Hopewell was an odd name for the ramshackle cluster of buildings bleaching in the sun. Hope*less* was more like it. Not that the word *ranch* applied either, Deanna thought, stiffening against Shep's wiry wall of muscle at her back. It looked more like a—

"It's a ghost town," he informed her, as if he'd read her thoughts. "But don't worry. I've never seen one ghost."

"That's very reassuring." Her situation had gone from desperate to bizarre. It was either wisecrack or cry at this point. "Just tell me you're not a serial killer."

Shep laughed behind her. "I'm not a serial killer. Just a poor rancher trying to get a small spread started."

An hour's ride from the nearest town, he'd said, and she didn't see a Jeep. Deanna opted to pretend that she was still back in her car and was out of her head, dreaming all this. After what she'd been through to date, this wasn't a large leap at all. She'd just nightmare-hopped from cops and robbers to back at the ranch, er, ghost town.

God, I know I've been a stranger, but please, I need help. Mama said You'd never give a person more than she could stand, and, Lord,…I can't take much more.

"Don't worry; you won't have to bathe in a barrel. The main house is beyond the livery stable at the end of the street, complete with indoor plumbing." Shep pointed to a thin line of poles strung from the opposite direction with a couple of heavy-duty overhead wires. "And we've got electricity…most of the time."

Somehow the conditional assurance of electricity didn't strike Deanna as a heavenly response to her prayer. But she hadn't prayed in so long, maybe God wasn't listening. Ignoring a sense of despair wedging itself between hope and desperation, she drew on the independent reserve that had moved her up the corporate ladder. *Think for yourself, Deanna.* She took in her rustic surroundings with a wary eye.

Push come to shove, she could follow the poles back to civilization like the cowboys always followed a railroad or river. She hadn't been raised in the city for nothing. She was a survivor. Still, try as she might, Deanna had yet to see the home the wires connected to because of the tall high-pitched roof of the last building on the street. Beyond it was an oasis of treetops and a working windmill. At least the pinwheel part moved, catching a slow breeze that eluded her.

"My grandparents modernized the mayor's house before I was born. Then my Uncle Dan took it over. Since I'm his only living relative, he left the whole kit and caboodle to me." Shep guided Patch down the knoll toward the small opening of what appeared to be a narrow main street.

The gentle timbre of his voice failed to ease her growing alarm. She held back the "Lucky you" that came to mind sooner than annoy the stranger carrying her into a remote ghost town where only God knew what fate awaited her. There weren't more than a dozen buildings. According to some of the faded signs still left above some of the doors, there was—or had been—a boardinghouse, a dry goods, and, of course, a saloon, with swinging doors still intact.

Eager to get home, Patch broke into a teeth- and head-jarring trot, which Shep put an abrupt end to. "Treat the lady nice and I'll give you an extra measure of feed," he cajoled the animal.

Ahead of them through the cluster of shade trees was a white clapboard house with once red, now faded, trim straight from a

Better Homes and Gardens nightmare edition. The paint was cracked and peeled. The remaining screens were buckled and patched. Well, it was in better shape than the rest of the town. Besides, who knew? Fifty years ago, it may have gleamed fresh from its modernization, but it was in dire need of another facelift now. Still, she could see possibilities…if she lived long enough.

"Home sweet home." Shep reined in his horse in front of the large livery stable.

Before Deanna could agree or not, a strange figure emerged from a concrete block building set slightly back from the street. It was a bearded man, clad much like her rescuer, except for one critical thing: He was covered in blood—fresh blood. As he raised his hand, the sun glanced off the meat cleaver he held.

The sight pushed her beyond her limit, an unadulterated fear filling Deanna with renewed strength. The scream that mustered below her heart drowned out whatever the man said. In a flurry of kicks and blows at Shep, who tried to restrain her, she landed on her feet in the dirt. Pain shot through her ankle as her heel twisted beneath her, but Deanna ignored it. She hobbled away from the startled, prancing horse that Shep abandoned in pursuit of her.

She fumbled in her purse for the pepper spray. "Stop right there or I'll shoot!"

Shep froze in midstep. His expression teetered somewhere between shock and amusement. Taking a step back, hands raised, he smiled and licked a trickle of blood from the lip she'd battered in her bid to escape.

"Slick, you've seen too many Westerns. Though I've never seen a cowpoke kayoed by a purse before," he added, a twinkle in his eye.

Deanna felt the rise of heat in her cheeks, but she held her ground. "Now take out that pistol and toss it over here…*slowly.*" Sheesh, she *did* sound like a veteran TV cowboy.

"What in tarn hill's goin' on here?" The other man, not the

least intimidated by Deanna's last stand, propped his hands at an indistinguishable waist and addressed Shep. "I thought you lit out after that stallion."

"Ticker, this is Miss Deanna Manetti from New York. The stallion ran her car off the road, and by the look of it, she'll be our guest for a few days." He returned his attention to Deanna. "Or maybe not."

Ticker—heaven help her; that sounded like a cleaver-wielding maniac's name.

He gave her a short nod. "Went Western on ya, did she? Reckon she looks a mite on the high-strung side." Ticker stared at her with a bemused expression. "Ain't they got butchers in New York, gal?"

"Butchers?" A ghost town with a meat market? She *had* to be imagining all this.

"Ticker and I are outfitters. The ranch is a dream on the side."

"Outfitters?" Confused, she took in their collective appearance. Certainly not outfitters of fashion.

"My partner and I take hunting parties up into the high country for elk and other game. Tick's been butchering and wrapping the last kill to ship back to our clients."

The other man snickered and made a tut-tutting or rather a *ticking* sound with his tongue. "Yep, by golly, I ain't kilt no human since…" He scratched his beard, absorbed in thought for a moment. "Since I don't know when."

With a mocking grin, Shep turned and started toward the open livery doors where his horse had bolted. "Just go on back to wrapping that elk, Tick. Maybe Miss Manetti will calm down once she sees she's not next in line for the freezer."

Bearing the brunt of their unabashed humor, Deanna watched until both men disappeared, one into the block building and the other into the stables. Weak with relief, she sank onto the remains of a plank walkway in front of the boardinghouse and buried her face in her arms, the pepper spray suspended in her hand. Her eyes stung from the emotional barrel race her mind had been dragged through and her head thundered fit to burst.

If "going Western" was another term for losing it, then she'd gone Western in a big way, punching and kicking fit for a big screen brawl. Where was the antiviolence marketing exec whose brass and sheer inventiveness won some of Image International's largest advertising accounts?

Men either cowered by the wayside at Deanna's first cool assessment or retreated after finding she had the steel to back it up. Now she wavered somewhere between nausea and hysterics, although how someone could be so hungry and sick to her stomach at the same time was a puzzle.

What have I gotten myself into now?

Massaging her temples, Deanna closed her eyes to the bright afternoon sun. Memory shorts of the grueling police interrogation played havoc with already ragged emotions. So help her, she had no idea that the bank transactions she made for C. R. Majors were illegal. She'd never suspected a thing.

"I made the deposits for C. R. on my way back to the office on Fridays as a favor, so that he could make his weekly one o'clock with the board of directors," Deanna had defended herself to the detective who arrested her right in the middle of a client interview.

She and C. R. always had a long lunch together on Fridays to go over her progress with the marketing team and, fool that she was, she'd thought that he enjoyed her company as well, since the discussion usually involved planning a date for the weekend. She didn't tell the police how the silver-tongued devil had flattered his way into her heart through her work or that she'd let her guard down at the promise of job advancement *and* romance with a man who appreciated the brain behind an attractive face.

"And you had no clue what was in the deposit bag Mr. Majors gave you?" Detective Riordan demanded.

So, instead of C. R. on the bank videotapes, it was Deanna

making the transactions that laundered illegal money through a reputable firm, once a week for the six weeks she'd been living in Great Falls. "I had no reason to look. He was the CEO of the company, so what right had I to question him?"

"Why didn't he ask the Accounts Receivable manager to make the deposits?"

"She was taking off on Fridays to get ready for a wedding. C. R. was boss over all of us. I didn't know what from why about the company's banking procedures. I was in marketing, not receivables. I hardly knew personnel in that department beyond an initial introduction."

Okay, so she did wonder at first, but C. R. had explained how the receivables department head was taking off to plan her upcoming wedding and that he, as her immediate superior, had offered to make the Friday bank run for her. Deanna had thought it a sweet gesture. The police weren't as gullible as she'd been.

"You were romantically involved with C. R. Majors, weren't you, Miss Manetti?"

"We dated," Deanna admitted. The heat that scorched her cheeks surely told the rest of the story. To her astonishment, the detective spread an array of photographs of her and C. R.—the afternoon at the park, a night at the theater, the Cattleman's Club, and the AR manager's long awaited wedding last weekend. In addition to the betrayal she already felt, violation added its two cents worth.

"When did you last see him?"

"There, at the wedding." She pointed to a picture of them dancing together. She looked like a starry-eyed idiot looking up at him. Although at the time, she'd felt like a princess walking on air in her designer suit and matching eelskin heels and clutch she'd purchased to complete the ensemble. She'd been clueless that her prince charming was a weasel. "He said he'd be leaving Sunday on a business trip to Toronto."

"And where did you two go after the wedding?"

"You mean you didn't get pictures of that as well?" Deanna shot back. Total strangers had watched her. Some of her most intimate moments had been tossed in her face on film. "C. R. took me back to my apartment. I made coffee. Then he went home to catch an early flight." After kissing her in such a way that she'd showered and was in bed before her heart resumed a normal beat.

Detective Riordan fingered another picture. "Did he say when he'd be returning?"

"Wednesday...today."

"I don't think so, Miss Manetti." The detective tossed the picture on the table in front of her. "You recognize the car?"

Surrounded by police and fire department vehicles was the burned-out frame of a Mercedes sports car. At least Deanna thought it was. "Are you saying that's C. R.'s car?" she asked, her voice straining past a pair of invisible hands that choked her.

"Forensics is trying to find enough of the body to identify," Riordan told her. "Car bombs don't leave much to work with."

A car bomb? Deanna had no ready reply this time. Her very breath had been kicked out of her by the vision.

"What we did find," the man continued, "was this little love note in your desk drawer along with a plane ticket to Barbados."

In C. R.'s familiar hand, the note read, "Darling, I await your arrival with our 'investment' to begin our life together in paradise."

Out of context, the note might have been a dream come true. Instead, it smacked of a deception so dark, Deanna could no longer look at it.

"Your ticket was bought by your boss the same time as his. Real cozy, eh?" the detective taunted.

Not knowing what to say, much less what to do, she'd just stared at the detective's worn shoes, trapped in a nightmare of someone else's making. This wasn't really happening to her. It couldn't be.

A sob worked its way out of her dry throat. As she opened

her eyes, the image of the shoes faded and transformed into a pair of dusty boots. She started, brandishing her pepper spray, but before she could activate it Shep snatched it away.

"Take it easy, Slick." He stepped back, hands raised as though to prove he meant no harm. "This way, no one will get hurt over a misunderstanding. I've had a taste of this stuff before, and once was more than enough, believe me."

Deanna eyed him with suspicion. "What was the occasion?"

Instead of answering, Shep chuckled. "You're jumpier than a frog on a hot rock." He extended a hand to help her to her feet. "How about some grub?"

Food. The idea was heavenly enough to assuage her ruffled humor. Shepard Jones could laugh all he wanted, so long as he fed her. Maybe then her head would be clearer and she could make up her mind just what to do about her precarious situation. Taking his hand, she struggled to her feet only to be startled by pain shooting up from her right ankle. Her right knee gave out, throwing her off balance against Shep.

"My ankle," she gasped, trying to explain her sprawling assault.

"Must have landed on it wrong when you dismounted." He steadied her with one arm about her waist. After what seemed a moment of indecision, he handed her back the spray canister. "Here, hold this and keep the cap *on.*" Without further ado, he swept her good leg out from under her and lifted her in his arms.

"You sure you trust me?"

"I guess we have to start somewhere." He shrugged. "Besides, where are you going to run off to?"

Deanna kept her fallback plan of following the electric lines to civilization to herself, tucking the spray back in her purse. But after the battering she'd given her rescuer with it, her purse didn't want to close right, adding insult to injury. This was a hundred-and-fifty-dollar designer clutch ruined, even if she had found it for twenty-five in a Fifth Avenue bargain basement.

"A good soak in some salts and you'll feel like a new person."

"I didn't say I was staying…after I eat, that is. You said there was a Jeep—"

The press of Shep's lips expressed his waning patience. He had every right to be annoyed with her. He was trying to be hospitable in an inhospitable place. That alone should win him an A for effort.

"I'm sorry. I should be thanking you, not asking you to do more for me."

"It was my horse that got you into this fix and you were pretty shaken up," he answered, with a guarded grace as he climbed the step to the porch of the main house.

"I didn't have to hit you." She touched the corner of his lip on impulse and he tensed in response.

Their gazes locked for the time it took the screen door he'd swung open with his boot tip to bounce back. It wasn't long by any means, but then, electricity traveled light speeds faster than second thoughts. Every one of Deanna's senses heightened along its charged path, the same awareness that seized him seizing her as well.

Beyond the dust of the trail and unshaven stubble were eyes that defied the label of brown. She watched, fascinated as a renegade *come hither* kindled in their gold-flecked umber only to be willfully doused by the mask of indifference claiming his face.

Once inside, he all but dropped her. "Make yourself at home. I'll get a tub for that ankle."

Deanna bobbed her head, still dumb from the shock, as he retreated through a narrow hallway into another room. He seemed to favor one leg. She hadn't noticed it before. Or was it just her imagination?

Hobbling over to a pine-framed sofa with plump plaid cushions of fifties vintage, she dropped down to take off her shoes and trouser socks.

"I figure I can start the grill and take a quick shower while you're soaking," he hollered above the sound of running water. "Then you can wash off some of the dust while I fix supper."

Deanna scowled in the direction of his voice. Clearly Shep was a man accustomed to taking charge, but at the moment, the only fault she could find with his reasoning was that it wasn't her idea.

She was used to being in control—at least until C. R. had come into her life. No way would she allow another man to control her life. Yet, she needed food or she wouldn't have the strength to control her next blink. She'd just play along until they reached a fork in the road of their intentions before showing him no one rode herd over her.

Ride herd? Fork in the road of their intentions? With a groan, Deanna buried her face in her hands. *Lord, puh-leeze help me find a way back East before I start chewing tobacco and taking pride in my aim back at the Hopeless Ranch in Buffalo Butte, the backside of the world! If I have to be herded by Shepard Jones, let me be herded home.*

Three

Once Deanna was situated with a foot tub, a cartoon character jelly glass of orange juice, and bag of pretzels to stave off starvation, her grubby but obliging host abandoned her. Like him, the house was laid back, fifties retro with knotty pine paneling and cabinets in the country kitchen-family room. Rustic wooden furniture with plump, masculine plaid cushions provided cozy seating near the fireplace. A large moose head hung over the stone hearth, flanked by other furry hunting trophies and a mounted fish frozen in mid jump. With no clue regarding the nature of their demise, blank expressions seemingly fixed on Deanna while death-silenced voices called out in warning to her.

That imagination of yours is goin' to be the death of you. Deanna could almost hear the exasperation in the observation her grandmother used to make of her. The way her heart was fluttering, maybe Grandma was right.

Looking away with an involuntary shudder, she took comfort that the only human representations among them were in faded pictures on the mantel representing a happier time gone by. Was the snaggle-toothed kid in the oversized cowboy hat her host per chance?

Along a sidewall, a stack of boxes—many still sealed with tape and labeled—suggested a recent move on someone's part. They reminded her of the ones in the spare bedroom of her apartment in Great Falls—before someone had torn them apart and emptied their contents from one end of the room to the other.

Oh, Deanna, what have you gotten yourself into? She swallowed the remaining bite of a pretzel stick and chased it with juice before resting her head against the back of the sofa. Nearby a voice crackled sharply amid a storm of static, startling her from her self-pity.

On a built-in desk sat a radio or scanner of some sort that fit the rest of these rustic trappings. As the transmission cleared, Deanna listened to a conversation of a father on his way home from town—wherever that was—reminding his son to get his homework done so he could go to a church youth meeting. She imagined a long ride home on some of the isolated roads she'd been lost on the last day or so and how comforting it would have been to have someone who cared to talk to.

Or at least someone who would talk back, she thought, remembering her furtive prayers. Maybe God just wasn't listening anymore, not that He'd ever actually *spoken* to her when she had been a little more regular in communication with Him.

A sound from the hallway where Shep had disappeared drew her attention to where a different man from the one who'd rescued her emerged from the back of the house. Now this was a guy befitting those incredible brown eyes that had held her hostage earlier. Clean-shaven, square-jawed, broad shouldered—Shep could have stepped off the pages of a rugged wear catalog but for the shirt he'd thrown on without bothering with the buttons.

It occurred to Deanna that he might be showing off his infomercial-perfect abs, but he'd tugged on his jeans without a belt as well and padded around in his bare feet. Buffed by hard work and long days in the sun, he didn't seem aware of his effect on the opposite sex. Deanna had seen enough men to know when one was putting on a show or just being himself…until C. R. The roller coaster of her frayed emotions took another dip.

"You got some spare clothes in your car?" her host asked, a vexed expression claiming his angular features. "If not I might find something you can change into, but they won't fit."

Deanna shook her head. "I hadn't planned on being gone overnight."

She hadn't planned *anything*. When she came home from the police station, already frazzled by hours of fruitless interrogation, she found her apartment turned upside down and inside out. Whoever ransacked the place had left a cryptic note saying they weren't through with her yet. Deanna shivered, arms crossed over her chest to disguise her discomfiture.

"Where's home then?" He helped himself to bottled fruit juice from the ancient round-topped fridge. Her grandmother had had a similar model. There was something oddly comforting about that and the general old-timey feel of the place.

"Originally New York," Deanna told him, distracted as she flashed back to the nightmarish scene at her apartment in Great Falls. When she called the police to report the break in, they'd treated her like the criminal, insinuating that she'd engineered the crime scene to draw attention away from their belief that she was in cahoots with the late C. R. Majors. And so she'd bolted without so much as a toothbrush, much less a plan.

"So what brings you to Montana?" Shep's query drew her back to the present. As he raised the drink to his lips, the late afternoon sunlight caught on a flash of gold lying against his chest. It was a plain cross, strung on a masculine weight chain.

"Checking out a job offer in Great Falls." Although a city in its own right, Great Falls had felt like a strange place with no long-time friends or even business associates. It wasn't her fault New York's heart beat in her chest.

He chuckled. "Well, you certainly took a wrong turn."

"So Pocahontas I'm not. With that zoo of animal heads staring at me, I'm lucky if I can remember where I am now."

Instead of taking offense at her stab at humor, he laughed. "You're just a bit frahoodled."

Frahoodled. That was a new one, but it fit just right. Deanna chuckled with him grateful for his good nature. "I guess so."

"So what brings you into these parts? You're a far cry from Great Falls. Just touring?"

"I was checking for a place to relocate, but I seem to have gotten off course." She'd sublet a furnished apartment in the city itself for a month to give her time to search for the right place.

Right place. It might as well be on the moon now.

"Boy, when you take a wrong turn, you make it a doozy." Shep snatched open the freezer door. "That's four hours away."

"I was just meandering to see what I could see and lost track of time." And she'd seen a gorgeous red stallion break in front of her car from nowhere in the middle of nowhere.

There was no point in telling Shepard Jones any more than he had to know. All she needed was another kink in this snarl of a mess.

The man took out two frozen steaks and slapped them on a plate. No more modern than the house itself, the plate was yellowed and cracked with age. Its pattern reminded Deanna of older, more carefree days when she'd set the table with a like design at her maternal grandmother's. Gram, who'd baby-sat Deanna while her parents worked, said the old dinnerware had come as a bonus prize in laundry powder boxes purchased long before Deanna was even born.

"Well, like I said earlier, I don't have anything to fit you, but I put out clean towels. There's a bathrobe on the back of the bathroom door. I can toss your things in the washer and dry them while you're cleaning up, if you want."

She sighed, grateful that Great Falls had left the discussion. Besides, to one who'd spent the last three days washing up at rest stops, the idea of a shower sounded heavenly. Dare she trust in that cross on his chest, that it represented the man? Or was she grasping at straws?

"Are you going to take me into town after supper?" She thought she saw the Jeep when he carried her into the house, but he'd had the bulk of her attention.

He stopped rummaging through a built-in bin of the knotty pine cabinets and let out a measured breath. "If you insist, Miss Manetti." Taking out two large potatoes, he straightened. "Miss Esther Lawson has a few guest cottages on the edge of town. If she's not booked up, you could rent one of them for the night. I can rouse her up on the radio to see, if that's what you want."

Except that Deanna had no money. As for her credit cards, even if the woman honored them, was it worth the risk that her pursuers could trace her whereabouts? It was that way in the movies.

She glanced at the radio and searched the jumble of wires and papers on the desk for sign of more modern communication. "What, you don't have a phone?" Everyone had a telephone.

"Not if I can help it."

"Not even a cell phone?"

Shep shrugged. "Sorry. Ma Bell gets on my nerves."

Heaven spare her. "What do you do in an emergency?"

"I have a radio. It's more reliable, 'specially in bad weather…and the telemarketers haven't figured out a way to utilize the air waves yet." He held up the potatoes. "Baked in the microwave okay with you?"

He had a microwave but not a radio. Deanna nodded. She was at the hind end of the world and stuck with a total stranger who decorated with dead animal heads. "What about your friend, er…Ticker?"

"Tick lives on the other side of town in an old travel trailer." Grinning, Shep added, "He's not much on social life unless it centers around a campfire."

Or skinning and cutting into bits some poor, defenseless animal. "I see." Deanna started to draw her feet out of the now-cool water in the foot tub when she realized she had no towel.

Seeing her predicament, Shep yanked off a few handfuls of paper towels and tossed them at her. "Sorry about that."

At least it wasn't an animal hide. She dabbed her feet dry, sinking with exhaustion and despair. What on earth was she going to do?

"Why don't you just wait till after you rinse off the trail dust and fill your belly before you decide?"

Deanna jerked her head toward her host. Was she so obvious?

"And if you're worried about sleeping arrangements, my aunt Sue's ghost would haunt me if I didn't give a lady my room for the night and bunk on the sofa."

Bless Aunt Sue's ghost for answering that question. Not that Deanna believed in such things. The late woman's nephew, on the other hand, was quite real. Although, to date, he had been the epitome of a gentleman and a good host. But was he a wolf in good host's clothing?

"People may fail you, Deanna darlin', but the good Lord never will." Shocked by the unexpected memory of her grandmother's words, Deanna glanced from the old refrigerator to the plate where two slabs of frozen beef thawed. That did it.

Her mind made up, she balled and tossed the damp paper towels in a thirty-gallon garbage can by the stove. She wouldn't trust the man, but how could she go wrong trusting in the Holy Spirit behind that cross, especially when it was backed by the faith of her devout grandmother and his righteous Aunt Sue?

"Nice shot."

Deanna managed a fatigued grin. "I've had lots of practice." Her office cohorts had given her a wastebasket with a basketball hoop to catch all the ideas that never made it past the drafting table.

"How's the foot?"

She tested it with her full weight and winced. "Sore, but it's better than before when I couldn't bear my weight at all. Thanks." She met his gaze from across the room.

Deanna saw no lightning bolt pass between them, but she felt its charge and retreated in all haste toward the back of the house.

Ahead was the open door of a bedroom—*the* bedroom, judging from what she'd seen of the outside of the small house.

"Hang a right. Left takes you into a closet," Shep called after her, once again anticipating her thoughts. "Wrong right," he teased, when she turned the wrong way on impulse.

"Why didn't you say it was the *other* one," she shot back.

Once inside the small bathroom, Deanna stared at the woman in the mirror, watching a crimson tide claim her face. "Young lady," she complained to her twin as she kicked the door closed behind her. "I hope you haven't jumped from one fire smack into another."

The way her cheeks felt to the touch of her cool fingers, she knew she had.

Four

Deanna had to admit, Shep was right about at least one thing: a shower. Aided by the two aspirin she found in her purse, it worked wonders for her disposition. Or maybe it was the clothes he had aired out in the dryer. Shep had nearly scared her witless when he'd knocked on the bathroom door and asked if she wanted them washed.

With a towel wrapped tightly about her, Deanna had edged the slacks and blouse through the crack of the door. "Sorry, dry clean only. For what I paid for them, they should be *self*-cleaning!"

A circuit overload had delayed her from drying her hair until the clothes had been fluffed in the dryer. As she waited for the lights to come back on after the fuse blew, Shep mumbled something about a step-above knob and tube wiring and meaning to upgrade someday. He must have thrown in one of those fragrant fabric softener sheets though, for she felt almost like new when she stepped out of the bathroom nearly an hour later.

Her stomach growled at the tantalizing scent of the steaks cooking on the barbecue grill on the back porch. She peeked through the screen door. "Anything I can do?"

"Nope." Shep took the scrumptious-looking meat off the grate. "Do you like your steaks warmed or more done?"

"Pink." Everyone had his or her own interpretation of rare, medium, and well done.

"Then take this one inside while I give this other one another lick or two on the coals."

"Sure thing."

A pitcher of tea—the real thing with bags suspended from the lift top—stood ready on the table. The red Formica tabletop had been set for two with a pair of matching glasses from a fast-food promotion and mismatched stainless ware. Deanna put Shep's steak next to a glass of tea that he had half consumed. As good as the grilled meat smelled, raw or not, she could have torn into it like a hungry dog, but helped herself instead to another pretzel stick. Since the steak had been frozen an hour earlier, it couldn't be much more than *warmed* as he'd described it.

A few minutes later, her benefactor joined her. Not only was her steak on the platter, but so were four ears of corn wrapped in foil that had been roasted on the coals.

"Worry a critter too much and it'll toughen up on you," he warned, nodding at the beef he set in front of her. "But see if that meets city specs anyway."

Deanna made a small incision and smiled. "Done to perfection…and none too soon." She chuckled as her tummy growled again.

She watched Shep retrieve baked potatoes from the microwave and juggle them to the table, tossing one on each plate with a boyish grin. Then, wiping his hands on his shirt, he took the seat opposite her.

"Mind if I say grace, Deanna?"

"Not at all. I am *so* thankful for this food."

She bowed her head as he began. "Lord, we don't pretend to know Your purpose all the time, but we thank You that You've provided for us one more day. May this food nourish our bodies as You nourish our souls. Amen."

"Amen," Deanna echoed, struck by the individual rendition of thanksgiving. But then, everything she'd seen about her host so far was original. C. R. had been such a stereotype, but she'd been too blinded by his sweet drawl and attention to notice. Deanna banished the thought before she lost her appetite. She needed all the nourishment she could get, for both body *and* spirit.

"So how'd this place get the name Hopewell?" She helped herself to a shameful dollop of block butter on her potato. Real tea, the familiar dinnerware and Formica table, block butter—it was like stepping back in time, except no one like Shep Jones ever sat across from Deanna at her grandmother's Formica table.

"It was a mining town until the small vein of gold beneath it ran out. I guess a lot of folks had high hopes that it would last longer. My uncle Dan always said he 'well hoped' it might amount to a ranch some day." Shep topped off his glass of tea. "That man could make a horse do anything he wanted."

The genuine admiration playing beneath Shep's long, lazy lashes was for his Uncle Dan, but it still made her heart do a somersault. Those lashes would be dangerous if he intended to flirt.

"He taught me a lot about animals, horses especially. People round these parts paid top dollar for any Hopewell horse. I'm hoping to keep that reputation."

"So this was a horse ranch then?" Deanna dug into the food on her plate rather than risk being drawn into the unfamiliar territory of his eyes. She needed to eat. Then she needed to think about her next move. The last thing she needed was the same kind of distraction that got her in this predicament to begin with—that of a man wielding a winsome Western charm.

"And will be again someday," Shep replied with a wistful look. "Not that we don't enjoy hunting," he admitted. "I guess I just inherited my uncle's love of horses as well as his ranch."

"You weren't raised here?"

He shook his head. "I was a military brat. My folks moved all over till they divorced. I went to school in D.C. where Mom moved and visited Dad at whatever base he was stationed. But I spent every summer here with my dad's brother and his wife."

"So that's you in the picture on the mantel?"

"Yep." He leveled a thoughtful look at her across the lazy Susan in the middle of the table for what seemed an interminable time before picking up the conversation. "After Uncle Dan died, his horses ran wild for two years. That sorrel that ran you off the road? I've been trying to round him up for nearly three months. He's an elusive son of a prairie biscuit."

"Is that how long you've been here?" Deanna nodded toward the boxes that prompted her observation.

"I guess I ought to finish unpacking one of these days," he admitted with a sheepish grin.

Deanna's toes curled under in the confines of her shoes.

"But enough about me. What kind of work brings you out to Big Sky from the Big Apple?"

She clenched her toes even tighter at the change in conversation. How much did she dare tell? "I managed an advertising campaign for a Great Falls company, and they offered me a position in their marketing department. I'm just out here checking it out before I do anything definite."

"What's the company's name?"

"Image International."

Shep scowled. "Never heard of it."

That was because it was in New York. Amtron Enterprises had lured her away to Great Falls—or rather, its suave CEO had after Deanna had put together a sweeping advertising campaign for his company. "That's because we promote our clients' services and products, not our own."

"Hmm." It was an innocuous sound, but it might as well have been a full interrogation as Shep contemplated her. Clearly his curiosity wasn't satisfied.

Deanna scraped the remains of her baked potato, avoiding his eyes. "So what are we going to do about my car?" The sooner she was away from Shep, the better. She didn't know exactly why, she just felt like a worm on a hot brick around him. Maybe it was the guilt his forthright manner made her feel. He harbored a fugitive, even though she was innocent. The irony that a shave and a bath had changed her perception of her rescuer from a serial killer to a knight in shining armor did not escape her.

"Actually, while you were in the shower, I radioed Charlie Long to pick your car up and take it to his garage for damage assessment. He's the mechanic I told you about earlier."

Deanna nodded. That was good, so why did she feel like someone was pulling the carpet out from under feet?

"The way the crushed fender had flattened your right front tire, I don't think you can drive it." Her reservation must have shown, for he added, "But if you want me to drive you into Buffalo Butte after supper, I'll do it. A trip to Great Falls is out of the question at this hour."

"Actually, I am a bit strapped for cash. So if you don't mind, I'll take you up on your offer of lodging tonight."

There it was again, that flicker of suspicion. Or was it concern?

"Is there anyone you need to get in touch with? Someone expecting you home maybe?"

"No, I…" Deanna thought quickly. It was better that he not know she had a place in the city because he may insist on taking her there—the last place she wanted to be at the moment. "I was staying with business associates in the city. Tomorrow I can call when we check on the car…not that they're expecting me back until after the weekend. They knew I was checking out the area."

Or at least pretend to call them. The idea turned in her stomach. She was sinking in a mire of lies and couldn't seem to escape them. It went against everything she'd been raised to be, but for now, she had no choice.

"Well, I can tell you repairing that fancy car of yours won't be a cheap fix, but Charlie will give us the best price."

"I've had a struggle making the insurance premiums to start with, fender bender or not."

So how do you happen to be driving a snazzy imported sports car if you're strapped for cash? Was that the question behind the curious appraisal fixed on her and he was too much of a gentleman to ask?

"But since I chased the red into your path, I feel kind of responsible, even if you were on my property."

"The car's not new, believe me. I was just in the right place at the right time." Okay, that much *was* true. "And the bank owns more of it than I do."

Another truth. Deanna had never been the kind to fall for any kind of scam, but when she did, she went all the way—losing her head and a good job, going into debt for a "new" pre-owned car because it looked hot, and ending up with a silver-tongued swindler.

Beginning to feel like she was on the receiving end of a twenty questions game, Deanna resisted the urge to squirm in her chair. After all, the guy deserved to know a little about the stranger he was taking into his home…just not everything. She gathered her napkin from her lap and made a show of dabbing at her lips, her attention wandering beyond Shep to the cabinet bulkhead. A small, embroidered plaque hung there, its background yellowed with age. The words, nonetheless, were clear: Father Knows Best. The stitched image of an open Bible implied which *Father*.

"But maybe we can work something out, since you can see I'm not exactly rolling in the green stuff either."

Thank You, Lord! Even though she didn't exactly deserve God's attention, given her lack of the same to Him, maybe He was listening after all. Regardless, she was grateful.

"Though I don't know how long a fellow can afford to feed you," Shep added with an impish glance at her plate.

"Well, since you feel *that* way," she rallied, buoyed to her feet both spiritually and physically. "I guess I'd better try to earn my supper and do the dishes."

"Deal. The soap's under the sink. I'll take out the scraps for the barn cat and check on Ticker…unless you need me for something else."

Deanna wanted to say, "No thanks, you've scrambled my thoughts enough as it is." Instead, she called out above the rattle of the dishes in the sink. "Go ahead. Just pretend I'm not here."

"I doubt I can do that."

Startled by his comment, she glanced over her shoulder to see him half in and half out of the screen door, staring at her in unabashed appreciation. Heat crept up from the open collar of her blouse as those brown eyes of his suspended her pulse and breath for an electric moment. Then, with a mischievous wink, she was released.

"Nope, it's not every day a man has someone to do his dishes."

Shep ducked out of the door, letting it slam behind him. The smile that had grazed his lips faded as he strode across the dirt yard down the narrow street toward the livery stable. He hardly paid any attention to the yellow tabby that fell in step with him, eager for the food scraps he'd gathered up in a napkin while clearing the table. He shook them out as he walked along, but his thoughts spun like a load in Aunt Sue's old washer, around the woman he'd left in his kitchen, kicking up enough ruckus to make his head hurt.

What was wrong with that picture besides the obvious— svelte silk and linen in a gingham setting? Salon-manicured nails in dishwater? Lost in the case of Deanna Manetti, Shep slowed as he approached the butcher shed.

Startling Shep from his introspection, Ticker emerged from the shed and bolted the door behind him. "Yep, I smell it too."

"What's that?"

"Trouble, with a big T. I was just comin' to check on you," his longtime friend and partner informed him.

"Not like that I hope," Shep snorted, as the man pulled off his apron and wadded part of it into his back pocket. "You already scared the daylights out of her." Twenty years Shep's senior, Ticker had helped Uncle Dan ever since Shep was a kid. Part Indian and part mule, his uncle used to say of his friend and employee.

Ticker grinned. "Reckon I did at that." He rubbed his ear. "Wasn't sure I'd hear right again after she squealed like a stuck pig." He looked toward the house. "She stayin' over?"

"From the looks of her car, not much choice," Shep said. "I'll take her into town tomorrow. Maybe I can get her a bus ticket to Great Falls till her car's fixed."

"Excitable little filly, ain't she?"

"Seems so." Shep glanced back toward the house at the end of the street. Behind it, the mountains colored the skyline with a dark jagged edge, above which a few cloven clouds reflected the rising moon. He loved to study the sky's canvas, which was ever changing, ever beautiful, whether fierce or fair.

Tonight he hardly noticed. His mind's eye was fixed on an oval face with lake blue eyes deep enough to dive into—except when they looked at him from the safe side of a can of pepper spray. Then they were blue ice, frozen in a mixture of fear and fight like those of a cornered animal. He let out a deep breath, as if to rid himself of the spell they'd somehow cast upon him.

"So it's like that, is it?"

Shep cut a sharp eye at his friend. "Like what?"

Ticker spat to the side and grinned. "Last time I heard you sigh like that, you was lookin' at the red stallion. Now it's a horse of a different color."

Blue. Shep closed the gate on that stray thought right away. "Nonsense. Tomorrow, she's out of here, one way or another."

The last thing he needed in his relatively happy life on the range was a woman, especially one city born and bred. His ex-fiancée had soured him on the sophistication that had once intrigued him.

"A man can't stay out of the race forever, ya know. A horse is nice and a dog is fine, but there's somethin' about a female that makes a man complete…leastways, if she's a good 'un like my Mary Ann."

Ticker's wife had nursed Sue Jones through her long ordeal

with a stroke. When Aunt Sue died, it was no surprise. But no one was prepared when Mary Ann Deerfield fell ill and succumbed to cancer a few months later.

"An' speakin' of critters, I gotta pick up Smoky from Doc Marine's place. Maybe that pup'll think twice the next time he comes across a porkypine."

"You going to take him with you on roundup?"

Ticker hired out every spring for roundup at the neighboring cattle ranch for extra money. While they split the outfitting income, Shep couldn't afford to pay his friend for his ready hand with the ranching endeavor. Tick graciously called it an even trade for land rent, but Shep knew better. If he let it, the free helping hand would bother him, but a man had to crawl before he could walk.

Shep had to repair the place before he could hire men to round up decent stock to start training. With his bum knee cutting short his successful career with the U.S. Marshals and ending his engagement to the woman with whom he planned to spend his life, Shep figured he had the rest of his life to fulfill the only dream that had survived a perpetrator's bullet. Meanwhile, his disability paid for the essentials. And someday, he'd do a good deed in turn for Tick or someone else.

"…if you don't mind," Ticker answered, drawing Shep back from the past.

Shep processed the words he'd heard but not registered, catching up. *Take care of 'im till I git back.* "Sure thing. The dog spends as much time at my place as yours."

Smoky was part Border collie, part shepherd, and all overgrown pup. Unlike his mother, a fine cattle dog of mixed blood, Smoky was given to bouts of playfulness, forgetting his responsibilities in bringing stray steers or horses back in line when they tried to break from the herd.

"Reckon I'll feed 'im in the morning, 'fore I leave. He'll find you."

A shapely silhouette appeared in the front door of the house.

Ticker started with that ticking thing he did with his tongue. Sometimes it was funny; other times, it was downright annoying.

"If there's anything left of you in the mornin', that is." His friend launched into a leisurely walk down the main street toward his trailer.

"You're an ornery son of a prairie biscuit," Shep called after him. Ticker answered with a wave, not bothering to look back.

When Shep looked back at the door, Deanna had disappeared. *Lord, I don't need this,* he prayed as he started for the house. But then, she'd be gone tomorrow. He was just giving her his bed for the night, not sharing it. How could being a Good Samaritan for one night hurt anything?

Five

Smoky chased the trailer behind Ticker's truck to the end of Hopewell's main street the following morning, yipping at his master as if to say, "Hey, you forgot something!" But when the truck didn't stop, the dog sat and watched the vehicle disappear. Shep knew how the animal felt. Ellen Sanderson had left him in the dust much the same way.

His fiancée refused to understand why Shep couldn't settle for a desk job in the D.C. office. She hadn't really known him at all. When she refused to even consider heading west with him to pursue his dream of horse ranching, he knew their love had been based on the false shine of the social life they'd shared. They took a great picture together—the diplomatic darling and her gussied-up escort—but the relationship had been no deeper than the paper the picture was printed on.

Shep bent down as Smoky trotted up to him for consolation. "Cheer up, partner." He scratched the shepherd mix behind the ears. "At least Ticker's coming back."

Big city and Big Sky just didn't mix. Much as Shep had enjoyed the excitement of being a U.S. Marshal, he'd never really been at home in the East.

"Tell you what, Smoke. You watch out for me and I'll watch out for you. How's that?"

The dog barked and wagged his tail. Whether it was because he agreed or was just glad for the attention was anyone's guess. Shep dodged a generous lick and straightened, looking at the house.

"What say we go see if our guest is stirring yet?"

Smoky fell in behind Shep's long stride with an uncannily timed yip. Either the dog actually understood the English language or he was the best con artist Shep had ever seen. The subject had been a source of debate between Tick and Shep on more than one occasion.

No one answered when he entered the kitchen-family room and said, "Anybody home?"

The breakfast he'd cooked and left on the pilot warmer of the gas stove hadn't been touched. The coffee was still at the same level in the carafe after he'd helped himself to a second cup before heading out to do chores. With a scowl, he glanced toward the closed bedroom door where Smoky acted as if he'd picked up a new scent, waiting poised, ears alert.

"Time to wake sleeping beauty," Shep quipped with a half curl of a smile.

He struck the door with three sharp knocks. "Hey, Slick, day's a wastin'!"

Smoky's lazy-tipped ears cocked as Shep placed his ear to the door. Not a sound. His lips thinned. Deanna's headache had returned when he came back to the house after speaking to Tick last night. Shep fixed her an ice bag for the knot at the hairline of her forehead, scrounged up a pair of new pajamas still in its plastic sleeve, then sent her to bed. Should he have kept her awake? Maybe the concussion was worse than it appeared.

He slammed his fist against the door, shaking it in its frame. "Deanna, rise and shine!"

Smoky, equally emboldened by a sense that something was amiss, added his two cents worth with a bark.

Shep gave his guest thirty seconds to respond before trying the doorknob. It was locked. How, he had no idea, since the old iron box lock had been painted open for decades. He stepped back, preparing to kick the door in when his better sense took over. Why bust the frame and risk injuring his foot in a battle with the time-petrified wood when nothing but a flimsy screen would be far more accommodating?

Rushing outside, Shep made straight for the open bedroom window with Smoky on his heels. Peering in, he made out a still lump of a figure smothered by the covers and pillows.

"Hey, rise and shine!"

The bed never so much as twitched in response. His pulse accelerating with concern, Shep produced his pocketknife and cut away the screen. Slinging it aside, he heaved himself through the window and did a head roll into the room over a pair of discarded high heels. Ignoring the pierce of the heels into the muscles of his back, he came to his feet and stepped toward the bed where a slender arm, swimming in pajamas, curled over a pillow covering what he assumed to be her head.

"Deanna?"

He knelt on the edge of the mattress. But as he reached for the pillow, the mattress shifted without warning from beneath him with an explosive whoosh. Unable to stop his forward momentum, Shep sprawled across Deanna, bringing her to life with a blood-curdling scream. A pillowed fist struck him full across the jaw. A knee came up with alarming accuracy, blanketed but sharp enough to trigger the instinct to retreat.

"It's okay; it's just *me!*"

A telltale hiss from Shep's left brought him back across the struggling, shrieking figure, pinning her to the bed. *Not the pepper spray!* With all his strength, he held the threatening sound down with a pillow.

"It's just me," he shouted over Deanna's muffled screams. "I'm *not* going to hurt you! I promise. Now let the spray go, or we'll both get hit."

A mumbled "What?" came from under another pillow.

"Let go of the pepper spray before it gets us both. I'm not going to hurt you," Shep repeated, his voice taut with strained patience. He'd have sent a male perp to la-la land by now.

It took a few seconds for his words to penetrate the obvious panic of the wildcat struggling in the tangle of blankets and pillows. And like a wildcat, Deanna Manetti packed more punch for the pound than appeared possible.

The kicking, punching, writhing, and hissing stopped.

"L…let me go. I…I'm soaked!"

Soaked? Rather than question what he thought he heard, Shep continued his clipped instruction. "I'm going to roll off you right now. You slip your arm out from under the pillow with the pepper spray and get up." His succinct and calm manner was a far cry from what he was feeling. He wavered somewhere between the urge to strangle his guest and relief that she was evidently fit as a fiddle.

The moment she was free, Deanna scrambled out of the bed. Snagging her foot in a knot of sheets, she stumbled and caught herself on the tall gun cabinet, rattling the contents. The glass doors had cost him a fortune. Thankfully, the metal reinforcement paid for itself, but the rocking of the base on the uneven flooring reminded Shep that he really needed to balance that thing. His focus shifted from the rocking tower of his prized collection to the young woman trying to steady it.

"Great—" she dropped the pepper spray canister to steady it—"I get to be the first gun accident where I'm crushed rather than shot by the bloomin' things."

Speechless, Shep stared at his guest. She was swimming in his pajamas, quite literally where they clung to one arm and shoulder as though she'd been hosed down. Water even dripped on the floor. "You *are* soaked."

"What, are you deaf as well as dumb?" Deanna snatched something from her ear—a wire of some sort. She cast a furtive glance from the locked door to the window, where remnants of the screen hanging from its frame explained his entrance before he could. "You *broke* in? Why?"

Shep eased to his feet, eyeing the pepper spray still within reach. "Because you didn't answer me when I knocked." Wait a minute. Why was *he* on the defensive in his own house? "Why on earth did you lock the door? I thought I'd proved that I wasn't going to assault you."

"New Yorkers know better than to trust anybody…especially if said person seems too good to be true, which is usually *not* the case."

Her upper lip was stiff, but the lower one gave her away. Not that it needed to. He'd seen the stark terror now thawing in her eyes. He forced the indignation eating at him from his voice. "You had a headache and a nasty lump on your forehead last night. I thought you were unconscious or something when you didn't answer," he explained. "So I broke in, but when I knelt on the edge of the bed to check you—"

Bewilderment claiming him, Shep tossed the covers back. There, lying in a wet circle was the ice bag he'd given her. A hint of humor tugged at the corner of his mouth as the facts all came together. "I guess I put my knee on that and slipped."

He glanced at Deanna to see her staring at the thing as well. She squeezed some of the water out of the pajama on her shoulder before raising her gaze to his with a sheepish grin. It tugged at the cutest nose he'd ever seen. "I didn't hear you because I was using the earphones on your transistor radio to shut out all the noise last night."

The transition of a sleepy, frightened little girl in need of comfort turning to imp played havoc with his thoughts. "What nose…*noise?*" Her vulnerability and his desire to assuage it made him stammer, setting off alarms along the wall protecting his emotions.

Her mouth twitched in yet another beguiling pose, sending his thoughts and reactions tumbling over each other like inept cops in a silent film. Suddenly, she stared past him, murmuring a startled, "Oh!"

Desperate for any distraction, Shep glanced over his shoulder in time to see Smoky bound through the window. He caught the yapping dog as it lunged up on the bed toward Deanna. "Whoa, boy. She's a friend."

Not that Smoky was acting anything more than excited and friendly. Nonetheless, Deanna appeared relieved and grateful for Shep's intervention, rewarding him with yet another smile.

"Where did he come from?"

"Smoky, meet Deanna Manetti. Deanna, meet Smoky. He's Tick's dog. I'm taking care of him till Tick gets back from the Double J's roundup. He's all bark and no bite…least I've never seen any bite in him. The most danger he poses is kissing you to death." Shep's pulse tripped. "Slobber drowning."

Slobber drowning? Sheeah, he was babbling like a pimple-faced boy on his first date. But then, the sight of Deanna standing in his pajamas, her shiny shoulder-length hair tousled, was hard to ignore. Half little girl, half imp, and all woman…

Shep turned away, tugging Smoky gently by the collar. He was thinking like some kind of pervert. "I'll fix you some more breakfast while you get dressed. Then we'll go into town and check on your car."

"More breakfast?" she asked as he struggled with one hand to slide the lock to the open position. How in blazes had she broken it loose from layers of paint? It finally gave with a loud click.

"I imagine the egg I fixed earlier is hard as a pine knot. I'll make another."

"Just put it in a sandwich."

"Whatever suits," he said, drawing the door closed behind him as if he couldn't do it fast enough. At Smoky's whine of a sigh, he glanced at the dog's quizzical look. "Don't even ask." Shep let go of the collar and retreated to the kitchen like a scalded hound.

The Jeep hit a bump in the road just as Deanna swallowed the last of her sandwich. When she had emerged from the bedroom after the bizarre wake-up call, her host had been eager to be on their way, so she grabbed a cup of coffee to go and ate on the way. No matter how hard she tried, she'd been unable to ignore the furry companion that had followed her every step since she left from the bedroom. On her way to the vehicle, she'd parted with half of her food. She couldn't help it. Unable to have pets in her New York apartment, she was a sucker for those pleading eyes.

"There's where you ran off the road." Shep pointed out her window as they drove by a dry embankment that looked as if a bite had been taken from it.

After a good night's sleep and a hearty meal, the surroundings were a far cry from the inhospitable landscape she remembered. All Deanna recalled were road, horse, and wilderness. She'd felt like King David must have when his friends turned against him, the sole living creature in an unfriendly wilderness, wondering why God wasn't hearing his pleas for help. Odd that the story would come to mind now. She hadn't thought of her old Sunday school lessons in years. But then she hadn't been in this much of a mess in years either.

Today the pastureland to the right and left of the dirt road seemed greener than the day before. She even spotted a scatter of cattle grazing on a gradual rise that swept toward the tree and rock covered hills beyond.

"This road leads up to a hunting lodge in the high country," Shep told her. "And dollars to donuts that's where that renegade stallion is right now, running with the mustangs." He shot a begrudging look at the scene fading behind them in the rearview mirror.

"I thought the mustangs were protected." Deanna had read something about that in *National Geographic,* hadn't she?

"They are, but the red isn't one of them. He was born and bred at Hopewell. He just likes to run with the wild crowd." Shep smirked over his stab at humor. "A lot of ranches let the bulk of their remuda of work horses run in the hills until spring roundup.

Then the hands round them up and remind them of their training for a few days before the real work begins."

At her quizzical look, he explained. "Rounding up the cattle
and weeding out the nonproductive cows and the calves bound
for market."

"Oh." So that explained why there were just a few horses in
the corral at Hopewell.

"The stallion and a few others have run wild since Dan took
sick, so Tick and I have our work cut out for us."

The Hopewell land ran on forever with its own network of
narrow and mostly unpaved roads before they reached a paved
county highway. Some were pitted, and jostled the all-terrain
vehicle so Deanna had to cling to the door, despite her seat belt.

According to Shep, the cattle she saw grazing here and there
were not his but were owned by neighboring ranchers who leased
the land from him. That certainly explained how such a large
place could have such a meager, not to mention spooky, center of
operation. She hadn't mentioned it, but that partly accounted for
her trouble sleeping. Who could get a good night's rest in a ghost
town?

"So what was the noise you mentioned earlier?" Shep asked,
as though reading her thoughts. His knack for doing that was
unsettling. "You know, what you tried to block out with the radio
ear plugs."

It was the first reference he'd made to his unorthodox wake-
up call. In retrospect, it was kind of funny, but he had yet to see
the humor in his rupturing an ice bag and scaring the bejittles out
of her. But then, neither had she until her mind replayed the incident while she was doing her hair and makeup. She'd been
snatched from a sound sleep, not sure if she was being smothered,
drowned, or worse.

"Are you kidding? I never dreamed the country was so loud,
especially at night with all those loudmouthed animals and
insects. When they weren't whistling, they were gargling. When

they weren't gargling, they were singing. When they weren't singing, they were squeaking. And I swear I heard at least three frogs being strangled before I turned to the radio to drown it all out."

"Yeah, we don't have fire and police sirens to drown them out like you do in the city."

Deanna cut a sidewise glance at her companion. From the twinkle in his eyes, he was teasing. "Well, in my book it certainly shoots the concept of quiet nights in the country."

"Just Mother Nature's lullaby. All the creatures singing out that all's well or warning of an upcoming change in weather conditions. The more you listen, the more you can tell what's going on in the world."

"You mean like Station Eight's siren is different from Station Twenty-Two's, so you know which district the fire is in?"

Shep grinned. "Something like that."

"But those poor frogs…well, it was just awful."

"They were probably just in love. It does strange things to creatures of all kinds, I guess."

Yeah, like causing an intelligent, well-adjusted career woman to make an utter fool of herself. And she had felt just like the frogs during the police interrogation, choking on the emotion that had led her into becoming the perfect patsy.

Shep accelerated to pass an old farm truck on the long, isolated road and waved as they went by. The driver responded in kind.

Losing herself in thought, she closed her eyes and leaned back against the headrest. *Heavenly Father, what am I going to do?* Gram would tell her to trust in the Lord, but Deanna hadn't let go of the controls of her life in ages. Snatched from her hands by circumstance and her poor judgment as they'd been, it didn't look like she had any choice now.

"That dame is gone like the wind. I swear, boss, I have no idea how she slipped through our fingers *and* the cops." The caller in the phone booth off the interstate that led to Great Falls hoped the poor connection combined with the roar of passing trucks would cover the fear cracking his voice. No one disappointed the boss and lived to tell about it.

The ominous silence on the other end thundered in the man's ear. He had to break it. "She musta slipped outta the parking garage when I went to the john. I mean, it was just me, ya know?"

"Were you also in the john when Majors blew himself up in his own car?"

The caller's pulse accelerated. It wasn't his fault. He'd followed the man all over the city and watched in shock as the car exploded for no apparent reason. "Nobody knows what happened there. *Nobody*…not even the police."

"But they will find out. Then I'll have to find out from them, because my own men are incompetent." His boss's words were as void of emotion as that rabbit-eating snake he kept as a pet in his penthouse suite.

At the moment, it felt like the cold-blooded creature was slithering through the caller's veins, approaching a heart seized still as one of the hapless animals the creature fed upon.

"Look, boss. I can't help it if my partner ate some bad Chinese and I had to answer nature's call."

"Of course not. It's perfectly understandable." The man even hissed his s's like a bloomin' snake when he talked slow like that.

"Yeah, well I appreciate that, sir. I surely do." But did the big man really understand? The caller looked at his reflection on the dirty glass of the enclosure, certain he looked into the face of a dead man. He ought to just hang up and split, head for some place like Florida or Mexico. Except that the man on the other end of the phone had a long reach. Birds of a feather worked together, and this lethal breed lived all over the world.

"I'll take over from here. It's time I called in a favor from a colleague in the DEA. When I know something concrete, I'll contact you. In the meantime, you and your partner stand by for my call."

So did the command mean go back and wait for a message by phone or from a gun? The boss man ordered murders with the same tone he asked for coffee refills, which he drank as black as his temperament when provoked.

"Oh, and don't eat any more Chinese food till this is over."

"You got it, boss. I don't even like the stuff."

The man in the booth wiped his forehead, wishing he felt as at ease with things as his tone suggested. With friends on both sides of the law in and out of Canada, there would be no escaping retribution if the man on the other end of the phone wanted it. Sheesh, who could help having a sick partner or going to the john?

"We *will* find her," his superior said. It wasn't a reassurance. It was stated as nothing less than a fact.

"I'll be waiting to hear from ya." Using his right hand to steady his left, the caller hung up the phone. He shivered, despite the warm spring evening. All the man could do was pray that Deanna Manetti and the money would be found soon, distracting the drug lord from petty matters like him. He might get away with a broken nose or lose a finger, but this Manetti dame was a dead woman walking.

Six

"Six weeks at the earliest, 'lessen I can find something else. I been callin' around all mornin'."

Deanna stared at Shep's "shade tree" mechanic in the late morning sun, her expression lying somewhere between a squint and a grimace. The only shade in Charlie Long's automotive junkyard was the overhang of his cabin. At the moment, they were in the fenced-in lot where he'd towed her crinkled car. *Six weeks?*

Beside her, Shep made some sort of grunt, no more pleased with the news than she was. "Might as well ask about having that faulty airbag replaced, too. Much as this baby cost, it should have worked and repacked itself."

"Dad-gummed foreign cars…" Charlie spat to the side, shaking his head. "They're snazzy enough, but they're biddies to keep runnin'." He chuckled. "Like some women, I reckon."

Deanna's neck grew hot as he shot a speculative glance at her. Ordinarily she'd have shot back that it was none of his business how she chose to spend her hard-earned money, but she needed to remain on the old coot's good side. "I didn't buy it new. It was a drug repo auction. I was just in the right place at the right time."

"Till now," Charlie observed in a wry voice. "It just don't pay to buy outside the good old U.S. of A.; I don't care how new a model ya get or how good a buy it is. Why, I wouldn't take one if it was given to me," the mechanic snorted. "Foreign parts is foreign parts and sooner or later a body's goin' to pay to get 'em… when and *if* they find 'em, that is."

Deanna nodded. How could she not agree? If she'd had an old American-made car, Charlie would undoubtedly have had a used part in the vast lot of rusting has-beens, or he could have found a new one right away. But her blue baby was so pretty, so snazzy. And she'd taken a leave of her senses with an atypical crush—in love with love, with life, and with a stylish Stetson. It was a far cry from the well-worn topper Shep tipped off his forehead in dismay.

"Just get it so it will run. I'll worry about the airbag expense later," she said with a sigh.

"Check out the airbag anyway, Charlie," Shep contradicted.

"Getting a price won't hurt," he explained to Deanna, "and if I'm going to fix something, I want it done right. Might have saved that knot on your noggin'."

Charlie's spontaneous smile diffused any further objection she could muster. It was almost a fatherly one, a protective kind that spoke of genuine concern. She had to steel herself to keep from latching on to the sentiment like a lifeline. Her parents were gone and the last shoulder she'd leaned on vanished into thin air, allowing her to fall flat on her face in a heap of trouble.

"I'll make more calls," Charlie offered. The eyes beneath the ample bushes of his brow narrowed as they shifted from Shep to Deanna then back to Shep.

"Thanks, Charlie. I know you'll look out for me. Always have." Shep reseated his hat, as if the matter was settled.

Strange. She had looked out for herself pretty well until recently. She prided herself on being able to stand and survive on her own. Talk about being an idiot. The past few days clearly had shown her how wrong she'd been. If Deanna wanted to rely on someone, she'd better look beyond her mirror like Gram always said.

Like Shep did. She recalled how easily he'd given God credit for getting him through another day, how trusting it had sounded. Oh, she could ask quickly enough, but could she earnestly *trust* like that? It defied logic to sit back and wait for God to take over, like letting go of a steering wheel and allowing the car to steer itself into or out of a collision. How could she not try to stop or avoid it? Staring at the accordion-pleated hood of her blue baby, Deanna had proof positive that even with both hands on the wheel, she hadn't been able to control her own destiny.

Shep's voice invaded the cloud of revelation enveloping her mind. "Just radio me when you hear something."

"Sure thing," Charlie replied. "I wanna get it out of here right quick. Invites vandals."

Ushering Deanna to his Jeep, Shep halted in midstep.

"Vandals?" He echoed her very thought.

An icy stab of alarm cleared Deanna's mind, riveting her attention to what the mechanic had to say.

"Yep. I can't figure it." Charlie jerked his head toward the fence where a patch of new chain-link fence beamed bright against the weathered rust of the old. "Cut clean through my fence like one of them criminals on TV and made straight for that snazzy job. I only put up the fence to keep Buck from tomcattin' around at night. But come quarter to three this mornin', he commenced to raise thunder. By the time I got out here, whoever it was had left his cutters and a right smart-lookin' jacket hanging on the fence in his hurry to get out. Saw his taillights as he headed away from town, tires a squealin' and Buck a yappin' after him."

Charlie glanced over at a bulldog with a drab fur coat at least two sizes too large at the collar. The face he turned toward them at the mention of his name reminded Deanna of an aged Winston Churchill sans the cigar.

Shep scowled. "Did you call the sheriff?"

"Naw, probably some drifter. I figured he saw this rig and helped himself to a closer look." Charlie grunted. "'Sides, if he came back for his jacket, me 'n' Buck would be ready for 'im."

"Yeah, if he was local, he'd have known about Buck." Shep turned to Deanna. "Why don't you take a look and see if anything is missing. You'd think he'd have at least snagged those hubcaps."

"He was more curious than greedy," Charlie informed them. "Had the trunk popped. Left the glove compartment open. I just stuffed everything back in there."

"You going to look?" Shep prompted when she made no move toward the car.

Deanna felt as if she physically pulled herself from the icy pool of panic that formed in her mind. He. Was *he* the one—or one of the ones—who'd trashed her apartment? Had someone found her? And if so, what was he looking for? It should have been obvious by now that she wasn't floating in cash, or she wouldn't be stranded out here.

Canada wasn't so far away. Deanna had seen enough crime television to know that with the kind of money she'd been accused of taking, she could have had false IDs made and caught a plane to anywhere. She walked over to the sports car with leaden feet and slipped into the driver's seat. Her hand shook as she opened the glove box. The owner's manual, along with all her maintenance receipts, were stuffed into the organizer in haphazard manner. She pulled them out and put them in order, wishing her life could be put to rights so easily.

The contents of her vinyl cosmetic bag that had contained a brush, spare lipstick, and a few personal products had been emptied and scattered into the far recesses of the glove box. Leaving them where they were, rather than call attention to the contents, she put the organizer over them and closed the compartment door. As far as she could tell everything was there.

What good would anything she had in the car be to anyone anyway, much less a vandal or a thief? The answer to that nearly paralyzed her.

They didn't want her car. They wanted her.

Shep leaned on the open door of the vehicle, peering in. "Anything missing?"

"N…no. I don't think so. Must have been a nosy vandal." Her attempt to laugh was shallow at best.

He stepped back. "Hey, Charlie, is that the jacket in the back?" At his nod, Shep reached behind Deanna and retrieved a crumpled and soiled silk-linen blend sport coat. "You're right; he must have been a well-dressed drifter," he said, checking out the label.

"Like as not that was either stolen or handed out at a shelter."

Deanna couldn't comment with her heart wedged in her throat. She'd seen the jacket before—on C. R. Majors. Except it couldn't have been C. R. because he was dead. Even expensive men's wear stores carried more than one of a particular design or color. Besides, C. R. wouldn't be caught dead—

She winced as Shep tossed the jacket in the back and helped her out of the car.

"Did I hurt you?" He released his hold on her arm.

"No, I'm just a little stiff from yesterday's accident, I guess." Somehow her rubberlike legs supported her. Part of her insisted the jacket was just a fluke. She was overreacting with nerves that were frayed to the point of snapping. Yet another more latent voice cried out, *God?* as if some heavenly voice was going to reassure her.

"The jack and spare are still there," Shep observed from behind her. He rifled through the contents of the trunk.

Unless C. R.'s jacket had been taken by his murderer. Unadulterated fear chilled the very marrow of her bones, oblivious to her desperate reasoning. But how had the man found her car when she didn't even know where she was?

"It's a real tire, too," Charlie observed in approval as Shep pulled out an old map that must have belonged to the previous owner from under the spare.

No, the one who searched her place couldn't have found her, she concluded, grateful that both men seemed oblivious to her dismay. It was simply impossible.

"Don't see much of that anymore," the mechanic went on. "Them flimsy little emergency jobs come standard now."

Shep grinned. "Not in these cars, Charlie." He handed Deanna her leather-encased portfolio. "Anything missing in this?"

As though expecting something to fly out at her, she peeked inside. Nothing inside was worth stealing, just plain paper and her drafting supplies. She had no real work in progress, having been on the job just long enough to acquaint herself with the current procedures and marketing personnel. At least her search gave her a chance to find her voice, if not any answers to the questions bombarding her.

"Nothing is missing that I can tell. Like Mr. Long said—"

"Make that Charlie," the older man interrupted. "I don't hold with much formality around here."

"Like Charlie said," Deanna flashed an appreciative glance at her host, "whoever went through the car must have just been curious." And he was likely some vagrant who lucked out at a shelter with wealthy contributors. C. R. didn't have the only expensive jacket in the world. She took a deep breath to override the sense of helplessness her lingering doubt instilled.

"Or thought there might be some money tucked away," Charlie speculated. "This model all but shouts big bucks."

"Well, it lies," Deanna said. "Just because it looks expensive doesn't mean it was." And just because the jacket looked like C. R.'s didn't mean it was. Appearances could be misleading. "I'm just glad they didn't damage anything when they found nothing worth stealing."

It *had* to be vandals…a fluke. Since she was certain that she couldn't find where she was on a map, the police or the people who'd ransacked her apartment couldn't either. End of story.

"Buck didn't give 'im much time to think beyond saving his hide." Charlie pointed to the bulldog watching them through the folds of his brow.

Buck didn't look like Deanna's idea of a junkyard dog, despite Charlie's talking as if the animal did more than sleep, eat, and cast a lazy eye over visitors. Somehow she pictured a Doberman or a rottweiler, not a pudgy pooch that hardly looked as if it could catch a burglar any more than its stub of a tail. Talk about appearances being deceiving.

"Nonetheless, you ought to report it, Charlie." As if his word settled the matter, Shep started toward the Jeep. "Never can tell about these things."

Deanna cast a quizzical look at Shep as she got in on the passenger side. His expression was fathomless, suggesting neither suspicion nor dismissal. From what she'd seen to date of her rescuer, if he were to err, it would be on the side of caution.

"Aw, I hate to bother Sheriff Barrett. And that deputy of his is more interested in listenin' to the scanner than doin' anything productive." Charlie followed Shep to the vehicle. "I been tellin' you, Shep, you ought to consider takin' the sheriff's place when he retires this fall. Lots of folks think that's right up your alley."

"It's not gonna happen, so save your breath. Hopewell needs all my time." Shep started the Jeep, giving it gas when it threatened to die.

"Don't hurt to think about it, does it?"

The Jeep jerked backward as Shep shifted into reverse. "I've got all I can think about right now without adding something else."

Lips twitching, the mechanic stepped back to give them space. With a keen glance at Deanna, he gave in to a lopsided grin. "Yep, I reckon you do at that."

Shepard Jones wasn't the only one with a lot to think about. Deanna fastened her seat belt as they accelerated out onto the highway toward Buffalo Butte proper. He couldn't possibly be any happier than she about her being stuck here without a vehicle for a minimum of six weeks. She'd thought for certain that Charlie could hammer out the dents, replace the flat tire, and she'd be on her way. Who knew her radiator and some special order thingamabob was trashed as well? Without adding auto theft to her rap sheet, she was stuck in the boonies where people left the g off of half the words that ended in -ing, dogs and guns were man's best friends, and dressed up for women meant clean jeans.

"Well, that settles that, I guess," Shep drawled. "I might as well take you back to Great Falls."

Deanna's breath caught, but it didn't stop the feel of the blood racing from her face to feed the panicked staccato of her heart. The only thing worse than being stuck here for six weeks was being stuck in Great Falls without a getaway car. She couldn't go back there. She just couldn't. She needed to lay low until she figured out what she could do.

"We'll hash it out over lunch," he suggested when she didn't reply.

After a short stop by the Farm and Ranch General, Shep took her to a vintage fifties railcar diner. The sign in front advertised a hot turkey sandwich and "fixins" for $2.99 as the special of the day. A shiny glassed-in entrance appeared to have been a recent addition, no doubt for climate control to the streamlined structure of time-dulled stainless steel.

As they entered, almost every head turned toward them, save those people who stared at the new arrivals via the reflection in the mirrors lining the diner walls. As she'd done since leaving Charlie's garage, Deanna warily searched each face, although she tried not to be as obvious as the curious townspeople. To her relief, none looked threatening—just the everyday rural sort.

Undaunted by the blatant attention, Shep ushered her to an empty booth around the end of the lunch counter by the restroom entrances, affording them some semblance of privacy.

Even though Deanna had just eaten her egg sandwich, the sight of the oversized pies in the glass display case on the counter and the smells emanating from the grill made her mouth water. The last time she'd eaten in a place like this had been with her grandmother when Deanna was a schoolgirl. The old diner at the corner of Maynard and Vandam had long since been replaced by a parking garage for a new medical facility. Somehow the similarity of

Buffalo Butte's Town Diner to the one from her past was reassuring.

"So what'll it be today, Shep darlin'?" A waitress—the only one as far as she could see—spoke to Shep, but her eye was on Deanna. She even looked like the Maynard Diner's Miss Fanny—heavy on the eyeliner and in a faded pink uniform with a spotless white apron. All that was missing was the little pleated frill in her tightly permed hair.

Shep grabbed a laminated menu from behind a miniature jukebox listing golden oldies and, glancing up, answered the inevitable question in her eyes. "Maisy, let me introduce you to Deanna Manetti. Deanna, this is Maisy O'Donnall. She and her husband run the best diner in town."

"That's because it's the *only* diner in town," Maisy shot back, not quite appeased by Shep's brief introduction. "Manetti? That's not a local name is it?"

"I'm from New York." Deanna extended a manicured hand. "Pleased to meet you, Mrs. O'Donnall."

"Lord 'a mercy, just call me Maisy. Last time I heard *Mrs. Anything* was right after I said 'I do.'"

"Miss Manetti is just checking out the place before she decides to take a job in Great Falls and relocate permanently from the East," Shep said. "Or she was until that blamed stallion ran her off the road and wrecked her car. She's been stranded out at Hopewell."

"Now I could think of worse folks to be stranded with." The wink Maisy gave him was outrageous.

"It's just till my car is fixed," Deanna mumbled, shooting an uncertain look at Shep. Where had *that* come from? Was it the answer to her shaky prayer or her desperation to stay at Hopewell until she had wheels again?

"Honey, if I was you, I'd take some irreplaceable thingamajig out of that vehicle and hide it, if you get my drift."

And Miss Fanny had also flashed that same flirtatious twinkle Maisy directed at Shep.

"Don't pay any attention to her," he said. "She runs on that way to all the men. And if they're single, her sole purpose in life is to herd them to an altar to alter their status."

"It's a scientific fact that married men live longer than single ones," Maisy rallied, her ample bosom swelling beneath the bib of her apron like that of a ruffled hen.

"Hey, Mais, where's that coffee?" one of the patrons at the counter called out.

"Now, Homer darlin', you know full well where it is," the waitress hollered over her shoulder. She turned back to Deanna with a woman-to-woman wink. "I'm making Shep's New York girlfriend here welcome. It wouldn't do for her to think we were antisocial."

It was almost like going back to the safety and security of another era...except instead of Gram, a tall, dark, and handsome cowboy sat across from her, a flush climbing up from his collar. Maybe Shep wasn't as impervious to his surroundings as he'd have others think. Or instead of being embarrassed, he was quietly fuming over her presumption that she was staying at Hopewell for the next six weeks.

"I'll have a burger and fries," he said quickly in an obvious effort to bring Maisy back to the point of their visit. "What'll you have, *Miss* Manetti?"

The earlier tease in his voice had hardened as well. She shouldn't have mentioned it in front of someone. Why couldn't she just let things develop without taking over the controls? This mess with C. R. scrambled her brain and undermined the faith she sought to dust off.

Deanna skimmed over the menu, unable to focus on the specials. Finally she seized upon a picture of a soup and sandwich meal. "A cup of the chicken soup looks good. Oh, and a diet cola." Her mouth had gone dry as the dirt on Hopewell's main street.

"Landsakes, gal, no wonder you got so many sharp corners. Men 'round these parts like their women more rounded, if you get my drift."

She squirmed under Maisy's disapproval. "I had a late break-fast." No doubt, the waitress would make her eat every drop of soup, just as Miss Fanny always had. After Deanna's loved ones had passed on, she thought people had stopped caring. Maybe that was why she'd been such a dupe when it came to C. R. and his seeming solicitous attentions.

Maisy shifted her attention back to Shep. "You want coffee as usual?" At his nod, she leaned over and said in a sawmill whisper, "Take care of this one and she'll round out nice as me."

"Well, you've done it now," he remarked, watching the wait-ress retreat behind the counter.

"Done what?" Deanna gave him a startled look. This was it. He would insist on taking her back to Great Falls.

"Now everyone within satellite range of Buffalo Butte will know that I'm harboring a waif from the Big Apple who doesn't have enough meat on her bones to tempt a hungry buzzard…leastwise, to Maisy's notion."

She mustered a laugh more of relief than humor, but it was short lived.

"You know, Deanna Manetti, I get the feeling that you're not telling me everything about your reason for being in these parts."

"W-what do you mean?" She struggled to keep her gaze and voice steady.

"First, you're riding out here in the wild with no idea where you are, as if you didn't even have a destination. You're as skittish as a long-tailed cat in a room full of rockers. You seem to be expecting something horrible to happen to you at any moment. And—" he took a deep breath before continuing—"you really have a problem with trusting anyone, particularly a man. Now you've either been watching too much TV or…"

Deanna's breath froze in her chest, the sip of water she'd just taken pooling in her mouth. She waited for the proverbial ax to fall.

"Or you are running from something, lady."

Seven

Shep's lips thinned into a grimace at Deanna's stricken silence. "I'd say you've had man trouble…maybe a relationship gone sour?"

Seizing on the excuse, she nodded, managing to swallow. Yes, that would work. Surely it came from heaven to his lips! Deanna resisted the urge to clap her hands in pious gratitude, swallowing the water instead.

"*Sour* is as good a word for it as any." That one *had* to be from God. She couldn't have put the notion in Shep's head. And for the most part, it was true. Framing her had certainly soured her relationship with C. R. At least God was speaking to Shep, if not her.

"And what about your job?"

"He was my boss." *Was* being the key word, as in dead. That part of her nightmare still didn't seem real, even though she'd seen the pictures of the charred remains of his car. She shuddered inside.

"Here's your drinks." Maisy set the soda and coffee on the table and left abruptly as though she knew this was no time to interrupt. "Food'll be up in a jiffy," she called over her shoulder.

Deanna couldn't freeze now. Her thoughts clicked, processing a believable scenario based on Shep's assumption. A week ago, her honesty did her family's raising proud. Now she couldn't tell the truth…at least not the complete truth. "I just wanted to get away from it all. In just six weeks, he…he took over my life, which wasn't what I expected when I came out here. Nothing was what I expected."

"In other words, East is East and West is West." The bitterness that surfaced in Shep's voice and expression took her by surprise.

"It wasn't *that* exactly. I was willing to give the West a try, but my prince was a snake in disguise." Her shoulders fell. So far, she hadn't told an outright lie. "He frightened me and I ran. Now I..." The blade of emotion in her throat was real. "Now I don't know where to go or what to do. I just know I can't go back to Great Falls...or New York for a while."

"Do you think he'll follow you?"

She saw where Shep was going, thinking that maybe the owner of the jacket had been her ex's. Deanna wished C. R. *were* all she had to worry about. But the one who'd broken into her apartment, not to mention the police, was a different matter. As for her car... No, that was a coincidence, nothing more.

"It's possible I'm being followed." What would happen if she told Shep the entire truth? His concern seemed genuine enough—a straight arrow given the respect she'd seen afforded him by those who knew him. If only she'd sought references for C. R. Majors.

"I have friends with the police. They'd take care of him."

"No!" Her panicked thought was out before she could hold it back. "I...I was hoping the old adage out of sight, out of mind, would kick in. I mean, once he sees I didn't return to New York, he'd have nowhere else to look, right?" Folding her arms on the table, she buried her face in them. "I can't believe I was so stupid to think I was in love."

A tear trickled down her nose and dripped on the table. She had to pull herself together. It wouldn't do to turn crybaby. She needed her wits about her. She needed—

"Been there, done that."

Sympathy and compassion were rich in Shep's voice and in the warm hand he put on her shoulder. "All you need is three hots and a cot until you get your thoughts together. Maybe that's where the Hopewell name gets its meaning. I know I've certainly taken refuge there since I was a kid watching my folks get divorced. I always left well again and filled with hope that things would be okay, if not in my eyes, at least in the Lord's. The Father knows best." It was the quote embroidered on the small wall plaque over the sink in his kitchen. Deanna raised her head, staring at Shep. Had God really heard her prayer? Was this His answer? Could it be this simple and straightforward?

"But any stray who comes to Hopewell has to pull her own weight," he advised her. "How does room and board sound in exchange for keeping house and giving me a hand when I need it?"

Relief flooded Deanna's mind, but with it swept in one tiny cloud of anxiety. It sounded like heaven, but the job itself was just the opposite to a woman who depended on the laundry down the block, food from a dozen local delis and restaurants, and a once-a-week cleaning lady to keep her apartment from being closed down by the Health Department. Her work had been her life, taking up and paying for keeping her singular household.

"Giving me a hand when I need it," he'd said. Make that *two* clouds, she amended as the rest of Shep's proposition registered. "But I don't know the least thing about horses."

"Ain't nothin' to know about horses that this fella can't teach you." Maisy leaned over and placed a bowl of hot soup in front of Deanna. Shep got his burger and fries. "Not that I was listenin'. And if I was, no need to keep such as that to myself, since everyone in here can tell the only horse you ever rode had to swallow a quarter to run."

"What, am I that green?" Deanna fell in with the ribbing.

Maisy chuckled. "Now, hon, you just got that citified look and manner, not to mention that accent. You call Shep's horses 'you guys,' and you just might spook 'em."

"I wish I knew what it'd take to spook *you* away," Shep said with a pointed look at Maisy.

"More'n you got, cowboy," the waitress fired back as she returned to the counter.

Deanna giggled. It seemed to ease the heaviness in her chest that had been there since everything had started to go wrong. It felt good, almost intoxicating. Shep Jones didn't exactly wear a white hat, but in that moment, he was her hero.

"She's a real character. Reminds me of someone I knew back in Brooklyn when I was a kid."

"Characters are all we grow out here," Shep told her with a grin that made her giggle again. Startled, Deanna put her hand over her mouth. Only half the schoolgirl reaction escaped, but it lit up mischief in his eyes.

"I didn't think you had a giggle under that streetwise facade of yours. Not to mention you've been white as old ashes since we left Charlie's."

Facade. He saw right through her. Deanna wasn't sure she wanted that with any man again—even a hero. Somehow she managed to pull a straight, stern face. "Facade, huh?" She pointed an authoritative finger at his plate. "Just eat your food before it gets cold."

In spite of his companion's confession, Shep had a niggling sense that he still didn't have the whole story. Or maybe his uneasiness was the result of the protective instinct she evoked in him. Taking in strays was a weakness of his, but this was a woman, not a cat or dog. Although, her spit and huff reminded him of a kitten, trying to intimidate for all it was worth out of fear. It was natural to want to coddle and reassure her.

And quite possibly dangerous. He must have taken leave of his senses to let her stay at Hopewell, much less offer her a job. The more he thought about it through the meal and a second cup of coffee, the more convinced he became. Deanna Manetti was definitely on the run and afraid of whoever was after her. The physical threat didn't bother him nearly as much as the emotional risk.

Despite her appeal, she was like his ex-fiancée—city born

and bred. And like Ellen, Deanna minced no words regarding her opinion of Big Sky country. As soon as she excused herself to go to the restroom, he slid out of his seat and headed for the old-fashioned wooden phone booth located between the restroom doors.

For all Shep knew, cultural and social differences could have been the issues that broke the proverbial camel's back between her and her estranged boss/boyfriend. She was here out of desperation, he decided as he dialed a familiar number.

"U.S. Marshal Service, Holloway speaking."

"Don't tell me you're still around, old-timer," Shep teased his longtime friend. "I thought you'd have hung up your six-guns by now."

Bob Holloway had run into the same sort of physical disability problem as Shep had, except his friend chose to take a desk job rather than leave the service altogether. Shep couldn't blame him for taking a sure thing rather than chasing a dream with a wife and five kids to support.

"Well, if it isn't the big game hunter. How are things in the high country?"

"Beautiful but troublesome." Shep glanced a few booths away where Deanna took her seat again. Maisy chatted with Deanna while she indulged in a slice of one of Town Diner's home-baked cream pies. The waitress insisted that it was on the house, a welcome to Buffalo Butte gift.

"Sounds more like a woman than an elk."

"It is. I need you to check out a Deanna Manetti—New York City, maybe Brooklyn with her accent...moved to Great Falls for a job with Image International. It's a marketing firm, I think."

"That it?"

"I have a license number and car to trace." Shep fumbled through his wallet for the note he'd made and gave his friend the data.

"Nice," Bob drawled. "A high-price city gal. You must have a weakness for the type."

"Once burned, twice shy. I just want to know what I might have to deal with," Shep explained, as much for himself as the man on the phone. "She's not been forthcoming with information. Claims she's running from a possessive boss/boyfriend."

"Don't tell me you've taken her in."

Wryness tugged one corner of Shep's mouth. "Didn't have much choice. It was *my* stallion that ran her off the road, even though she was on my property."

"And you felt obligated—"

"Yeah, yeah. Just call the sheriff's office in town and have him contact me when you get the info, okay, buddy?"

"Watch your back," Bob cautioned.

"I usually do."

The warning prompted a distracting rush of unwelcome memory. Shep hung up the phone, snatched back to a time he'd tried to forget. He'd been so busy watching his back, and that of the witness in his custody, that he'd failed to see what the DEA agent assigned to the joint operation was doing. Before Shep knew what was going down, he'd taken a bullet in the knee while protecting a female snitch.

A full-scale gunfight had broken out. The other agency hadn't bothered to tell the Marshals that the witness assigned to their transport and protection was being used as bait to draw out the big fish. His gung ho partner got a promotion. Shep got an award and forced retirement from active duty.

He'd returned to the high country to reconcile the bad turns in his life. Psalm 18:33 became his mantra: *"He makes my feet like the feet of deer, and sets me on my high places."* There Shep reevaluated his life, his love, and rediscovered the closeness he'd once known with God, before his busy life had come between them like a time-stealing, attention-grabbing predator.

Was Deanna Manetti a different kind of predator, either by design or by chance? Barely healed himself, Shep struggled with the inner voice that urged him to take her in. Why would God put another woman in his path after the last one had come between them?

Shep opened the folding door of the age-darkened phone booth and met Deanna's smile. It wasn't an invitation, but there was a part of him that wished it were. It was that part of him that scared him more than the possibility of some gun-wielding, jealous boyfriend.

Lord, lead me not into temptation, he prayed as he stepped up to the table and took the check. "Well, Slick, are you ready to hit the road?"

Nodding, Deanna gathered up the small purse from the vinyl seat beside her.

"Don't you forget the community hall meeting Friday night," Maisy reminded him. "Bring Deanna too. Maybe she can come up with a way to stir more interest in our Craft Days fund-raiser."

Even though he was committee chairman, Shep had forgotten. Deanna was disrupting his life in more ways than he could count.

"Better watch out for this one," Shep said, with a sigh. "If the government had Maisy O'Donnall on their interrogation team, she'd unravel the secrets of the criminal world like a crocheted blanket."

Maisy snorted with indignation. "I'm just bein' friendly to this nice young woman. Not that she'd have a secret to her name."

Was that a check of alarm Shep detected in the deep pools of his guest's eyes or the shot of sunlight reflected on the diner's shiny door opening to admit a new customer? Reservation clouded over his playful humor as he followed Deanna to the checkout. He hoped he was mistaken.

Eight

D o you need to call anyone before we head back?" Shep
held open the door to the Stop and Save Market where
they picked up a few groceries.

"*One lie begets another.*" Gram's sage observation haunted
Deanna as though whispered straight into her ear. *Gram, bear with
me and…and, Lord, please forgive me. I know You've given me refuge.
I'm just trying to hold on to it.* She chose her words with care, stick-
ing to the flight-from-a-relationship-gone-sour scenario she'd
sketched earlier. "The only one I might call is the one I dare *not*
call."

The fact was she had no one to call, no one to turn to. Her
chivalrous host was her only friend, and that was based on false
pretenses.

"What about family back home in the Big Apple?"

"No one close anymore. Just a distant relative or two." She'd
never been a social butterfly. More like a business bee, she had
friends only in the context of work. Time hadn't been there for
others. After Gram's death, her extended family's gatherings had
stopped. With Deanna's parents gone, she had no one close with
whom to keep in touch.

Heavily populated as it was, New York had been a lonely
place. No wonder she'd been such an easy pick for the first guy
brave enough to breach that no-nonsense wall she'd erected
around her almost nonexistent private life.

"Well, *I'm* having second thoughts already," Shep quipped as he deposited the three bags of groceries into the back of the Jeep.

Second thoughts? Deanna abandoned her morose evaluation of her life with a startled look.

"I don't know if I can afford to feed you," he teased. "Looks like I'm feeding a herd of rabbits."

Picking up on the friendly debate, which had started at the produce counter when she suggested they purchase more than one kind of lettuce for a salad and something other than apples for fruit, Deanna rallied in relief. "Fruit and vegetables are part of the basic four food groups, but your lettuce has little nutritional value. And in case you hadn't heard, beans don't make the fruit and veggie grade." Or did they? She tried to recall a home economics lesson long since moved to the recesses of her memory about the placement of legumes. They went with meat and proteins didn't they?

"I had vegetables and fruit already…plenty of both."

"In cans, dusty cans at that." Deanna had seen them when she put away the dishes last night. "Everyone knows that fresh salads and produce are far more healthy."

"And more trouble," Shep pointed out with a stubborn quirk of his lips. "Especially when a man doesn't know if or when he'll have time to cook. I just got tired of throwing stuff away. If it's in a can, it's always good. It's not like I have a market within spitting distance like you do."

If not for the mischievous light in those bourbon brown eyes of his, Deanna would have retreated. The last thing she wanted was to jeopardize her temporary reprieve from life on the lam.

"That's where health-conscious planning comes in," she told him with brazen authority as he backed out of the row of parking spaces that ran parallel to Buffalo Butte's tree-dotted main street.

Surely, Martha Stewart was choking somewhere at that very moment, given Deanna's helter-skelter home life. It was more than literal miles away from this small town, U.S.A. But for the street vendors and delicatessens so prevalent around her previous workplace and neighborhood, she'd be eating out of cans and the frozen cardboard boxes she'd spotted in Shep's freezer, too.

"But those two cans of Chef Luigi's macaroni and franks don't count, I guess."

Caught, there was nothing to do but fess up. "When it's on sale, one can indulge on occasion."

"Oh, I get it." Shep cut a sidewise glance at her. "Breaking the rules is okay when it suits you."

His question struck the bulls-eye of her conscience. Were they still talking about food? Squirming mentally, she forced a grin. "Okay, I admit it. I've been a Chef Luigi addict since child-hood." At the raise of his brow, she added, "What, do you think cowboys have the monopoly on an unpredictable schedule? It's a quick meal in a pinch."

Shep lifted his hand, acknowledging the wave of the young man sweeping the pavement in front of a pharmacy/soda foun-tain. Everyone here not only knew Shep but obviously liked him. The more she saw of him, how could anyone not like Shepard Jones?

Deanna felt guilty deceiving such a nice guy, but what choice did she have? Would he be so nice and understanding if she'd said she was on the run from the police and God only knew whom else? Would he believe in her innocence when the facts the detec-tive had presented her were almost enough to convince even her that she was guilty?

With an involuntary shiver, she turned away to stare at the lazy roll of the pastureland as they left the equally slow-paced town.

"You too cold?" Shep's inquiry gave away the fact that his attention hadn't wavered from her. Under other circumstances, it would have been flattering, even hoped for.

Deanna shook her head. "Somebody must have stepped on my grave," she offered, repeating one of Gram's sayings.

"I'm a fresh air fiend anyway." Shep cut off the air-conditioner and rolled down the windows from his console.

"Yeah, me too. Nothing like a lungful of diesel fumes to kick off the day." Deanna couldn't keep a straight face at the sharp look aimed at her. It softened with a white-toothed grin.

"If it blows your hair too much, just holler."

"Spoken by a man who must know his way around women." What kind of woman made a man like Shep tick?

"Nope, just their hair. Consideration of that is one of those universal rules integral to man's survival. You know, like never leave the toilet seat up."

With a laugh, she focused on the country surrounding them while Shep fiddled with the radio. He probably went for the fresh-scrubbed and wholesome as milk type—someone who was equally at home in the kitchen and the stable instead of the deli and the office. Definitely not her.

Resigned, she enjoyed the wind whipping her hair about her face and eyes. Although it had been cut for just such abandon, whether clipped up off her neck or down as it was now, Deanna rarely had the chance to test it. The rushing air seemed to carry away her problems, enabling her to appreciate her surroundings and the country music station's corny parody of the *Perils of Pauline.*

The villain tied Sweet Sue to the railroad tracks. The train was coming. Things couldn't look any more hopeless. Corny as it was, Deanna related to Sweet Sue's desperation. In her mind she could see C. R. with the black cape and sleazy mustache framing her and then the ransacking and then…just like in the chorus of the radio song, "Along Came Jones"—Shepard Jones, that is.

She gave her companion a startled look and burst out laughing. "Get outta here."

"What?" he asked, clueless.

"Along came *Jones.*" She waved her hands, directing and singing along with the chorus. "Get it? I mean, is that weird or what?"

Shep's mouth thinned to more of a grimace than a smile. "I don't see the connection. I ran you off the road and then rescued you. The name is the only similarity, and Jones is one of the most common names—"

"Forget it. It just struck me funny." Men! No sense of whimsy. She settled against the headrest once more as the song gave way to an advertisement for some bug killer for farm and ranch use, but at the announcement of the upcoming weather and news brief, her relaxed humor turned to alarm. What if her story was aired? *God, spare me please. I just need a little time…*

She listened, breath still, for her name, but the broadcast leaned more toward national and international headlines. In no time at all, the music started again. Once again, she could breathe easily and savor the moment in silence.

Although there were no horns blowing or hordes of people waiting impatiently at every corner for a light to change, the ride took Deanna back to carefree hours spent in the taxi with her dad. While city born and bred, he'd been a cowboy at heart. Country music and TV Westerns were a mainstay at the Manetti household. What would he think now if he saw the coppery sea of cattle grazing on a sun-parched plateau in the distance instead of rush hour traffic frozen around him? She could almost hear him singing along with the radio, belting out lyrics about being footloose and fancy free in the middle of Montana. Had she been chasing his dream and not her own?

"The cattle look like their coats are polished," she observed as the Jeep passed them by. "Are they yours?"

"The cows aren't, but the land is. I lease it for grazing to one of the bigger spreads. Helps pay the taxes at least, till I can get up and running with my horses."

So Hopewell was much bigger than its meager home place suggested. Although he fell back into silence, Shep's remark triggered the latent entrepreneur in her. With this kind of collateral, there were any number of opportunities Shep might consider as a means to fulfill his dream. Why he wanted to train four-legged beasts that would eat him out of house and home, not to mention fill a litterbox in one visit, was beyond her, but it was possible.

Even though Deanna was clearly out of her element, she wouldn't mind the all's well euphoria of this windblown country-song moment and the companionable presence of her host as part of her life. In the back of the Jeep as the road became rougher along with the landscape, a symphony of rattling paper and plastic interspersed with the occasional bottle-tapping timpani played like a lullaby, while the bags of groceries kept time to an upbeat rendition of Western swing.

At Shep's intrusive chuckle beside her, Deanna realized she'd lost herself in woolgathering longer than she thought. Worse, she'd started singing aloud with the chorus again, not just in her mind.

"I wouldn't quit my day job for a recording contr—" Shep swerved the Jeep with a clipped, "Well, I'll be a—"

Before embarrassment could claim her, their vehicle was bouncing like a speeding taxi over road construction across the shallow ditch running parallel to the road. Her exclamation of astonishment had hardly rolled off her lips when Shep steered the vehicle straight up a dry grassy incline. With the grinding and groaning of gears echoing the outrage of the jouncing, banging grocery bags in the back, she finally saw the reason for his sudden and erratic behavior. Grazing at the edge of some scrub trees crowning the hill was the sorrel stallion that had forced her off the road the day before.

"What are you going do?" She braced herself against the dash of the vehicle with her hands.

Ahead, the horse lifted its head, ears pricked. It stood frozen for a moment, like a magnificent statue glistening red in the sun, then reared on its hindquarters in defiance. Its golden mane and tail unfurled as it bolted, racing along the wood's edge and down toward a steep-sided valley.

"Corral that son-of-a-prairie-biscuit," Shep steered the Jeep after it.

"In *this?*" Glad for the seat belt that kept her from bumping her head on the roof, Deanna glanced sideways at her companion. There was no telling exactly what he said under his breath, but the renegade stallion had shattered his laid-back attitude.

The sorrel left a trail of dust, amplified by the Jeep pursuing it. Head bent in determination, Shep maintained a tight hold on the wheel and Deanna held what breath was not jolted out of her. The Jeep careened over a raised slab of rock on the floor of what was turning into a canyon with higher and higher rocky cobalt sides. "You can't possibly catch him in this."

"No, but if I can herd him into the draw up ahead, there's an old gate there that just might hold him until I can get back with Patch. You game?"

His excitement *was* infectious. Or was it the challenge Deanna found impossible to ignore as she nodded, grinning like a fool. Thank heaven they were strapped in a Jeep with a roll bar...and that they hadn't seen the mustang again yesterday while riding Patch, who had no such safety devices.

Each time the stallion pivoted and tried to run back, Shep steered the Jeep into his path to head him off, honking with a horn that sounded like it hadn't quite cleared puberty. She thought the vehicle surely would turn over, but it soon became obvious that the cowboy at the wheel had done this before and knew just how far to push it. All he needed to do was wave his hat out the window and holler—

"Yee-hah!"

...exactly what he just did, she thought, as startled as she was incredulous. Gripping the dash with one hand and the window frame with the other, Deanna definitely preferred to ride the trail from her dad's old La-Z-Boy.

The stallion tried doubling back again, this time with more determination than ever. It was almost as if the animal sensed the trap ahead. With Shep leaning out the window and whipping his hat overhead in big circles, his long stretch caused his foot to slip off the gas pedal and the Jeep threatened to die.

He jerked the vehicle out of gear to slow down. "Take over," he shouted, unbuckling his seat belt and reaching for the door handle.

"Get outta here!"

In a flash, Shep braked and was out running toward the charging horse.

"No wait, not really—" she called after him in disbelief.

Waving like a wild man, he blocked the stallion's path where the Jeep couldn't maneuver.

Deanna fumbled at her own seat belt for what seemed like an eternity. She climbed into the driver's seat as the vehicle, left in neutral, began to drift. Frantic, she stared at the worn sketch of the gears on the shift knob. It had been years since she'd managed the gearshift on the family's old station wagon. In fact, she rarely drove in the city at all, having had to store her car in a garage in Jersey due to the high cost of parking.

Ahead of her, the stallion moved like an express train toward Shep. Its ears were laid back, the stretch from its head to tail level. Hooves pounding the earth, the horse sped closer and closer, but the cowboy just stood there.

"What, have you got a death wish or something?" Deanna revved the engine the way her dad did when waiting for the red light to go green.

To protect the man from being splattered like a bug on a grill of a moving car, she jammed the shift into first gear. Her mechanical steed roared and jumped forward, but the front wheels struck a sharp rut, the wheel jerking in her hands.

"Whoa, speed bump," she gasped. Easing up on the accelerator, she shifted into the next gear before cracking down on it again. As the gears found their teeth, the Jeep surged ahead in sporadic persistence.

Andretti, eat your heart out. She engaged the third gear and the fourth with NASCAR determination. Ahead she saw the stallion less than a length away from trampling Shep down.

No way she could intercept it. Deanna gripped the wheel, bracing for the inevitable when the sorrel pivoted with a sharp right, rolling Shep to the side. Or had the man jumped? She swerved into the path of the horse to head it off, wondering if it could jump a Jeep with the same ease it had brushed off its master.

"Cut him off!"

A glance in the side mirror confirmed that Shep was up and cheering her on. Maybe the animal was afraid of vehicles, she thought, heartened by the encouragement. After all, Shep wouldn't urge her into the path of those thundering hooves if it weren't.

"Heeyah!" Caught up in the excitement, Deanna dared to release her left hand from the wheel to wave at the oncoming horse. If only Pop could see her now.

The mustang was coming head on and something was flying from its mouth, as if it were snorting and blowing puffs of lather like some rabid wild thing. Snatching her hand back inside, she seized the wheel with the panic that shot straight from her clenched fingers to the feet she locked on the brakes. The tires dug into the dirt, throwing the rear end every which way in a whirlwind of dust, while she struggled to keep it straight.

It was impossible on the dry, rock-studded terrain. As if a giant had picked up the back of the Jeep on one side, the vehicle lurched in a precarious tilt.

Deanna's scream was cut short by the slam of the rear wheels on the dirt. Something glass shattered in the back. The whole vehicle bounced a couple of times, but somehow, she regained control. As she shifted down to slow her reckless pace, the transmission growled and shrieked in bone-chilling protest.

"Not reverse! You'll drop the transmission!"

She barely heard Shep's warning. All she knew was that she had to stop and let the horse go wherever it darn well pleased.

Again Deanna hit the brakes and closed her eyes. Moving at a slower speed, the vehicle came to a jerky halt, coughed, sputtered, and died in a surrounding cloud of dust. She braced for the horse to run it over, for the crash of metal and foam-snorting muscle. Instead, Shep's voice penetrated her fear-frozen state.

"Hold tight, Slick."

Opening her eyes, Deanna saw that the stallion had turned once again, and Shep was on its heels howling like a banshee. Weak-kneed, she stumbled out of the Jeep, watching the horse head into an offshoot of the valley. Just visible in the overgrown brush nearby was an old gate made of rusty wire and boards split and weathered by the elements. The minute Shep reached the gate, he dragged it across the opening, closing the mustang in.

Her mouth dry and her heart beating a mile a minute, Deanna stood by the hot vehicle as Shep approached it. He was smiling at her, not the least perturbed that she'd almost busted his Jeep's transmission. She stepped out of his way to avoid his purposeful stride, only to be gathered up in his arms and swung around.

"We got him!" Shep whirled her about once more. Suddenly, he gave her big kiss on the cheek. "Not bad for a city gal. I'll make a wrangler out of you yet."

City gal…wrangler—what was wrong with this picture? The answer was lost, swept away by the rush of his infectious excitement. All she knew was that she wished she could preserve the moment. Instead, she bobbed her head like one of those spring-necked toy dogs that rode in a car back window.

Robbed of breath by the triumphant high—or was it the dancing gaze that dipped into her own?—Deanna stood in the wiry circle of Shep's embrace. His damp, work-hardened body pressed her softer one against the warm metal of the vehicle. Her heart fell over itself with the male essence of dust, sweat, and soap assailing her nostrils.

The sun kindled a sobering light in the umber-dark look that slid from her eyes to her mouth. Deanna's knees quivered like gelatin. She was no femme fatale, but she knew when a man was going to kiss her. She held her breath, bracing and yet knowing that she would yield the moment his lips touched hers.

Leaning ever so close, Shep brushed her cheek to cheek as he reached around her, inside the Jeep, and retrieved a coil of rope from behind the driver's seat. "I better secure the gate before he takes a notion to bolt."

Feeling as intelligent as one of those dippy toy dogs, Deanna tried to pull herself together as Shep turned away. "Sure," she called after him, unsure of anything.

What the devil had just happened? It was one thing to wax nostalgic with her charming, good-looking host, but somewhere between daydream, reality, and roundup, her imagination crossed a line she hadn't even seen—one she vowed she'd never cross again.

Nine

While Shep reinforced the blooming gate with the blooming rope, Deanna focused on rebagging the scattered groceries, as though that would distract her from the emotional riot over what had just happened…*or not happened*. It wasn't as if she'd been waiting all day for Shep Jones to kiss her; she mopped up the juice from a bottle that had cracked against the spare wheel well. Everything else had simply scattered, like her wits. But unlike her wits, the groceries were unscathed…except for the juice.

By the time she repacked the supplies and slid into the passenger seat, Shep returned to the Jeep. His mischief had returned along with that toe-curling boyish grin of his. Behind him, the stallion circled in its makeshift enclosure, snorting with indignation.

"I can't believe we got him." He gave Deanna an appreciative look as he turned the key, oblivious to the flip-flop it instigated in her chest. "Much obliged, partner."

It was probably just the adrenaline rush from all the excitement that caused her irregular heartbeat.

The vehicle roared to life under its master's acceleration, muting her hapless, "No problem."

At least she didn't owe him a new transmission for her inadvertent slip into reverse while still rolling ahead. Right now, all Deanna wanted was to get away from the spot where she'd nearly made a fool of herself. When would she ever learn how to read men, really read them? She thought that he was going for a kiss, not a stupid rope.

The Jeep struck a bump, reminding Deanna to fasten her seat belt as she grazed the headliner with her head. After dropping the visor to see to the condition of her hair and finding nothing but an old map clipped to it, she used the side view mirror instead. She was a little pale but didn't look too worse for wear, at least on the outside.

And it could be worse, she thought, tucking a lock of hair behind her ear. If she had dropped the transmission, they might—heaven forbid—have had to rely on the stallion to get them home. With a shiver, she glanced in the side view mirror where the horse was now reduced to a tiny image in their dusty wake.

Home? The word stuck in her mind. *They* weren't going home. Shep was. She had no home. Deanna swallowed the sudden well of self-pity rising in her throat before she lost all dignity and cried. She was made of sterner stuff.

"So how'd you like your first roundup?" Shep fiddled with the tuner on the radio again.

"Great!" Deanna answered with forced enthusiasm to cover the fact that her heart still hadn't settled on a normal beat from the near miss with the horse, not to mention the near kiss. *The man thinks horse, so talk horse.* "Weren't you afraid that stallion would run you down?"

Shep pulled his hat down low to protect his eyes from the western sun, but his mouth was sheepishly tilted. "The thought did cross my mind, though to step on a man goes against a horse's grain. All it usually wants is out."

"But does the horse know that?" She was going to be just fine. Nearly getting run down by a wild stallion was enough to make anyone a basket of nerves. And it certainly was the closest to living on the edge Deanna had ever been. "Like maybe he never read the training manuals, you know?"

"Those of my personal acquaintance did. That's all I can tell you for sure."

At least he put on no pretense. Unlike C. R., this cowboy was what he was and made no apologies for it. Not that she had seen a thing he needed to apologize for. The guy sitting next to her was the real McCoy. If only she'd met him first.

It was another half hour before they reached the main street of the ramshackle ghost-town-turned-homestead. Smoky ran out to meet them, barking and tail wagging. Breaking away from a few of the horses grazing in a fenced pasture behind the old barn, Patch—the one-eyed horse—came trotting up to the front corral. His nicker split the air as the motor of the Jeep died.

"Looks like Old MacDonald's welcoming committee," she said, as a yellow tabby cat leaped up on the hood and stared at them through the windshield. "But, if I have my nursery song right, you're short a chicken, a cow, and a pig."

"Tick's got a couple of laying hens down by his trailer, the cows are grazing elsewhere, but the only pig around here is in the freezer." Shep grabbed most of the bags in the back of the Jeep and started toward the house, once again all business. "Do you mind getting the rest? I want to saddle up and go after that red before he breaks out. He doesn't have enough room to work up a jump, but he's a wily buzzard."

"Just leave the bags on the stoop and go on," Deanna assured him. "I'll put together some supper while you're gone." Salad and…*something*.

"Much obliged, ma'am."

The real McCoy, Deanna thought, quite taken once again by the simple, sincere avowal. And that drawled *ma'am* tickled her fancy.

"How about if I wash down the Jeep, too," she called after him as he strode toward the barn. For some reason she was feeling ambitious. "I can't even tell what color it is."

Shep stopped at the livery stable door and tipped his hat.

"Keep this up, Slick, and I just might take a mind to keep you."
With that, he disappeared inside.

Fumbling for a ready reply, she slipped into the house
instead, but not without stumbling over the threshold. Of course
the talk about keeping her was just teasing, nothing more. She
had to keep things in their proper perspective with Shepard
Jones. No more mistakes.

"The last thing you need, Deanna Rose Manetti, is another
complication in your life." From the kitchen window she watched
Shep lead Patch out of the barn and swing up on the mare's back.

Broken in by wear, his jeans gloved his body like a second
skin. *Calvin Klein, eat your heart out.* Deanna checked an inadvertent sigh when he glanced toward the house and waved a sun-
bronzed forearm in her direction, as if he sensed she was looking.
Could he be as aware of her as she was of him?

"Oh, enough already."

Instead of dropping her fascination with Shep, Deanna
opened the cupboard doors above the kitchen counter. One could
tell a lot about a person by what he kept in his cabinets. Instant
coffee, some artificial creamer, a box of sugar cubes, and a few
basic staples rested on yellowed lace-edged shelf paper—the sort
Deanna hadn't seen since her childhood in Brooklyn.

A simple man with simple tastes, but not quite in the twenty-
first century. It would be Manetti and Rubbermaid to the rescue.
And a good Starbuck's brew would put that jarred mess to shame.
After all, the way to a man's heart…

"So who wants a way to his heart, Gram?" she argued with
her grandmother's reminder embedded in her memory. In
Deanna's line of work, simple was easier, cheaper, and usually
more effective. "I'll just earn my room and board by organizing
him. It's safer that way."

Ten

By the time Shep rode into the stable yard on Patch, a scrumptious smelling meatloaf simmered in the oven, surrounded by small red potatoes and some onions Deanna had pulled from the garden at the side of the ranch house. Stomach growling, she glanced once more at the simply set table, now adorned with some wildflowers that grew along the garden's edge, and popped the tray of homemade biscuits into the oven to cook with the finishing main dish.

"Never put the bread in until you see the whites of their eyes," she said in satisfaction as she hurried to let her barking companion out.

As she followed Smoky to the livery entrance where Shep tied up his steed, both were covered in trail dust.

Deanna didn't have to guess the reason for the grim line of Shep's mouth. There was no sign of the stallion he'd set out to bring in. "Got away, huh?"

"Yep."

Shoving his hat up from a furrowed brow, Shep raised the stirrup to unfasten the girth. Patch shuddered when he lifted the saddle and blanket off her back, revealing sweat-soaked hair matted in little ripples and swirls. The horse nuzzled him, almost in a consoling manner as he removed her bridle.

"Ah, I know, girl." He rubbed her neck with broad, capable hands. "You're disappointed, too. We're gonna knock him on his backside one of these days."

Deanna watched the exchange between horse and master and felt an odd pang of envy. Then, catching herself, she rolled her eyes toward the cobweb-infested ceiling of the barn. She'd reached an all-time low, envying a horse…after spending the afternoon talking to a dog. She'd be a flaming Dr. Doolittle before she got out of this mess.

"Maybe a nice hot supper will make you feel better," she suggested with mustered cheer.

"Can't hurt."

Now *that* was better. Her stomach acted up again, but this time it was from the apologetic grin directed at her.

"Matter of fact, it sounds downright tempting. If it's half as good as it smells, you got yourself a job."

All Deanna smelled was hay, horse, and sweat-soaked leather, but she accepted the compliment eagerly and prayed Shep was right. She'd thrown it together from the memory of watching her mother and grandmothers in the kitchen—soup mix and breadcrumbs in the meatloaf with ketchup for a topping. And of course, the meal wouldn't be complete without biscuits like Gram used to make. If Shep had cookbooks, they were well hidden.

"So the rope didn't hold, huh?"

"The rope held." Shep tossed a scoop full of grain through a feeding window into Patch's stall.

"Maybe Patch isn't fast enough," she offered, envisioning the smaller horse trying to catch the bolting red. Since Shep was gone all afternoon, he must have given the stallion a good chase. "Did you hurt your leg?" she inquired upon seeing him wince when he picked up a dusty green hose curled in the dirt.

"Nah, it's an old war wound that acts up when I do more running than riding."

"You were in a war?"

"Figure of speech. As for Patch," he continued, "I'll put her up against the stallion in the *long* run any day. Some horses are built for speed and others for endurance. But speed wasn't the problem."

Shep lifted the handle of the faucet. Water poured from the hose nozzle into a galvanized trough. "Nope, that renegade kicked the old gate to pieces. The rope was the *only* thing that held. I'd hoped he would keep, at least until I could get back there. I spent most of the time tracking him up into the hills. At least he's away from the roads. All I need is another accident to account for. No offense," he added quickly.

"None—" Deanna finished with a shriek, jumping back from the brimming hose he offered her.

"Want a drink?"

She shook her head.

"You gotta get over that nervousness. The horses can sense it and it'll affect them too."

Under her watchful eye, Shep helped himself to a few hearty gulps before turning off the flow. Where it had washed away the dust from his face looked like a clown's smile of tanned whisker-stubbled flesh. Instinctively, Deanna traced it with her finger.

"Bozo the cowpoke. Cute!" she teased, before catching herself. She took a step back, striking the post where the saddle hung, and would have stumbled had Shep not been fast on his feet, wrapping an arm around her waist to steady her.

"Whoa, Slick! Didn't anyone ever tell you horsing around in a barn can get you in trouble?"

"More than I'm in already?" she shot back, her throat suddenly in need of that drink of water. And she thought the temperature normally dropped as the sun started down. This close to Shep Jones, hers rivaled high noon.

"Never can tell."

Deanna's ears roared. At first she thought it was the blood rushing to her face, but Shep's disconcerting attention switched to something beyond her in the ranch yard. She glanced over her shoulder to see a pickup come to a stop, driven by another man wearing a Western hat.

The moment Shep's arm left her waist, she moved away with

a guilty flush. Giving her a surreptitious wink, he turned to meet the visitor climbing out of the truck cab.

"Clyde Barrett, you old dogface, what brings you to these parts?"

"I tried to raise you on the radio," the older man answered with a grin at Deanna, "but this city gal said you weren't in."

She stepped forward under the simultaneous appraisal of her companions. "I'm sorry, but I'm not much of a radio operator. I didn't mean to hang up on you."

The man laughed and brushed aside her apology with a wave of his hand. "You didn't hang up, ma'am. You just didn't give me a chance to get a word in."

"But I held down the button."

Their visitor chuckled. "Shep, if you're going to keep this little gal around, you gotta teach her how to use a radio so she can earn her license…or break down and git a phone." Clyde's pained grimace at the latter suggestion told Deanna she was in the company of another Stone Age remnant.

"I see what you mean," Shep said. "If you hold down the button, Slick, the person on the other end can't transmit. You only hold the button down to speak, then let it go so you can hear the answer."

"I'm so sorry. I feel like a dunce." As many police movies as she'd watched, she should have been able to figure that out.

"Shoot, Miss—"

"Manetti," Shep filled in for his friend, offering an apologetic look to Deanna for forgetting his manners. "Clyde Barrett, this is Deanna Manetti from the Big Apple."

"From what little I heard, I figured she was from someplace like that." Clyde extended his hand. "Pleased to meet you, Miss Manetti. I don't reckon a city gal like you would know her way around a radio. We hams are a dyin' breed."

"My pleasure, Mr. Barrett." Deanna raised her brow in confusion. "But I thought you said your name was Charlie on the radio."

"That's the phonetic alphabet we use for our call sign. Mine's kilo-seven-lima-oscar-X ray…K7LOX," Shep said.

"Oh shine, boy, she can call me Charlie anytime. Been called a lot worse," Clyde snickered.

"Did you come out here to flirt or just to hold up my first home-cooked meal in a coon's age?"

"My biscuits!" Deanna gasped. Without so much as an adieu, she sped off toward the house at a full run, her only comfort being that the smoke alarm she'd wiped off earlier hadn't gone off…yet.

"She's a flighty filly, ain't she?"

"A thoroughbred for sure." Shep's gaze lingered after Deanna's hasty retreat until she disappeared inside the house with the slam of the screen door. "Long-legged, sleek, and swift," he added with an unwitting sigh.

And too full of cute and spunk for *his* good. If Deanna had been one of his buddies, he'd have clapped her hard on the back in his rush of excitement and maybe shaken her arm till it was about to fall off. Instead, he kissed her, dumb as a drowning goose in the rain. A peck on the cheek was innocent enough until that unguarded glance at her lips called for something more intimate. Not that he even had feelings for her, he argued with himself.

Clyde snatched Shep from the stew of his thoughts with a smug snort. "Boy, you got that same *gotta have* look in your eye as you get when you talk about that stallion Dan turned loose in the hills."

Shep groaned inwardly. He'd learned early on that there was no point in arguing with the old lawman. As a kid, Shep came to know the sheriff of Buffalo Butte—and vice versa— while doing civic duty for shooting out the town's only stoplight with his new air rifle. Every Saturday that summer, Shep had to clean the sheriff's office and jail. Aunt Sue blamed his fascination with law enforcement on the bond that formed between the juvenile and the lawman.

"Maybe, but I know where to draw the line." Yes, exactly where he'd drawn it. And twice now, he'd come within a fool's breath of crossing it. If he hadn't caught sight of the rope when he did…

The annoying smirk on Clyde's lips showed he was no more fooled than Shep himself. "Well, that's good to hear."

There was something about Deanna that went beyond physical attraction, something a lot scarier than chemistry. That quirky accent and seeing the West through her incredulous city eyes made him laugh—something he'd begun to think he'd forgotten how to do. Then there was that vulnerability behind her spunky, wiseacre veneer that beckoned to his protective instincts like a silent but dangerous *come hither.*

He knew nothing about Deanna Manetti, but what Shep did know was enough. The sooner she was gone, the better. What could God have possibly been thinking in sending him another *Ellen,* unsuited to the hard life he loved? Hadn't he given it all over to God—his hurt, his disappointment?

"Maisy brought over one of her pies to my office…" Clyde was saying in the background of Shep's introspection. A body never could rush the aging sheriff when he was bound on visiting.

Granted, Shep knew the Bible bit that said as he treated the stranger in need, so he treated Jesus himself, but was he being asked to plough the same heart ground all over again? He'd barely recovered from the first time.

"I tell you, that husband of hers has a handful, but he eats good."

Although Deanna wasn't exactly like Ellen, another voice cropped up, drawing Shep deeper into thought. The feisty New Yorker adapted quickly enough today, even if she did nearly drop his transmission on the ground. Ellen wouldn't have even tried. And Deanna liked country music…

"…I'd no more finished the last bite when the phone rang," Clyde droned on.

Shep checked himself. Never mind what God was thinking; what was *he* thinking? Spunk or no, a future out here with someone like Deanna was as futile as building a house on sand…and he'd eaten enough grit in the collapse of his previous relationship to last a lifetime. His best bet was to stick with the stallion for any kind of future. Horses he understood.

"…thinkin' she's in a heap of trouble and I'd just hate to see you get throwed again."

Clyde's remark jerked Shep from his tail-chasing introspection. "What?"

"I said, I'm glad to hear it, 'cause I'm thinkin' she's in a heap of trouble, and I'd hate to see you get throwed again. You know," the sheriff teased, "like off a horse?"

Trouble. Shep heard the word. His brain processed it, but he still stared at Clyde as though it were Greek. Shep gave himself a mental shake. "What kind of trouble?" It wasn't like he hadn't suspected *something,* so why did he feel like he'd just been mule-kicked in the belly?

Lord, I told You this was more than I was up to. I have every reason to be leery of this mess.

"Not sure." His friend shrugged, hooking his thumbs in his waistband. "But the DEA is sending someone here to talk to you about her. My office, tomorrow, first thing in the mornin'."

Drug Enforcement Agency? Now Shep knew there was more to Deanna's problems than a lovers' spat or an overbearing boyfriend. Bob Holloway's inquiry on his behalf must have triggered the Feds' interest. Still, she certainly didn't look or act like a user or a pusher—no needle marks along the soft, slender length of her arms. But then neither had the last witness he'd been assigned to protect. The grim reality was that Clyde's news also explained the reason behind the fear that Shep sensed beneath her feisty exterior.

"So who's after her, the law, a cartel, or both?" If it was the law, she'd be okay. Otherwise, Deanna was a murder victim waiting to happen.

Clyde sighed, scuffing the dirt with his polished shoe. "I told you all I know, son."

"I appreciate it." Shep reached out to shake Clyde's hand. "So, what were you going to do on the radio, leave that message with *her?*"

"Not much chance of that," Clyde grunted turning to leave. "I was just gonna give you a heads-up that I was comin' out." He winced as he slipped into the driver's seat. "I'm gettin' too old for this."

"You still got a few years left in you." Stepping up to the car, Shep closed the door and peered through the half-open window. "I'll see you at eight sharp tomorrow. I doubt she'll be going anywhere if I have the Jeep." Not as afraid of horses as she was.

"Yeah, well, you mind you take care of yourself and watch your back, just in case them DEA are right about the folks she's involved with." Clyde gunned the big engine of the police car.

Stone still, Shep watched as his visitor turned around and headed out the main street, the same way he'd come in. He didn't like being used, which was exactly what that city gal was doing. If he hadn't followed his professional instincts and called Washington, he might not have found out until it was too late. Shep started for the house. Maybe God sent an answer to his quandary after all—*hands off.*

Eleven

The white porcelain backsplash was spattered with the charred debris Deanna cut away from what was left of her culinary attempt. Shep was inclined to have it out with her then and there, but knowing that if she lied before, she'd lie again held him in check. That and the tear-glazed eyes she raised to him as he approached her checked his raw impulse.

"I'm here under false pretenses," she announced in a voice so small it begged for reassurance.

Shep stopped in midstep. Had she heard his conversation with Clyde?

"I can't cook worth butkus!" Deanna slam-dunked the biscuit she was working on into the garbage can next to the gas stove. "I usually ordered out or ate salad, but how hard can it be to make a biscuit?"

Following her glance to the table, Shep spied the large bowl of greens decorated with pepper rings and fancy cucumber slices. "I like salad," he ventured cautiously, uncertain yet as to which of her personas was going to prevail—Alice in Despair or Valkyrie of the Burned Biscuit. More disconcerting, neither resembled the pepper spray packing mama, who'd stood him off yesterday, or the indignant sleepyhead, who'd held him at bay with a pillow this morning.

"I just got distracted and forgot the time." She sniffed, rubbing her nose with the back of her hand.

Burned never looked as cute as it did on Deanna's upturned,

forlorn face. He reached for a towel and mopped some of the charred crumbs she'd been scraping off her nose. "Don't fret. The salad, the meatloaf, and those…" Shep grasped for an identification of the shriveled bits surrounding the lump of meat with clotted ketchup topping. "Vegetables," he decided, "will be just fine."

"I've never been a homemaker." Deanna sounded like her entire life had been a failure. "But I can cook with a book. I mean—" She grabbed a paper napkin and blew her nose. "If you can read, you can cook, right?"

"That's what I've found." Shep was glad the Feds were coming to save him. He just hoped they came before he forgot how mad he was.

"But I can clean," she went on, "and I'm very good at organizing."

"You wouldn't be successful if you couldn't…organize, that is." Now *that* was intelligent. "Look, you just have a seat and let me finish up here, soon as I wash up a bit."

"But dinner will be cold."

Like that could make it worse. Shep fought down a chuckle. "Just put it back in the oven. It'll stay warm from the residual heat."

He started for the bathroom, pulling his shirt over his head. Maybe she'd left ketchup in the bottle to get dinner down.

"Are you too disappointed?" she called after him with a crescendo of emotion in her voice.

"Nope, don't sweat it. I've seen worse than that."

Shep closed the bathroom door behind him and looked at the mirror. "You're a lying son of a gun," he accused the twin staring back at him. He hadn't seen a meal done quite to that extent, even when Tick overturned a fry pan of fish in the campfire.

And he *was* disappointed. But the latter had nothing to do with food, he realized, flipping the water on at the sink. It had to do with deceit and all the past it dragged up.

Shep lathered and rinsed his hands and arms, then buried his

head under the lukewarm flow, rinsing away the dust as vigor-
ously as he mentally dismissed the memories. Giving his squeeze-
dried hair a dog shake that splattered the mirror, he reached for
the clean towel on the back of the bathroom door, when he
caught a whiff of an unfamiliar scent.

It wasn't exactly unpleasant, but it wasn't perfumy like a bathroom lotion or cleanser. Shep smelled the towel. That wasn't it.
Confounded, he sniffed like a bloodhound homing in on the
scent until he reached the door itself where it was strongest.

That city gal had to have scrambled more than his wits,
because if Shep didn't know better, he'd swear he smelled butter.

By the time Shep returned to the kitchen, Deanna had pulled herself together. She forced an overbright smile and shrugged.

"Sorry I went all wimpy on you. I'm not really a crybaby. I just
wanted to make it up to you for your taking me in and turning
Hopewell into a shelter where I can regroup my thoughts."

"It's no big deal, Deanna."

She turned away hastily and took the meatloaf out of the
oven. "I promise I'll do better tomorrow. You'll have a meal fit for
a king."

This time tomorrow Shep wouldn't be grappling for words to
put her mind at ease. Deanna Manetti would be in the custody of
the DEA. "Any idea what you'll do when you get your car fixed?"

"Go back to New York, I guess." She thumped the meatloaf
she put on the table with her finger and wrinkled her nose. "Better
get a sharp knife. It's kind of dried out."

"I'm sure it's nothing ketchup and applesauce can't fix."

Shep took a carving knife from the drawer by the stove and
plied it to the meatloaf. "Though I've sawed through firewood that
wasn't this hard," he added with a quirk to his mouth.

His humor put a smile on heretofore trembling lips. "You're a
good guy, Shepard Jones," Deanna said. "I'd begun to think that

even God had forsaken me when your horse ran me off the road. I had nowhere to run. And then *along came you—oo—oo."* She mimicked the song they'd heard on the radio.

Deanna's choice of words in describing her plight was a direct hit, striking a painful chord from his past. After Ellen broke their engagement, he hadn't been able to run home to the high country fast enough, crippled knee and all. It was just the place he needed to heal, both physically and spiritually.

"You can't outrun God, especially here in Big Sky country. That old saying 'head for the hills' works for all God's creatures, man included." Heaven knew he told it straight. "The wilderness always has been a refuge for saint or sinner." Man, he was starting to sound like Reverend Lawrence. "What I mean is that the farther you are from the distraction of life in general, the easier it is to feel God's presence. That's why David—even Jesus—got away sometimes, you know. Just to feel closer. And take my word for it, up there on the mountain top, surrounded by God's untarnished creation, it's hard not to think of Him."

"Yeah, if one of God's creatures doesn't eat you before you can pray to be saved."

Not even Deanna's half smile could hide the sense of loss and desperation Shep witnessed in her eyes. Beyond the wet glaze that some women could produce at will, her very spirit cried out to his kindred one.

In that instant, Shep not only knew her pain, he knew this was no criminal. She was just a frightened, lost, and lonely soul—and that spooked him more than looking into the cold conscienceless void of a hardened assassin. On the brink of a leap he wasn't sure he wanted to take, Shep put the knife on the side of the platter as though its slight weight might carry him over. *Lord, I can't do this.*

"I'll get the ketchup." Deanna turned stiffly to the refrigerator, unaware that she'd offered reprieve. "I mean," she said to the interior, "I thought I was happy *with* all that distraction. Now I'm not so sure. This enough ketchup?" She held up a half bottle of the red save-anything sauce.

Ketchup was good. Glad to be returning to neutral ground, he breathed a little easier. Maybe his luck would last until tomorrow, when choice was removed from his hands. "For starters. But I'll get the *pièce de résistance.*"

In their effort to sidestep each other, Deanna heading for the table and Shep for the cupboard, they nearly collided.

"Yo, cowboy, this kitchen ain't big enough for the both of us."

Montana wasn't big enough for the two of them. As though she were toting a loaded six-gun instead of a ketchup bottle, Shep bypassed Deanna and fumbled through the cabinet for a jar of... What was he looking for?

A jar of applesauce caught his eye. Yes, that was it.

Lord, just help me make it through the night, Shep prayed as he returned to the table. And maybe when the setting sun coming through the kitchen window didn't bathe her in its angel aura, he'd be just fine.

An overcast sky cast a cryptic gray cloak over the morning skyline of the city. From the penthouse view of Ontario Imports, the high-rises appeared as stark and still as tombs against it. Below, tiny humans and miniature vehicles worked, silent as maggots in the asphalt bowels of the city streets. Insignificant in the overall scheme of things.

Seated at an oriental desk of carved teak, a man in a tailored gray suit turned from the vista. Fifteen years ago, Victor Dusault was one of them. Today he sat in a god's seat, silver wings distinguishing his once pitch black hair at the temples like medals of honor. At his command, the drugs his men smuggled into the country were turned into money, and money, after being laundered through some of his legitimate corporate investments, into power.

A soft, gliding sound drew his attention from the outside world to a glassed-in cage that took up one entire wall of his suite. Ama, a gift from one of his key Mexican associates, slithered off a length of dead log and over the floor of the habitat toward the feeding door, where a small white rabbit quivered, frozen to the spot.

It was a natural law. Power begat power. The strong drew it from the weak. Dark eyes narrowed in anticipation, the man waited for the nine-foot boa to make its kill when the phone rang. With little more than an annoyed glance away from the cage, he turned on the speakerphone.

"Yes?"

"We found the woman," a voice crackled on the other end of the line.

Now this news was worth distraction. Swinging his leather chair about-face to the desk, he folded his hands in satisfaction. "Where?"

"She's taken up with an ex-U.S. Marshal near a hole-in-the-wall called Buffalo Butte…still in Montana," the answer came. "The Marshal became suspicious of her behavior and called an old buddy to check up on her story. One thing led to another."

Victor smiled, an unnatural expression that strained the taut set of his mouth. "It's always nice to have the authorities help us out."

"We aim to please."

"You know the procedure. Don't kill her until she tells you where Majors put the money." Majors was an idiot to trust anyone, much less a woman. There was no room for trust in female characteristics, not in fickle, frivolous, or fun. A half smirk settled on Victor's mouth. But then, what could one expect from a peon who double-crossed a powerful man like himself?

The position to which Victor had elevated Majors as CEO of Amtron Enterprises simply proved too tempting. His only regret was that he couldn't personally show others, who might think of getting away with a similar scheme, what happens to anyone who disappoints Victor Dusault.

"My guess is she'll lead us to more than the money."

Victor tapped impatient fingers on the corner of his leather desk pad, waiting for his informant to continue.

"Someone else is very interested in her whereabouts besides us and the authorities."

The tapping stopped, his fingers fisting. "I don't have time for word games."

"Majors is alive," the caller answered hastily. "His body wasn't in the charred vehicle."

This was better news than finding the money. Money Victor could replace. The opportunity for revenge came only once. "Sloppy of him," he said, masking his delight with indifference.

C. R. Majors was such an amateur minor player; he hardly deserved Victor's personal attention. A pro would have at least put another body in there to buy time. Call it an alternative answer to the homeless problem. "So she outsmarted him, eh?" Deserving or not, the double-crossing little twerp was going to get his full atten-tion for as long as it took for a bullet to close the distance between Victor's gun and Majors' head. As for the Manetti woman—

"Not quite." The eagerness on the other end of the phone line reflected Victor's own. "We found a tracking device on her car, and it wasn't one of ours. If it were, she'd either be singing at the top of her voice or no longer with the living. It *had* to be Majors. I say we wait and catch the proverbial two birds with one stone."

"*You* say?" He hated working with government agents. They had trouble recalling where the bulk of their paycheck came from.

"I *think.* I meant to say I think. It's your call, sir."

"Just sit on this little love nest until both birds are home. My team and I will be waiting for the word."

Astonishment echoed in the caller's voice. "*You're* coming across yourself? What if it's a setup?"

"Then it would be extremely tragic for you." Victor needn't

elaborate. The silence on the other end told him his informant understood completely. "You know the information we'll need. Don't call without it."

"No, sir." The connection went dead.

Behind Victor, the sun broke through the morning cloud cover, reflecting his much improved humor. Now his denied urge to squeeze the life out of the little fool heartbeat by heartbeat lived again. Victor could almost smell the stench of fear seeping through Majors' pores—the fear that precipitated the last breath of a man who looked death in the face.

The leather of the chair creaked as Victor swung his attention back to the habitat. A disappointed sigh escaped his lips. He'd missed the kill. The rabbit was gone. Satisfied, the snake constricted the muscles beneath the diamond and oval patterns of its brown and cream skin around the unresisting remains.

Survival of the fittest. Animal or human, the same rule always applied. Which was why Victor used his money and power to stay fitter than the next man—or woman, as the case may be. He looked forward to the same satisfaction as his pet, growing stronger on the weakness of his prey. At this point, the money was secondary.

Twelve

S hep pulled his Jeep headfirst in front of the sheriff's office, scattering a small puddle left over from the early morning shower. The sun had come out shortly after the rain and glared off the wet road the entire drive into town. Unaccustomed to wearing sunglasses—they only got in a cowboy's way—he winced from the blinding light that worked its way under the brim of his hat. That and guilt over the searching looks Deanna had given him across the breakfast table had worried the fire out of him.

When he'd emerged from the shower first thing that morning, fresh dressed and shaved, Shep had found his tousled houseguest preparing breakfast in her robe. As much as he'd seen Aunt Sue in the same getup on many a morning, it had never hit him like a cross between a kick in the belly and the flu. Worse, he almost liked it.

Nothing he said sounded right after the lie he told about going into town for some forgotten supplies, so he'd stuck to little more than polite conversation. He insisted the omelet she'd made was delicious, even if he'd left part of it untouched. And it was. It just didn't go well with the casual deceit sometimes required by his former profession.

Shep would like to think he fooled her, but the half-frightened expression on her face as she stood in the door and saw him off left him unsure. The only thing he was sure of was that the sooner this was over, the better.

"There's our boy now, right on time," Clyde Barrett announced when Shep entered his office to the eighth strike of the courthouse clock.

"Clyde," Shep acknowledged, waiting for his eyes to adjust to being inside.

His chair scraping on the hardwood floor, Clyde got up and cleared his throat. "Shepard Jones, meet I.S. Special Agent Voorhees. He's the fella handling your little gal's case."

"Not *my* little gal." Did Clyde say *Voorhees?*

At Shep's disclaimer, the agent stepped into his line of sight. "Long time, no see, buddy. How's the knee?"

Shep heard Clyde's introduction as well as recognized the agent extending his hand to him, but he had a hard time believing either. Gearing down to avoid the ice patch instinct of what lay ahead, Shep turned without a word and hung his Stetson on the paneled wall next to the door. Unlike the rest of him, his mind was in overdrive, jerking him into the past where his last encounter with Jay Voorhees lay incredibly fresh.

There was Jay, years younger, hovering over Shep's stretcher as the paramedics loaded him into the ambulance with his knee blown to bits.

A fierce anger Shep had thought long buried flashed over, curling his fingers into tight fists against his palms as he stared at Voorhees's outstretched hand. From beyond the heated turmoil, a voice reminded him that he'd forgiven the man. It had been part of his healing process.

"It reminds me it's there now and then," Shep replied, completing the handshake out of polite obligation, nothing more.

He *had* forgiven Voorhees, hadn't he? It wasn't as if Jay had intended to end Shep's career and engagement. The ambitious agent had simply pushed the envelope of risk, ignoring Shep's instinct and protest. It had all been the result of the same-old, same-old interdepartmental competition common to different agencies forced to work with each other.

Shep was to protect the DEA witness against a major drug

trafficker. As head of the DEA investigation, Voorhees was Shep's senior, there to make certain the U.S. Marshal succeeded in his assignment. Shep's wariness of the forced partnership had been justified by too little shared information and too much fervor to advance a career.

"You two know each other then?" Clyde remarked in surprise.

"We've worked together before." Shep shifted a riveting look back to Voorhees. "International Services, eh? You've been moving up the ladder." Voorhees had been a Special Agent assigned to the Intelligence Center in the District of Columbia, where Shep worked. His loose-cannon approach evidently hadn't hurt his career.

"I'm in the highest percentile for conviction rate. That kind of record speaks for itself," Voorhees answered without a modicum of modesty.

"Well, I'm glad to have played my part in your success." Shep's wry drawl sent his memory fast-tracking back to the past, defying his notion that he'd let it go and let God.

The desk clerk had clearly been out of his element when they checked in at the Interstate Motor Lodge after a twelve-hour drive. Although reservations had been made and paid for by the agency under their assumed names, the clerk had to start the check-in procedure over three times. Then he had trouble finding the right keys, the whole while wiping sweaty palms on his shirt and saying he was new at the job.

While his explanation seemed reasonable, it just hadn't felt right. As a precaution, Shep suggested they just go elsewhere on their own when he returned to the car, but his partner nixed the idea. Voorhees joked that if it were a setup, they'd catch the hit men too. At least Shep had thought the agent was joking at the time.

That night Shep slept in a chair behind the only entrance with one eye and both ears open—a move that saved their lives. He'd heard or rather sensed their stealthy approach in time to send the witness into the bathroom with Voorhees. When the intruders burst in, SWAT style, semiautomatics firing, Shep took them both out from behind, but not before a ricocheting bullet caught him in the knee. Two dead men and hospitalization for Shep later, the witness testified, putting a major hitter in the drug world away. Voorhees got a commendation and a promotion. Shep got a commendation and a disability discharge.

"Oh, I've earned a few on my own since then," Voorhees said, pulling Shep back to the present. "Heckuva bad break for you though."

Voorhees was as full of himself now as back then. Shep maintained indifference to hide his quagmire of emotions. "Goes with the job, I guess."

Clyde broke the awkward silence that followed. "Can I get you some coffee, Shep?"

"No thanks. Let's just take care of Agent Voorhees's business and let me get back to my own. So what's the story on Deanna Manetti, Voorhees?"

"Maybe embezzlement, maybe money laundering, maybe poor taste in lovers…or maybe all of the above."

Shep took the first two in professional stride but mentally tripped over the word *lovers*. It wasn't as if it was news that Deanna had made a bad choice in men, but the shabbiness implied by Voorhees's word choice didn't fit Shep's perception of her. She needed help, not persecution.

"…car bomb, but forensics found no body," Voorhees went on. "My guess is, he double-crossed the Canadian cartel and faked his death to throw them off his trail."

"Whoa," Shep said, throwing up his hands to gain time to catch up. He was *not* Deanna's keeper…not now. "*Cartel?* Deanna was laundering money for a drug cartel?" Beyond skeptical, Shep was incredulous. "She hasn't got a dollar's worth of change to her name, unless it's stashed somewhere else. I flipped through her purse."

Had she lied about being strapped, too? Considering her state when he found Deanna, she hadn't. If she'd had money, a woman like her would have lit out for anywhere but Buffalo Butte.

"You can take the man out of the job, but you can't take the Marshal out of the man." Coming from anyone else, Voorhees's observation might have been flattering. "But we checked the car this morning…nothing."

The agent helped himself to some of Clyde's coffee from the pot that always brewed next to the restroom door. Three packets of sugar later, not to mention enough creamer to make latte an inadequate description of his concoction, he stirred it as though lost in thought until it threatened to brim over the side.

Too much thought, Shep noted with suspicion. If his instinct was right, the prolonged pause in the conversation meant Voorhees was already withholding information of some sort. Most likely he was deciding what more Shep needed to know and what he didn't. Interagency distrust at its best, Shep thought, taking in every nuance of the agent's behavior and assessing it.

"Someone ransacked her place while she was being questioned by the local police," Voorhees said at last.

"Maybe it was the boyfriend." Shep found Voorhees's word *lover* too distasteful to use. "Which would prove right there that she was just a dupe being used by him. Any prints?"

"Place was clean as a whistle," the agent told him. "I don't think Majors was that professional. I mean, the guy blew up a car with no body."

"At least he didn't kill someone innocent." Substituting a body would have bought him a little more time to operate if the people he swindled thought he was dead—time for him to split with the money, while authorities and his cronies chased after Deanna. No wonder she'd bolted. She must have been frightened out of her wits with the law *and* unknown thugs after her.

"Are we talking a small-time disgruntled perp or a cartel looking for her?" Shep asked.

"Or the lover," Voorhees said. "But there are implications in the investigation that we're talking big-time drug operators and money laundering. Personally, I vote for the lover."

"Who's to say Majors didn't take the money and isn't living the high life in a Mexican resort or some other remote paradise? That makes more sense to—"

"A man matching C. R. Majors' height and build was picked up by a security camera in Manetti's apartment building *after* his alleged death. Blasted hat hid his face, but my bet is on him. The cartel would have taken out the camera first. It's not like it was hidden."

Going to Deanna's place after the fact? Something must have gone wrong, if Majors intended to frame her for his crime. Otherwise, he'd have been nuts to tarry after his *accident*. "Okay, so he's definitely not a professional."

"A greedy little white-collar twerp," Voorhees agreed. "He used Deanna Manetti to pull off this caper and left her holding the bag—quite literally, we think."

Shep wrestled against accepting that Deanna was knowingly involved. "So something went wrong with his plan to frame her and make off with the money."

"No, evidence points to her being part of the scheme and planning to follow him later with one of the tickets he bought to the Caribbean."

It wasn't making sense. Something had to have gone wrong. "Did he use his ticket?"

Voorhees shook his head. "That's why we think he's still around somewhere and that she's our key to finding Majors, not to mention our only link to the money."

And the drug ring's only link. Majors was penny-ante, but the involvement of a drug cartel sent a chill raking down Shep's spine. Deanna's situation grew more ominous by the minute. Greed usually led to foolhardiness. Majors not only pulled the wrong tiger's tail, but he was taking Deanna along for the ride.

"So why don't you just take her into custody? Why go through all this with me?" Shep acted like he couldn't see what was coming. The ice patch of his direct involvement in the case was widening by the second, and there were no guardrails.

"Because we want him more than we want her. She wouldn't tell the police anything before anyway...claims she made the deposits to the account as a favor, that she had no idea what was going on."

"So Deanna's just bait." History was repeating itself. Voorhees was still ignoring the bird in the hand for more in the bush. "Majors can finger the ringleaders in the cartel, if they don't take him out first."

Voorhees grinned. "That's the big picture, Jones...which is where *you* come in."

Shep clenched his jaw, bracing as he hit the slippery slope in his mind. He'd already heard more than he wanted to know, the momentum toward the point of no return.

"I understand the woman is stranded at your place until her car is repaired, right?"

With a short nod, Shep pulled up a chair and straddled it, leaning on its back with folded arms. "And you want me to keep a lid on things until this Majors tries to contact Deanna." He wasn't going to go along with it, but he was curious. "Just how do you expect him to find her? You can't possibly believe they chose this little fly speck on the map as a meeting place...*if* she is even guilty of complicity."

Which is something Shep seriously doubted. For all her smarts, Deanna Manetti had a gullible side. It was more danger-ous to someone like him than any combination of beauty and brains. Shep had been called to aid and protect the innocent, to champion justice. It was an inherent part of him, even if he wasn't quite as idealistic as he'd been when he entered the Marshals.

"No," the agent acknowledged, "but Majors knows where she is—or at least where her car is."

"Now hold on a minute." Shep straightened in anger. It was just as he suspected. The car search *had* told them something. "If you want my help, Voorhees, you'd better tell me everything you know or suspect. I don't like surprises." What was he saying? He had no intention of getting involved.

"We didn't find money when we searched her vehicle, but we did find a tracking device mounted under the hood of the trunk. Great way to find each other if plans go awry, don't you think?"

So that was who had broken into Charlie Long's garage. It also explained why the alleged vandal hadn't taken any of the car's equipment. The stereo alone would bring more than pocket change. But did Deanna know she was being tracked? At first she'd been pale as last night's ashes, but after Charlie's explanation, she seemed to have gained her color back.

If this wasn't a quagmire, there was no such thing, Shep fumed, as angry at himself for being drawn into it as he was at Voorhees for tugging at just the right strings, in just the right order, to pull him in. Except that Shep wasn't likely to be the only one herded into this patch of quicksand.

"As friendly as folks are here in Buffalo Butte, all this Majors has to do is ask about the car, and he'll find out all he needs to—"

"Now hold on, boy." Clyde stopped Shep as he sprang from the chair. "Ain't nobody tellin' anything to any strangers about your houseguest. Cantankerous Charlie wouldn't if he could, and I spoke to the folks at the diner, the feed store, and the grocery this morning. Told 'em the gal was in Witness Protection, it was their civic duty to keep what they knew to themselves, and to send any strangers who wander in asking questions straight to me."

Great. Within the span of a few hours, Buffalo Butte had become a town of special agents for the U.S. government. Shep knew the townsfolk wouldn't talk after the sheriff's explanation, but that didn't mean they wouldn't try to *help* either. From Agent Voorhees's groan of realization, he and Shep were at least of the same mind on that—civilians had no place in agency business unless it was unavoidable. And it *was* unavoidable now…unless Shep refused to go along with the plan. It *was* his choice.

"Meanwhile," Voorhees said, taking Shep's silence as compliance. "I want to set up a surveillance of your place. You can tell your pretty guest we're geologists testing the area for minerals."

Uncle Dan had sold the mineral rights to Hopewell, not that there was anything left worth mining, so the charade would seem reasonable to Deanna—or anyone who might ask—*if* Shep went along with the plan.

"And since you've obviously won her trust, we want you to try to get her to talk."

"I'm not wearing a wire." Shep didn't like it, nor any aspect of the entire scheme. He'd left his job behind him. He certainly didn't want to work with the man whose reckless ambition had cost him that job in the first place.

"It would go a long way toward building the case," Voorhees pointed out.

And while Shep was accustomed to being put at risk, he didn't like the idea of Deanna being used…even if she had used him. "Like I care. I'm not living under your microscope in my own home. You'd just have to take my word on what she says, if she says anything—"

"I hear you don't even have a phone," Voorhees interrupted.

"If I decide to help at all, I won't need a phone. I have a radio."

"We'll give you a phone. We have to have some way to keep in contact."

"I didn't say I'd help."

Voorhees met Shep's glare head on in bold study. "So she's got to you, has she?"

Shep clamped his fists to his side to check his impulse to knock the patronizing smile off of the special agent's face. "Whatever happened to a person being innocent until proven guilty?"

Granted, he could see how easily Deanna might play him for a sucker and a place to hide out, but she wasn't *that* good an actress where her fear was involved. It had been vividly real. He'd seen it beyond her eyes, where lies could not abide.

"Maybe I need to rethink this plan," Voorhees goaded. "I suppose you could tell her that you've made arrangements for her to stay at that bed-and-breakfast for propriety's sake."

And leave Deanna to the mercy of Jay's ambition, not to mention jeopardize Esther Lawson and the citizens of Buffalo Butte? Shep wavered. At least at Hopewell, just he and Deanna would be at risk. Tick had already left for roundup at a neighboring ranch.

"All we're asking is that you plant a few listening devices." The agent shrugged. "Hey, it could prove her innocence in this. . . unless *you* have something to hide."

This was a no-win situation. Shep was condemned if he did and convicted if he didn't.

"If I were a swearing man, I'd tell you where to go, Voorhees," Shep ground out slowly.

Jay lifted his brow. "Then you really have changed since that day I put you in the ambulance." Reaching into his coat pocket, he withdrew a cell phone and handed it over to Shep. "Numbers are programmed in. List is in the directory."

Shep *thought* he had changed. Now he wasn't so certain, because at this moment, he felt everything he'd felt back then and more. Dropping the unwanted phone in his pocket, he turned before he was tempted to give in to a repeat performance. "I'll keep the phone. You keep the bugs." He grabbed his Stetson off the peg by the door and set it firmly on his head.

It might be a no-win situation, but Shep wasn't going to let Voorhees know it. Besides, half a loaf was better than none. At least he wouldn't have strangers listening in on every word spoken in his own home.

The radio played loudly from the bedroom as Deanna finished off a peanut butter and jelly sandwich for lunch and surveyed her progress. The windows were washed. The curtains were in the washer. The cabinets looked brighter. Once she had new shelf paper, she could tackle the insides. All in all, the whole room looked and smelled television commercial clean and fresh.

"Martha Stewart, eat your heart out," she challenged, taking up her plate and heading to the kitchen sink.

From the rug in front of the door, her furry companion raised his head.

"You're not Martha Stewart," she said in a playful tone that set Smoky's tail wagging. "You're Smoky, aren't you, boy?"

Grateful for his company, she walked over to the overgrown pup and gave him a good scratching behind his ears. As if on cue, the dog promptly dropped and rolled over for a belly rub.

"You are rotten," she said, laughing as his hind leg started thumping the floor. "But I don't have time to tickle you. I don't know when Shep will be home, but I gotta get these curtains hung."

Sheesh, she even sounded like the happy homemaker. Not that there was anything wrong with that. Deanna had a great respect for the women who maintained a household and raised children to boot. It simply hadn't been a role for her.

Inadvertently her attention shifted to the mantel where a little Shep, clad in full cowboy regalia—six-guns and all—gave her a snaggletoothed grin.

"Oh, enough already!"

Deanna hurried to the washing machine as if the prospect of domestication nipped at her heels. She loved other people's kids, but how could she even think about being someone special's honey and having children when she'd made such a mess of her life? It might sound good, but it just wasn't workable—whether Shepard Jones was the catch of a lifetime or not. He'd drop her like a hot brick if he got wind of her trouble with the law. Unlike C. R., this guy was a straight shooter. He'd even come to a complete stop at a four-way the day before when the only thing that moved for miles were cows in the fields.

Forcing the issue out of her mind, she reached inside the machine and began pulling the curtains out. It was their third washing, and this time the white was finally white and the red…was pink. With a groan, she shook one out, but her dismay only grew when it fell apart, as if she'd rent it in two.

Now what was she going to do? Shep couldn't fix *this* with ketchup or applesauce, no matter how much of a gentleman he tried to be.

As Deanna cast an accusing glance at the empty bleach bottle, Smoky erupted into fierce barking in the kitchen. The dog was growling and pawing to get out when she reached the screen door and looked down the long narrow main street of the ghost town; something she'd been avoiding, lest her imagination run wild with her. At the far end, dust lingered in the air, although what had stirred it was nowhere in sight.

She supposed Shep might have come up the back way, but if it was him, why hadn't he pulled the Jeep up in its usual spot by the house? In the pasture beyond the livery stable, Patch looked up curiously from grazing but made no move to meet her master as she had yesterday. And wasn't Ticker's trailer on the other side of the street? Besides, Shep had said Ticker would be gone for a few days.

Painfully aware of how alone she was, Deanna was reluctant to let her only companion out, no matter how much he pawed and barked.

"Sorry, Smoky, but I need you more in here." She eased the front door shut and locked it.

If someone came up and knocked, she simply wouldn't answer it. She'd hide in the bathroom and let Smoky's barking convince him no one was home. Most likely it was a friendly neighbor dropping by for a visit, but Deanna was afraid to take that risk. Besides, a friendly neighbor would come right up to the house, not hide in his vehicle.

Thirteen

I t seemed like an eternity passed in the four-watt night-lighted confines of the bathroom. The dog continued barking, his excitement waning as he raced from the kitchen to the bedroom and back, only to start again. Finally, curiosity got the best of her. Deanna opened the door and listened. The Beach Boys crooned a lively tune on the radio, interrupted by an occasional bark from the dog, as if Smoky, too, questioned whether the need for alarm was over.

Deanna tiptoed to the bedroom, instinctively hunkering down to her knees when Smoky resumed barking at the window. Peering around the curtain she spied someone coming out of the livery stable—a man, tall and lean in faded jeans and a T-shirt. He took his time, looking all around, as if casing the place. A beat-up Western-style hat shaded his face, hiding his age, although the rest of his outfit did little to hide the fact that he was in good physical shape.

Down on the Jersey shore, she might have admired the tanned bulge of bicep as he put his hands on his low-slung jeans in seeming contemplation. Today, it evoked a different response. He was big, strong, and totally capable of anything he had in his mind to do. She shuddered, recalling the overturned furniture in her apartment and the broken drawers. What if somehow—

Her heart stopped as the stranger turned abruptly, staring dead on at the house. He couldn't possibly see her, but Deanna drew back against the wall and tried to push Smoky away from the bedroom window before the dog leaped through the buckled screen.

"Down, Smoky!" She lunged for the dog's collar, losing her balance and sprawling on the cool wooden floor empty-handed. Smoky vaulted over her and made for the porch door. A scramble and peek through the curtain revealed the visitor walking straight to the house.

With a strangled cry, she crawled back to the bathroom as fast as her surely bruised knees and hands would allow. Once inside, she eased the door shut, leaving just enough of a crack to keep tabs on what was transpiring. By now, Smoky's excited bark had grown fiercer, even threatening. He sounded as though he could chew up and spit out the stranger from the boots up.

The man knocked loudly on the kitchen door, despite the dog's ruckus.

"Yo, anybody home?" The old metal doorknob rattled over Smoky's low growl. "Hey, take it easy, boy. I'm not gonna hurt you."

Of course the stranger could see inside the kitchen, thanks to her housecleaning binge—not a curtain at either window. That might not have made a difference before she washed the glass in them, but she'd made it easier to see what might be worth stealing inside. Deanna strained to listen above Smoky's warning, picking up what she thought were retreating footsteps on the porch.

Her breath of relief lodged in her chest as Smoky abandoned the door, racing past her for the bedroom window. Was the intruder there? Easing out of the bathroom, she inched along the hallway wall and peeked around the bedroom door to where Smoky had taken up guard.

"Here you go, boy."

Deanna flattened against the cold plaster at her back. *Heavenly Father, he was back!*

"Smells pretty good, huh?"

Afraid to look, but more afraid not to, Deanna peered through the hinge crack of the bedroom door in time to see the now silent Smoky sniffing something at the screen. Now *there's* a real guard dog. In disbelief, she watched the man pry the screen open enough to slip a large dog biscuit through. Western security left a lot to be desired, she thought, wishing for the alarm system and window locks at her New York condo. She didn't even have a phone to call for help.

This guy really knew what he was doing. Smoky took the biscuit and laid down on the scatter rug, chewing his traitorous little heart out, while the stranger carefully removed the screen. "Got more where that came from, buddy." One…two…three more biscuits landed on the rug next to the dog. With little more than a grunt, the stranger hoisted himself up on the windowsill.

Gee, eat favorite treats or take out a guy big enough to break a dog in half? It was a no-brainer. Why she'd ever longed to have a dog eluded her at the moment. She edged back to the bathroom and closed the door without a sound, thanks to the healthy dose of cooking spray she'd put on the hinges the other day. With luck, the intruder would never know she was inside.

But if something did go wrong, what would she do? Deanna glanced at the tub. Hide behind the shower curtain? Her overactive imagination played the infamous shower scene from an old Hitchcock movie, nipping that idea in the bud. If a confrontation were in order, she'd at least see what was coming at her.

A rattle of doors from the other side of the bathroom wall froze thought and breath. The gun cabinet. Oh great. Now she had an armed burglar to deal with.

What am I going to do? She stared at the useless bolt on the bathroom door. It had no keeper to lock into. As long as the burglar had dog biscuits, nothing but a well-buttered door was between Deanna and the gun thief in the other room. She should have brought a knife with her from the kitchen. She should have holed up in a room that had an escape route. She should have—

The bolt of a rifle clicked and reclicked, cutting off her second thought. Had he loaded one of Shep's guns?

God, don't let him shoot the dog—or me, for that matter, she finished, awash with a sense of foolishness. She ought to let the dog pray for itself. She ought—

She was panicking. She tried forcing breath through her fear-strangled throat. Glancing about for anything she might use to defend herself, she quickly assessed her arsenal: a plunger, a toilet bowl brush, a few men's toiletries. Useless, all useless—unless she was going to pin an armed man to the wall with the plunger and brush him to death.

Her frantic gaze came to rest upon a small book lying open on the back of the commode. It was a devotional like the ones Gram used to read daily. *Oh, God, I really need Your help.*

Deanna grabbed it, desperate for some instruction. The bold-face type at the top of the page read, "I can do all things through Christ who strengthens me. Philippians 4:13."

"But, Lord, it would be so much easier if I had a gun to even my odds." Without thinking, she leaned against the lid on the tank. Time stood as still as Deanna's heart at the scrape of raw iron to raw iron. The words of the verse echoed in her mind again and again until suddenly, they offered more than comfort.

Brightening, Deanna lifted the porcelain-coated top from the back of the toilet and raised a silent prayer beyond the rust-dotted exhaust fan in the ceiling. *Thank You, Jesus!*

The lid was heavy, but not too heavy to lift. If the stranger did find her, she'd be able to manage only one swing, so it would have to count. In one step, she backed against the wall to the side of the door as footsteps sounded in the hall. If the man just took the guns and left, she'd remain right where she was, but if he so much as—

The knob beside her turned and the door flew open against the adjoining wall. Deanna's thought launched into action. Hard as she could, she swung the heavy lid upward and into the face of the man who stepped through the doorway. The dull clang of it striking the intruder in the face sent vibrations up her trembling arms. It was followed by two successive thumps—that of her victim and that of her weapon striking the floor in the little hallway.

In the remote light from the bedroom door and kitchen, Deanna retrieved the lid lying on the stunned man's chest in case she needed it again, when she saw blood seeping from his nose. As the downed figure felt for his face with uncoordinated hands, she lifted the lid once again as a precaution.

He groaned, his fingers brushing his nose, and then his hands fell limp upon his chest.

A sick, sinking feeling threatened to take out Deanna's knees. "I've killed him."

She dropped the tank lid with a clang and grabbed towels from the rack on the wall. Kicking the hunting rifle he'd carried beyond reach in case he regained consciousness, she knelt and raised his head before he choked on his own blood. No, she needed to tilt his head back to stop the bleeding. Or should she try to sit him upright? Why hadn't she paid more attention to the first aid class in her Scout troop instead of selling more cookies than anyone in the entire district?

Now finished with his treats, Smoky trotted up to where Deanna frantically rolled a towel and stuffed it under the unconscious man's head. Head cocked in seeming uncertainty, the shepherd mix gave a short, inquisitive bark.

"Oh hush up, you wuss. If you'd done your job, I wouldn't be—" Before she could finish, her unhelpful, unpredictable companion bolted back into the bedroom, overtaken by yet another fierce surge of barking.

Was there someone else out there? To Deanna's dismay, Smoky's outburst suddenly grew fainter and fainter. The dog had jumped through the open window. Dare she hope he'd drive off the intruder?

Half frozen with fear and half with hope, she heard what sounded like a vehicle door slamming. The fickle animal must have heard its approach and now, of all things, ran out to greet the driver. Smoky might be man's best friend, but he definitely wasn't this woman's.

Dear Lord, make it a friend.

No sooner had the prayer formed in her beleaguered mind than a man's voice hailed her from outside. "Deanna!"

"Shep!" *Thank You, God. Thank You, thank You, thank You!*

Springing to her feet, she nearly tripped over the tank lid to meet her knight in shining armor as he raced into the house with Smoky at his heels.

"What the—"

She threw herself into Shep's arms, babbling in relief. "Burglar…broke in…dog biscuits…worthless ball of barking fur…" The words poured out, incoherent against Shep's chest, her tears soaking into the warm cotton of his shirt. "Your guns…"

"Take it easy; it's okay." Shep pried Deanna from her death hold around his neck, his voice soothing sweet to her ears. "Everything is all right, but I need you to pull yourself together, okay?"

Shep was right. He was here and he was right. It *was* okay. She'd survived and Shep was here. Deaf to her thoughts, her lungs struggled with large hiccoughing gasps while her pulse thundered in denial between her temples.

"I…he…I k-killed a man." Try as she might, she couldn't make her babble coherent.

Shep held her back at arm's length, staring in confusion. "What?"

Hapless, she pointed toward the dimly lit central hall.

Brushing her aside, Shep hurried to the side of the still, bloody-faced intruder. As he put his fingers to the man's throat, Deanna's released a squeak of a whisper. "Is he dead?"

"No, but he's going to wish he was," he told her grimly. "Turn on the hall light and then get some ice in a bag…and more towels."

It took a moment for the order to register. Shep's level voice and methodical actions effected a semblance of calm on the storm-pitched sea of emotion in her brain. Everything would be fine. Shep could handle the stranger, should he regain consciousness. Shep could call an ambulance on his radio. Shep could fix everything.

Still trembling, she backed away from the men and fumbled for the switch. With a click the hall filled with light.

"Oh no!" What little comfort Deanna had begun to feel was shattered by Shep's explosive outburst. "For the love of—"

It was probably just as well that she didn't understand the rest of what he said as he pulled the unconscious stranger upright and dragged him against the wall, so that it supported his back.

He shot the frozen Deanna a riveting glare. "Get me that ice!" The scarcely checked hostility in his voice startled her into action.

Behind her, she heard the victim moan.

"Easy, Ty, just sit tight," Shep said, returning to that soothing, all-is-under-control tone. "We're going to take care of you, buddy."

Ty? Buddy? Her stomach did a slow rollover as Deanna stumbled to the refrigerator and yanked it open as if she were being sucked into a raging vortex of desolation and it was her only escape. The cool metal door offered support, but not against the winds of condemnation lashed at her from within.

Smoky's barking had been a greeting, not a threat. She'd nearly killed one of Shep's friends. How could she explain that all she could think about was the people who'd set off a car bomb in C. R.'s car and ransacked her apartment? That the *best* she could have hoped for was a burglar and not an assassin?

The burn of ice against her groping fingers hardly registered as she tugged a tray loose from the frozen grip of the freezer shelf. All she felt was a desire to crawl into the freezer and close the door behind her until she was too numb to register anything at all.

"Deanna, what are you doing?" Shep demanded from the hall.

But there was no escape. Not for her. Not this time. She dumped the ice onto a kitchen towel, watching the brittle cubes fall, cracked and broken as the hope she'd begun to find at Hopewell.

Fourteen

T yler McCain looked like death warmed over as he lay
on Shep's bed, propped upright on pillows. Shep had
managed to get Buffalo Butte's own rodeo star cleaned,
bandaged, and in a fresh shirt. Now he tried to convince the
sandy-haired broncobuster to let them take him to the hospital.
He didn't think Ty's nose was broken, but Shep thought his lip
needed stitches on the inside.

"I've had worse than *thish*," Ty declared, his voice distorted by
the swelling of a split lip.

"I am *so* sorry, Mr. McCain." Deanna pressed the ice bag,
which Shep found when her makeshift one fell apart, to the
young man's mouth. "I honestly thought you were a burglar stealing Shep's guns. If you hadn't come into the bathroom where I
was hiding—"

Ty moved the bag aside. "I told you, it's perfectly under*sh*-
tan*d*able. If I wa*sh* in your position, I'd have done the *shame* thing.
Though I don't rightly know if I'd have thought to flail the dick-
en*sh* out of *shomeone* with a toilet tank lid." The charismatic smile
that Shep had seen make seasoned cowgirls trip over their own
ropes broke into a wince. "I'll never live *thish* one down, buddy."

"You shouldn't try to talk," Deanna chided, easing the cold
pack back. "Now you hold this, and I'll get another ice bag for
your eye and nose. That one is almost melted."

"*It'ch* fine. I gotta get back to my buddies at the hotel."

Shep overrode him. "Go ahead and get another, Deanna. If

you can't get him to the doctor with a split lip and concussion, maybe frostbite will do it."

The stricken look she gave Shep made him feel guilty for the acrid note in his jibe, but she wasn't the only one with unsettling secrets. Besides, she'd practically packed his friend in ice in her effort to make up for the damage she'd done. And she had been trying to protect his guns.

When Shep pulled up by the house and saw Smoky vault through the open bedroom window, he'd felt an icy dagger of dread run through his chest, given what he knew about the people after Deanna. Only years of experience made him stop long enough to retrieve the long-handled flashlight/nightstick he kept beneath the driver's seat.

On hearing the sheer terror in Deanna's answer to his hail, he thought certain he'd have to use it, but instead of finding her at the mercy of some drug thug, he'd found an old friend in need of protection from her.

"I don't think you ought to be driving," Shep spoke up. "Why don't you let me take you back to your friends? Deanna can follow me in the Jeep." He had to go back to town anyway. Maisy O'Donnall had hailed him over to the diner as he left the sheriff's office to remind him of the church fund-raiser meeting that evening. Shep would skip it, but he'd been elected the chairperson.

"Nah," Ty declined. "Just radio Esther and have one of them come get me."

"I've got to go back to town anyway," Shep informed him, ending the subject with the finality of his tone. "But I will raise her and have her tell your friends what's going on. They can kick around town and plan on heading out tomorrow if you're up to it."

Tyler and some of his rodeo cronies had taken a few days off to go hunting. Since Ty and his father, who had one of the nicest spreads in Montana, had a falling out over Ty's wanderlust in the rodeo circuit, he kept most of his belongings at Hopewell. That was why he'd parked behind the livery stable to pick up his camping gear. But Shep kept all the guns on Hopewell locked in his gun cabinet. When Ty found the door locked, he'd just come in the same way he and Shep used to when they were wayward teens not wanting to awaken Uncle Dan and Aunt Sue. He knew Smoky from previous visits, although it took a few dog biscuits to reacquaint himself with the ruffled dog.

"Couldn't think of that pup's name for the life of me," he'd told Shep and Deanna as they tried to clean him up, "But I *shaw* that tin of dog *bischkets* on the porch and remembered what a *shucker* he was for them."

Ty had no idea when he decided to wash some of the gun cleaning oil off his hands that a frightened female armed with a toilet tank lid was waiting for him. If she'd hit him head on, Shep wasn't so certain a hospital could have helped him.

"Besides—" Shep gingerly lifted away the expired ice pack from over his friend's eye—"you've lost most of today anyway. And it's gonna be wet tonight according to the weather band."

"You're the boss man," Ty conceded. "If things were different here, we'd love to have you come along. Might spot that red you've been after."

"Nearly had the rascal the other day," Shep said. "No, I have to shore up some things around here before I can bring him in."

"You just *shay* the word, and me and the boys'll come up and help. I'd love a chance at bustin' that one."

"Appreciate the offer, partner." Shep turned toward the door, calling over his shoulder, "Now stay put till we're ready to leave."

Deanna passed him in the central hallway on her way back with another ice pack. Avoiding Shep's gaze, she hurried into the bedroom. Once again, he heard her apologize. Right now Shep had to build up a trust of another kind, and it wasn't going to be easy, knowing what he knew now. He took up the radio mike. Trust was hard to build on a false foundation.

It took a while before Esther responded and promised to give the traveling circuit riders the message.

"And keep an eye on him, Esther. He took a hard knock," Shep advised.

"I will, but you haven't forgotten our meeting tonight, have you?"

"No, Maisy reminded me this afternoon." With all that was going on, it had slipped Shep's mind until then. The church needed a new roof, and the citizens of Buffalo Butte weren't exactly rolling in dough enough to do it out of pocket. "I'll see you later."

As he signed off, Shep glanced out the kitchen sink window at the stable, thinking about bringing Ty's truck around when it dawned on him that there were no curtains on the rusty white rod over it. In fact, there were no curtains at *any* of the kitchen windows. He'd been so absorbed with taking care of his friend, he hadn't noticed.

"I've never seen a rodeo," Deanna was saying in the other room. "I mean, I saw one on television, but..."

She had that same note of awe as the wide-eyed teenaged girls who stood in line to get autographs from the circuit riders. It used to amuse Shep, but for some reason, it annoyed him at the moment. With a disdainful set of his mouth, Shep interrupted Ty's open invitation to come as his guest anytime.

"Deanna, where are my kitchen curtains?" He hadn't technically bought them, but he *had* inherited them. Thus justified, Shep crossed his arms and stared out the sink window at the barn where Patch helped herself to a drink at the watering trough. When the mare finished and meandered away and he'd still heard no answer, he turned to ask again but stopped short at the sight of the distraught young woman standing in the hall.

"I washed them," she answered in a small voice.

Instinct bade Shep hold his tongue, but it didn't stop a finger of anxiety from skimming the back of his neck. If her manner was any indication, she'd done something terrible.

"And they fell apart." Her chin quivered, but she mastered it. "They were yellow with age and I bleached them…apparently too much. I know I sound like a broken record," she said, haplessly tossing up her hands, "but I'm sorry."

Trust, an inner voice reminded him. He was supposed to win her trust and biting off her head was not the way to do it. Besides, it was hard to tell how old the curtains were. More than likely his Aunt Sue had been the last one to wash them. Disaster seemed waiting around every corner for this woman to waltz blithely through it.

"Guess they needed replacing anyway." Terse as his admission was, Deanna seized on it.

"You can see through the glass in the windows now." The spark of hope lighting in the desolation that possessed her face disbursed the remainder of Shep's irritation, even though he didn't recall *not* being able to see out of them.

"Oh yeah. They look good." Actually he'd thought they looked good before, too, but why hurt her feelings? It was bad enough that he was going to spy on her and win her trust. The whole ride back from town, he'd argued with himself and God about his obligation to allow Deanna Manetti, a wanted woman, to stay at Hopewell. He owed the DEA nothing, especially not Jay Voorhees. He owed her nothing, save a car repair, which he could honor while she was under someone else's watch.

Yet, for every argument Shep came up with against sheltering her, he kept thinking of the Scripture about as one does to the least of others, so one does to Christ. What if God had turned him away when he'd been on the run? True, it hadn't been from the law, but it had been from life. In the wilderness of the high country, Shep had slowly healed, both physically and emotionally. He reestablished the relationship with God that had faded.

Maybe he could help her by this charade. The idea certainly took some of the bitterness out of working with Voorhees again and made Shep feel a little less guilty to boot.

"I saw Patch out there looking at the house. Guess she's hungry." Shep glanced out the window to see if the horse was still in the corral. She was. "If you can keep Ty down till I get my chores done, we'll take him to town and grab some dinner. I have to go to a church meeting after that, but it won't be long."

Deanna glanced down at her rumpled clothing. "I'm afraid I'm not decent enough to go anywhere. Not even a dryer sheet will help now."

The knees of her slacks were soiled where she'd evidently been scrubbing the floor. It had never occurred to Shep to try to find clothes for his charge.

"We'll pick up some clothes, too. For now, just rummage through my things and see what you can make do with."

Shep wished his enthusiasm was a bit more genuine, but most of his assets were on paper. He was cash poor. Slapping on the Stetson and picking up the flashlight he'd left on the kitchen table earlier, he started outside. "Keep him down, now," he called back as the screen door slammed behind him.

"I will…thanks."

"No problem." Shep suppressed the nagging anxiety in his voice, but it wouldn't leave his mind. Not only was his pocketbook at risk, but his sanity as well. He felt like the rope in a tug-o'-war of conflicting emotions.

He knew full well what he needed to do—what God expected him to do. *But, God, I didn't destroy Your sanctuary the way Deanna Manetti is destroying mine.*

The church community hall was warm and inviting with its knotty pine paneled walls and Currier and Ives print curtains. The committee members gathered around a row of folding tables to discuss how to raise money for the church's maintenance fund. A cross breeze from the open windows carried the scent of freshly brewed coffee and the lilacs that had grown into a fragrant hedge on the side of the building. Dressed in a borrowed T-shirt and pair of jeans cinched at her waist with the belt from her linen-silk blend trousers, Deanna listened as ways to meet the need for the new roof were debated.

"Even our biggest bazaar or church dinner won't raise the money we need," Maisy O'Donnall pointed out. "We still have a room full of crafts from the last one."

The friendly waitress from the diner walked over with Shep and Deanna after they'd finished their meal—a pot roast special. Esther Lawson caught up with them before they reached the church at the end of Main Street. She'd left her sixteen-year-old granddaughter with Tyler, who complained about staying behind while his friends drove over to Taylorville, Buffalo Butte's larger, more urban neighbor.

"I told young Tyler that if he didn't stay put, he wouldn't be going anywhere in the morning," Esther sniffed primly.

It came as no surprise to Deanna that the lady was a former schoolteacher and had taught most of the townspeople under forty, including Shep while his dad was stationed overseas. Esther had a sweet, kindly face—definitely a looker in her day—but her ramrod straight posture hinted of a backbone of steel. Deanna had no doubt that Tyler was following her orders to the letter.

When Shep had asked Maisy and Esther where the best place to buy ladies' clothing was, the two began clucking like mother hens over her. There was no need for Shep to take Deanna to Taylorville; plenty of nice things were in the church rummage sale boxes that would fill the order. Before the meeting started, Shep carried out a box of clothing just Deanna's size, some of the pieces with tags still on them.

"Honey, the Lord knows what size we all wear," Maisy said, when Deanna marveled at her good fortune. "And Juanita Everett is always buying things a size too small, if you get my drift. Fills the church box and empties her husband's pocketbook, not that it's any of my business."

"Now, Maisy, idle talk breeds mischief," Esther cautioned.

Unruffled, Maisy laughed. "Shoot, Esther, that's all I ever do. I suppose that's why I'm so ornery."

Deanna suddenly had two mothers, one a prim lady, the other an outrageous flirt, and both the answer to a prayer she hadn't even asked. Overwhelmed by the friendly support, she glanced out the window at the little white-steepled church across the parking lot. She knew now that she'd forgotten God's size, but He hadn't forgotten hers. If only she knew what He had in mind for her. He knew she was innocent.

"What we need is exposure," the former schoolmistress declared, drawing Deanna back to the conversation at hand. "Maybe we could pack up and head over to the big Smart Mart in Taylorville and have a sale there."

"The problem is, even if they'll let us set up at the store, we don't have enough people with enough time to staff a bake sale or craft table for as long at it would take to raise the money," Reverend John Lawrence said.

The reverend sat next to Shep, who'd been chosen as the chairman of the maintenance committee. Maybe this time, she *had* found someone she could trust. Maybe their chance meeting wasn't chance after all. If God knew her dress size, He surely knew what she needed in a man. Of course, she'd thought C. R. heaven-sent at first.

Lord, I'm so confused.

"What if we did the job ourselves?" Shep asked during the lull of prospective ideas. He looked around the table. "Most of us have to be a bit handy with tools on our farms and ranches, and the labor is the costliest part of the bid."

"If we don't have time to staff bake tables, where'll we get time to put on a new roof?" one of the younger men at the table challenged. He was the one who helped Shep load supplies at the Farm and Ranch General Deanna's first day in Buffalo Butte.

"If folks used to raise a barn in a day, Seth, I imagine a group of us could slap on a new roof in one. Maybe your dad could get the building materials at cost for the church?"

"I imagine we could work something out."

"Some of my boys would be willing to put in a Saturday," a gentleman with thick straw-colored hair ventured. "I imagine we ranchers could show you farmers how it's done."

Even if he and Deanna hadn't been introduced, she'd have recognized J. B. McCain, Ty's father. They had the same chiseled features and coloring, except that the senior McCain's hair was heavily peppered with white.

"That so?" A tall red-cheeked man about the same age remarked from the opposite side of the table. Like most of the men here, he had a white line along the top of his brow engraved by the constant presence of a baseball cap. "I reckon my crew knows a thing or two your cow chasers haven't even thought of."

"So why not have a contest?"

It wasn't until all heads swung toward Deanna that she realized she'd voiced her question aloud. While a burglar might intimidate her, a conference table of entrepreneurs didn't faze her at all, unless she counted Shep. He looked as though she'd just started the range wars all over.

Deanna threw up her hands. "It would be a *good-natured* challenge. It would garner more interest, get more people to come see your wares and watch the competition."

"I know all the cowboys in the area would come, just to see us show the farmers how it's done," J. B. snorted.

"So'd the farmhands," his adversary at the opposite end chimed in. "Just for the fun of watching you eat crow, J. B." He glanced at the minister. "What do you think, Reverend?"

Reverend Lawrence smiled, accentuating lines carved by time and an enduring sense of humor. Pale blue eyes twinkling, he nodded at Deanna. "I think this young lady might have found a good way to get some of these fellas to finally come to church."

Fifteen

S *anctuary.* Although Deanna hadn't exactly been to the church proper, which sat across a parking lot from the community hall, she felt the sanctuary offered by its congregation and readily accepted the minister's invitation to attend the Sunday worship. What was it Gram had said when as a child Deanna had asked if God lived in their church? *"No, child, God lives in the people. Special as it is, the church is just a building. It's the people who bring God in."*

She wasn't sure if she'd stumbled across Hopewell and Buffalo Butte, or if God had recognized her voice after such a long silence, but she longed to believe the latter. No, she did believe it. The line from a hymn drifted through her mind in confirmation. *All things were possible.*

Deanna looked through the windshield of Shep's Jeep at the long narrow strip of road ahead of her. A few days ago it was the road to nowhere. Now it felt like the road home…at least for a while. She shoved the temporal aspect of her circumstance to the back of her mind with a wistful smile.

For every person she'd met to date, Deanna knew or had known someone just like them back home in her childhood Brooklyn neighborhood, good down-to-earth folks who lived their best and cared for others. They made her feel like one of them. Maisy and Esther had outfitted her in clothes. Esther even offered to take her to Taylorville to find new curtains for the kitchen after hearing about that fiasco, but Shep insisted on taking Deanna himself.

"I thought that was the way of it, Shepard," Esther had said with a schoolmarm's smugness.

Deanna cringed inwardly for her host. She knew their relationship was as platonic as platonic could get. Until her car was fixed and she was on her way, it was simply an economic necessity for them both. If anything sprang from that, it would be worthless, founded on a lie. She squirmed beneath the guilt that suddenly clouded her sense of security.

"The wind too much for you?" Shep asked, startling her from the dark turn of her reverie.

"No, it feels super." She chuckled. "In New York, you put down a window and get an unfiltered dose of diesel and gasoline fumes. Although I admit, I always found the smell of city traffic to be invigorating...you know, like there was enough fuel in it to give me extra miles to the breath. Hey," Deanna defended herself at the skeptical brow Shep cocked at her. "It was what I grew up with. It made me tick."

"And what makes you tick now?"

The question came out of nowhere, nailing Deanna to a proverbial threshold, one she wasn't sure she wanted—no, dared—to cross.

Shep put on his blinker and turned at the weathered sign marking the long entrance to Hopewell. A turn signal in the middle of nowhere with no other vehicle in sight. This guy was so by-the-book it was incredible.

"I think I've lost my ticker," she answered after a thoughtful silence. "Like I'm in some kind of rootin', tootin' Oz and I can't find my ruby slippers to get back home."

A sting annoyed her eyes. She looked away, pretending fascination with a grove of trees in the far pasture until she mastered the well of emotion that was more like an unruly sea lately—rising, sinking, churning, drowning. *Lord, I am so pathetic. I don't even know myself. I only know I'm in over my head…*

"What in the world?"

Shep's exclamation struck her like a cold splash, clearing away one wave of emotion for another. At the approach of the main street toward Shep's house, a shiny new motor home stood in the headlights of a beat-up pickup. Some men stood against the door of the RV, held at bay by someone or something. Surely not Smoky, she thought, her veins suddenly shot with an icy dread. That canine's incessant barking had no more than a dog biscuit's worth of backbone behind it.

The three men by the motor home squinted as Shep's Jeep lights compounded the glare in their eyes. Deanna had never seen them before. The tallest had an athletic build with longish fair hair wrapped behind his ears. Another looked as though he'd been plucked from a computer keyboard—close-cropped hair, wire-rim glasses, rumpled cotton dress shirt loosely tucked into pleated trousers. It was the third man who seemed in charge. Clad in a well-fitted suit of nondistinct color, he ventured one step forward, hand raised in a cautious wave as Shep brought the Jeep to a halt in front of them.

"Mr. Jones, are we glad to see you. I'm Jay Voorhees from the government geological survey team. We spoke the other day about our running some tests on the mineral contents of your property?"

"I never heard of 'em," an obstinate voice declared from the blind side of the pickup. "Caught 'em snoopin' all around the place."

Deanna listened, groping for a reason to assuage the heightened alarm gripping her chest. All she could think of were the men who were looking for her…or the police. *Will I ever have another moment's peace?*

"I was just telling this gentleman we were looking for an electric hookup when he surprised us."

"I reckon he did." Shep chuckled as he climbed out of the

Jeep and started toward the disconcerted group. "Mr. Voorhees, this is my outfitting partner, Ticker Deerfield." Raising his voice, he called out to the man hidden by the pickup. "It's all right, Tick."

Shep's simple assurance was enough to loosen the breath stuck in Deanna's chest. Her pulse even registered as he continued to explain. "I spoke to these folks a while back about the mineral rights Uncle Dan sold to the government. Knew they were coming, just didn't know when. Sorry I forgot to say anything about it."

Deanna stayed put in the Jeep, no longer frozen with fear, but from the toll it had taken on her strength. Her legs felt as stable as the melted ice pack that had given way when Shep knelt on it and it had sent him sprawling across the bed during her first morning at Hopewell.

"What brings you here anyway?" Shep asked his partner. "The roundup isn't over, is it?"

"Naw," Tick answered sheepishly as he stepped into view from his hiding place. "I couldn't get no sleep with some of them young fellers yappin' and lollygaggin'. Figgered I'd catch a couple good hours of shut-eye and then roll 'em out before sunup to see the error of their ways."

There was something about Tick's half-bearded grin in the headlights that further comforted Deanna. Funny how a few days ago, she'd been certain he was, at the least, an ax murderer. Now he looked like a guardian angel packing iron. Rifle lowered in one hand, Tick extended the other to Mr. Voorhees.

"Sorry I gave you such a scare. 'Course you're wastin' your time, if you're lookin' for gold. This ain't no ghost town for nothin'."

"There are *other* minerals aside from gold, Mr. Deerfield. That's what we're here to survey," Voorhees replied.

Deanna leaned against the headrest of her seat and closed her eyes in thanksgiving for Shep, for Tick, even for Buffalo Butte. She didn't know how her problems would be resolved, but at least she was no longer alone. It was going to be all right.

All things were possible.

For the first time in a very long time—maybe back as far as when she'd stopped going to church to finish an urgent project or sleep in from working late the night before—she actually relaxed.

Shep wondered if there would be anyone in Buffalo Butte who was not "in" on Deanna Manetti's case by the time it was resolved. He'd felt obliged to explain to Tick, who echoed Shep's instinctive reaction—she had to be a victim of circumstances and bad judgment.

"Well, she come to the right place. You 'n' me both know what it is to be run hard by life and put up wet. Man nor beast don't git no closer to their Maker than up here in these parts. Reckon that's why the good Lord made these mountains and sent the little filly our way."

Ticker didn't go to church proper unless he was roped into it, and he never talked much about faith. But he kept a worn Bible in his pack and studied it beneath a cathedral ceiling of sky, surrounded by untarnished creation. When Shep's partner did talk about his faith, the words stuck in Shep's mind, same as they did when the experienced older man spoke of his instincts.

"If it was me," Tick went on, "I'd be leery 'o' that Voorhees fella. Wouldn't surprise me if he wasn't crooked as a dog's leg."

While Shep didn't think Jay was crooked in a legal sense, he agreed the man's motives were skewed by his ambition. Had God sent Deanna to Hopewell, expecting Shep to offer her refuge and help?

"Inasmuch as ye did it not to one of the least of these, ye did it not to me."

The words from the book of Matthew and Tick haunted him later as he lay cramped and bound in more ways than one on the sofa. The workout shorts he'd donned for decency's sake twisted about his waist, tightening like a noose each time he turned over. The sofa itself just wasn't long enough to accommodate his frame. With little alternative, he stuck his feet out the side past the wooden armrests, hoping to avoid getting a crick in his neck.

In the central hall Deanna stood by the washer digging through the boxes the church ladies had given her like a kid digging through cereal boxes for a hidden prize. She had an uncanny ability to roll with the punches she'd been dealt, but the bottom line was that Tick was right. She needed help and protection, the same as God had offered them in their time of need.

That and what he now knew made it impossible for Shep to harbor a grudge for too long over her deceit. But merciful days, she was just too cute for his comfort in his oversized jeans and shirt.

His ex-fiancé wouldn't be caught dead in that getup. Nor would Ellen have fit in so well at the community hall meeting, much less paid enough attention to contribute anything. Deanna's idea had lit a fire under the committee to accept his. The last time Shep had mentioned doing a project themselves, the idea was shelved without much interest.

Something as simple as adding some friendly competition between the farmers and ranchers kindled its appeal. But then, selling ideas was her game, he realized, diverting his gaze to the ceiling as though watching his engaging guest might become addictive.

"Oh!"

Deanna's breathless exclamation drew Shep's half-lidded attention to a purple silky something she held up in the overhead light. Separating it into two pieces, she held the shorter against her chest as though measuring for size. Shep had no doubt the nightgown that came just above the knees would fit. And the color would shade those voluminous blue eyes of hers toward violet.

"Think you'll be much longer?" he asked, turning away from the light with an impatient jerk as though it bothered him. Shorts akimbo, he raised his hips and wrangled them aright with an indignant snatch, but staring at the sofa back didn't help erase the provocative image conjured in his mind. He could already picture her in the figure-skimming silk.

"I'm sorry," she exclaimed, her delight with her new things infecting her voice. "I was so involved with these things—they are just lovely—"

"Well, some of us have to work tomorrow."

"Now wait one minute, buster. Like I didn't work today? Like—" Deanna broke off as though she'd been whipped into silence by guilt. "Sorry."

He was being a jerk, but he couldn't help it. Something had put a burr under his saddle—or some such place. The light went out with the click of the switch. The soft padding of her bare feet faded as she retreated toward the bedroom.

"I'm just going to take a quick shower," she called back to him. "Maisy said she'd washed all these things before boxing them for the church sale, so I don't see any need to wash them again, do you?"

"Not if you intend to wear them."

"Okay, wise guy," Deanna shot back readily at his reference to the late kitchen curtains. "I'm a few hours older and a wash load wiser now...and at least your clothes didn't fall apart. They are clean, folded, and in the basket by the dryer, thank you very much."

"Thank you very much, *Miss* Manetti. Now I have to get some shut-eye so I'll have the energy to wear them. Good night."

"Good night, *Mr.* Jones," she mimicked, the proximity of her voice taking Shep by surprise.

He glanced over his shoulder in time to see her ponytailed profile flit into the bathroom, the silky ensemble tossed over her arm.

"Sleep tight. Don't let the bedbugs bite." She closed the door behind her. A few seconds later the shower came on.

Oh yeah, he was going to sleep *tight*…like an overwound watch. There were federal agents in his yard and a charming criminal in his shower. Piece of cake.

In the semidarkness of dawn, a piercing whinny sliced through the white noise of the radio, jolting Deanna upright from a dreamless sleep. Never had she heard such a noise—like someone was chopping wood with a hammer. Rolling out of bed, she peered out the window at the silhouette of the ramshackle buildings, expecting to see them flying apart, board by board.

The tall A-framed livery stable, which, with only one of its double doors open, stood like a one-eyed, pointy-headed monster on the verge of exploding with the shrieks of horses and the smashing of lumber. From her limited knowledge of TV Westerns, only fire or a wildcat caused that kind of terror in a horse.

In the other room, the scrape of a chair and a muffled exclamation told her Shep was just as alarmed. The porch door opened and slammed in his wake as he darted out into the yard, barefoot and struggling into his jeans. From the other end of the buildings, a barking Smoky barreled around the corner ahead of Ticker, who was as fully dressed as he'd been the night before, rifle in hand.

Excitement clearing the sluggishness from her mind, Deanna pulled on the matching robe and rushed out onto the porch just as Shep reached the half-open side of the barn door. Suddenly, he lunged aside. From out of the black interior, a dark horse streaked past him. Deanna looked down. She was barefoot, and the horse was galloping straight for the house. She ducked back inside.

The thundering of the horse's hooves competed with men's shouts as she scrambled to find her shoes. By the time she emerged again, the livery stable lights both inside and outside had been turned on. Arms folded across her chest against the morning chill, she wobbled, stockingless, in her fashion pumps toward the open door. "Can I help?"

Slowing at the door with second thought, she spied one of the men from the shiny trailer hustling around it, struggling to don his jacket.

"Thunderation," Ticker shouted above the heavy-hoofed scramble inside the barn.

But it was an ungodly sound that warned Deanna to sidestep in time to avoid the animal that trotted out of the barn—not a horse, but like one.

"Molly, you buck-toothed daughter of…" Ticker, hot on the animal's trail, stumbled and caught himself. "If I get my hands on your scrawny neck…"

"Hey!" the geologist from the trailer shouted, waving wildly to avoid being run down by the irate critter.

Molly turned in a scatter of dust and headed toward the house, but Ticker and Smoky herded her back toward the barn…and Deanna. Eyes growing with each snort and bellow of the mule, Deanna could almost feel its hooves pounding into her chest. The vision spurred her frozen limbs into action. Darting around the closed half of the barn door for cover, she slammed hard into the man trying to open it.

Reality slowed into clips of awareness, punctuated by the staccato of Molly's hooves and the bizarre dance of arms and legs trying simultaneously to catch each other. Deanna clung to Shep's solid torso as they tumbled, gravity refusing to stop. Shep was atop her, shielding her from the hooves that took a fleeting pause along with Deanna's heart, and then resumed somewhere beyond their heads. Had she blacked out?

Shep's voice penetrated her daze. "You okay?"

Deanna nodded. She hadn't enough wind in her lungs to answer. She kneaded his chest as if to prove that she was still alive and not a mangled mess from Molly's hooves. Relief uncoiled her fear-drawn muscles in one sweep.

"Deanna?" Shep rolled away from her in alarm.

The abrupt withdrawal of his warmth exposed her to a cool rush of the early morning air, prompting her to open her eyes. "What?" She lifted her head from the dirt floor, looking about wildly. "I'm alive, aren't I?" She clutched at her chest, as if to be sure. "Where'd that animal go?"

"Out the back." A hand appeared in front of her face. It belonged to one of the geologists, the one in the suit. "Can I help you up, Miss Manetti?"

Something about the way he said her name sent a shiver along her spine. She stared at him for a moment, disconcerted, and then accepted his help. "Thank you, Mister "

"Voorhees, Jay Voorhees."

"Yes, I'm sorry. Mr. Voorhees." Deanna straightened her robe and brushed as much of the dirt off as possible. They hadn't been formally introduced last night, but she'd heard Shep tell Ticker the geologist's name.

"Can I help you into the house? You look as if you're about to swoon."

"Swoon?" She ran her fingers through her hair. New Yorkers didn't swoon…did they?

"I got her," Shep spoke up, no question at all in his voice or his actions as he slipped an arm around Deanna's waist.

"You can help me with the mule, young fella," Tick called from where he dug into a barrel with a metal can. "All you gotta do is shake this feed to get her attention, and she'll follow you right back to her stall there."

The older man pulled a splintered stable door out of the way. It looked as if it had been kicked to bits. So did one of the other doors, but a solid bar blocked the way of a beige horse with a dark mane and huge black nostrils that quivered as it whinnied. Suddenly, it pulled back and circled inside the stall, as if looking for another way out.

"Reach inside and dump it in her feedbox," Tick said, not the least concerned that the horse next door looked as though it would try to bolt through the sturdy bar at any moment. He pointed to the box just inside the opening of Molly's empty stall. "Stand back, and she'll trot right on in, happy as you please. Then just slide that bar across to keep her there."

"I'll be back in a minute, Tick." Shep pulled Deanna away from her leery study of the snorting, whinnying horse. Even Patch—the horse she'd heard had walked without flinching through firecrackers tossed in mischief during the last Fourth of July parade—was becoming restless

"No rush," Tick assured him. "We got everything under control." The older man directed Voorhees out the back door where Molly disappeared, while he moved to head Molly off from the other side in case she decided to act mule stubborn.

"Just remember," Tick reminded the greenhorn, "all you got to do is get her attention with that feed. O' course, with that blamed stallion sportin' about, she ain't actin' like herself so keep an eye out."

Sixteen

W hat happened back there?" Deanna leaned into the crook of Shep's arm as they walked toward the house. She loved horses—on television and at a distance. But up close, they were too big for comfort. Would she ever get used to them?

"The bay is in season and that red came courting."

Deanna hardly heard Shep's answer. Like she was going to be around long enough to get up close and personal with a horse.

"The vixen kicked down the door to let him in, and Molly… well, she just got caught up in all the excitement." Shep let the door slam behind them, flipping on the light. "Sit down before you fall down and let me take a look at that knee."

Knee? What knee? Deanna looked down, tugging her robe out of the way, to see caked-on dirt and a trickle of blood down her shin.

"What made you run out there in the first place?" he asked, heading for the sink. He took a clean cloth from the drawer and ran it under the faucet.

"Well I…" Why *had* she run out? She was terrified of horses. "I guess I just didn't want to be left alone." Now that was lame, really lame. But then she'd been lamebrained ever since she'd heeded the call of the West. Shep's explanation of the chaos finally caught up with her.

"Did you say the girl horse kicked down the door and not the stallion?"

"The *mare*," Shep amended, his wry but disarming grin spreading as he squeezed the excess water from the cloth and knelt in front of her.

"The shameless hussy!" Deanna exclaimed, adding with second thought. "Although, I guess I wasn't a whole lot better."

Shep's head came up so sharply, he nearly bumped Deanna's.

Heat flushed her face. "No, n-not *that* way," she stammered, wishing she had a rein on her tongue. "I meant that I'd made it easy for a guy to lead me astray, away from my home and a good job and…and now I have nothing but a beat-up sports car. You know, like I had a sports car life envisioned and wound up with a wreck."

Deanna grimaced at the sting of the wet cloth he pressed on her open cut despite Shep's gentleness. Why hadn't she met the Jeep man before the sports car one? She hadn't needed speed. She needed durability—someone to weather the terrain of life.

"I should have been content with public transportation and my job in New York. But the idea of being in love and in charge of a department with a big salary and fancy vehicle has me jobless and up to my neck in debt for a car that won't run."

"'Stay away from the love of money; be satisfied with what you have.' Deuteronomy, I think," Shep added after a short pause for thought. "Sometimes moving up in the world isn't worth it. But hey, at least your car can be fixed." He rose and walked back to the sink.

But could her life—not to mention her heart? Deanna bit her lip as it quivered under the weight of her hopelessness.

"And who knows, maybe we can do something about your life, too."

"Like a complete overhaul?"

"Nah, I think you've still got a few good parts intact." Shep took a Band-Aid and some antiseptic from a first-aid box he pulled from under the sink. "Besides," he said, looking out the window as he rinsed the cloth under the faucet. "The rest of that verse goes, 'For God has said, I will never fail you. I will never forsake you.' He's the master mechanic. He can fix anything."

"Yeah, but I left Him. I haven't exactly been in regular touch."

"Been there. Done that. Came home with my tail between my legs," he reflected with a halfhearted grunt of humor. "But He took me back…a lot quicker than I'd come to Him."

Shep wrung the cloth dry and shook it out, before taking up the other supplies. When he turned, the rippled planes of his chest had been splattered and streaked by the force of the water splashing from the sink.

If God was using Shep to save her, He could be making a real mistake. The most reverent thought that came to Deanna's mind at that moment regarding the straight-shooting rancher was *Holy cow*.

"You look good in dirt," she quipped, unable to dislodge her gaze from his searching one. She'd fallen for gorgeous before, but this was gorgeous *and* good.

At Shep's disconcerted expression, she grimaced. Sheesh, she wasn't much better than that mare. Here this guy was talking seriously about God and she was flirting— kicking down a protective door she hadn't finished building yet. Broadsided by a double shot of remorse and panic, she groped in silent prayer for help. *God, are You there? I need some help here. I don't know what I'm thinking. No, I'm not thinking, I'm just doing, and I'm not even sure why or how…or if I should be having these thoughts at all. Have You sent just a shepherd to protect my hide or a Shepard for my heart? I don't want to get hurt anymore.*

"So do you."

Shep's belated, husky reply, his closeness, melted away the psychological bar she kept trying to put between them. Or was it his touch? One hand cradled the back of her calf as he gently applied the antiseptic. The sting registered, shattering the spell holding Deanna breathless and still. "Oh, oh!" she gasped, erupting with a frenzied huffing and puffing to cool the burning wound. "You're killing me here."

The Band-Aid he applied firmly over her wounded knee finally assuaged its outrage. The heat of his hand ironing it onto her skin sent pinpricks of awareness all the way to the nape of Deanna's neck. Then he took it away.

Talk about mixed signals! Her senses flashed and pinged like a tilted pinball machine.

"There," he said, as though caught in the same electric freeze-frame as Deanna, at least on the surface. Was his heart doing flip-flops like hers? Were they supposed to be doing flip-flops?

"You mean you aren't going to kiss it and make it better?" she blurted out. Her pulse accelerated even faster at her spontaneous reply. Her mother and Gram kissed boo-boos and made them better. If Shepard Jones did, her brain would scatter like a dandelion gone to seed. Shep's throaty "Nope" checked the clamor of her thoughts but failed to rescue her from the warm cinnamon depths of his eyes where she floundered, unable to escape.

If there was another saucy reply floating around somewhere, it had sunk to the bottom of her think tank, beyond retrieval. She rose with him as he straightened to his feet. At first she thought it was Shep's eyes that coaxed her from her seat, but his hands reinforced them. Through the silky material of her robe, their gentle persuasion raised gooseflesh in their wake. Goose bumps when she was anything but cold. Go figure.

With the crook of a work-roughened finger, he cupped her chin, tilting her head back so she could almost feel the night's growth of bristle on his face. His breath warmed her lips. As he pulled her even closer, the silk of her gown and robe did little to allay the effect of the masculine torso pressed against her. She could feel his heart beating counterpoint to hers, a dizzying sensation if ever there was one.

His kiss was more of a caress, as tender as the touch of his fingers had been to her battered knee, yet it raised her senses to a state of awareness that transcended earthly senses. He wanted more; Deanna knew it. She wanted more as well. Like Eve with the apple just within her grasp, Deanna inhaled the sweetness of pure temptation, almost tasting it.

"Is there a future worth chasing here?" Hoarseness riddled Shep's whisper of the same question that haunted Deanna's mind.

Holy Cow. Is there? Was there? Could there be—

"Well, we got it." The out-of-the-blue statement shattered the magic moment suspending the two of them. Shep all but recoiled as the helpful geologist stepped into the kitchen, followed by a loud bang of the door.

"Don't they teach you to knock in *geology school?*" he grumbled, crouching down to pick up the first-aid supplies abandoned on the floor.

"Sorry, I figured you'd want to know about the mule." Voorhees tossed up his hands in surrender. "Guess I'm not the only one who got caught up in the excitement." He backed out the spring-loaded screen door, adding with a laconic twist, "Except mine was with a mule."

Shep inhaled, stoking his breath for the thunder she saw gathering on his face, but Jay Voorhees disappeared before it erupted, his footsteps fading in retreat. When Shep turned back to her, his expression was as hard as the thick oak bars across the stable doors.

Her stallion was about to bolt…but not if she beat him to it. Pivoting away, Deanna beat a leisurely path to the bedroom as if nothing at all had transpired.

Nothing had, she told herself as she shut out the walking, talking temptation that had brought her to the brink of…of what exactly? She walked to the edge of the bed and dropped on it, bouncing as though to jolt the answer from its dark hiding place.

"Is there a future worth pursuing here, Deanna?"

Her future was either on the run or in prison for a crime she didn't commit. His was chasing that four-legged Romeo all over creation. The futility of a relationship slammed Deanna like a freight train. C. R. had tied her to the railroad track, but when

Jones had finally come along, it was too late. The wheels had cut her heart in two.

She'd have laughed at the mental picture, but it hurt too much. *God, please…take it away.*

Grabbing a pillow, she hugged it to her chest, as though that might ease her pain. It didn't. There was no relief. No matter what Shep *or* Deuteronomy said, Deanna couldn't shake the doubt and its consequential guilt that repeatedly overwhelmed her. Sure all things were possible, but were they probable?

God, where are You? Did You send Shep my way just to show me what I might have had if I'd been more faithful?

Outside, an engine roared from the far end of Hopewell's only street where Ticker's departing pickup cast a cloud of dust over the visitors' travel trailer. Blinking tear-blurred eyes, she searched the stillness of the ghost town through the window. Its sun-bleached buildings glowed iridescent in the morning sun now peeping over the horizon. On the outside, it looked alive, but inside it was as abandoned and empty as she felt—and haunted by what might have been.

Shep didn't bother to go back to bed. He'd hardly slept anyway, cramped as he was on the sofa. And his knee ached as though someone had shoved a screwdriver under the cap and left it there. He must have aggravated it when he pulled Deanna to the ground and scrambled to shield her from Molly's hooves. Popping a couple of aspirin from a tin he kept in the livery, he washed it down with fresh water from the hose.

What on God's green earth had gotten into him? One minute he was trying to bandage her bloodied knee and the next, he'd pulled her into his arms and kissed her. And that question about a future—that was a masterpiece. It was like pulling a perp's gun from inside his jacket and asking, What's this, buddy? He already knew the answer and so had she, given the way she skedaddled.

He owed Voorhees a debt of gratitude for stopping what could have been a disaster. So why did Shep feel the urge to punch the man's face? Was it professional embarrassment at having been caught doing something that went against their training? Or was it that Shep still couldn't accept Voorhees's charge that Deanna was a crook, not the victim?

"Morning!"

Shep glanced up from the stable door he'd been repairing to see the subject of his preoccupation appear in the opening of the barn, Tick's dog at her side. Or maybe it was that Deanna Manetti was as out of place here with him as a hothouse rose in the desert. He'd never seen jeans that glittered before, but the sun in the open doorway glanced off their curve and taper, holding his attention longer than he intended.

"Mornin'." Shep shifted his focus to the project at hand. Some of the planks in the door had been split and needed to be replaced, but most of them could be simply renailed and braced.

Cutting a wide path around the barred openings of the now empty stalls, Deanna approached him. "So what do you want me to do today?"

He looked up from the broken door in surprise.

"I mean, the house is clean, and I've torn up everything I can in there, so I thought I'd start on the barn," she explained with an exaggerated shrug. "Gotta earn my keep, right?"

Shep acknowledged her with a grunt. "Just don't spook the horses with those fancy jeans." Heaven knew they spooked him— or at least the feelings they provoked did.

"Okay, they're too flashy for the boardroom or the stable, but they were free and they fit." She flanked her concession with an impish grin. "So what do I do?"

Shep thought a moment. "You think you can reach just under the bar there and grab those water buckets? They need emptying, rinsing, and refilling with fresh water." He'd turned the animals out to drink at the water trough in the corral, once they'd been fed, but hadn't gotten around to giving them fresh water inside. "And the stalls need to be cleaned out and fresh straw put down."

"Will do." Not quite as chipper as before, Deanna glanced uncertainly into one of the empty stables. "You don't think the horses will come back while I'm in here, do you?"

"I doubt it, but I'll close the corral gate just in case, how's that?"

"Sounds great. Thanks."

If only she weren't so appreciative, so agreeable and willing to tackle anything, so—

Disconcerted, Shep leaned the damaged door against an old sawhorse and closed the doors. When he came through the last one, he noticed Smoky had found a place in the shade and, eyes bright with curiosity, watched Deanna tackle the first water bucket.

She struggled with the hook that held it suspended at the horse's head level. On seeing the rubber pail was nearly full, Shep started to offer to take it down for her, when she released it.

"I got it," she grunted, lowering it to her arms' limit.

Returning to the repair of the stable door, Shep took up a nail to replace one of the bent ones he'd removed earlier, but he couldn't help watching Deanna's awkward waddle toward the back door of the livery stable with the sloshing bucket balanced between her knees. With a grin, he took up the hammer and started a downward swing when a shriek accompanied the emptying splash of water outside.

The end of his thumb exploded in pain, making an expressive hiss that leaked through Shep's clenched teeth.

"*Eww,*" Deanna wailed, "what kind of an animal does *that* in his water bucket?"

Eyes watering, Shep tried to squeeze the agony out with his other hand, jaws clenched in silence. If he wasn't so angry over his recklessness, he'd have laughed in anticipation of what had grossed the city gal out. It was a fact of life with livestock. With a horse's intake and output valves on the same plane, manure some-times found its way into their water containers, even when hung on the jamb.

"That is the most disgusting thing I have ever seen."

Just wait till you see the stables. His response never went beyond thought, for Shep feared more than those words lurked behind his grating teeth, waiting for the chance to find voice. He rolled his eyes up at the dust-laden, cobweb-strung ceiling. *Lord, this is not going to work.*

Unaware of his pressing affliction, Deanna rinsed out the bucket, her face screwed in disdain. Most noses weren't that cute wrinkled up like that. Shep finally let out the breath he'd seized upon the sharp impact of the hammer. When he thought it was safe, he eased up on the pressure on his thumb, allowing blood to throb back into it. It hurt like the devil.

"What's wrong with you?"

The innocent widening of Deanna's curious gaze only added to his aggravation. Maybe he shouldn't talk just yet, he thought, clamping down on words again. When it was obvious he had no intention of answering, she waddled back with the refilled bucket and set it down in front of the stable.

"You banged your thumb?"

Those expressive blues fixed on him were deep enough for a guy to fall into.

"Let me see it."

Shep clenched his hand against his chest. The last thing he needed was the source of his pain treating it. "N…no, it's fine."

"Come on; let me see."

"It's fine."

"You're white as a sheet and sweating bullets." She reached for his hand. "Now let me see."

That did it. "If you hadn't been babbling on about horse—" he paused in midsentence— "*droppings* in water, I wouldn't have done it in the first place."

He didn't think it was possible, but his accusation made her eyes widen even more with incredulity…or indignation.

"Well, pardon me for my ignorance about the decided lack of horse hygiene, Forrest *Grump*. I didn't know talk was forbidden in the barn. I guess stupid *is* as stupid does."

Deanna's muster of defiance cracked with the slight quiver of her upturned chin. "You will not hear one more word from me. I mean, heaven forbid you have another boo-boo. You might bite my head off and spit down my neck."

Shep knew a no-win situation when he saw one, and he was steeped in *no-win* up to his neck. Still, he felt compelled to try. "Look, I'm sorry. That was the pain talking. Just forget it, okay?"

"Sure, no problem."

The words said one thing; Deanna's voice said the opposite. Shep took up the hammer and pried off a loose splinter with the claw, watching as the stubborn city gal struggled to hang the full bucket. She lifted it twice, but after using her knee as a bolster, got it on the second try. The gentleman within pointed a guilty finger at him, but Shep ignored the voice. The way he saw it, he was condemned if he did, convicted it he didn't—either way he was going to pay.

Seventeen

I s your knee bothering you?" Deanna asked as she put the large salad she'd made on the table along with two dressings.

With the boost of an antihistamine for watery eyes, she'd finished her stable cleaning and put fresh hay in each stall. To her amazement, the smell of the fresh hay was refreshing in a down-home sort of way, like fresh sheets on a bed. Not that she'd want to roll around in it, considering what she just shoveled out, but this evening the horses should enjoy stretching out and reveling in the scent and feel of the newness—unless they had allergies.

"It gets a little stiff when I can't stretch it out," Shep acknowledged, heading for the bathroom to wash up for lunch. "It'll work out."

Deanna glanced guiltily at the sofa where her gracious host had spent the nights since she'd been stranded there.

"You know, there really is no reason you shouldn't sleep in your own bed. After all, it *is* your house, and I'm not exactly an invited guest."

The running bathroom faucet drowned her out. A minute later, Shep emerged, his hair damp and neatly combed. The edges of his rolled-up sleeves were slightly damp from where he'd evidently rinsed his hair and face without the benefit of a cloth. Somehow the reckless dunk-and-towel-dry look became him.

"I was taught to give ladies the best seat, and I guess that goes for a bed as well. Aunt Sue wouldn't give me a moment's peace if

I didn't." He assessed the salad before sitting down.

"Something wrong?" she asked.

He hesitated, then shook his head. "It looks good. I just think I'll fix a sandwich to go with it."

"I'll do it."

"Sit!"

Deanna obeyed the sharp command as instinctively as the dog that waited next to the table in hopes of a dropped treat. "I guess hard physical work demands a different diet than white-collar jobs."

"I guess your white-collar beau considered all this rabbit food with no protein a meal?"

Shep slapped together two slices of bread with a chunk of cheese in the middle and sat down without bothering to cut it in half like Gram always did. "Around here, it's a side dish." He lowered his head, prompting Deanna to do the same, and offered a short grace.

Deanna reached for the salad dressing as Shep took a bite out of his sandwich. There was a loud silence as she tossed the oil and vinegar among the greens. The veggies crunching as she ate her first forkful sounded like some kind of food grinder, no matter how softly she tried to chew. After what seemed like an eternity, she swallowed.

"Look, I'm sorry—" Shep began as if he'd been waiting for a lull in the mastication.

"I'm sorry—" she said at the same time.

Deanna blushed as their gazes locked and gave in to the smile prompted by Shep's grin.

"Ladies first." Shep sat back expectantly.

"I was just going to say I'm really sorry you hurt your thumb. It looks awful." She shivered involuntarily. It did. The nail was black now and the flesh was a screaming red.

"And I was going to say I'm sorry for being a Forrest *Grump*."

"I have a smart mouth," she said with an apologetic shrug.

"And it slips into gear before the brain. I gotta get that worked on."

Shep brushed aside her apology with a wave of his sandwich. "I deserved it." He put down his napkin next to the salad bowl. "For a city slicker, you did a good job today. I didn't think you'd last past the first stall…only heard you gag once."

Embarrassed, Deanna rolled her eyes toward the ceiling. "It's just…I mean, not just defecating in their water bowl, but in their beds and lying in it?" She shuddered. "What, horses have no shame?"

"It's just the way horses are." He looked at Smoky. "Dogs don't exactly meet human standards in hygiene either. That's why they call them animals."

"Good point. I just wasn't prepared. I certainly never saw such things on Dad's Westerns, which is—was—the full extent of my horse education." She paused in thought, her fork in front of her mouth. "I figured you fed them with a bag on their nose, gave them water from a creek or your hat, slapped a saddle on them, mounted with a running leap, and hi ho Silver away. I guess that's what I was expecting—a TV ranch." She shrugged. "And who'd have thought a wheelbarrow was so hard to steer?"

Shep laughed. She'd put too much manure in the barrow and not only narrowly missed running Smoky down, but almost dumped it in the barn entrance.

"It's an art," he conceded.

"Yeah, well I'll get it." Deanna hated for something like that to get the best of her, especially when it looked so easy.

"It's not like you'll be using that skill when you leave here."

Shep's observation dropped like a wet towel over the barely reestablished camaraderie between them. So it was just as Deanna thought earlier. He wanted her out of his life. He was just too polite to let on, obliged as he felt to put her up.

"True," she admitted, "but maybe it will be like riding a bicycle. It will always be there, should I need the skill."

Shep finished his sandwich and the salad, the latter most likely out of politeness, and went out to work with the mare. Deanna watched him for a long while through the kitchen window as he talked to the animal, coaxing it with motions of his hands or feet. Whatever he was teaching, he did so with a gentle patience while Patch watched from the outer pasture like an old pro observing a rookie.

She recalled how the horse always ran up to greet Shep. *You'd almost think I was jealous,* Deanna thought with a pang, *jealous…of a horse!*

"That does it. I've *got* to do something to save my sanity."

Smoky turned from his watch by the front door as if she'd spoken to him. His tail twitched in answer.

"But what?" She walked over and gave her furry companion a friendly scratch.

Framed by the door, the picture of Hopewell's lone street lined with buildings of a bygone era lured her attention from the dog. A hint of a smile took over Deanna's lips, reflecting the idea the scene sparked in her mind.

The jury was still out on whether she'd come to the right place for refuge, but looking at the ghost town through the eyes of an entrepreneur, she suspected there were possibilities here that Shepard Jones never thought of. Regardless, a little exploring wouldn't hurt. And just in case— She began to scrounge through the paper and magazine rubble atop the radio desk. It wouldn't hurt to take a notepad along…and the *fearless* watchdog, now on his feet, watching her in anticipation.

Eighteen

Early that evening, after a quick shower and change, Deanna rode with Shep toward Taylorville. She and Smoky had checked out the main buildings along the street, but the Hotel Everett had captured Deanna's imagination with its rich Victorian trappings. There had to be a fortune's worth of antiques and building materials if Shep wanted to sell it piece-meal and demolish it. But restored, it could be worth that much and produce income to boot.

There were still gorgeous carved dressing screens and some original furniture in the rooms upstairs and the lobby. Its elegance and the dust—not to mention the fright the young geologist with the buff body gave Deanna and Smoky when he descended the grand staircase—took her breath away.

After admitting that her footsteps had given him pause for thought as well, the living, breathing *ghost* apologized for scaring her and renewed an apparent friendship with her watch mongrel. He left Deanna with visions of dollar signs dancing in her head. With the right backing, she'd wager the ghost town could make more money than all the horses Shep could train or breed in a life-time.

"Well, there it is," Shep announced as they approached a sign that read *Welcome to Taylorville*. "The *big* town."

Putting her idea aside, Deanna took in the city ahead. Taylorville was a big town by Buffalo Butte's one-stoplight stan-dard. There was actually a bypass around the business section of the city, but the Smart Mart store was at the intersection of the bypass and the old route on which the town had been built at the turn of the century. Its architecture was certainly larger and more modern than the Victorian quaintness of Buffalo Butte. Signs from some of the national fast-food chains dotted the highway, separated by businesses that had outgrown the city limits.

Shep pulled into one of the burger places next to a truck dealership for a quick supper before shopping at the Smart Mart. Although silent while she did the stable chores that morning, muscles Deanna didn't even know she had now shouted at her in protest of their abuse as she eased gingerly into one of the wooden booths across from her host. The adrenaline rush of her exploration and speculation must have masked her misery until now. While Shep filled their drink cups, she dug an aspirin from her purse and discreetly took it rather than admit her greenhorn misery.

"Do you know how much fat is in one of those?" she asked a few minutes later as the cowboy lifted a double slab of burger smothered with all colors of condiments to his mouth.

"No, and I don't care. I'll work it off."

His lean frame testified to that, she mused, taking a bite of her grilled chicken sandwich.

A gaggle of preschoolers passed by in a helter-skelter stampede toward a table across the room where birthday balloons had been set up. A harried mom and dad brought up the rear, arms loaded with presents.

Shep shook his head. "It'd be easier to herd cats," he remarked under his breath.

"You don't like kids?" It shocked Deanna. Somehow she thought that his patience with animals might make him a good dad.

"I love kids...in small numbers."

Why that tidbit of information made her feel better was beyond her. Their relationship didn't stand a chance of getting that far.

"How's your Chicken Lite meal?"

"Not bad." Conscience bade her add, "Not as good as yours looks—that is, if you scraped a half pound of ketchup off it."

"What about the fat in those fries?"

Deanna put a protective hand over the super size order of tasty fries. "French fries are sacred. Besides, everyone knows a body needs *some* fat intake."

Challenging the skeptical lift of Shep's brow, she shoved a few into her mouth as if to prove it.

"Sacred, huh?" That rakish grin of his was enough to curl her toes. It had to be fattening or something equally corrupting.

"Whenever I got sick, Pop always brought home the best French fries from the local grill—not that I ever met a fry I didn't like. Hot…cold…I could always be tempted with a French fry."

"I'll have to keep that in mind."

Deanna nearly choked on her half-swallowed potato. Was there some double meaning here, as if he might *want* to tempt her? She chased the fry down with a long sip of soda. Nah, he was just teasing her. A sudden pop of a balloon from the birthday table across the room startled her from her whimsy.

"Not nervous are you?"

Deanna shook her head. The slow ka-thumping renewal of her heartbeat reminded her of her earlier scare that day. "You know, that surveyor guy scared the bejittles out of me this afternoon. I was in the old hotel and Smoky broke out barking—"

Shep scowled. "Voorhees?"

"No, it was the quiet blond guy."

"He didn't bother you, did he?"

"No, we talked for only a minute. Seems I scared him as well," she said in an effort to defuse the tension drawing Shep's hands into a fist on the table. His playful teddy bear humor had turned to that of an irate grizzly. Maybe Shep didn't like the idea of the survey for some reason.

"What was *he* doing in there?"

"The same thing I was, I guess—exploring."

"Did he question you?"

Deanna began to feel like food wasn't the only thing being grilled. "No, it's not like I'd know anything about the place anyway."

Could it be that if the geologists found something worth mining, it was a problem?

"Well, if you see him snooping around the house, let me know."

"Why? Have you got a pot of gold hidden under it?" When Shep didn't share her jest, she became serious. "What would happen if they found gold or copper or whatever? Would they tear up the ranch?"

"The government owns the mineral rights. I'm not sure what a discovery like that would entail. I'd have to check the agreement Uncle Dan signed. I just don't like strangers snooping around my home without asking. *You* were invited."

Deanna wondered what Shep would say to the idea that had struck both her and the surveyor as they'd looked around at the vintage setting. "What would you say if I told you that you have a gold mine all right, but it doesn't have any gold? Just the potential for making money."

Shep gave her a quizzical look.

"If I were you, I'd restore Hopewell and open it as a frontier town where families could not only stay, but learn about the Old West. Kind of like Williamsburg, Western style."

"Right." He snorted. "And where is the gold going to come from to finance such a thing?"

"You'd have to put together a corporation with investors...a partner at least. I've seen it done a zillion times. One puts up the hard assets—in your case the town—and the others the liquid assets or the cash."

"It'd be like living in a circus."

"Do you want to live in that little house forever?"

"No, I've got a place picked out for a homestead someday," he answered slowly, "but—"

"One would pay for the other." Deanna leaned forward as the idea took hold. "You could start off by remodeling the hotel. There's not a hotel within forty miles of here. Miss Esther's isn't even open half the time. The men you take hunting could stay there at the first. Later, when there's more to do, they could bring their families. And the wife and kids would have plenty to do while they hunt. Just imagine, staying in a real ghost town. We could have a pool and make the saloon a restaurant and maybe even have shows."

"Whoa, slow down, pardner." Shep threw up his hands. "When you get on a horse, you ride it hard, don't you?"

"It's just something I think would fly. It would take some checking out, for sure, but I could do that for you…get statistics, find out the pros and cons—"

"Not if you're going back to New York."

The laconic reply pulled the rug out from under Deanna's excitement. She could do it from New York…if she wasn't rubbed out by thugs or put in jail by the authorities.

"Well, look who we have here," someone exclaimed, breaking the charged silence at the table.

Reverend Lawrence stood next to their booth holding his dinner tray. Next to him was a petite woman with a sweet, grand-motherly smile and gorgeous white hair.

"Ruth, this is Miss Manetti, the young lady who came up with the idea for the roof-raising contest. The word's out, and we've got more volunteers than we need," the reverend exclaimed in delight. "Miss Manetti, this is my better half, Ruth."

Deanna received a warm handshake. "Pleased to meet you, Mrs.—"

"Ruth, dear. Or if you must, Miss Ruth will do." The sprite-like twinkle in Ruth's eyes and the lotion softness of her hands reminded Deanna instantly of Gram.

"Miss Ruth, Reverend, sit down and join us," Shep offered after introductions were made.

"Thanks, but no thanks, son," the reverend said. "After forty-two years, I've learned that every once in a while it's good to take Ruth for a big night out, just the two of us." He gave his petite wife a squeeze with his arm. "And this is it, so you folks'll just have to make do on your own."

Deanna watched as the minister found a table and helped Ruth to her seat before taking his own. "They are precious," she marveled as the pair shared one extra large slush with two straws. "With that snow white hair and those twinkling blue eyes, they look like a matched set. Even her dress is the same shade of blue as his collared shirt. Guess they're among those lucky ones who met and married their match."

Would she ever sit across a restaurant booth some day with her match mate?

Deanna glanced back at Shep, surprised to see him contemplating her. Was there a kindred thought behind those gorgeous, incredibly intense eyes, or was it just a renegade French fry that caused the quickening in her gut?

"You got a little sun today."

It was a fry. At least the sun exposure would cover the heat that crept to her cheeks as she pretended to study her lightly pinkened arm.

"At least it doesn't clash with my outfit." She pointed to the gaudy pink-and-lime polka dot of her hand-me-down capris, a grin masking her melancholy. A body would have to be blind not to see how mismatched she and Shepard Jones were.

"Maybe we should pick up some suntan lotion while we're at it."

"What, you think I'll be around long enough to get a good tan?"

She was grasping at straws and for what? Her muscles ached. She thought the habits of horses were disgusting. She *was* a fish out of water.

Because in spite of all of the above, another argued, she was enjoying her venture into rustic living under Shep's watchful eye. Granted, it was usually a grumpy eye, but at least she had his attention. And he had apologized.

"Are you through?" He nodded at her half-eaten sandwich and the few remaining fries.

"I filled up on soda, I guess." The hot and cold ebb and flow of her emotions had dashed her appetite along with the fleeting sparks of hope. "Speaking of which, I'd better check out the little girls' room."

She started to gather up her trash, when Shep preempted her. "I'll get it. You go on. I thought we'd stop by the garage on the way home and see if Charlie's had any luck finding those parts for your car."

Why don't you just crank him up on your radio? Whenever she forgot there was no chance for a future at Hopewell, Shep was quick on the draw to remind her. Keeping the acrid thought to herself, Deanna retreated to the bathroom door, punching it open. One minute she thought he wanted her to stay, the next, he made it obvious he wanted her to leave. Plucking petals from a daisy was more reliable than the mixed signals she detected.

Shep stood talking to the Lawrences when she emerged. Refusing to become one of those women who cried their hearts out in the ladies' room, she'd fortified herself by a mental vent of her exasperation with the man. And he didn't even know he'd been told off.

She listened as they fixed the date of the roof raising to coordinate with the end of one of the area's big roundups. Ruth had a handle on the women's end of things—food, bake and craft tables, and entertainment and game booths for the children. Beneath that grandma exterior, Deanna sensed executive material.

"So what do you think of the West, dear?" the reverend's wife asked when all the bases for the fund-raiser had been covered.

"It's definitely not home, but it has its pluses."

Reverend Lawrence patted her on the arm. "Just remember, Miss Manetti, home is where the heart is."

"Or where you hang your hat." Shep tipped his to Mrs. Lawrence. "Folks, we'll see you tomorrow in church."

"I look forward to it," Reverend Lawrence called after them.

Shep opened the passenger door for Deanna and then walked around to the driver's side. Her legs weren't nearly as stiff getting into the Jeep as they'd been earlier getting out. Maybe the aspirin had helped. Unfortunately, the ache she suffered from now had no ready pill to relieve it.

Nineteen

Shep followed Deanna in silence at the Smart Mart. He couldn't put a finger on what had dampened her humor, but something had. The resilient spirit he admired in her, that grin-and-bear-it way she rose to any occasion had given way to a seemingly forlorn silence. She wasn't a coward by nature, but a can-do person. So why did she run, and from whom? Had her romantic interest in her boss been the final straw, adding betrayal of the heart to framing her for his crime? Something wasn't right about this, but what it was, he had no idea—and she wasn't talking.

At least he knew the source of the burr in his humor, he thought, waiting while Deanna read the label on yet another brand of yogurt. He'd been happy with Hopewell as it was, moving along as he could toward his dream, but obviously that wouldn't move him ahead fast enough for someone who was running with the big money dogs. Maybe he *was* chasing his tail rather than a dream.

One thing was for certain—he would have never thought of turning Hopewell into a Western vacation spot. Where he saw dilapidation, Deanna saw opportunity. Shep would enjoy sharing his passion for horses by teaching greenhorns to ride like he had at nearby stables back East when he was assigned to the D.C. office, but there was a big hole in her plan—his decided lack of liquid capital. Building the ranch his way, a little at a time as he could afford, was attainable. His was safer, both for his heart and his pocketbook—especially if she moved back East.

"Do you have to read the ingredients on every label of everything on the list?" he snapped, disappointment and discomfort contributing to his testy humor. He shifted his weight unobtrusively from his aching knee to his good one. "Beans are beans. At this rate, we'll close the store."

"But some have more fat content than others, and the pricing is misleading. It's a major marketing tool. You have to compare the price per lot to get the cheapest with the right content when you have more time than money."

Shep winced inwardly at Deanna's lash of reality. "Like me?"

His cryptic question seemed to puzzle her. "Like *both* of us."

Except he hadn't been driving around in a car that cost more than most people's homes. Her silk blouse and trousers probably cost more than one of the tailored suits left over from Shep's more lucrative days in the service. He hadn't traveled in circles like hers since he'd left D.C.—and Ellen.

"Well, let's save money *and* time," he said, glancing at his watch. "I want to stop by Charlie's and see how much longer I'll be buying bean sprouts and all-natural yogurt."

Deanna flinched as though he'd physically slapped her. The raw hurt on her face made Shep feel twice as condemned. Her eyes pooled with tears as though pumped there by her quivering chin. Remorse locked horns with the anger and frustration that had provoked Shep's barbed response in the first place. He was taking his own shortcomings out on her.

"Look, Deanna—"

She cut his apology short. "If I had somewhere else to go and the means to go there, I would, *Mr.* Jones."

Burying her attention in the grocery list as though she couldn't quite make out her own writing, she walked stiffly down the aisle.

"Deanna, wait—"

Shep's effort to apologize was pointless. Each time he caught up with her, she tossed something in the cart and flitted off again like a bird that'd allowed the cat too close. Grim-mouthed, Shep followed in her icy wake. Not until they reached the drapery department was she forced to stop.

"Which one do you like?" She pointed to the entire row filled on both sides with curtains of all shapes, sizes, and colors. Her upper lip wasn't exactly stiff, but the wounded jut of her chin had become so.

This was going nowhere but downhill…and fast. "You pick something out…*please.*"

"I need to read the labels for material content, so that washing doesn't ruin them," she mumbled self-consciously. "And to get the right sizes."

Shep leaned on the handle of the cart as if he had all day. "Take your time. I *mean* it," he said as obligingly as he could.

After a moment's pause, the wary brow she raised at him faded. Clearly humoring him, Deanna began to dig through the racks of curtains with the thoroughness of a crime scene investigator. Not a package escaped her critical examination. Sooner than speak to him, she chatted to herself. One style was perfect, but it didn't have the right size. The right-sized curtains didn't seem to match the decor in the room. The ones that matched were a material that required dry cleaning.

"You don't want dry clean only curtains in your kitchen," she pointed out, finally acknowledging he was there. "Especially with all the windows you have."

"Of course not," Shep agreed, distracted by the increasing irritation of his knee and the conflict between guilt and his impatience. Of all the times for him to have skipped his medicine.

Climbing in the high country didn't aggravate it half as much as walking on city concrete, but then, God created the former. The majesty alone was enough to distract him from his discomfort—something the big department store was sadly lacking.

"Okay, I've narrowed it down to two choices."

Shep sent a prayer dart heavenward. *Thank You, Lord.*

"Which do you like? The white with the checkered green trim isn't quite as kitcheny as the one with the fruit on the hem, though I think either one would brighten up the wood paneled walls." She held up the two packages so Shep could see the pictures on them.

"Either one is fine and dandy with me." He glanced at his watch. They'd been in the store over an hour. If he took the spare pill he kept in the Jeep as soon as they got out, it might be too early to take another one at bedtime.

"You didn't even look. It's *your* house." Her terse disapproval was eighty-grit sandpaper to his diminishing patience.

"Then get the white ones." It never occurred to him that letting her make the decision was a wrong approach. From the angry sparks flecking her eyes, he was going to wind up wearing them.

"*Which* white ones?"

"The fruit. I like fruit."

"Fruit it is."

Shep let out his breath in relief as Deanna put the other package back.

"Although the check would lend itself more to the family room part of the kitchen," she countered thoughtfully. "I mean, how will all those animals look surrounded by dancing apples and pears? Checks are more masculine, like a master-of-the-hunt motif."

As if he walked on eggs, Shep ventured guardedly. "I totally agree. I hadn't thought about the compatibility of the trophies and the curtains. The checks are far more appropriate for wildlife than the fruit."

"Now you're patronizing me." Deanna snatched up six packages and slammed them into the cart. The force jammed the knee Shep had favored.

His agony was not lessened by the fact that she had no idea what she'd done, but somehow he reined the explosion of pain just short of it reaching his tongue. It occurred to him to run the cart over his good foot as distraction, but instead, he threw up his hands in surrender, trying hard to react in the opposite direction of his primary urge to shake her till her eyeballs rolled.

"No, I'm not." His controlled calm could have aced an Oscar. "I think the check is so right that we should get these pillows for the sofa to replace those ratty old brown ones that put a crick in my neck." He reached down, despite his discomfort, and added two checked pillows displayed beneath the curtains. "And what about a rug? One for the door and one in front of the sink? They'll cover those worn spots in the linoleum." If the woman wanted to shop, then by golly, he'd shop. He scanned the display a moment and found a set of dish towels and a dishcloth to match. "And what about these?"

Deanna shrugged. "It's your money. But while you're at it, there are some potholders that match, too." She pointed to the set with a grating sniff.

Shep pulled the set off the hanging bar and tossed them into the cart. "There! I think we have every blessed checked thing in the store. No, wait." He took off with exaggerated glee toward placemats on display farther down the aisle, ignoring the aggravation to his aching knee. Picking up two, he added them to the checkered heap in the cart. "What do you think?"

"They're easier to maintain than a tablecloth."

"My thoughts exactly." Good thing they'd chosen checks over fruit. The latter would have withered from the chill in her response. With a pained smile, Shep pushed the cart to the checkout. Deanna followed him.

"I'll be outside," she said, breaking her cross-armed silence as he started to put the goods on the black conveyor belt.

Trapped between guilt and grudge, Shep waited as the register blipped its way toward an escalating total. Good job, Jones. Now they were *both* miserable. Avoiding the curious glances of the clerk, who had to have been deaf and blind not to notice the thick tension between him and Deanna, Shep looked at the magazine rack behind him.

10 Tips for Men: How to Make Her Want You. The article title leapt off the display at him. Once certain no one was paying any attention to him, he picked it up and flipped through the pages in a nonchalant manner until he reached the cover feature.

"Hey, do you want that woman's magazine or what?"

"Nah, just looking." He put the magazine back as if the same wildfire spreading up his neck and face had set it ablaze, too. As he turned toward the register, he caught sight of fresh-cut flowers displayed on a metal stand next to the candy display. Above them was a sign reading *Romantic Bouquets.*

"That'll be one hundred twenty-two dollars and thirty-seven cents," the young clerk said, her speech slightly distorted by the braces brightening her smile. "Do you have any coupons?"

"No." Shep couldn't recall the last time he'd spent that much in one place since leaving Washington, but a few more bucks wasn't going to break him now. "But I'll take a bunch of these flowers, too."

He handed them to the clerk and fished out his wallet as she rang up the final tally. Shep had always wondered who bought fresh flowers in a food-and-everything-else market. Now he had a pretty good idea.

What a fool she'd been, Deanna thought, staring straight ahead as Shep turned onto the dirt road leading to Hopewell's main street. They had stopped at Charlie Long's garage, but the older man wasn't home. Limping noticeably, Shep got a drink from the vending machine in front of the garage and took a pill he'd found in the Jeep console. If he'd only said something, she'd have insisted on coming back another time.

As it was, the groceries rattling in the back of the Jeep made more noise than the two of them together. Shep concentrated on the road ahead. Deanna leaned into the wind rushing through the open passenger window like a dog, hair flying away from her face. Unlike a blissfully content pooch, she hoped the wind would dry her tears and cool her scalded cheeks or at least disguise her misery.

All those silly notions that Shepard Jones might somehow be interested in her were nothing more than wishful thinking. He didn't want her around one second more than she had to be. And after she'd tried so hard to prove her worth.

Deanna let out a shaky breath and dug with her finger for a runaway tear that had whipped from the corner of her eye into her ear. Great. Now she lived an old country song she used to mimic by holding her nose and wailing something about tears in her ears from lying on her back while crying over a long gone love. Her relationship with C. R. had been a sham. Now even the hope of finding someone to share her life with seemed dashed.

God, I need You now. C. R. made me feel stupid. Shep makes me feel worthless.

These things were foreign to her, a successful businesswoman and…and what? What else was she good for? What had she ever done to help anyone other than herself since Girl Scouts? The money Deanna made went toward making her life easier so that she could work harder. She had no family, no friends to speak of, at least beyond her work associates. With most of them, there was no time to share her heart's desire.

Deanna held on to her seat belt as though it might keep her from sinking deeper into the whirling mire of despair. Her mind wandered back to a childhood Sunday school lesson on the apostle Peter. He'd successfully walked on water and then nearly drowned when he was distracted from his focus on Christ by the storm. She'd colored the picture of him thrashing in the furious sea, reaching for Christ's hand.

Jesus, I can't see Your hand, and the waves are breaking over my head.

They passed the surveyor's trailer, squat and dimly lit, parked next to Ticker's dark one to share the water supply and septic.

When Shep stopped his truck in front of the porch, Deanna got out and made a dash for the house as if those stormy waves clawed at her heels with frothy fingers. As usual, the door was unlocked—something this three-deadbolt New Yorker had yet to get over—so she let herself in. Shep could get the bags. Right now, she didn't want to face him. She just wanted to be alone.

But what about his knee? He *had* to be in pain to lose his easy-going nature. Deanna looked longingly at the bed she wanted to throw herself upon in a fit of dramatic misery. Heaving a sigh of surrender, she turned to go back outside. She might not be able to see God's hand, but an angel surely whispered in her ear like a cartoon cherub, halo a bit crooked, robe wrinkled, but deter-mined to keep her in line.

"Where were you when I met C. R.?"

"Say what?" Shep placed an armload of bags on the table as she reentered the kitchen.

It felt as if a swarm of fire ants climbed to her cheeks. "Nothing. Just mumbling to myself. I'll get the rest of the bags. You sit down and prop your foot up."

That he didn't argue made Deanna feel much worse. By the time she brought in the bags with the curtains, Shep reclined on a stack of pillows with an ice bag on his knee.

"I'm much obliged, Deanna."

The contrition on his face bled some of the coolness from her polite, "You're welcome."

Shep made no effort to hide his watchfulness as she put away the groceries and unpacked the checkered kitchen accessories that had *checkered* what had begun as a lovely end to a hard but enjoyable day.

"If you don't mind, I'd like to wait until tomorrow or Monday to put these curtains up," she said, taking them into the hall wash area. "I read in one of those women's mags in the dentist's office once that you can get wrinkles out of fabrics or clothes by fluffing them with a wet towel in the dryer."

"No problem, it can wait. Do you mind letting Smoky in? He's scratching at the door."

"Sure." Deanna went to the door and opened it. "And just where were you when we drove up?"

Once inside, Smoky responded to her playful tone by shaking all over, depositing grass and sticks that had clung to his thick coat onto the floor.

"Ah, I see. Been collecting weeds, have we?" She poured some dog food into a dish and gave him water in another.

"You're going to spoil him," Shep warned, a lazy smile tilting his lips. "When Tick gets back, the dog won't know where home is."

What a refreshing change it was from the tight-mouthed, clenched-jaw profile he'd maintained during the hour's ride home. A schoolgirl awkwardness suddenly assailed her. "I haven't had a pet since I was a—" she bumped the rounded corner of the red Formica table—"kid."

Boy, once the romantic in her was awakened, the clumsy idiot just wouldn't learn. It just kept springing back up with that stupid grin, waiting for another blow like one of those punching bag clowns.

"Would you mind pulling my boots off?" At her wary hesitation, Shep pointed sheepishly to his knee.

"I guess I owe you at least that much after dragging you all over the department store with your sore knee." She grabbed one of his boots and worked it off. "You wouldn't have had to shop for curtains anyway if I hadn't ruined them." Taking extra care with the inflamed knee, she wriggled the other off. "And your knee wouldn't be in such bad shape if I'd stayed out of the way. I don't know what possessed me to run out like I could help." She carried the boots over to the stone hearth. "No wonder you want to get rid of me. I've been a royal pain, huh?"

A shifting on the sofa and the crinkling rustle of cellophane turned Deanna from straightening a landslide of horse and hunting magazines into a neat pile. Shep sat up, his bum leg propped on the coffee table. In his hand was a bouquet of fresh flowers.

Deanna blinked, but he was still there, drop-dead gorgeous and carrying flowers no less. *Shepard Jones and flowers.* Her heart did loop-to-loop at such a dizzying speed that she didn't know if she was going to faint or take off after it.

"What's this?" Sheesh, that big-nosed moose over the mantle could have done that good and it was dead. "I mean, I can see they're flowers," she admitted in an attempt to shake the dipsy-doodle from her brain. "But what for?"

Twenty

he sign said *Romantic Bouquets,* but I'd call them Penance Posies." Shep crooked his finger, beckoning her over. When she simply stared at it in distrust, he pleaded, "Just humor a man in pain…*please,* ma'am "

A crooked finger wasn't exactly an extended hand, nor did it belong to Jesus, but it did belong to a Shepard. Or was she a drowning soul grasping at straws? Deanna took a step. Besides, it wasn't fair, packaging that "please, ma'am" with that sexy drawl of his. Once within Shep's reach, she hesitated again. Her heart couldn't survive another nosedive tonight.

Taking her hand, Shep coaxed her down to the cushion next to him. "I thought they'd say 'I'm sorry' better than I could, my not being so flowery with words." He lifted two flowers with broken necks, shoving them between their unscathed counterparts. "Although it looks like they aren't going to do much better after being hidden under my pillow."

Uncertain which was going to leak first, her eyes or her nose, Deanna lifted the colorful assortment and pretended to smell them with a loud sniff. Shep handed her a tissue from the end table. As she wiped her eyes and blew her nose as daintily as her emotion would allow, she realized she was going to sneeze.

"Is something wrong?"

Deanna drowned Shep out with an "Aah-choo!" so loud, it startled the dog lying nearby.

"Allergies." She sniffed as Shep handed her a fistful of Kleenex.

The hay she'd spread in the stable that morning hadn't seemed to affect her, but something about fresh flowers always made her eyes and nose water. "I can't go to a wedding or funeral without taking an antihistamine."

"Hah, that figures. So much for making you feel better."

"But they do. I just can't put my face in them." She put them on the coffee table, the corners of her mouth twitching. "What a pair of clowns we are. Our motto should be: 'The harder they try, the harder they fall'."

"We hit the ground pretty hard this morning."

At the mention of that fiasco, Deanna turned in sudden earnest. "But I have been trying to pull my weight, honest. I really want to fit in."

Humor vanished from Shep's expression. Putting his arm on the sofa back behind her, he leaned closer. "Why, Deanna?"

Be still my heart. As if her heart ever listened! With Shep within kissing distance, it was beating itself into a puddle of mush. "Because…"

"Because what?" Shep brushed her lips with his as though to tempt the answer from them. Circling her waist with his arm, he blocked her escape.

As if she wanted to.

"Because for some reason, I really like this place…not to mention you." The meltdown had already started, her brain going first.

His gaze held Deanna's in a sweet, searching captivity. "Even when I'm a jerk, like tonight?"

Not wanting to break the fairytale-like spell by saying something stupid, she nodded. Something wet tickled her cheek. A tear?

Shep caught it with his lips.

She watched, mesmerized as he removed the salty essence of her pain and fear. But he didn't take them away, he pressed his lips to hers, sharing. Such a simple gesture to offer such untold comfort, assuring her that she was no longer alone, that he was there for her. His embrace, his gaze—both pleaded in a voice that spoke louder than words. Even above the sweet rush of blood to her ears, she could hear it. *Trust me.*

God knew Deanna wanted to. She needed to trust as a desperate soul in trouble, as much as the woman he awakened in her longed to yield to his touch. Or was it her touch as she explored the capable ridges of his back? He eased her back onto the sofa, but Deanna was swept there by the realization that a man like Shep could take her to places that made her heart and body sing, and her soul as well.

Pillows cushioned the warm, dizzying free fall of awareness—pillows and the ice she'd discarded. Bolting upright with a shocked gasp from the cold invasion of her senses, Deanna banged Shep's mouth with her head and shoved him away.

"What the—" Caught off guard, he rolled to the floor between the couch and the coffee table, landing with a startled grunt.

With an involuntary shudder, Deanna produced the ice bag from behind her, holding it up for him to see.

Without the benefit of the chill factor, it took Shep a moment to register what had happened. When it did, he let out a wry laugh and pulled himself up. "It figures."

Deanna scrambled to help him avoid any strain on his knee. "You're bleeding." She reached for the box of tissues they'd flattened in their sweet fervor. She hadn't even noticed them. What in the world had come over her...over *them?*

Shep touched the back of his hand to his lip, coming away with fresh blood. "Someone must be trying to tell us to go to bed."

Deanna looked up from dabbing his lip with a startled "What?" Surely he hadn't said what she *thought* she heard.

"Not the same one," he clarified. "Me here and you in there."

Frustrated, he raked one hand through the tousle of his hair and pointed to the bedroom door with the other in speechless effort to climb out of the hole he'd inadvertently dug for himself.

Impossible as it seemed, Deanna was warmed more by his clumsiness to set things right than his very persuasive seduction. Her by-the-Good-Book Shepard had more depth, not to mention moral fortitude, than all the men she'd ever dated put together.

"You're off the hook," she said when she could no longer keep a straight face.

Relief lightened the crimson flush of his face. "I just wanted to convince you how sorry I was, and—" he heaved a hapless sigh—"I guess I got carried away."

That grin…that toe-curling, belly-quickening grin—who could resist it? "Yeah, well that makes two of us. I was just trying to say you're forgiven and *BOOM!* Go figure."

Whatever had possessed the two of them wasn't through with her yet. Deanna couldn't bring herself to break away from Shep's contemplative look. Like him, she grinned in clownlike silence until Cupid, or whatever it was that came over them showed mercy.

"So," she said, making the first move away from temptation. She handed him the ice bag. "Put this on that knee. I'm turning in. Tomorrow's gonna come early, ready or not."

Walking on air, she entered the bedroom and closed the door. A stupid grin still fixed on her face, she looked at the bed in an entirely different light than earlier. The lonely, desolate place in which she'd expected to spend the night now looked like cloud nine, where dreams of Shepard Jones would keep her company.

Sunday morning was filled with the giddiness of a honeymoon— or what Deanna imagined one to be. Shep was cooking breakfast when her alarm roused her from the comfort of her bed. After putting on a dress that looked like it belonged to one of the sitcom moms on the oldies television channel, Deanna entered the kitchen to find the table set and the cook serving a steaming breakfast—a Western omelet, grilled toast, and French-fried potatoes.

"Wow. You've been busy." She sat in the chair he held for her. "And my favorite food no less. Is this still penance?"

"No."

His mischievous look was enough to make her forget the food. In a crisp white oxford, tie, and pleated dress trousers, this guy could grace the cover of *GQ* any day. If he were wearing the smart tailored jacket that was hanging on the back of his chair, he'd be James-Bond-goes-West devastating.

"Ah, I see." Deanna shook off the image before she tripped over her tongue. She narrowed her eyes in feigned suspicion. "You're trying to tempt me, aren't you?" Playfully, Deanna looked behind her and under the table. "There's an ice bag around here somewhere, isn't there?"

Shep didn't answer, but the curve of his mouth and the devilment in his eyes spoke volumes.

And she thought it was hard to eat with Old Bull watching her. The patty of butter she cut from the block fell off her knife before she could get it to her toast.

"Butter fingers," Shep teased, as Deanna's knife clattered on the floor in her effort to catch the patty before it landed in her lap. "You really aren't at home in the kitchen are you?"

"That's butter *thumbs,* wise guy. You try buttering your toast with a bug-eyed bull moose staring down his nostrils at you…not to mention his beady-eyed buddies."

Shep laughed. "Trust me, the moose and his buddies are beyond wanting your breakfast."

"Then why do you sit with your back to them?"

"Because I can see down Main Street from this chair."

Deanna pulled a dubious face. "I hear ya. Next you'll be telling me that you don't sit with your back to the door so you won't wind up like Wild Bill Hickok."

"What do you know about old Wild Bill?"

"Hey, Pop and I read and watched every Western there ever was at least once." A nostalgic smile lighted on Deanna's lips. "We were cowboys at heart, even if Pop rode a taxi instead of a horse and I took the subway for my stagecoach. I went through a tomboy phase that drove Mama nuts—no dresses, just jeans and those Western shirts with piped trim on the pockets. I could slap leather with the best of them, even Tommy Triglia, who grew up to be the hood next door."

"I can't picture you as a tomboy. You're so…"

"Svelte and charming?" Deanna took up a forkful of omelet, part of which promptly fell in her lap on its way to her mouth.

"Exactly." Shep watched her mouth as she chewed, as though charmed, making it nearly impossible for her to swallow.

"Finishing school—" A renegade crumb constricted Deanna's voice and made her cough.

"That explains that charming cross between uptown girl and girl next door."

Shep handed her a glass of water, but his study of her made her first swallow defy the law of gravity when Deanna took a drink. Only by sheer willpower did she override the anomaly.

And she thought the moose staring at her was bad.

Later, as she watched Shep walk around the Jeep after closing her door for her, Deanna noticed his limp had improved considerably. The night off his feet and on ice must have eased the inflammation. Recalling his glib response to her question as to what had happened to his knee, she wondered what kind of war wound he'd suffered. Most likely a horse rolled over on him.

He glanced at her once they were on the road. "You ever think of learning to ride?"

Deanna wrinkled her nose. "Maybe." If she was around long enough and had lost every brain cell she had. Where she'd gotten her citified idea that real horses were just moving versions of their arcade counterparts—clean, saddled, and ready to go—was beyond her. And never had she seen a television horse with a dirty coat and tangled mane. "If you can find one that won't soil its water—or worse, its bed, and then roll in it."

"You're something else, Slick."

His chuckle smacked of wonder more than derision, spawning a warm fuzzy feeling in her tummy. High on Shep's company, Deanna relaxed against the headrest until they passed the *Welcome to Buffalo Butte* sign. As if waiting in ambush behind it, anxiety swept down, blasting away at her giddy contentment with second thought.

Watching the families filter into the white, steepled building from the parking lot, Deanna struggled between longing and panic. She wanted to go to church. As a child, she'd always felt a little closer to God in His house. Maybe there, He'd make His intentions clearer. Was He answering her prayers or punishing her by showing her what she'd forfeited for her neglect of a spiritual life?

While she was still a little pink from her exposure to the sun the day before, Deanna was certain there wasn't a drop of blood beneath the color as she fell in with the friendly stream of parishioners. Her heart was pulling it from all quarters, just to keep beating. Shep had no idea that the shepherding hand he put at her back was all that kept her from bolting like the red stallion. Then it was too late.

Inside, it seemed as though the entire congregation swarmed around to welcome her. Yes, she had been stranded at Hopewell when a horse ran her off the road. Yes, Buffalo Butte was a far cry from her native New York. Her accent? Brooklyn with Irish-Italian influence. Her profession? Marketing consultant. No, she and Shep had no plans to make it a permanent arrangement. Why? Job opportunities weren't exactly brimming in these parts. Besides—

"Well, if I were you, honey, I'd think hard about pursuing my career over a good man. Our Shepard is quite a catch," Juanita Everett whispered, her volume rising with that of the organ, which signaled the start of the service.

A short scramble later, Deanna sat between Shep and Maisy

O'Donnall, dazed by the barrage of questions and warmed by the friendly reception. Up front, the mayor's wife sidled past three of her sisters to take her place in the choral ranks behind the podium. Deanna would have had to be blind not to recognize the woman who'd donated so many of the clothes the church provided—the loud ones, at least. Juanita's floral red-orange suit from her winter vacation in Hawaii screamed *Aloha* from the front row of the choir.

"It's a cryin' shame the choir doesn't wear their robes after Easter," Maisy whispered to Deanna after the candles had been lit. "If she don't blind us, we'll sure as shootin' have to see them dimpled knees of hers winkin' at us through the whole service."

When the special music selection was over, the minister stepped up to the pulpit. Maisy elbowed Deanna, snickering as Juanita shifted from one hip to the other, fiercely tugging on her straight skirt until it could at least be seen below the flowing drape of her shawl-collared jacket. Although she smiled in response, Deanna was too nervous for any humor to be genuine.

After the invocation and responsive reading, the congregation sang an upbeat traditional hymn. Since there was a shortage of books, Deanna shared Shep's. Their joined voices stood out from the rest in her ear as they sang—his masculine one, her feminine one—blending as God designed. The words declared that their hope was built on nothing less than Jesus. And He was *her* last hope. All other ground was sinking sand. Only God and the Shepard next to her kept her from being consumed by the quicksand she'd gotten herself into.

She considered Shep as he sang the chorus without looking at the words—clean cut, fresh shaven, and dressed to the nines, or rather from boots to bolero. She thought him handsome from the first time she'd seen him cleaned up, but something was different. It wasn't the suit, or even the discovery that he had a decent voice. It was something else…a sense of confidence maybe, or was it joy? From out of the past, a song Deanna used to sing in the children's choir came to mind—"This Little Light of Mine."

The answer smacked her in the face. She should have known from the Bible he kept by the recliner or the devotionals she found in the bedroom and bathroom. Or the way he took a total stranger into his home without some ulterior motive. It was his faith. Unlike C. R., Shepard Jones's beauty was more than skin deep. Beyond the physical, it came from his soul.

Indulging a flight of whimsy, she imagined the two of them as a couple, worshiping at the family church, surrounded by friends and neighbors. It was just like that morning, when they'd cleared the breakfast table and done the dishes together. The last time Deanna had felt this sense of right, she'd been a child, surrounded by loving family.

God, I don't want it to end.

But it had to. It was inevitable that either the law or C. R.'s shady associates would find her. If she prayed, she should at least pray for something possible.

"All things are possible through Jesus Christ." Reverend Lawrence's words from the pulpit reinforced the voice that had been echoing them in Deanna's mind. Dare she hope it was God and not Memorex?

On either side of Deanna, Maisy and Shep joined the congregation in an "Amen."

"With that truth in mind, let us present our burdens and concerns for others," the minister proceeded. "Are there any additional requests for others besides those on the prayer list printed on the back of your programs?"

Shep flipped it over scanning the names, but Deanna could no longer read it. *All things are possible through Jesus Christ.* The last three of the minister's words kept bouncing around in her brain. Her eyes stung, while an invisible vice closed in on her chest, making it hard to breathe. *All things are possible through Jesus Christ.*

Through Jesus. Was that the missing ingredient?

A hand covered her shaking one, squeezing it. It was her Shepard, her kind, gallant knight, for the moment *not* in denim. "Are you all right?" he said under his breath, head bowed in reverence to the minister's prayer.

Deanna nodded. She dug in vain through her purse for tissues, realizing that she must have used the last ones at the wedding reception. Just a little more than a week ago, it felt like a year ravaged with fear and despair.

Shep handed her his handkerchief. "Go on; it's clean," he teased. Around them, the congregation echoed the reverend's "Amen."

Maybe she'd made a mistake coming to church. With her guilt for staying away and all that happened of late, her emotions were too volatile. Desperate, Deanna practiced a technique of breathing she'd learned in a yoga class to regain her composure. She couldn't allow herself to become a blubbering basket case and humiliate, not just herself, but Shep as well.

"Paul prayed that the Ephesians might grasp how deep the love of Christ is," Reverend Lawrence said, commencing the sermon after reading a verse from the large Bible on the podium.

Amplified by the wooden acoustics, his voice filled the room with a holy authority. His words were not just heard. Deanna could *feel* them. They brushed her bare arms light as angel wings, lifting the downy hairs on her skin.

"The apostle wanted them to know this love that surpassed their knowledge and understanding, that they might be filled as only God could fill them." Reverend Lawrence gave a little laugh. "Sounds good, doesn't it?"

It did, especially to a beleaguered soul drained of all spirit. Deanna let out a shaky breath.

"But I'll bet that Seth and Becky Farley didn't feel that kind of love when Becky was diagnosed with breast cancer." The young man who'd helped Shep carry some feedbags out to the loading dock at the Farm and Ranch General and the pretty woman next to him nodded, smiling. "And what about you, Mayor, when your grandson nearly died from a tractor accident. It sure didn't feel like God's love when the doctors told you he might not make it, did it?"

"No, sir, it did not," a heavyset man with jowled cheeks said.

"When bad things happen to good, innocent people, when we are pushed to the very limit of our endurance, I don't care how strong your faith is, doubt can shake it, and you will become involved in a spiritual battle between good and evil that will take no prisoners. One or the other will win." The minister leaned forward on the podium, looking around the room. "My question to you is: Which one will triumph over you?"

Twenty-one

"Which one will triumph over you?"

The question riveted Deanna to the back of the bench. Which was stronger, her doubt or her faith? Her feelings or her knowledge? *Lord, I don't know. I know I want my faith to be stronger.*

In the midst of her confusion, a strange warmth penetrated her awareness, as though a comforting arm braced her back instead of the old wood, curved and worn smooth by saints long since gone. Its reassuring welcome seemed to say, *Hey, you came here, didn't you? That took faith.*

Or was it desperation? Doubt countered, reluctant to surrender its grip upon her conscience.

A voice slipped through her awareness—a testimony of faith strong enough to hold a family together. "When our youngest son was imprisoned for drug trafficking in California, even Ruth and I, with all our knowledge and faith in His Word, felt like God had ignored our prayers for him. We'd done all we could as parents and left the rest to a God…who must have taken a vacation that week."

The minister skimmed the sea of faces in the congregation with a twinkle in his eye that belayed his previous statement. Behind him, Juanita Everett still struggled with her skirt. A baby cried out suddenly on the other side of the room, resulting in a flurry of activity to assuage it.

"Plugged that one pretty quick," someone from the other side of the room snorted, evoking a ripple of amusement among his peers.

Deanna could picture a pacifier bobbing up and down as the child suckled it, but her focus was on Reverend Lawrence. His thick, white hair gleamed in the sun cast through a palladium panel over the stained glass windows behind the choir and sanctuary. Although he wore a pale blue suit with a clerical collar, in lieu of a formal white robe, the light made him look like a divine messenger, waiting patiently until the congregation was as quiet as the baby.

"I imagine more than just a few of you have felt the same way…as if your prayers weren't reaching God's ear…as if surrounded by a dark and stormy sea while He slept."

Deanna's heart squeezed out a resounding yes above the clamor of confusion in her brain. That was exactly how she felt. Reverend Lawrence might be looking the other way, but he was speaking to her heart—no, to her weary, flagging spirit, battered by the doubt the reverend mentioned and compounded by her own self-reproach. She'd made some bad choices, like not pursuing her spiritual needs.

"No matter how old we are, we often tend to be like the little boy who sat at his mother's knee, watching with fascination the passes of her needle and thread as she embroidered.

"After studying the twisted tangle of the many-colored threads the mother had taken such great care to stitch, he became puzzled. Why, the child asked, was she working so hard on a helter-skelter work of knots and loose ends that resembled nothing at all?

"I'd say that's a pretty good description of how our lives appear at times, wouldn't you?"

Deanna nodded emphatically at the rhetorical question. Oh yes, she could see it now.

The minister continued after a reflective pause. "Laughing, the mother drew her son up on her lap and showed him the work from the topside—a beautiful piece of art coming together one thread at a time."

Deanna's chin sagged as the point of the story registered. *The tangled strings of life below are threads being masterfully woven according to the plan of the Great Weaver. Great. Just when she sees a glimmer of hope, the minister tells her she has to go to heaven before she can look down and understand. But then, the loose ends of her life would probably expedite her journey by hanging her.*

God, this isn't exactly the encouragement I was hoping for.

"After His fervent prayer in the garden of Gethsemane, Jesus Himself hung on the cross, His human pain blurring His spiritually perfect vision. For that moment, all He could see was the bottom of the Father's embroidery as He cried, 'My God, my God, why hast thou forsaken me?'"

Deanna looked past the minister at the stained-glass depiction of the Savior on the cross, nails driven through His hands, a crown of thorns forced upon His brow. Why should she, with all her admitted flaws, deserve more consideration than He, who was without sin?

"God did not forsake His Son," Reverend Lawrence averred without doubt. "Although, at that moment…driven to a point beyond human endurance, Jesus *felt*—" he made air quotes with his fingers—"abandoned by the Father. The key word here is *felt.* Feelings and faith are sometimes at odds in our lives, dear ones. Jesus *felt* abandoned, but He *knew* He was not," he explained. "Jesus *felt* doubt, but even while blinded by His suffering, He reached for the thread of His faith buried in the middle of the tangled knots and loose ends of His Father's embroidery. See the difference?"

But Deanna thought doubt was the sign of a poor believer. And she'd been filled with it.

"How do I know this?" The minister smiled. "Because next in the seven sayings of Jesus from the cross is 'I thirst,' which I take to mean He longed to feel God's reassuring hand, God's water for His spirit. And even though He was given vinegar and brine instead, He still reached for that hidden thread of faith, trusting that it was there. He surrendered Himself to God's will. 'Into thy hands I commend my spirit.'"

Surfacing amid the words came a message that felt like precious water to Deanna's dry spirit. *It's okay to doubt. It's only human. Just don't give up.*

"'The Lord, He is the One who goes before you. He will be with you. He will not leave you nor forsake you,'" Reverend Lawrence declared loudly. "You can bet your bottom dollar that Jesus knew that quote from Deuteronomy and believed it with all His heart and soul. It was His earthly senses, trapped in a human body, that cried out, "'My God, my God, why have you forsaken me?' Not…" He struck the podium with his fist. "His…" He struck it again. "Spirit." He waited for the words to sink in. "That was pain speaking, *not… His. faith.*"

One could almost hear a pin drop. It seemed to Deanna that even the normal shuffle of people in their seats was stilled by the impact of Reverend Lawrence's words. He broke the somber spell with a grin.

"Now I know that no one in this church ever said things that he or she didn't really believe or mean when he slammed his finger in a car door or struck his thumb with a hammer."

Beside her Shep laughed outright with the rest of the congregation at the minister's tongue-in-cheek observation. "Or when his knee felt like a nail had been driven through it by a grocery cart," he said in an aside to Deanna.

"The more spiritually mature of us have conditioned ourselves to respond appropriately with an excited gee willikers or something as harmless. Any hands?" he asked facetiously.

A few ventured up tentatively. Deanna's was not among them.

"Others call out for God in a prayer that only the Holy Spirit can translate," he added, rolling his eyes toward the ceiling. "And others curse God, as if it were His fault you weren't paying attention. In other words…" Reverend Lawrence resumed when the varied reactions of the listeners stilled. "You say things you don't really mean or believe in because the pain blinds us to God's presence…and you can be sure that God has not abandoned you like it feels. He's hearing *every word you say*."

A few Amens mingled with humor rose from the congregation.

Reverend Lawrence silenced them by raising his hands and his voice. "And Glory be to God for showing us that, even though Jesus is the Son of God, He was also human." He turned his notes over as if he were through with them. "Why," he asked pointedly, "is this so important to you and me? Because Jesus knew that we, too, would feel abandoned, even though we believed in God's Word, and He wanted to assure us that *it's only human*. He didn't want a wedge of guilt to separate us from His unconditional love and understanding. He wanted us to know that He had been there, without the benefit of His godly powers…just like you. He wanted us to know that He understood."

Like her, Deanna thought, her mind racing with the current of her emotions rather than against it. Like her, Jesus had been pursued by the righteous and the not so righteous. Like her, He'd prayed to be spared, but God hadn't answered His prayer the way He preferred but according to God's plan.

But, God, I don't know if I can accept Your will like Jesus. I'm not that strong. I'm not worth the dirt under His toenails.

"Each and every one of you is precious enough to Jesus that He died for You. You don't have to be worthy for His Grace. And that's a mighty good deal, since none of us are."

Gooseflesh rose on Deanna's arms. This was too weird, even for her. It felt as if the minister was reading her mind without even looking at her. But she knew better. The irony was not lost on Deanna.

What she felt and what she knew were at odds…just like her feelings of abandonment were at odds with the Word she pro fessed to believe in. God hadn't abandoned her. He'd been with her all the time, waiting for her to reach up in faith for the hand she could not see. He'd sent her a shepherd.

"Remember, God doesn't expect us to be perfect. He knows from experience how hard that is within the limitations of the human form, even for the Son of God. All He expects is for us to reach up for Him in trust, admit our shortcomings, ask forgiveness for them, and try our best."

A sob caught in her throat. Deanna blew her nose in a lame attempt to cover it. At Shep's inquisitive look—how could he miss the fact that she was in tears?—she quipped, "If I'd known how good church was for my sinuses, I'd have attended every week and skipped my allergy shots."

The minister glanced over at a board on the wall where the music selections were listed and announced the page number of the last one. The organ began to play softly above the shuffle of pages and feet as the congregation rose.

"As we sing, I want to invite you to lay your burdens down at the altar of God. There may be someone heavy on your heart. Bring them here. You may be overwhelmed by concerns of your own. Nothing is too big or too small for our God. Or maybe you've felt like Jesus, overcome by pain and persecution…"

In her mind's eye, Deanna saw the interrogation where the police had hammered the nail of accusation with merciless questions through her fear-stricken heart.

"By rejection and humiliation…"

They'd made her feel like trash…C. R.'s throwaway, a criminal…

"Abandoned by God."

There'd been no one to turn to, and God hadn't answered her pleas—at least she couldn't see that He had.

"Then come here and claim God's promise. He's reaching down for you right now, waiting for you to take His hand."

"Are you sick, honey?" Maisy, her heavy makeup accentuating the concern on her face, put a comforting hand on Deanna's arm.

She couldn't answer. A blade of emotion was slitting her throat from the inside out. And Reverend Lawrence—no, God—was offering a balm.

"He's saying, My child, I've been there. I know what You are feeling. I understand."

The reverend extended his hands to the congregation. "Come, beloved. There is always room at the cross for you."

With the crescendo of the organ, the people began to sing the hymn. Each word strengthened Deanna's conviction that it was no coincidence that she wound up in Buffalo Butte, with this man, in this church. For the first time since its onset, the storm had cleared. And through it, Deanna saw a nail-scarred hand reaching out to her. All she had to do was take it—trust in it.

Shep wasn't sure what came over Deanna back at the church—contrition, the Holy Spirit, or maybe a little of both. She not only sniffled through the sermon, but when Reverend Lawrence gave the altar call, she went forward, so visibly shaken that Shep had gone with her. When Maisy and Esther flocked to either side of her like mother hens, he stepped aside in relief. Maybe it was a woman thing.

"I'm so sorry," Deanna said for the umpteenth time as he pulled up to the ranch house. "I felt like an idiot, crying like a baby in front of the whole church. It would have taken a plug big as a wagon wheel to shut me up."

Shep couldn't help but smile. She may have lost her composure, but not her Brooklyn accent and wisecracking wit. "People cry at the altar all the time."

"The way I was carrying on though, I scared the others away…like it was catching." She blew her nose on the ball of tissues Shep grabbed as they left the church. His handkerchief had reached its limit, too. "Miss Maisy and Miss Esther must think I'm some kind of lunatic."

"Maisy and Esther know all about your trouble. That's why they ran to your side."

Deanna's tear-reddened eyes sharpened. "What do mean *my trouble?*"

Shep recovered quickly from his slip. "You know, your new job not quite what you expected and then getting stranded out here. What else?"

"Isn't that enough?" She opened the passenger door to get out. "I was so sure that my life would work out here. I rented out my New York apartment, went in debt to buy a car that's way out of my league, even at a bargain, and left a job I'd worked *eight years* to get. I have nothing to go back to."

"Then stay here." Shep's mind went blank with shock. Was that *him* speaking? No, it was God. If he'd had any doubts about helping Deanna, the Sunday message erased them. Yes, he was weak. He'd just put his own life back together again. But Shep wouldn't save Deanna. God would—possibly through him. It didn't hinge on Shep's ability, just his trust in God's Word.

The Jeep door frozen in her hand, Deanna looked as if she were still caught in his initial shock.

"You kind of have a way of growing on a person," he added, stumbling over the feelings that accounted for his offer as well. If he was going to trust God, he might as well trust Him with his heart, too.

Deanna's chin started to quiver again, her eyes filled once more. Then, with a wounded cry, she slammed the door and ran into the house.

Shep looked after her, speechless. Had he said something wrong? He replayed his offer in his mind, searching for the reason behind her strange reaction. Telling a gal she had grown on him might not be the smoothest compliment in the world, but it was still flattering…wasn't it?

Bewildered, he climbed out of the vehicle to follow her inside when Jay Voorhees hailed him. Frustration hissing through his teeth, Shep leaned against the open door, forcing the man to come to him. After all, he wouldn't have a bad knee if it weren't for Voorhees.

"Having a lovers' quarrel?"

"What do you want, Voorhees?"

"Come on." The DEA agent's smug derision was enough to make Shep wish the Bible said *punch* the other cheek. "*Penance Posies?*"

Shep felt the blood leave his face. How in the devil—

"She must be one hard-hearted Hannah to still be mad after that line."

The answer to Shep's unspoken question slammed home. His pulse rebounded in an angry rush, scorching everything in its path from neck to scalp.Voorhees planted listening devices, violating their agreement not to use them, violating Shep's closely guarded privacy. Every word said in the house last night—or for who knew how long—had been listened to and recorded. It took all of his religion and self-control not to throttle the government agent then and there.

"You have until three to tell me what you want; otherwise, get out of my way, you double-crossing, eavesdropping—"

"How was I to know she didn't have you wrapped around her finger by now?" Voorhees cut him off. "You know we couldn't take your word on it. You know policy. You're out of the loop now."

His past service counted for nothing? Even as Shep rebelled, he had to admit to the validity of the man's statement. Still—

"I was hoping she might have said something helpful while you were away," the agent went on. "The money laundering connection of the embezzlement story hit the news this morning, but we withheld your girlfriend's name. All the public knows is that a junior marketing executive and the CEO of Amtron Enterprises have been charged with embezzlement of company funds and laundering drug money. No mention was made of Majors' surviving his fatal accident or the Canadian syndicate connection. So as far as the bad guys know, no one's caught their scent."

Shep processed the new development, buying time to cool off. "We haven't had the TV on, but then, you already know that."

Voorhees was unruffled by the sarcasm. "The lab verified that Majors' prints were on the car and the tracking device, so we're stalled until he comes out of the woodwork."

"Or the syndicate cleans up his mess." Shep nodded toward the travel trailer. "Those guys would be better off as lookouts than eavesdroppers."

"They're doing both, pal. No need to worry. When Majors shows up, we'll be all over him."

"A two-bit white collar perp is the least of my worries. It's his friends that bother me." Shep couldn't figure out how the mob would know, but experience told him that they had ears and eyes in more places than the authorities could even guess.

Voorhees leaned against the doorjamb of the vehicle with one hand, taking a look inside. "I tell you, we are on top of it. All you need to do, you lucky dog, is stay on top of Miss Manetti."

Names unfit for any ear came to Shep's mind; names he'd stored while recovering from the surgery and rehabilitation, when it was anyone's guess if he'd ever walk without a cane or walker. They surfaced so fast and furious that they piled up, tying up his tongue.

Shep clenched the open Jeep door, blindsided by an urge to defend Deanna's honor and the anger he'd struggled to put behind him in the months after the accident. He thought he'd come to terms with the past, that he'd forgiven the man. Voorhees didn't know what he did then any more than he knew what he was talking about now.

But reason wasn't cutting it this time. "I know my responsibility," Shep said with a deceptive calm. "Just make certain you know yours."

He gave the door a sling and pivoted before he saw Voorhees jump clear to keep from having his hand caught in it. Shep couldn't help the satisfaction twitching on his lips at Voorhees's startled oath. Like with most ill-gotten things, the pleasure was short lived.

Once inside the house, self-recrimination set in. Evidently, his spiritual growth was valid only when it wasn't seriously tested. His isolation on the ranch, among friends and neighbors, had given him a false sense of accomplishment.

I'm sorry I let You down, Lord. I need Your help to deal with the likes of Jay Voorhees. How I feel like treating him and how I know I should treat him just don't agree. But I will try to do as the Good Book says.

The knotty pine planks of paneling Uncle Dan put up when Shep was six took on a satiny glow in the light of the noonday shining through the sparkling clean glass. The warmth and light offered a reassurance Shep didn't feel he deserved.

"What was that all about?" Deanna emerged from the bedroom. She'd changed from her dress into casual slacks and a flowery shirt.

Despite her ill-fitting clothes, Deanna had a natural beauty most women had surgery to acquire. High cheekbones, tall and not too thin like the women on the covers of the magazines at the grocery store, Deanna was round in all the right places. And those baby blues could make a man wrestle a grizzly bare-handed—or punch out a certain government agent.

"He's just being a pain. They want to poke around a bit longer than they'd told me."

"They've stayed pretty much out of the way, haven't they?"

"Skunks stay pretty much out of the way, too, but I don't want 'em around."

Deanna laughed. "I guess the city would drive you crazy."

"If you have the right people around you, I guess it doesn't matter where you live."

The moment the words were out, Shep cringed inwardly. Now they were also on tape.

"Home is where the heart is."

Shep wanted to kiss the whimsical curl of Deanna's lips. He wanted to hold her and comfort her, to take away the pain that had wrenched sobs from her...to protect her. If only she'd tell him what really happened so he could help prove her innocence.

"I have an idea." He stepped up to her and slipped an arm about her waist. "You've done nothing but work since you've been here. Instead of cooking supper, why don't we make some sandwiches and have a picnic? I'll take you up to the spot I've picked to build on one of these days."

The way her face brightened, he wished he'd thought of it before now.

"What a lovely idea. I'd love to, but..." Her face fell. "I was just going to lie down for a while." She put her hand to her temples, shaking her head in confusion. "I just...I don't know. All that boo-hooing must have knocked the cheese from my ravioli, I guess. Do you mind too terribly?"

"Of course not." How could anyone mind that little-girl-lost look? Shep wished he could hold her while she slept. He wished he could take away all the worries that exacted their toll on her face. *God, help me help her. Show me how.*

He took Deanna by the shoulders and turned her. "You march off to bed. I'll take care of supper."

"No, all I need is—"

"In these parts, ma'am, when the weather clears, the men take over Sunday supper. It's an unwritten law." He guided her through the bedroom door. "Just a man, food, and fire—like in the Flintstones."

"There's romaine, cucumber, radishes, and scallions in the fridge. I can make a salad when I get up to go with the meat."

"That's not people food," he grumbled good-naturedly. "That's what the meat eats."

"You are hopeless," she declared, standing back as Shep turned down the bed.

The flip of the sheet sent up a whiff of the scented lotion they'd purchased at the Smart Mart. His bed had never smelled so good nor looked more inviting than when Deanna sat on its edge. She stared up at him, back stiff, uncertainty in her eyes.

Amid the trust and confusion awash there, Shep sensed a kindred longing that could easily have been tapped if he were the man he'd been before his accident. What felt right often trumped what he knew to be right when it came to women. In the end, he lost the girl and the game.

Shep nixed the kiss he'd intended to plant on her nose, instead managing a husky, "Sleep tight, Slick."

"Thanks, Shep." The contented purr of her voice and the soft rustle of the bed beneath her weight licked his retreating heels like a fire to dry brush. Like a spooked calf trying to outrun it, his mind darted in one direction and then the other.

Supper. He needed to get out the chicken and marinate it. Jerking open the refrigerator door, Shep basked in the cool blast of air, looking inside without really seeing the groceries Deanna had organized as she unpacked them the evening before.

He needed a clear head to help her, to coax the little Irish-Italian charmer into telling him her side of the story so that he could help her, not seduce her so that she'd resent him later.

This game was for keeps. While Shep hated games, especially where the heart was involved, circumstance and conscience forced him to play. What if God had turned him away when he sought the sanctuary and healing of Montana's hills? He had to ignore the panic of getting burned again by going back into service and the risk of falling for someone so different that a future together was as likely as pigs flying.

This was no longer a matter of the heart and soul—it was one of life or death. This leap of faith was going to require him to put all on the line.

Twenty-two

A loud clanging brought Deanna up with a start from a dreamless sleep. For a split second she wasn't certain where she was or if a train was about to run her over. Then the present came flooding back to her—the interrogation, running off the road, the cowboy carrying her off to a ghost town, her emotional display at church, Shep tucking her in. The tall, lean cowboy was in every flashback with a lazy grin, a devilish smile, a passionate kiss…

Choosing to dwell upon the latter, Deanna pulled the spare pillow to her chest with a sigh just as the clanging sounded again. Whatever kind of bell it was, it was loud enough to wake up the ghosts all over Hopewell.

"Dinner's ready, come and get it!"

And the man cooked as well. Shep was too good to be true. *Lord, I know in my heart that You've brought us together for a reason. I just have to be patient for the answer to my prayer for love like Mama and Pop had. But I'm hoping it will be with Shepard Jones.*

"Food's getting cold. Move it, sleepyhead." Shep stood in the open doorway, apron splashed with barbecue sauce.

"What time is it?" Deanna mumbled through a yawn.

"Four o'clock and ticking like the devil for five."

"Give me five minutes," she said, tossing back the covers.

After washing her face, straightening her sleep-rumpled clothes, and brushing her hair, Deanna made her way to the kitchen. The first thing that struck her was that the windows were no longer barren. The off-white curtains with their gingham check trim were perfect...almost. The ties had been wrapped tight as a rodeo calf's feet around the tiers, so that light came in on both sides of each panel. Over the sink window, one tier hung halfway down from the valance rod, leaving the rest of the window bare.

"I ran them through the dryer with a wet towel, just like you said," her host beamed proudly.

Maybe she'd forgotten to pick up a valance. "They certainly brighten the room, don't you think?"

"If I'd known what to do, I'd have replaced them a long time ago," Shep observed. "But if you take a notion to fiddle with them some—Aunt Sue was always pulling up those ruffles on the top—it won't hurt my feelings. I wasn't sure what to do with the belts."

Deanna wanted to run to the grinning galoot and give him the hug of his life, but she didn't want to scare him off or do anything that might spoil the moment. "I'll be glad to fiddle with the belts," she assured him as he pulled out her chair for her with a flourish.

"Now you just sit right here, ma'am, and I'll get the food from the grill."

She just loved the way he said *ma'am.* "Wow, talk about above and beyond! You're going to spoil—" she broke off abruptly, suspended halfway to her chair seat. Eyes wide in disbelief at the sight of the bull moose over the mantel with a gingham check blindfold, or rather, valance, she collapsed the rest of the way down in laughter. "You're..." She searched for the right word. Crazy? Wonderful? Surprising? *"Unbelievable."*

"I didn't want old Bull to ruin your meal." Pure mischief danced in his lingering look as he backed out the back door.

Deanna took the time alone to inspect the room. He had certainly been a busy bee while she napped. The curtains up, the scrumptious looking spread on the table, the delicious smelling chicken on the grill—she glanced up—and the ridiculous looking moose. She giggled. Nothing could ruin this, even if old Bull ran through the kitchen right now, valance flying in the wind from his giant antlers.

"How about a walk?" Shep suggested later after helping with the dishes. He'd insisted, despite Deanna's objection that the cook shouldn't have to clean up.

"As much as I ate, that's a great idea," she replied. "Although I'll probably waddle more than I'll walk."

Whether a tribute to the chef or to the fact that she'd skipped lunch, she'd had seconds of everything—not counting the chicken wing she scarfed up while clearing the table. She never ate *three* pieces of chicken, no matter how small they were.

"Teasing aside, I like a woman with a healthy appetite...especially when it all goes to the right places." Gallantry personified, Shep opened the door and with a sweeping gesture of his arm, prompted her to go first. It was just as well her back was to him. Hot as her face grew, she was blushing like an addlepated schoolgirl.

Smoky met them on the porch and happily preceded them to the barn. Patch whinnied expectantly from the corral.

"Aw, look," Deanna said with satisfaction. "She sees the carrots I grabbed on the way out."

"She might smell them," Shep corrected, "but my bet is, every time I walk toward the barn, she's hoping it's mealtime."

"I'll bet she smells them." Deanna shook the carrots in front of her just to make certain.

Whether Patch really did smell them or not, the mare obliged her with another nicker of anticipation.

"See," she declared in triumph.

"You're slick, Slick." Shep's wry grin belied his suggestion that she might be right.

Still, combined with the electricity of his gaze, it caused her to tingle all the way down to her toes with something more than satisfaction. At the steady of Shep's hand, the awareness intensified. The horse eagerly grabbed the vegetable stick with teeth that looked like a row of yellowed piano keys. Shep or no Shep, she pulled her hand away. Patch bit through the carrot, losing half, so Deanna picked it up and tried again.

"Come on," Shep cajoled in a voice that made wild horses his pawns. "I won't let you get hurt."

Like a warm, breathing shadow fitted to her back, Shep placed one arm about her waist, the other bolstering hers. At that moment, Patch's piano teeth could have taken off her arm at the elbow and Deanna wouldn't have noticed.

"That's another thing about horses. They're a jealous lot." Shep nodded to where Molly edged up for her share.

Deanna fed the last carrot to the mule and even mustered the courage to scratch the dry bristle of its forehead. One wary as the other, the mule and Deanna pulled away from each other at the same time.

"Don't move," Shep counseled her, his breath upon the back of her ear. "Just hold your hand up and wait."

Sure enough, the mule swung its head back so that Deanna could scratch it again. When she rubbed Molly around her ears and beneath her halter, the animal heaved a wet sigh of bliss.

"You've cowboyed up right fast, Slick."

Deanna looked at him askew. "I'll take that as a compliment."

"It means you're getting the hang of ranch life pretty quick. When you aren't running from them, you have a way with animals. Smoky trails you like a shadow."

"Well, I've always loved pets," she admitted, "but I think the way to their hearts is food. When I was little, I wanted a career at the Bronx zoo, so I could feed all the animals. That was before size became so intimidating."

"I'd say it's a sign of your generous and trusting nature. Animals can sense it."

It could also be a handicap. So should she throw the proverbial baby out with the bath water and never trust again, or had Shep saved the trait before it was too late?

"So what kind of pets did you have?"

"A cat, which had to be kept outside, a guinea pig, a turtle, goldfish, and—" she belted out in frivolous song— *"a parakeet in a pear tree."*

"Did you have to get rid of any pets before you came west?"

Deanna picked up a stick and toyed with it. "I haven't been home long enough to have a pet since high school, although I condo-sat with a few for traveling friends."

"Anyone special…aside from the jerk you're running from?"

C. R. was a black cloud that refused to go away, even during sunny moments like this. She shook her head. "Not really. I didn't have time…building a career, you know?" Deanna snapped the stick in two and tossed the pieces over the fence, the way she'd tossed away all her effort and sacrifice. "And when I do take the time, I wind up with nothing…except God," she hastened to add.

"God is enough."

Shep's conviction stopped Deanna in her tracks. She waited expectantly for him to elaborate. Instead, he kept on walking, forcing her to keep up with him. What was it the minister said about knowing and feeling? She knew God *was* enough. She *felt* like she needed more.

"I found that out after I busted my knee," Shep finally volunteered, adding dourly, "which resulted in my relationship with someone—who I thought had hung the moon—going sour."

"What, was she nuts or something?" Deanna bit her lip, but it was too late. She'd already incriminated herself.

"No." Shep let her ready quip slide like a gentleman. "Ellen was a diehard city girl who didn't know the meaning of the word *compromise,* especially if it meant leaving the glitter and bright lights. All elegance, no substance."

The bitter edge of Shep's voice struck a kindred chord in Deanna, even though his ex wasn't a crook. C. R.'s betrayal had hurt as much as it frightened her. It was the hurt that made her empathize.

"I imagine you know exactly how she felt."

Nailed by Shep's direct gaze, Deanna hesitated. Was it accusation or curiosity behind its frosty wall? "I know how *you* felt," she declared. "I left the city behind, remember? And I'd hardly call this outfit *elegant.*"

Instead of sharing her wry humor, Shep drew further into a contemplative shell. Leaning on the fence rail, he lost himself in the flamingo pink of the western horizon. There was little else to do but join him—and savor the moment.

This was the kind of Montana she'd sought, taking in the panoramic postcard beauty before her. White-tipped mountains above the dark green tree line drew the lazy, sun-soaked clouds about them like a cloak. The evergreen skirts were studded with blue-gray rock and garlanded by strips cleared for roads here and there.

Spilling near the foot of the hills was a glistening ribbon of water Deanna hadn't noticed before. It lazily wound through the large pasture, where wildflowers presented their colors in homage to the majesty of the sun.

"You'll never see a skyline like that in the city."

Shep spoke to no one in particular, but Deanna answered anyway.

"It *is* beautiful." She rested, chin propped on folded arms on the rail next to Shep.

Some kind of birds sang for all they were worth from the cluster of shade trees along the bank. Hidden by shiny leaves, they made the gray-barked grove their stage for Mother Nature's enjoyment. Annoyed by Patch's close proximity, Molly kicked up her heels and bolted across the waving meadow grass, ears laid back. Her dark brown coat glistening and black tail swishing, she was sort of pretty, for a mule.

Molly lacked the grace of the horse that started after her...and the speed. As if in a race, Patch swept past the mule, splashing through the shallow stream first. Then, as though having second thoughts, the spotted cow pony pivoted abruptly and walked back to have a drink.

"So what caused your relationship with the man of your dreams to go sour?" Shep asked after a long spell of silence. "Did you see it coming or were you blindsided like me?"

"Blindsided, definitely." Like now by that question. Why wouldn't he leave her past alone and enjoy the moment?

"So it's definitely over then."

"Over, finished, *dead.*" Deanna cringed inside at the mental image of C. R.'s charred car. "Look, I'd just as soon not talk about him, okay?"

"No problem. I understand."

She doubted that but appreciated Shep's consideration anyway.

"Just one more question."

Deanna stiffened, waiting.

"You said you left the city behind. What are the chances of your giving the West another chance?"

If she hadn't been leaning on the rail of the fence, Deanna would have collapsed in shock. Was Shepard Jones saying what she *thought* he was saying? Her mind did a two-step—two cheers forward, one doubt back.

"I..." What if she were reading more into his words than was really there? "I guess it depends on my motivation to stay. I have to work—"

"What if you had a job here?"

Was the man joking? She couldn't read his face, turned toward the sunset as he was. All she saw was his profile—the weathered ridge of his cheek, the pronounced square of his jaw, clenched in...what? Apprehension?

"What, you want to hire me as your maid? After ruining the curtains and burning your meals?" she exclaimed with exaggerated incredulity. "Bill Gates wouldn't take a risk like that."

He finally laughed. Some women might have been insulted,

but she was realistic when it came to homemaking. It wasn't her thing. She admitted—

"I want more than a maid, Deanna." Shep stopped her thoughts dead in their tracks. He turned, taking in her blank expression. "I've been thinking about your idea of turning Hopewell into a resort of sorts."

So he wanted a marketing consultant. Deanna checked her disappointment. Guys like Shepard Jones didn't propose to people who'd lied to and used them.

"And I think it's a good one—if I had the right partner." Shep placed his hands on her shoulders, searching her gaze with an intensity that reached for her soul. "I need someone I can trust with my dream, not someone who'll run off and leave me holding the empty bag."

Like C. R. had done her. Strange, but the cut to her pride was no longer as deep and raw as it had been. Shep could make her forget C. R. ever existed. The thought of walks like this—of watching the sun slip behind the mountains each evening, pulling the blanket of night over it—was like a balm to her wounds. *God, is this it? We're to be partners?*

"And who knows where we can go from there."

She tilted her head back as Shep stepped closer.

"Great things can be built with trust, Deanna, *if* we lay it on a foundation of faith." His hands were warm where they touched her back. "I would ask you only to be honest with me, nothing more, nothing less. No more blindsides."

What was he getting at? A change of mind like his ex, or did he suspect Deanna of being dishonest?

"If you don't think you could stand life around here, tell me now. Our Montana winters are long, cold, and often lonely." Shep hesitated, almost swaying in his boots, as though he stood on a precipice trying to decide whether to leap or leave. Suddenly he leaned toward her, pressing his forehead to hers—eye-to-eye, nose-to-nose. "I'd do my utmost to keep you warm and happy…as…as your husband, of course."

Husband? Half her mind simply refused to accept the mind-boggling idea that he even wanted her out here, much less that he'd consider marriage.

Yes, he said husband, the other half confirmed. If Shep leapt, it would be by the book.

But it's impossible under the circumstances.

All things are possible through Jesus, if you believe…if you trust in God's promises. Remember?

Burying their differences, the two opposing voices finally merged. Shep did say husband. He wouldn't say it if he didn't mean it. And he wouldn't have her any other way. And neither would she.

The news traveled through her veins, spread by the jungle drum of her pulse, while Deanna's heart played leapfrog with her tongue. It was her turn to leap—no, to *trust.* If she was going to trust in God, she'd have to trust in His Shepard as well. Yet the words piled up in the back of her mouth, wedged by excitement. There was little choice but to answer with her lips.

Deanna slowly spelled out her answer to Shep with a kiss that left no room for interpretation. *Yes, yes, yes!* The fingers she ran through his thick hair added to the chorus, singing in a language all their own. He was exactly what she'd left the city for—a good, honest, hardworking cowboy. God had turned the cloud of C. R. into a silver lining—Shep. And here and now, in his arms, was a moment to die for…

Not lie for. Three short little words, yet their impact was that of a wrecking ball, taking down the hope she'd built upon the sand of deception. The roof of euphoria crashed to ground zero, leaving nothing but the dust of what might have been.

Or was this a chance to make a clean start? Would she build something so precious as this on sinking sands of deceit, or would she do what she knew was right? The choice was hers.

"What's wrong?" Shep's voice was husky with desire as he

nuzzled her ear. Deanna heard him inhale the scent of her shampoo and test the softness of her skin with his lips. The hot rush of his breath burned upon her neck.

God, what do I do? Tell him and trust that he'll stick with me?

Backing away, Shep caught her chin in the crook of his finger, raising her face until the waning sun glistened a blinding brightness in her eyes. "What is it, Deanna? Tell me."

She couldn't see the concern on his face, but she felt it. Like one of his horses, she found herself wanting to succumb to his will, to confess. But what if she lost him? What if he turned her in? After all, he still had the tags with the warning that it was unlawful to remove them on his pillows. He stopped completely at stop signs in the middle of nowhere, with no vehicle in sight for miles.

"It can't be all that bad, Slick."

When his effort to tease a smile back to her clenched lips failed, Shep drew her gently against him, sharing his strength and assurance. His shirt caught the tears that streaked down her face.

"God will never leave you nor forsake you, Deanna," he whispered against the top of her head. "Nor will I. Tell me what just threw up that wall. Maybe together, we can take it down."

But what could he do? Shep was too good and noble to be involved in this. He'd taken her in with complete trust. An invisible fist squeezed her chest as though to dislodge her confession.

God, I confessed to You. Isn't that enough?

"I can't help you if you won't tell me."

What? Do you want your life to become a rerun of the television fugitive story and risk throwing away your every chance at happiness?

It was the first time Deanna ever realized that God was speaking to her directly—and He had a Brooklyn accent. He was also right. She gave herself a mental smack. Of course He was right. He was God. Whether now or later, Shep was going to find out. It was better now, before she loved him even more.

Better confess now, because whether Shep kept his word or

not, God would keep His and stand by her. Deanna just had to step out onto the thrashing water of her emotions and ignore the storm. Battered by fear, weary of the guilt that pulled her under, she had to reach through clouds of doubt, to where she could not see—to climb upon the waiting Rock. All other ground was sinking sand.

Sinking sand or the Rock?

Twenty-three

Maybe we should go back to the house, because at least one of us is going to have to sit down."

From the little he knew of Deanna's trouble, Shep had to admire her resilient humor. It was her life ring when she was in over her head. But returning to the house with its electronic ears was out of the question. He wanted—no, needed—to hear what Deanna had to say without others listening in.

He pointed to the cottonwood grove in the middle of the sweeping pasture. "If you don't want to miss this sunset, there's a couple of rocks over there."

Deanna hesitated. "What about the horses? I mean, you think they'd try to run us off or something?"

"Not a chance." As if to prove there was nothing to fear, he climbed over the rails first and extended his hand. "Because they know who we are, they might mosey over to see what we're doing, but they won't bother us."

Was the panic lighting Deanna's face as he helped her over the fence due to horses or their subject? He promised he'd never leave nor forsake her, but what if she admitted she'd been Majors' partner as well as romantically involved with the man? What would he do then?

"Ohhh, here they come."

Taking the small hand reaching for his, Shep gave her a reassuring squeeze. Exactly as he expected, Molly and Patch came within fifty yards of the grove and watched curiously as he and

Deanna made a seat of a suitcase-sized rock overlooking the rushing stream.

"There are two kinds of creatures in this world—predators and prey. Like I told you before, horses fall into the latter category, which makes them cautious, not to mention skittish."

"But what preys on a horse?"

"Man, big cats, wolves—"

She held up her hand. "Okay, that's enough. All I need is something else to worry about."

"It doesn't even have to be a real threat. A horse will spook over anything it perceives as out of the ordinary. A thoroughbred threw me once because it spied a tractor sitting at the edge of a field. The thing wasn't even moving."

Deanna looked past Shep, downstream where Molly and Patch had meandered. Only Molly still acted interested in them. The mule stretched out her neck, nostrils flared and twitching.

"Is she mad or what?" Deanna asked warily.

"Horses smell trouble. They can't really see who we are, but they can certainly smell us. That's what Molly is doing, taking a second look...or sniff."

"I should be so lucky," she snorted daintily. "If I could have smelled trouble..." The despair filling her eyes twisted Shep's heart with unseen hands. Her shoulders sagged under its weight. "I don't know where to start."

"How about with the jerk who abused you?" Shep already knew about her New York job and that Majors had hired her away from it.

"C. R." Deanna kicked at a small stone, sending it splashing into the streambed. "He didn't physically abuse me, like I let you think. He emotionally betrayed me, letting me think he wanted me to be more than the new marketing manager. And...I don't know. I'll be thirty soon. Maybe my biological clock scrambled my brain, but I fell for his claims that Montana would not only provide job advancement, but that it was a great place to raise a family."

So she wasn't one of those professional women who had no time or room in her career for kids. At least that made Shep breathe a little easier.

"Well, I swallowed it all—hook, line, and sinker."

Her voice breaking at times and hard as cold steel at others, Deanna told her story.

"Two weeks, he sent flowers, took me to nice places. We had lunch together every day when he was in Great Falls. Afterward, I usually stopped by the bank for him to make a deposit, since he always had one o'clocks with the board three days a week and it was on my way back to the building."

Shep wanted to ask how far Majors went to convince Deanna of his affection but held his tongue. Never rush a confession that's moving along on its own. More often than not, a talkative perp would volunteer answers to questions that hadn't even been thought of. Someone who was inherently honest, as he believed Deanna to be, wouldn't know how to cover up a partially exposed truth. Nor would she think of trying.

"We even went to Toronto for a weekend—strictly business, mind you," she stipulated, a flash of color rising to her cheeks. "He wanted me to do a presentation for this major account he'd been trying to get. We spent the nights tweaking and working in the changes they asked for. I was so flattered by his compliments on a job well done that I didn't really wonder why he made no move toward romance beyond a good-night kiss."

Deanna glanced from the submerged stone to Shep. "After working till 4 A.M. and having to present the work at nine, a kiss was an accomplishment."

"What, was he nuts or somethin'?" Shep's imitation of Deanna made her grin.

Focused on the stone, she continued. "The week before I wound up here was crazy. C. R. was back and forth from Toronto, so that Friday was the only day we actually made a lunch date. Even then, it was rushed. So I made his deposit as usual and took the rest of the afternoon off to shop for a coworker's wedding gift. We'd taken up a collection.

"After the Saturday wedding, everyone danced till late at the reception. It was so much fun. I really liked the people I worked with. And C. R. even talked about how we'd do this or that differently...when we decided to take the plunge," she explained. "The other marketing personnel even saw something between us, the way they kept teasing us." Deanna swallowed hard, as if the emotion in her voice had thickened to the point where she couldn't speak. "I mean, I wasn't the only one fooled."

Shep put his arm around her shoulders with a squeeze. "Hearts can make a fool of anyone, Slick. I'd even put my money where my mouth was and bought the ring. When Ellen accepted it, I was certain it was a done deal."

Her brow shot up. "The ditz didn't keep it, did she?"

Ditz. Shep had never thought of Ellen like that. If one of them had been a ditz, it was him for thinking he could transplant his hybrid flower into the wilds with nothing more than love. "She gave it back and I returned it."

"You ever notice, of all the great poets and scholars, not one ever answered Shakespeare's question about whether it's better to have loved and lost than never to have loved at all? I mean, the last one can hurt, but the first one feels fatal."

"Yet, here we are."

Deanna searched his gaze, starved for a morsel of reassurance. "Yeah, well that's all well and good, but don't take off your running shoes. The story's not over yet.

"Early the next morning after the wedding, C. R. left for a Monday business meeting in Canada—or so I thought." Her face mirrored her reaction to what followed—astonishment when the police took her downtown and interrogated her about C. R.'s whereabouts and the contents of the bank deposit box, then horror compounded by hurt as it sunk in that, not only had she been betrayed, but she'd been framed as well.

Shep's spirit soared in triumph. He knew it. Deanna was the dupe, an innocent victim.

"C.R. embezzled more than 3 million dollars from the company, and he'd used me to make the deposits." She shrugged her shoulders. "I didn't even look in the bag. Yeah, it was big and heavy, but it was from our biggest account. Dumb as turkey, I just handed it to the clerk at the counter and carried the slips back to him."

Deanna ventured an uncertain look in Shep's direction, as if expecting him to react in some dreadful way. Features schooled to show attention without judgment, or the relief he felt at her professed innocence, Shep waited for her to proceed.

"The police had pictures from the bank camera of me making the deposits. The clerk identified me as Mrs. Majors. I didn't see any harm, so I didn't bother correcting her. I thought it was kind of nice. That's how stupid I was."

"Stupid and vulnerable are not the same thing," Shep offered in her defense.

Nonetheless, the more Deanna told him, the grimmer it looked for her. The pictures of her and C. R. implicated a relationship and partnership. C. R. had disappeared, leaving her holding an empty bag. Anger flushed through Shep's veins. Deanna was a savvy young woman, but the generosity and eagerness to please that Shep found so disarming had left her prey to a calculating coward.

"Then—" Holding Deanna in his arms now, Shep felt the sob that wrenched from her chest. "Then they showed me C. R.'s car, all burned up. And…and that mean detective says I double-crossed C. R. and t-took the money and….and k-killed him with a car bomb."

She pulled away and blew her nose on the second fresh handkerchief Shep had handed her that day. Told in spurts of emotion, her situation took a turn from bad to worse. She was not only accused of murder and embezzlement, but the police accused her of ransacking her own apartment to throw suspicion away from her.

"Sure as the Pope prays, I didn't embezzle any money or plant a car bomb. I never so much as lit a firecracker in my life. And I know butkus about who could have wrecked my apartment. All I know is that I was scared and nobody would believe me."

Her last words tipped her over her emotional edge, driving her back into Shep's waiting arms. No wonder she'd run. She thought C. R. Majors was dead and whoever killed him was after her as well, thinking she had the money. Shep held her tight, kissing the top of her head and whispering reassurances that, even as he made them, gave him pause for concern. He believed Deanna, but how could he prove her innocence?

"What am I going to do, S-Shep?" Deanna leaned against him as if her fight had drained along with her tears. "I…I turned it over to God this morning, but I'm still scared. I can't see a future for us past the end of my nose, much less what you said you wanted."

"You are not going to do anything…yet," Shep decided. "There's clearly more to this than what you know."

"No one believes me anyw-way."

"I do."

She lifted her tear-razed face from the cradle of his shoulder, looking as though she wanted to believe but was afraid.

"And I have some old friends—" How much should he tell her? She was already frightened out of her wits. "Friends from the service," he said carefully, "who can help get to the bottom of this. The Great Falls police sound like they are over their heads." And Jay Voorhees was too gung ho to worry with the little details that might prove Deanna innocent. Even Majors was small change for him. All Voorhees wanted was the big fish, the man behind Majors.

Professionally, Shep understood. But he also understood the danger to the parties being used as bait for the prize catch.

"Is that how you hurt your knee, in the service?"

Shep couldn't believe that in the midst of her own quandary, Deanna could even think about his knee. "Yes." It wasn't a lie. It simply wasn't the entire story. "And the guys I served with owe me. If anyone can help you, it's them."

Wonder surfaced on the troubled blue of her eyes. She took his face between her hands. Her lower lip trembled.

"I thank God for you, Shepard Jones. I know He sent me to you." The corners of her mouth quivered into a smile. "You are my earthly shepherd. I don't deserve you, but I am so thankful God doesn't give us what we deserve. Like, instead of a saint, I'd have that mean-spirited detective on my side."

Shep tightened the circle of his arms, drawing Deanna to her feet, so that he knew the feminine length of her, soft and inviting against him. "You give me too much credit," he said, his voice suddenly gruff with awareness. "Holding you like this, looking into your eyes, watching your little chin tremble…" He leaned down and brushed the tip of her nose with his lips. "Believe me, I'm feeling *anything* but saintly, Deanna."

The kiss he gave her proved it.

"We got a solid line on Majors." There was no hello or introduction in the voice coming over the cell phone.

Victor Dusault pressed it to his ear, no longer interested in what caused the traffic jam in which his limo was caught. His initial indifference upon answering the call vanished at the mention of the man who'd double-crossed him. "What do you have?"

"A Visa charge in the town down the highway from Buffalo Butte. Majors was sporting a baseball cap pulled down over his eyes, but he was so nervous while he waited at the ATM that he looked right up at the hidden camera."

Cornered, scared—exactly how Victor wanted his victims to feel in their last hours. And C. R. Majors was living his last hours, whether he knew it or not.

"…doubts about the woman," the caller said, drawing him back to the conversation.

"What kind of doubts?"

"If she'd agreed to meet him after this thing went down, why is Majors dragging his tail? Or why hasn't she made a break for it?"

"Because he thinks she's being watched. The man is an amateur, but he's not stupid." Dusault leaned against the seat as the limo pulled forward, the traffic finally clearing ahead of it. "It really doesn't matter whether she's innocent or not. She's obviously the key to getting our hands on that little double-crosser, not to mention my money. So what's the game plan with the Feds?"

"Same as you, sir. Waiting for Majors to make his move on the woman."

Victor reached into his jacket and took out a gold case and withdrew a custom-wrapped cigarette. Lighting it, he waited as the caller continued.

"We tail 'em everywhere they go, but it's been a no-go so far." There was a pause on the other end. "Could happen anytime now. With that bank thing, Majors must be getting desperate."

"Indeed." Victor blew a smoke ring and watched as it dissipated in the draft of the air-conditioning. "Then that's it, my friend. Look's like I'll be hearing from you again soon."

Flipping the cover of the cell phone shut before the caller could hang up, Victor picked up the remote for the television mounted in the console between him and the driver and turned it on, tuning to the twenty-four-hour weather channel.

He hadn't risen to where he was by leaving the smallest detail to chance. It was the kind of thing that separated the man from the beast. A man needed to be suitably dressed to kill—and the killing hour was approaching fast.

Twenty-four

Will Addison was one of those can-do people whose amiable personality and reputation as a straight shooter had won him the confidence of, not just the men in the D.C. branch of the U.S. Marshals, but key players in other government agencies as well. What Shep's former director didn't know at Shep's first call that morning, he could find out and quickly. By the time Shep finished putting up the signs for the weekend roof-raising challenge and barbecue—courtesy of J. B. McCain—Will called him back on the complimentary cell phone Shep stored under the seat of the Jeep.

"These guys are into a little bit of everything," Addison told Shep. "Drugs and guns are like love and marriage—they just seem to go together. The ring leader is a French Canadian named Victor Dusault."

Shep could picture his friend sitting in his Constitution Avenue office, folders piled like leaning Towers of Pisa around a desktop. One drawer would be pulled out to make room for an open box of fresh chocolate dipped donuts. By Friday, the stale remains would be softened by a dip in the office coffee, which could soften a stainless steel spoon equally well. Crumbs undoubtedly sprinkled his oxford shirt and tie, not worrying Will in the least.

"What doesn't fall off will make a good snack later," he'd say, an ever-present twinkle in his eye. His nature ranged from humor to deadly intent, depending on the circumstances.

"There's some kind of Internal Affairs investigation going on, so watch your back, Shep."

"Crooks *and* crooked agents?" Shep scowled at the road ahead.

That morning Agent Voorhees was beyond acknowledging the possibility that Deanna was the innocent victim Shep claimed she was. He was too furious with Shep for disabling the listening devices by playing his CD player. Shep was too close to the forest to see the trees, Voorhees claimed. She was playing Shep as the chump, using Hopewell and his hospitality as a safe house until she could rendezvous with Majors.

Voorhees had told him, there was nothing new. They just had to be patient until Majors surfaced. Lie number one.

No, the syndicate didn't know Majors was alive. That was either lie number two, covering the Internal Affairs investigation, or Voorhees was an idiot not to recognize the possibility.

Dusault's men were lying low because of the investigation to cover their laundering tracks. Shep would sooner believe they were subsidizing the Tooth Fairy. The syndicate was looking as hard for Majors and Deanna as they could, if they weren't already on their way, tipped off by the plant in the agency.

The bimbo was the key. Except Voorhees's word for Deanna hadn't been as tactful. Shep's knuckle had now scabbed over where it had grazed the agent's teeth. In spite of the extra pounds Voorhees had put on, he was still quick. Otherwise he'd have needed some dental work and Shep could have been arrested for assault. As it was, the other two men in the trailer were between them before a second punch could be thrown.

Lord, maybe I am too close to this for my good and for Deanna's. Reason flew right out the window with turn the other cheek. But how much am I supposed to forgive from this jerk?

Yet, even as he demanded his answer Shep knew it. *Seventy times seven.*

"As for the girl, there's not even a parking ticket on record for her," Addison said, piquing Shep's attention with new information on Deanna. "Grew up in a deteriorating working-class neighborhood, rose above it to a Manhattan high-rise and the upscale crowd. Ambitious, but not afraid to work for it."

Trying to remain objective, Shep ignored the leap of elation he felt. Every crook had a clean record at some point in life. "What about proof against her? She told me she made the deposits."

"She told the truth. They have her on camera. What they don't have yet is who withdrew the money," Addison said. "It's gone…cashed out."

"Majors?" Shep guessed.

"They're working on the film to identify the person who withdrew it, but it was a dark-haired woman with shades and a hat—not your young woman," Shep's friend pointed out. "She— if it was a she—knew enough to keep her back to the camera."

"If it was Majors," Shep speculated, "then he's long gone with the loot, and we're waiting for nothing. Voorhees is just spinning his wheels."

"Don't think so. The DEA has a record of a bankcard cash advance in Taylorville just this morning. Majors wouldn't risk using a corporate card if he had 3 million in cash. Sounds like he's grasping at straws now."

Voorhees hadn't bothered to tell Shep that—and he'd had time to update him before Shep lost his temper. What else was he *not* sharing?

Seventy times seven, Lord? Shep clenched his fist so tight around the wheel that his knuckle started to bleed again. The sight of the blood trickling down the back of his hand brought to mind the greatest example of forgiveness known to mankind, snuffing out Shep's anger like a smoky candle, so that the light of reason shone brighter and clearer.

"So Voorhees is running this investigation-turned-stakeout to apprehend Majors as a witness against bigger fish with a syndicate plant in the middle of his plan?" Talk about burning a candle at both ends. "He's crazy."

"Like a fox," Addison said. "He'll get the perp, the plant, and a witness against the syndicate. Voorhees will be running the St. Paul district before this is over."

"If he doesn't get knocked out in the crossfire." Like Shep had. Voorhees's ambition had ruined Shep's career. If everything didn't go exactly as planned, it could very well do the same to his. The man needed protection from himself.

Shep held the phone away from his ear at a sudden burst of static, courtesy of the power station he approached. "I'm losing you, Will, but I owe you big time."

Shep couldn't quite make out his friend's reply—something along the lines of anytime. "Call me if anything new crops up. I'll keep checking for messages."

"Got your…ber…here—" Pure static surged in Shep's ear, obliterating his connection.

Cutting off the cell phone, he shoved it back under his seat.

If Majors had been in Taylorville, he either knew where Deanna was or was on the verge of locating her vehicle at least. And thanks to his bank withdrawal, not only did the DEA know his whereabouts, but so did the syndicate he'd double-crossed— which made it twice as dangerous for Deanna, however she was involved. The question was: How stupid was C. R. to make such a blunder? And if he wasn't stupid, then what was he up to?

Should he tell Deanna? His heart wanted to, but his professional side reined it in. Including him, there were four men watching out for her. She was already scared witless, not knowing who was after her. Would she be better off knowing it was a crime syndicate? Shep didn't think so. As for C. R., Deanna truly believed he was dead. Should she be warned that he was not only alive, but looking for her?

Again, his training contradicted his heart. What was to keep her from bolting again, away from the one person who believed in her innocence? And if she was guilty…

Shep braked the Jeep, tires squealing as they dragged past the entrance to Hopewell. Great. In his emotional quagmire, he'd nearly forgotten where he lived. Frustration bubbling to an all-time high, Shep backed up and wheeled the vehicle sharply onto the long dirt road leading to the ranch. The fact was he trusted Deanna. He just didn't trust his ability to make a sound decision regarding her best interest. Never having been at odds with himself like this, he saw only one solution: Stick to the rules. They were black and white. His emotions were too gray to rely upon.

Deanna ran out on the porch as he pulled the Jeep in front of the house. Covered with dust, she looked as if she'd been rolling around with the horses in the corral. "Did you talk to your friend?"

"He's put someone on it. We just need to sit tight until he gets back to us." He wiped a smudge off the tip of her nose as relief flooded her face. "Besides, I gave him my word that I wouldn't let you get away from me."

"I think your word is safe, Shepard Jones. Wild horses couldn't drag me away when you look at me like that. I just wish I'd told you sooner...trusted you like you trusted me."

Now who was the deceiver? His conscience cringed. But this was the best way he knew to protect her...and she needed his protection.

"Don't tell me the house is *that* dirty, or have you gone into demolition?"

Her initial anxiety vanished, replaced by a saucy look that reminded him of a cat with a mouthful of canary. "No, but the old dressing screens I got out of the hotel were."

"Dressing screens?" Shep had no idea what she was talking about but figured he was about to find out soon enough.

Taking his hand, Deanna led him to the door. "You aren't the only one full of surprises. Now close your eyes." She waited for him to comply before leading him inside.

"You haven't done anything to Old Bull, have you?"

"Old Bull is his bug-eyed self again, and the valance is where it belongs, but that's not it."

By Shep's guess, they passed the kitchen table, sofa area, and were now in the central hall. He smelled the detergent. She had done some washing.

"Okay, now you can look."

"I'm afraid to," he protested. "Your track record hasn't exactly instilled confidence—"

"Ta-da!"

Shep opened his eyes to see Deanna pointing proudly into the bedroom where not one large bed but two smaller ones stood, snug against opposite walls. Dividing the room in half were two dressing screens placed end to end and supported by a dresser on one side and a chest of drawers on the other.

"Now you won't have to sleep folded over on that lumpy old sofa." Deanna fairly sparkled with pride beneath the smudges on her face. "And your aunt Sue and my Gram's spirits can rest that we're not doing anything indecent, immoral, or as Gram would say, *disgraceful.*"

The way Deanna wrinkled her nose thawed Shep's initial surprise so fast that he had to check his thoughts before they crossed the line Deanna had drawn with furniture and word. It had been hard enough to sleep on the sofa, especially after last night.

Out of sight was not out of mind. Knowing someone who'd willingly gone into his arms, melting soft against him and burning warm with his kisses, was sleeping in his bed, the womanly scent of her sweetening his sheets and pillows had played havoc with his imagination. Now it would waft across the room, making him as aware of her as the sound of her moving and breathing beneath the covers.

"Don't you like it?" Disappointment tugged down the upturned corners of her lips.

"It's fine. Just fine," Shep reiterated mechanically. "Looks like it did when Aunt Sue and Uncle Dan used the room." It wasn't enough. Shep could see it in her fallen face. He grasped for some words of assurance.

"I only did it because of your knee," she said in defense of her action. "I wasn't trying to be pushy or take over."

"Of course you weren't. Believe me, I appreciate it." He took her hands and drew her to him. "It's one of the most thoughtful things anyone has done for me, and I'm acting like an ingrate. It's a fault and I'm sorry."

A mix of wonder and adoration kindled in her expression. Gently, she framed his faced with her hands. "If that's your only fault, Shepard Jones, then I know God sent you to me, straight from heaven. My own guardian angel…I mean…*shepherd.*"

Shep prayed Deanna was right. But if she was… "I kind of like that role," he admitted with a nervous laugh, "but if I'm going to live up to it, then I'd best just thank you for being so thoughtful and stay on the couch. You see, Deanna…" He cupped her chin, his beating heart about to plunge recklessly into the uncharted waters of her confidence. "Neither of us needs more complications than we already have right now, and if we were that close, I might start feeling more like the wolf than the shepherd."

The week passed quickly for Deanna, even without her customary multiple telephone access, faxes, computers, and television to distract her. Until she found the latter hidden in a cabinet built into the stone fireplace wall. Alone in the house, Deanna tuned into a local station news program, fearful of what she might hear, yet having to know.

The announcer read the story about an ongoing investigation into the car bombing of an Amtron Enterprises executive suspected of embezzlement in Great Falls. Relief flooded through Deanna when the announcer's pause indicated the end of the story, but it was premature. He resumed with, "Further investigation regarding the connection of the company to a drug money laundering scheme is underway by federal authorities."

Drug money! Were drug lords the ones who'd ransacked her

apartment? The very idea seemed to draw the strength from her knees, forcing Deanna to the sofa before they gave way completely. She knew when her apartment had been trashed that things were bad, but this was worse than she'd thought. Far worse.

Deanna wiped at the tears forming in her eyes as if to make the situation go away. There was nothing she could do to undo what was already done. Tears wouldn't help, nor would panic. She had to think rationally.

Anthony Manetti hadn't raised his little girl to be a wimp. The veteran New York taxi driver prided himself over Deanna's spunk and aggressiveness, while he credited her endurance and tenacity to his wife, who started in the garment industry as a cutter and moved up to manager and stockholder in a male-dominated business world. Deanna was the "cream of both crops," as her dad would say.

Maybe curdled cream. She blew her nose on a tissue from a box on the end table. Thank God they weren't here to see her now. And thank God Shep didn't watch television and that her name wasn't mentioned.

But why? Deanna frowned, puzzling over the omission. If this was drug related, maybe the authorities wanted to find her first, like as a witness, except that she knew no more about who C. R. was involved with than she did before. Why turn herself in when the police wouldn't believe that she knew nothing about the embezzlement? They wouldn't believe that she didn't know about the drug ring either.

Shoulder's drooping beneath the overwhelming burden, Deanna fell against the sofa back. The fact was, her goose was cooked no matter which way she turned. The proverbial fat would hit the fire sooner or later. All she could do was enjoy the time she had now. It wasn't her thing to put off meeting a challenge head on, but until she could figure out something else to do, it was her only option.

In the week that followed, she almost enjoyed the routine at the ranch, despite wondering when her name would be released or when she'd be found. With a fervor she didn't think possible, Deanna mucked the stables in true cowboy fashion, even braving to give the horses treats from the garden while Shep worked on repairing the corral behind the livery. Together, they groomed the animals, Shep building her trust in them and vice versa.

Each night after the dishes, Deanna found a simple recipe from a cookbook in a box marked *Books* that Shep hadn't bothered to unpack and prepared the cuisine the next day. She offered to unpack the moving boxes stacked along the wall, but he was adamant that she leave them be.

"Most of it goes into storage anyway. I've unpacked all I need."

Was this increasing distance due to the strain of having taken on her burden, worrying about his friend's progress in clearing her? Just the mention of it wound him up tight as a spring. That Deanna understood all too well. Regardless, she counted her blessings each night, and the cowboy was number one on her list.

Toward week's end, Ticker Deerfield returned from roundup and heralded them with tales of rebellious cows and greenhorn shenanigans over a crescent roll and crusted Beef Wellington Deanna had made from a recipe on the canned rolls. The more she laughed, the more the old-timer would embellish until tears ran down her face.

"You'd be a perfect storyteller around a campfire." She could just picture Ticker in buckskins, keeping city slickers like herself spellbound or in stitches.

"Shoot, ma'am, I was born spinnin' yarns, so my mama said."

It was hard to believe how badly mistaken she'd been about Ticker, Shep, Hopewell, and Buffalo Butte. The people and town were just friends and a home she hadn't discovered yet. And she'd have never discovered them, if not for her trouble. God had made them the silver lining of her cloud, even though she hadn't seen or felt His presence at the time.

"More yarn than substance," Shep teased, more relaxed in Ticker's presence than he'd been all week.

Ticker also brought the news that Charlie Long had found the parts he needed for Deanna's car in a junk auto lot in Wyoming. It would save Shep five hundred dollars over the new. They were being shipped via truck and should be in the beginning of next week.

With Charlie's news that she'd be on the road again in another week also came his advice. "Sell that foreign bucket of bolts while she's ahead and get a good used American made vehicle." The man also sent her portfolio with Ticker.

"Said he don't want to be responsible for anything in the car," Ticker explained as Deanna cleared the leftovers from the table. "Charlie's a queer old dog."

This, from a man who was taking Molly up to a hunting cabin the next day because the *town* was too crowded for him, Deanna mused later. Shep and Ticker had gone on the nightly rounds, leaving her to amuse herself.

While she boiled potato cubes for salad for tomorrow's Buffalo Butte roof raising and barbeque, Deanna opened her portfolio and took out a sketchpad. The pencil she began to doodle with felt foreign to her work-calloused fingers, as if it had come from another world.

Still, by the time the potato salad from *Betty Crocker's Best Recipes* was sealed in a large Tupperware container, Deanna's doodling had come together. It was a sketch of the hotel lobby, not as it was, but as it could be. Skylights replaced some of the tin panels in the vaulted ceiling, flooding the open area of the first floor as well as its perimeter second floor balcony with a natural light to supplement the electrified replica chandeliers. Instead of piles of junk and boxes, Victorian settees, chairs, and even gaming tables were arranged in groups around the lobby. Elegant feathery plantings flanked the great archway into the round tower of the dining area. Across the middle of the richly carved walnut desk, a smear of mustard provided the only color.

Now she remembered why she didn't cook and work at the same time, Deanna thought, studying the rough sketch as though looking into the future. But with planning and care, the two worlds of marketing and homemaking could be combined, just like the Old West atmosphere with the twenty-first century amenities. Sure, there'd have to be concessions from each to make it work, but the end result would be worth—

Outside the porch door, Smoky barked, startling Deanna from her introspection. She thought the dog had gone off with Shep and Ticker.

"Just wait till I catch you half asleep sometime, pooch," she threatened as she went to the door to let him in. "Payback is..."

Just as she reached for the door handle, Smoky vaulted off the porch and raced around to the side of the house, his barking becoming fiercer.

"Shep?" The dusk-to-dawn light on the gable of the livery stable illuminated the street in front of the house, but the far side and back were in the shadows. "Smoky, what is it, boy? Is that barn kitty trespassing again?"

The dog had grown very territorial after Deanna discovered the yellow tomcat in the livery. Now the shepherd mix mongrel stood at the back corner of the house, the hair around his neck raised stiff as an Elizabethan collar.

"What's with the dog?" Shep emerged from the barn in a trot, Ticker not far behind.

Deanna heaved an exaggerated shrug. "Probably the barn cat is out there. Why don't you go around the garden side and call him?" She dropped down to her knees. "Come on, Smoky."

"Deanna, get in the house and stay there."

Startled by the sharp edge of Shep's voice, she rose, but he ducked around the side of the house, a long flashlight brandished in hand, without seeing the blank look she gave him. Gradually, her shock gave way to alarm. Did Shep know something he wasn't telling her?

"Best do as he says, missy," Ticker told her. "Could be that dog's cornered a porkypine or worse, a stinkin' skunk. He won't chase nothin' worthwhile."

Recalling Ticker's earlier tale of how Smoky wound up at the veterinary hospital having needles plucked from his hide, she let out a breath of relief and headed for the safety of the house. Skunks, porcupines, wolves, big cats—welcome to the Wild West, city gal.

Behind her, Ticker threatened, "Dog, if you get sprayed, I'm gonna shave you nekkid as a newborn!"

The mental picture of the *nekkid* dog was too horrid, not to mention funny, to dwell on. With a giggle, she walked to the rear window where the long beam of Shep's light flashed among the small grove of volunteer trees that shaded the backyard. Emboldened by his presence, Smoky rushed to join him with Ticker not far behind, still grumbling.

"See anything?" she called out through the open window.

"Not yet."

Shep's terse reply gave Deanna pause for concern once again, until reason prevailed. If she were stalking a skunk or porcupine, she imagined she'd be a bit uptight, too. Returning to the table and her sketch, she began to put her drawing materials away. She didn't like tipping her hand on an idea before it was ready for presentation, even if it was a far-fetched *what if.*

But then, until last Sunday, her entire future was a far-fetched *what if.* With God and the shepherd He sent her, impossible was no longer a valid word in Deanna's vocabulary. As long as she believed, all things were possible.

Twenty-five

I'm going to be up on the roof of the church most of the day, so you two had best be on your toes," Shep instructed Jay Voorhees and his men. The older technical agent would remain behind with Ticker in case Majors showed up at the ranch, while Voorhees and Agent Jon Kestler kept an eye on Deanna. "There's over two hundred and fifty people expected in the plaza today. It's the perfect place for Majors to make contact with Deanna."

"You really think he was at the house last night?" the senior agent queried, brow arched in skepticism.

Shep answered with steel-jawed impatience. "*Someone* left footprints at the back bedroom window. If the three of you had stayed away from the house like I told you, I'd know for sure."

By the time Shep and Ticker had looked among the trees and returned to the house, Voorhees and Kestler had tracked up the area when they joined the pursuit. There had also been evidence that someone had tried to pry open the back screen, which had been painted shut for years. Chipped paint was scattered like snowflakes around the window and on the sill. Confound it, they knew better.

"Maybe you can get a partial footprint," Shep said, voice ripe with accusation. "That is, after you eliminate yours. The window is a long shot with the paint peeled off like this, unless the perp touched the glass." Unless one or more of them contaminated the scene on purpose.

"We couldn't have known where the guy had or hadn't been," Kestler objected. "We heard the commotion and ran out to help."

"Help?" Shep exclaimed. "Like you kept me informed that Majors got a cash advance in Taylorville?"

The disconcerted exchange of glances between the two men convicted them. "Seems you still have friends in high places, Jones." Jay Voorhees's dry remark did little to improve Shep's humor.

"Seems you still like to keep your own people out of the loop." Was Voorhees the mole?

"You're not *our* people, Jones," the agent reminded him. "Your cooperation warrants you information on a need-to-know basis. Your personal involvement with Miss Manetti gave my chief second thoughts regarding that much. We've been after Victor Dusault for the last five years. The man runs everything from drugs to firearms and launders his money through operations like Amtron Enterprises. He finances nonexistent product development and marketing through someone in house like Majors, who transfers the money back through a Swiss account for a percentage."

"Until he got greedy and brought in a naive girl from New York to sucker into making the deposits in his private account instead." No, Jay was too ambitious for his own good, but Shep didn't think he was criminal. "It's her face on the camera; naturally everyone thinks she's in it with him."

"Now you're catching on."

"But it wasn't Deanna who withdrew the money. The female had her coloring, but not her build or features. I know that, too." Kestler had been nosying around, but then a stakeout could be boring. As for the other guy, who knew? The tech wiz hardly ever left the trailer.

"She's our only solid connection to Majors," Voorhees explained. "Turns out we were right. That tracking device we found in her car shows someone else thinks she's involved."

It didn't make sense. Unless Majors picked up the money in drag and had it, but why follow Deanna? If he gave it to her with the intention of meeting later…nobody would be that stupid. She was the most viable suspect, captured on video. That left Deanna as the patsy with Majors and possibly a female accomplice setting her up. But again, why follow her?

At the short blast of the Jeep's horn, Deanna's signal that she was ready to leave, Shep pointed a warning finger at Voorhees.

"Look, we never have cared much for the way the other works, but we got the job done. Don't let her out of your sight."

"You know, Jones, I hope for your sake Manetti is innocent."

Not trusting his ears, Shep spun on his heel.

"I mean it. I can't see it, but I do mean it."

Seventy times seven. The reminder stopped Shep's stinging reply. Who knew, maybe there was hope for Jay Voorhees as a humanitarian yet.

Lord, I know it's not up to me to judge the man, much less exact the pound of flesh he owes me. I have to forgive him. I really thought I had. But this time, it's not about me. It's about Deanna. Help me keep her safe. Send angels. However You want to handle it. Just protect her.

There was no parking space anywhere on the plaza in the center of Buffalo Butte. Cars and trucks closed ranks along the side streets as well as behind the businesses lining the large shaded square. People kept arriving with lawn chairs and blankets to watch the competition. Two giant dump trucks waited on either side of the pristine white A-framed church to receive the debris from the old roof. Two flatbeds, courtesy of Seth Farley's Farm and Ranch General and the lumber supply in Taylorville, were loaded with the new materials.

In the tree-shaded plaza in front of the church, a carnival atmosphere pervaded. Tents set up by local vendors and civic groups sold crafts, baked goods, and food and refreshments to the gathering crowd. A troupe of church clowns from Taylorville came to entertain the children with pony rides, face painting, and zany shenanigans. What had started off as a volunteer labor project had grown into a fund-raiser that possibly would pay for the materials as well.

Deanna stood, head bowed, next to the Whet Your Whistle tent with ladies of the congregation and listened as Reverend Lawrence launched the event with a prayer of thanksgiving and blessings for those who'd made the affair possible. Gathered around him were the volunteer cowboys and farmhands, divided earlier into two tag teams.

Afterward, when the Reverend gave Deanna credit for the competition idea, which kindled the wildfire growth of the event, she grew warm from head to toe. She wasn't embarrassed. This was the kind of thing she did every day for a living. The warmth came from being included as one of their little congregation— Buffalo Butte's own, he'd called her. Next to her, Esther Lawson squeezed her hand as if to second the minister's words. Deanna's Amen was wrung straight from a heart overwhelmed with thanksgiving of her own.

After the blessing was over, the minister and ex-construction boss, wearing jeans and a T-shirt that said *I work for a Jewish carpenter,* slapped on a baseball cap from Farley's Farm and General and walked over to one of the trucks, where he honked the horn long and loud, signaling the work to begin. The gathering scattered like spooked sheep, but each had a mission.

Deanna remained long enough to watch the strapping young men climb up the ladders like monkeys and nail braces in place until they knelt against the peak of the roof. Armed with flat bars and belts hung with assorted tools slung low on their hips, they began a coordinated attack on the buckled and faded shingles from both sides.

After moving a safe distance to the Whet Your Whistle refreshment booth to help Esther Lawson and Maisy O'Donnell sell sodas, it was hard for Deanna to tell which of the sweat-glistening, tanned specimens in beat-up black Stetsons on the roof was her Shep…until she spied a green checked dish towel hanging out of his back pocket.

"Aha, I told you so, Esther." Smug, Maisy added, "Those two have it bad."

Both women grinned at Deanna.

"Honey, the leaves above us just waved with that dreamy sigh of yours," the diner's part owner teased. "Have you set a date?"

"Maisy, you're embarrassing Deanna. What's she going to think of us?" Esther chided, invoking her schoolmarm authority.

"That we're nosy, meddling old women…at least I am. So…?" Maisy's raised brow turned the curve of the penciled-on arches over her eyes into pointed chevrons.

"No, we haven't even talked about a date," Deanna admitted, reluctant to count chicks before they were hatched. Her situation was still as tenuous as walking on eggs. "We're taking it slowly. After all, we've only known each other a couple of weeks."

"My Chuck and I knew we were meant for each other the first time we met," Maisy told them. "He told me on our first date that he was going to marry me."

"What did you do?" Deanna asked.

"I told Mama to start making my wedding dress," she declared with a wicked giggle. "I wasn't going to be one of those silly young women the minister always preached about who got caught without my lamp filled with oil and ready for the groom."

"Does your family know about our Shep?"

"I'd like three sodas and one kiss from the little lady in the blue dress," someone drawled behind Deanna, sparing her from Esther's probing question.

Realizing that Esther and Maisy were both staring at her blue shirt-waisted *I Love Lucy* style dress, her face grew warm. Tyler McCain stood on the other side, flashing a dazzling smile at Deanna when she turned. The black-and-blue swelling around his nose and eyes had diminished, leaving just a faint yellow trace of her attack.

"Hey, it's the least you owe me after knocking me off my feet," he reminded her, pure devilment dancing in the pale green of his gold-fringed eyes.

"I'll get the drinks for you, honey," Maisy offered, while Deanna's wits assembled like an army of stooges.

"I-I thought you and your friends had gone back to the rodeo circuit," she stammered, still looking for a ready reply.

Ty leaned against the counter, enjoying her fluster too much for her liking. "When we heard about the shindig down here, we decided to come back and support our local community. We're setting up for some barrel racing and relays this afternoon in back of the community hall."

"Here you go, Tyler McOnery." Maisy set three Styrofoam cups brimming with soda on the counter.

Deanna extended her hand. "That'll be three dollars."

"What about my kiss?" the sandy-haired rogue exclaimed as he placed the bills in Deanna's hand.

"This is the soda booth," she answered, pointing across the way at the bake table where Juanita Everett, Ruth Lawrence, and two other ladies seemed to be doing a brisk business.

"Kisses are sold over there—dark *and* white chocolate," Deanna rallied, recalling the gorgeous candy kisses cake she'd seen on display earlier. "But it's going to cost more than that silver tongue of yours can conjure up. Like twelve bucks."

Ty lifted Deanna's money hand, which was still folded between his, up to his lips. "Touché, *ma cherie.*" With a wink and a parting tip of his hat, he gathered the three sodas in his hands and walked over to a picnic table where two other cowboys watched from a distance. At his exaggerated shrug, his friends laughed at him.

"Is he as big a ladies' man as he *thinks* he is?"

"Bigger when you count all his money," Maisy informed Deanna. "Just like his daddy before him, which is why the two of them constantly butt heads like addled bucks. Too much alike," she explained. "Proud, stubborn, good-lookin', and rich."

"But money isn't love. His daddy learned that too late, bless his heart," Esther observed, stepping up to help another customer.

And so the morning passed. Her companions learned about Deanna's life in New York and a sketchy account of her disastrous move to Great Falls, while Deanna learned who was who in Buffalo Butte, complete with back stories, between customers.

After his wife had been admitted to a nursing home with a debilitating stroke, J. B. McCain left Ty's mother for a woman half his age. Ty never forgave his father, despite the top-notch care and daily visits J. B. continued until his first wife's death. Nor had the young man accepted his new stepmother of seven years.

Juanita Everett was as flamboyant as she was generous, the opposite of her husband. "The man's honest," Esther was quick to point out, "just frugal."

"He has to be," Maisy exclaimed. "Juanita's weight fluctuates so much, she needs a complete wardrobe in three sizes."

At noon, another shift of volunteers came on to relieve the Whet Your Whistle crew. As Deanna handed over her money apron, someone hailed her from behind. It was one of the bulbous-nosed clowns there to entertain the children. His iodine red hair stood up everywhere except from the rubber balding from his painted forehead to his crown. There, a bright yellow hat that would have fit a doll was held in place by a thin black elastic chinstrap.

"Got a light?" he asked, an unlit cigarette hanging from his fire engine red lips.

"Sorry, I don't smoke," Deanna told him. "And maybe you ought to think twice about it, given your present company." She nodded to the three painted cherubs behind him.

The clown glanced over his shoulder in surprise, his red smile growing. "Well, well," he exclaimed, taking in his entourage with an encompassing sweep of his hand. "A round of sodas then."

"That'll be four bucks," she told him as he handed three of the drinks to the little ones.

"You don't have change for a hundred, do you?"

Deanna looked at the crisp bill he fished out of a deep pocket in his green overalls. "Sorry, we need our change for the stand, and my purse is in the car," she added in jest.

"Try the Lions' raffle table," Maisy suggested from the back of the stand. "They'll have it, with all those five dollar books of tickets. We'll trust you to come back and pay us."

"My lands, yes," Esther said, topping off the clown's drink after he'd taken a long sip. "And that's on the house. You look like you're about to melt in that getup."

"I'm forever indebted, ma'am."

Deanna, who'd started away, did a double take, her attention triggered by the familiar quip—or was it the voice?

The clown pulled the little hat up and let it go, the elastic snapping it back in place and causing the daisy in the band to bob on its spring stem. "Good day, ladies. I shall return."

She was just being paranoid, she decided when he stopped on the way to the raffle booth and made a balloon animal for a wide-eyed preschooler. A horn blew in one of the dump trucks, signaling the end of the first contest. Judging from the cheers on the cowboys' side of the roof, the ranchers were ahead. Leaving Esther and Maisy to have lunch in the cool of the church hall, Deanna sought out Shep in the bare-chested throng around the galvanized bucket of canned and bottled drinks provided for the workers.

Hat cocked back on his head, he rolled the ice cold soda can across his forehead and over the back of his neck in an effort to offset the sun beating down on the open area. "We won by one throw of shingles," he told her, staring up at the exposed barren plywood sheathing. "Some of the boys from Woolsy's Construction in Taylorville are going to patch a couple of soft spots during lunch. Speaking of which, I'm famished."

Shirt slung over one shoulder, he put a possessive hand at Deanna's back and ushered her across the street in front of the church to the plaza. Never in her life, had Deanna felt more secure than among God's people under the watchful eye of her earthly Shepard.

After purchasing two pulled pit beef barbecues with O'Donnell's famous slaw, they tried to find an empty picnic table to no avail. Instead, Shep staked out a shade tree and spread his shirt on the grass for Deanna to sit on. Nearby, a push merry-go-round spun delighted squeals from the children riding it. The children, the watchful parents, and the antics of the clowns provided live entertainment as they ate the delicious food prepared by J. B. McCain and the Cattlemen's Club.

"This is the biggest attendance Buffalo Butte has ever had for any civic or church event," Shep said, resuming his seat at the foot of the tree after disposing of their plates. "Seth has one of his clerks running folks back and forth to cars parked on the outskirts of town on a tractor-pulled wagon."

"I've seen it circling the plaza and wondered where the people were coming from," Deanna said. "I sold a tray of drinks to a family from Great Falls. I guess that notice Esther put in the *Meridian* brought people in from all over."

"No, your idea of a competition is what sparked the interest."

The admiration in his gaze caused a quickening in her stomach. It might have rolled over in delight, if she hadn't eaten so much. Now she wanted to take a nap—in Shep's arms. Deanna sighed dreamily, imagining his sun-bronzed warmth, the interplay of the muscled pillow beneath her cheek. Altogether, the picturesque small town, the cowboy, the shade tree, and a blanket of grass combined for an old-time movie-perfect setting.

God, I thank You for this moment and pray that it's a preview of our future together, that someday, we'll be watching our children on the merry-go-round, attending our church function…

Three long beeps of the horn brought the lunch break and her secret prayer to an end. Shep inhaled deeply, as though mustering enough energy to get up. Flexing his arms and shoulders, he groaned. "I have a feeling this kind of work is going to tell on us tonight."

"Want me to rub you down in that horse liniment you used on the mare?" Having abandoned his shirt, she reached out from her standing position to offer him a boost up.

He rose, a perfectly wicked grin flashing white across his face. Playful, he pulled her against him and lowered his forehead to hers. "Better not," he cautioned, the words rumbling from deep in his throat. "Might make me too frisky for my own good." He kissed the tip of her nose and backed away reluctantly. "At least the idea'll give me one up on the rest of the fellas this afternoon."

Twenty-six

While the roof of the church grew before the eyes of the cheering crowd, Maisy, Esther, and Deanna filled in as gofers for the various church booths. As far as she could see, the ranchers and farmers were matching shingle for shingle to the point that the contest might well be a draw. Naturally, she gave an enthusiastic whistle each time she passed the Stetson-dominated side.

Behind the church and community hall on the public ball field, Tyler McCain and some other young men were taking names for a barrel race and relay competition to be held that evening during the private steak cookout his father sponsored for the volunteers and their families. He'd even talked his father into posting a hundred-dollar purse to be split between the winners.

"That boy'd bust his tail for a hundred-dollar prize but won't work up a sweat for real money," J. B. McCain derided when Deanna delivered a tray of large sodas to the men assembling a big barbecue pit behind the community hall. "You wouldn't have any banner ideas that would lure that show-off back to Buffalo Butte and the Double M, would you, gal?"

"Sure." She followed up her flippant answer. "Turn Hopewell into a working Western town resort and put Tyler in charge of a rodeo show for the tourists. He'd have work and play, plus he'd be close to the Double M."

To her astonishment, J. B. appeared to be taking her seriously.

"Hey, I'm just kidding," she said hastily. "It just popped into my head, you know."

J. B. motioned Deanna away from the confusion of the grill. "Anything else popped into that pretty little head of yours?"

Embarrassed that she'd put her mouth in motion before engaging her brain, Deanna shared her thoughts regarding Hopewell—fixing up the buildings as lodgings for tourists, gearing the shows toward family entertainment, providing some dude ranch type experience in riding and running a ranch.

"Of course, I'd have to do the demographics to see what the competition is and if there's enough interest to keep it going, sufficient investors willing to take the risk, et cetera. I haven't really thought it through."

"What does Shep say about all this? Last I heard, he was set on breeding a hardy mustang line and training workhorses."

"He listened." Why did she have to say a word? Shep was intrigued but not sold.

"He always was the cautious type."

"Sometimes that's a good thing." Heaven knew she could have been more cautious with C. R. Majors.

"And sometimes it can mean the difference between making a fortune and making a living."

And that was a key factor in her reckless decision, moving to the top in a male-dominated world. Recalling Esther's observation of J. B. McCain, how he thought money was the key to everything, Deanna couldn't help but relate to the man. "Guess it depends on a person's priorities."

J. B. pulled her aside as a pair of boys just missed running into her. Absorbed in their chase, both risked losing the shaved ice from their snowcones.

"I haven't had a snowcone in ages," she said, ending the uncomfortable conversation. "I'm going to find out where they're making those."

"I think they're shaving ice in front of the hardware store so they can share the electric hookup with the Chuck Wagon," J. B. called after her.

Shep was on the ground crew handing up supplies as Deanna passed through the parking lot between the church and community hall. Hard as it was to believe, the roof was already half done, at least on his side. Slipping up behind him, she tugged on the key chain hooked to his belt. "Can I have the keys to the Jeep? I need to get my purse."

Due to the nature of their duties, Shep had locked both her purse and his wallet in the vehicle so they wouldn't have to worry about keeping track of them while they worked.

"Go ahead, but take one of the ladies to go with you," he advised over his shoulder, never missing a beat in the rhythm of the human chain passing bundles of the new shingles along to those on the roof.

Unable to resist, Deanna planted a surreptitious kiss between his shoulder blades and hurried off before she got the blame for Shep's dropping his pass of the building materials.

While Shep's caution was sweet, the place was crawling with townspeople, including the parking lot. Besides, the church women were busy as bees as it was. Keys in hand, Deanna made her way around the opposite side of the church past its tree-lined cemetery to a back lot, where Shep had finally found a place to park.

The back lot was packed with assorted trucks, SUVs, and the trailers that had transported the ponies. The maze was perfect for a group of kids who were playing hide-and-seek in and around the vehicles. Between two large elms outside the chain-link graveyard fence, a dozen or so horses were tethered, the transport of choice for many of the volunteers from close by.

Two teenaged boys, who had been assigned to keep the animals watered, led the horses two at a time to a big trough by an old-fashioned pitcher pump for a midafternoon drink. Montana's answer to a bicycle rack, Deanna wisecracked to herself as she searched for the row of vehicles they'd parked in. The lot hadn't been filled then, so it looked different now. She thought it was in the first two or three rows.

As she meandered down the second row, she spied the front of Shep's trusty dusty steed on wheels, but upon reaching it, she stopped short. A clown, the same one who'd asked her for a light earlier, was climbing out of the back window. Certain that Shep had locked up, it could only mean one thing. Fire flew into Deanna.

"Hey, Bozo, what do you think you're doing?" she demanded in a loud voice, hoping to draw attention from those nearby.

Half in and half out the rear window, the clown peered over the roof of the Jeep, bemused at first, until he spied Deanna's indignant approach. Leaping to the ground, he stumbled over his oversized shoes. Something went flying from his hand, landing in the dirt ahead of him.

Recognizing her purse before the clown grabbed it up and scrambled to his feet, Deanna broke into a run. "Thief!" she shouted, running out of her heeled designer slippers in determination. There wasn't any money in the bargain basement bag, save a five-dollar bill that Shep insisted she take, but it was a matter of principle. Besides, she'd seen a purse just like it in Saks for over a hundred dollars.

"Stop that clown," she hollered at the boys watering the horses. "He's got my purse!"

Instead of helping, the two boys stood agape at the sight of a barefoot woman, full skirts hiked above her knees, chasing a clown around the back corner of the cemetery. Hot on his heels, Deanna could only hope the cowboys setting up the parameters of the competition would recover faster.

"Thief," she screamed with what little breath she could afford. Bozo started for the thick crowd watching the roofing contest between the church and community hall and then changed his mind, striking out across the barrel-studded ball field, headed for the high grass and brush beyond.

The moment's hesitation and his oversized shoes gave Deanna the advantage. Her heart beat with each step she took across the hard-packed field, thundering in her ears as if she had four feet instead of two. Her burning lungs were assailed with as much dust as oxygen, but the thief was almost within her reach. Just another inch and she'd have him.

Impatient, Shep stood with an armful of the warm, rough shingles, looking up at the team on the roof, which for some reason had stopped working. "What's the holdup?" he shouted, his thoughts mingling with those of the other outspoken members of his team.

"Blow the horn," Reverend Lawrence ordered from his supervisory perch on the roof's peak. He repeated himself twice before someone had the presence of mind to obey him. The one long beep was the signal for all hands to stop where they were.

"They can't be finished," one of Shep's teammates exclaimed from the ladder.

The ranchers had at least three more rows to the crown. Shep made a megaphone with his cupped hands. "What's the problem?"

The team leader on the ridge near the back of the church climbed to his feet, straining to look at something behind the church. "Looks like Ty McCain's roped himself some clown and a woman in a blue dress in the back lot by the ball field."

Blue dress? Shep stiffened. Deanna's had matched her eyes. Surely—

"Shep!"

"Shepard!"

From somewhere in the crowd, two women were shouting his name. He peered over the sea of bobbing, turning heads when Reverend Lawrence called out to him in an incredulous tone from his lofty station near the steeple.

"My heavenly days, Shep, it looks like *your Deanna.*"

"Shep!" Reaching through the crowd, Maisy O'Donnall brushed Shep's arm as he shoved through the bystanders between him and the ball field behind the cemetery. "Wait!"

Esther Lawson inserted herself into his path. "Shepard—"

"Not now, Esther."

He practically lifted the retired schoolteacher out of his way rather than run her over, then plowed ahead. A clown...what had Deanna said about a clown smoking in front of some kids? And where the devil were Voorhees and Kestler? They'd certainly been gawking at him and Deanna during lunch. Shep had wanted to kiss the mischief off Deanna's lips more than he wanted the food, but not with those two as witnesses.

At the thinned edge of the crowd, he broke into a dead run toward the group of cowboys gathered around Ty McCain and the dark bay quarter horse that Shep had trained for his friend. The pressure of the hunting knife Shep had tucked in his boot reassured him he'd have a weapon if he needed it.

What in the world were Deanna and a clown—?

He slowed to an approaching lope. "What's going on here, Ty? Deanna?"

At the sound of a plaintive "Shep!" he elbowed a slow-moving cowpoke out of his way in a protective surge to get to her, rescue her, soothe the tremble in her voice.

There, in the middle of the crowd, purse held over her head as she tried to tear her way out of the rope tangle with the other hand, was the lady in the blue dress and a clown. The latter struggled with frenzied hands to pull up his large baggy pants from around his ankles, while a furious Deanna kicked at him. Suddenly, she brought her knee up under his chin and, taking advantage of the daze suspending his reaction for a split second, batted him with her purse.

"Take that, you nose-honking, purse-snatching bozo!"

It struck Shep that the clown needed more help than Deanna.

He sprawled backward, still tangled in the rope, almost taking her with him. Grabbing the sputtering, kicking fury by the waist, Shep yanked her free of Ty's lasso and held her tight as her angry assault dissolved into tears.

"It's okay, darlin'," Shep cooed against the top of her head as she buried her face in his shoulder. Beyond them, the clown tried to staunch the blood trickling from his lower lip.

"He b-broke into the Jeep an…and took my purse!" she sniffed, pointing behind her without looking at the downed perpetrator.

"I tell you, Shep, you got yourself a regular wildcat there," Ty McCain called out from his saddle. "I rode out to help her, but by the time I let go of my rope, she had the varmint by the suspenders, slinging him out of his drawers."

Two of Ty's friends pulled the groggy comic figure to his feet. "I think you need to meet our town sheriff," one said, pulling a large silk handkerchief out of the perp's baggy trousers and handing it to the bleeding man.

"This is a hundred-dollar bag here," Deanna raved, as if trying to justify her uncharacteristic aggression. "I only p…paid twenty for it," she admitted to Shep, "but that's not the point."

She was terrified of horses but thought nothing of running down a thief and recovering her property bare-handed. What a character. "Well, you have it back and everything is okay, right? He didn't hurt you, did he?"

"He…"

Stopping her quivering complaint long enough to pluck the wet towel tucked in the back of Shep's jeans, she pulled away on her own and loudly blew her nose. Before Shep and everyone else, her adrenaline-fueled hysteria swung from helpless and vulnerable back to aggressive and furious again.

"That coward wouldn't dare." Deanna glared at the thief. "You coulda just dropped it, you know."

"*You* could have just let him have it," Shep chided, the rash-

ness of Deanna's pursuit swinging his initial alarm toward annoyance.

"Maybe that's how you operate out here," she averred, "but in
my old neighborhood, you learned to stand your ground against
punks like this or be stepped on." Wiping her hands on her hips,
she marched over to where the clown stood mute, holding the
bloodied wad of silk to his mouth.

"You ought to be ashamed of yourself!" Her admonishment
would have done any Irish-Italian mother in Brooklyn proud.
"Smoking in front of kids and stealing from honest people like
this. Just who do you think you are, *Mr.* Bozo?"

With that, Deanna grabbed the rubber edge of the clown
mask and ripped it off the man's face. The glower of her gaze fal-
tered, as she took in the light brown hair, packed wet against his
head by the mask and wig combination. A voiceless exclamation
of disbelief parted her lips.

"It's me, Deanna."

Clearly shaken, she reached for Shep, the clown's stony confession tightening her grip on his arm until the pinch became
unbearable. Disengaging the death grip, Shep took her into the
protective circle of his arms, inserting himself between her and
the ghost from her past. Only C. R. Majors could draw the angry
blood rush from her face, leaving her white as the paint on his
mask.

"But he's dead." Deanna's voice was little more than whisper,
a squeak of disbelief. Trembling as though suddenly chilled to the
bone, she clutched Shep, unable to climb deep enough into the
haven of his embrace. "I don't understand. I saw his car burned
up. The detective told me he'd been in it," she rambled against the
lightly furred depression of his chest. "He said the people C. R.
double-crossed had killed him and he'd protect me from them if
I told him where the money was. But I didn't know anything
about it. I was innocent and he…he…that lying, conniving—"

"Whoa, there." Shep grabbed Deanna before she flew at

Majors in a resurgence of outrage.

"Why?" she demanded of the man who'd not only betrayed her heart, but framed her for a crime she didn't commit. "Why did you do this?"

All Shep's training was put to the test as he held the woman scorned at bay. Arms and legs flailing, vying with each other to get at the crook who'd victimized her, it was like trying to calm two cats with their tails tied together.

"Check him for a weapon," Shep ordered in exasperation, "and somebody find the sheriff, *wherever he is.*" With Ty's rope pulled tight about Majors' hips, he wasn't likely to get away, but he could have a concealed weapon, not to mention a kitchen sink, in that getup.

Where in blazes were Voorhees and Kestler? They weren't supposed to take their eyes off Deanna.

"Shepard!" Esther shoved her way toward Shep, her eyes as wide as her glass frames. "We have them."

Have them? Shep's thoughts echoed as Deanna gave up her struggles.

"Easy, Miz Lawson," one of her former students said, steadying the older woman, while she made a gasping recovery from her run across the field.

"Have who, Esther?" She wasn't making a lick of sense, but at least her appearance had a sedating effect on Deanna.

Still breathless, Esther waved her hand in a frantic bid for more time and then pointed to the community hall. "Them…wait." The retired teacher drew in a deep breath and closed her eyes, reminding Shep and doubtless others, of her time-proven cure for hiccoughs or an overdose of excitement. Everyone waited as she let it go until it was completely expended.

"Two men…been following Deanna…all day," she managed. "Maisy and…and I…locked in the food pantry."

"They locked Maisy in the pantry!" Deanna exclaimed, as bemused as Shep.

Esther shook her head. "Maisy gone…to get sheriff. Me…" she said, clasping her chest. "To get you."

"Wait a minute," Deanna said. "You're saying that you and Maisy locked two men who were following me in the pantry?" The puzzled furrow of her brow deepened. "But why would—" She looked at Shep, searching for the answer to her question. Then, as if she'd spotted it, her eyelashes fluttered and her eyes rolled upward beneath them, chasing the raw terror it invoked into the oblivion of unconsciousness.

Shep caught the full weight of her body in the circle of his arms before she slumped to the ground, and with the help of a bystander, he managed to hoist Deanna's limp figure in his arms. This whole operation had turned into a three-ring circus. The perp was a clown, tackled by his victim, and roped with her by a cowboy on a horse. Shep's elderly ex-schoolteacher and the town gossip locked two DEA agents in the food pantry.

Rising above her discomfort, Esther Lawson took immediate charge. "Shepard, bring Deanna into the community hall where it's cool. We keep a first-aid kit with smelling salts there." Turning to lead the way, the older woman clucked like a mother hen to herself. "Bless her little heart, at least the worst is over for her now."

Shep fell in behind Esther, not nearly as relieved. The worst might be over for Deanna, but something told him it was just beginning for him—in the third ring.

Twenty-seven

Deanna stirred by the time Shep had her firmly in his grasp.

"Easy, Slick," he said against her forehead. "I've got you. You're safe."

"I'm not usually a swooner," she mumbled, still a bit woozy.

"It's not every day a gal sees a ghost."

"But it wasn't a ghost that I was worried about. All I could think about were those faceless men who wrecked my condo—the ones who wouldn't give me a chance to even say I was innocent."

"Excuse me. Excuse me." A paramedic from an ambulance on duty for the affair broke from the crowd and came straight for Deanna and Shep. "Have we got a heat stroke here or what?" He found a pulse on her wrist and watched his watch.

"I'm okay re—"

"Quiet please, ma'am."

Deanna waited until the young man got his reading.

"You wanna put her down, buddy, so I can check her out?"

"No, I don't want to be checked out. I'm fine." She couldn't be finer—in Shepard Jones's arms.

The young man shrugged. "It's your call. Pulse is good."

"And I *can* walk," she told Shep.

"I imagine you *can*, but there's no need to." His gaze testified without question that they were of the same mind on that subject. In his arms was exactly where Deanna belonged.

"It's okay, folks," the paramedic announced. "You can start again anytime."

He parted the sea of onlookers clustered between the church and the hall ahead of Shep and Deanna. Curious faces swept past in fast-forward, so that if any were familiar, Deanna had no time to recognize them.

"Shep, you want me to fill in for you?" a young man with a handlebar mustache called out from the throng.

He nodded. "Appreciate it, Vic."

"You need me?" Reverend Lawrence called down from the roof. He seemed torn between his responsibilities as minister of the church and foreman of the roofing crews.

"Everything's under control," Shep assured him.

With a "You take care of our little lamb now" the good reverend signaled the man at the wheel of the flatbed to honk the horn.

It was still blowing amid the cheers of the volunteers and their supporters as Shep stepped into the cool of the air-conditioned hall where Sheriff Clyde Barrett, flanked by a grim Maisy O'Donnall, removed a chair that had been wedged under the doorknob of what appeared to be a closet.

"You voted for me to be sheriff, Maisy," the man chided, "so what on earth possessed you to take over my job?"

"Esther and me didn't have time to go gallivantin' all over the plaza," she declared in their defense.

Deanna grabbed Shep's arm as the sheriff, gun still holstered, slid back the deadbolt and opened the door. What if the men were armed?

"Sorry about this fellas," the officer apologized. "The ladies meant well."

Surely she'd escaped one bizarre situation and landed in another. Instead of the sleazy thugs she expected, the geologists from Shep's ranch emerged, soaked in sweat from their confinement in the non-air-conditioned enclosure.

"These guys aren't thugs," Deanna told her friends, warmed by their benevolent intentions, despite the mistake. "They're the guys who have been doing geology tests or something at Shep's ranch."

"Oh, my word." Esther looked stricken, but Maisy wasn't as easily convinced.

"If they're geologists, I'm a rocket scientist," the diner waitress declared. "What does a geologist need with a gun, 'cause the pudgy one has one. Saw it right off at the drink stand when he reached in his jacket for his wallet."

"Mrs. O'Donnall is right," the man Shep referred to as Voorhees admitted. "But the sheriff can vouch for us that we are special investigators for the government. That's all anyone here needs to know," he said with an authority that nipped in the bud the questions forming in Deanna's and likely everyone else's minds.

The government? Deanna glanced at Shep, disconcerted. Had he known these men were government agents? His schooled expression held no answer for her.

"Well, I for one am so sorry, sir." Esther clapped her hands together as though praying for forgiveness. "We were just trying to keep Deanna's abusive boyfriend from finding her, and we thought—"

She'd only told the two women that she'd left a bad relationship, so what possessed the dears to think she needed protection? Had Shep said something to them behind her back?

"What I'd like to know is how in kingdom come did you two federal boys get hoodwinked by two of our finest senior citizens?" The sheriff's poorly concealed snicker brought a flush of color to the men's faces.

"Who are you callin' a senior citizen?" Maisy railed, throwing the sheriff in the same fire as the agents.

"Now that was just a figure of speech, Mai—"

"They must have seen us tailing the suspect—" Jon started at the same time as the sheriff, stalling both.

"Excuse me." Deanna took advantage of the pause, not certain she'd heard right. "Did you say *suspect?* Like in me as a suspect?" The possibility that the police called in the FBI or whatever to track her down sent a shiver down her spine.

"I'm afraid so, Miss Manetti," Agent Voorhees confirmed.

"Sheesh, am I on the Most Wanted show, too, just for taking a colleague's bank bag to the bank for him?"

"Anyway," Jon picked up, "the ladies called us in to help get a heavy box down off the top shelf in the pantry. Next thing we knew, the door was locked and the lights went out."

"You could have kicked it down." Shep's derision curled one side of his mouth.

"That's a solid wood door, buddy," Voorhees pointed out, "not to mention church property. We beat on the wall and shouted until some kids overheard us and promised to find the sheriff."

"Giving this guy a clear path to get his hands on Deanna," Shep shot back as Voorhees brandished a pair of handcuffs from his coat and walked over to the mute clown in the custody of Ty McCain's associates.

Deanna's thoughts tripped in confusion. Were the geologists the guys in high places that Shep told her could help her?

"Looks to me like Majors was in more peril than our Miss Manetti."

The agent's wry observation failed to amuse Shep. Deanna could almost hear his teeth grating under the pressure of his twitching jaw muscles.

"Gentlemen," Voorhees said to the men who turned C. R. over to him, "I thank you for your help, but I'd just as soon clear the room of all parties not directly involved in our investigation. It'll all come out eventually, but for now, the less you know, the better. That goes for you as well, ladies," he added for Esther and Maisy's benefit. "Just keep what you've seen under your hat until the investigation is over. Some of you could be called as witnesses later, and we don't want any slip of the tongue to invalidate some-one's testimony or harm the prosecution."

The clamor of emotions in Deanna's mind numbed her to Esther's kindly, "Keeping you in prayer, sweetie," or Maisy's wink as they followed the other good citizens out of the hall. The geolo-gists—no, government agents—had shown up right after her arrival at Hopewell.

"As for you, *Bozo,*" Agent Voorhees addressed C. R. "you are under arrest. You have the right…"

Shock numbing her ability to sort out her confusion, Deanna became distracted as the man in charge read C. R. his rights. Jon left to get their vehicle, instead of taking the sheriff's offer to hold C. R. in the local jail. Low profile was the aim. His chief wanted them to wrap this thing up without word leaking out that could jeopardize other investigations. First on the agenda was picking up their partner and the tech trailer at the ranch. Then they'd be on their way.

"On your way where?" It was too much for Deanna to take in. The geologists were government agents and C. R. was not only alive, but had followed her to—to what, steal her purse? "So since you have C. R., does this mean I can go free?"

As long as she was cleared, she didn't have to understand. God sent her to Shep. Surely He wasn't going to take her away now that she'd found happiness.

"You're still suspected of collaboration, Miss Manetti." The senior agent gave her an apologetic look. "You did make the deposits."

"But I didn't know what was in them." Deanna jumped to her feet heading for C. R. The least he could do was clear this thing up. "Tell him, C. R. You owe me that after the stunt you pulled. Tell him I didn't know anything about the blooming money…that you snookered me big time."

"Deanna didn't know anything about it," he said, expression-less.

"Now *that* was real convincing," Deanna quipped with a dour look. "Sheesh, I know it's the truth and I wouldn't believe you."

There had to be a way to resolve this. But how? Question after question stirred in her mind, overlapping with flashbacks of all she'd been through. No one would believe her. "Wait a minute. How did you even know where I was? Even *I* didn't know where I was."

"He put a tracking device on your car," Voorhees explained. "Something like the fancy models have standard that can be used to trace a stolen vehicle."

"I know what a tracking device is." Deanna glared afresh at the man who got her into this mess. After what he'd done to her, he was lucky she'd just busted his lip. "You have got some nerve, Majors. Do you have any idea what I gave up to move out here? Or worse, what I've been through since I listened to your puff and nonsense about opportunity for success *and* romance? Hah!"

"If Miss Manetti had nothing to do with your scheme, Mr. Majors, then why did you go to so much trouble to find her?" Agent Voorhees asked.

"Yes, *exactly,*" Deanna chimed in.

C. R. looked at Deanna. "She's one of the most passionate women I've ever met. Can you blame me?"

Deanna gasped. "You take that back!" He made it sound like they'd been intimate.

"Of course, I had no idea she was so violent." He ran his tongue over his tender lip.

"Violent? I'll show you violent." In two short steps, she gave him a sound slap. "Now you tell the truth, you lying, conniving, thieving son of a gutter rat."

"Hey, what about my rights?" C. R. demanded of Agent Voorhees. "Keep her away from me."

"I thought Miss Manetti's *passion* is what brought you here."

Deanna felt validated by the agent's cryptic turn of phrase. "So why did you really hunt me down? I certainly don't have the money. Somebody tore apart my condo looking for it, and the police blamed me." Just recalling it made her want to grab C. R.'s lower lip and pull it up over his head. "And I've been mucking stables and wearing this Lucy dress and psychedelic handoffs just to earn my room and board. I was afraid to use my credit cards. Cut off my arm, why don't you!" she exclaimed. "So if my wanting to rip off your head and spit down your neck is passionate, then I admit it. I'm *very* passionate. I'm so passionate I could—"

"Easy. He's not worth working yourself into a tizzy." The sympathetic touch of Shep's hands on her shoulders checked her ballooning fury. She turned and leaned into the circle of his waiting arms.

"So now what'll we do?" she asked, laying a weary head against Shep's shoulder. "I don't want to go with them. I shouldn't have to. I'm innocent."

"In that case," Voorhees said, "you won't object to my searching your purse."

The purse. Of course. Whatever C. R. was after was in her purse. "Not at all. All I know is you won't find any money… except the five you gave me," she said to Shep.

Agent Voorhees took up the dusty purse Deanna had left on the table in her angry confusion. But after opening it and dumping out all the contents, nothing was revealed that didn't belong there—a few folded tissues, a spare lipstick, folding hairbrush, and a wallet containing Shep's five, her license, and assorted medical and charge cards. Stymied, the official ran his fingers inside the expensive clutch, along the seams, and discovered its single zippered compartment. Aside from dental cleaning gum, a safety pin, a ball of lint, and a small tin of aspirin, there was nothing else.

"Not exactly the Denver mint, is it?"

Unphased by her dry observation, Agent Voorhees started patting C. R. down.

"What, you think he might have it on him?"

Voorhees pounced on Deanna like a cat on a mouse. "And what would that be, Miss Manetti?"

Trying not to shrink from the agent's grilling look, she shrugged. "How should I know? Whatever it was he was trying to steal my purse for."

"What I'd like to know," C. R. spoke up, his speech a little slurred by his swelling lip, "is how you feds caught up with us so fast."

Deanna bristled. "Don't you say *us*, you creep."

"So how *did* you find me?" C.R. repeated as Voorhees finished patting down his back. "Did you follow her and wait?"

"That's about the size…"

"Marshal Jones tipped us off," the agent said.

"Marshal?" A shower of icy pinpricks lifted the gooseflesh on Deanna's skin from head to toe. Her mind staggered over the ragtag timeline of events. No one could have followed her. She was lost…desperate and lost when she ran off the road on Shep's ranch. Then two days later, the geologists appeared. Except they weren't geologists like Shep said…lied.

"*Marshal?*" Deanna repeated, not wanting to believe her shepherd had betrayed her. But Shep was a rancher. No way could he fake Hopewell and set up Buffalo Butte just to trap a fugitive. That had to be real. "Like in a *police* kind of marshal?" she asked Agent Voorhees.

"Ex-marshal, Deanna," Shep clarified…like that somehow made his calling the federal agents on her all right. He turned her so that she had to look him in the eye. "I knew you were in some kind of trouble, and I wanted to help."

"When did you call them?" She felt sick to her stomach, or maybe she was going to pass out again.

"I called in the first day we came to town, but that has nothing to do with—"

"No, don't." Deanna backed away from Shep, wishing she would pass out. And when she woke up again, none of this would have happened. "Not another word. I wouldn't believe anything you said anyway."

Things like *I love you. I want to share my dream with you. Would you consider giving the West another chance?* She bit her lip as hard as she could, but nothing she did or willed stopped the glassy hurt gathering in her eyes. *I ran away to the hills, too; God healed me. God is enough.* What kind of a man would use God to further his lies?

Voorhees came to Shep's defense. "He was just doing his duty, Miss Manetti. If he hadn't tried to win your trust and get you to talk, he'd have been guilty of aiding and abetting a criminal."

"If you're trying to help me, Voorhees, I'd appreciate it if you stop now."

Invisible fingers of conviction constricted around Deanna's throat, forcing her to swallow the cold, harsh lump of reality. As its poison digested and spread, she stared in anguish at her fallen knight—her fallen shepherd. "You knew all along."

"Deanna, I was professionally obligated to cooperate—"

"So that's what you call it." Her nostrils flared with the distress of her breath. What a pathetic sap she'd been, so desperate for love that she'd taken the fall, not once, but twice. "Well, you did it real good, mister."

Shep reached for her. "Deanna—"

"Don't you come near me, Shepard Jones, or so help me, I'll…I'll…"

What could she do, take Shep and an armed federal agent on? Looking about like a trapped animal for any means of escape, Deanna spied the open closet door.

"I'll be in here until our ride comes."

She spoke to Agent Voorhees, not Shep. He wasn't going to exist in her world. Yet halfway inside, raw emotion overrode her will. Deanna peered around the door at the handsome Judas. "You knew that C. R. was alive, didn't you?"

His silence shouted admission from the thinned line of his mouth. Deanna felt she needed to run, to retreat before she made a total fool of herself, but she had one last round of condemnation to fire, its fuse burning, painful, within the innermost chamber of her being.

"You know, lying and leading me to think that I was safe and…and even loved was low enough, Shepard Jones, but…"

Her voice broke, choked off by a sob Deanna was determined to suppress. Its razor-sharp barbs cut all the way down. "But that guy…" She jabbed a finger at C. R. "…was a prince, compared to what you did." Tears trickled down her cheeks with a will of their own. "He used love to fool me, but *you used God.*"

Deanna drew in a ragged breath, glowering at Shep's tall blurred figure through emotion-razed eyes. "He broke my heart, but you—" Bitterness seeped into her mouth, saturating her voice. "You…broke…my…spirit."

Ducking into the stuffy darkness of the small enclosure, Deanna shut the door behind her. There without prying eyes and false wagging tongues, she could cry. There she could wear her bruised and battered heart on her sleeve. There she could plead for God to remove her broken spirit from its bleeding, beating ruin, never again to be healed. She couldn't—wouldn't—bear its breaking again. God had to understand. It hurt too much.

Twenty-eight

"Deanna!" Shep stuck his head in the door of the sedan, cutting Jay Voorhees off from getting into the driver's seat. Deanna had refused to come out of the closet or accept the agent's offer to allow her to ride back to Hopewell with Shep. Eyes swollen and nose red, she looked away from him, staring out the tinted window in the backseat. Agent Kessler separated her from the cuffed C. R. Majors. Much as Shep hated an audience, he had no choice but to say what he had to.

"All I ask is one thing." When she refused to look at him, Shep forged on. "Don't do the same thing to me that the authorities did to you. Don't judge me guilty until you hear me out."

"Isn't that sweet—" Majors grunted, slammed by the backhand of Deanna's purse before Kessler could even react. Her aim was incredible, considering she'd not even moved her unseeing eyes from the dark window.

Majors swore through the fingers he pressed to his fresh bleeding lip. "She did it again! You keep her away from me or I won't tell you anything."

"Just shut up or I'll move up front and let her at you," Kessler warned in disgust at the whining perp.

"Just think about it, Deanna," Shep pleaded. "That's all I'm asking." Having been in the center ring of this circus long enough, he backed away to let Voorhees take the wheel. Aside from thumping Majors, Deanna had been in a zombielike state since she emerged from the pantry.

"See you back at the ranch, buddy," Voorhees called through the open window of the car as he shoved it into reverse.

I'm not your buddy.

Shep checked the annoyed retort. It was as pointless as his plea to Deanna. Even if he could convince her that he'd acted in her best interest, there was her tirade about being stranded on the backside of the world, cleaning stables, and wearing hand-me-downs when she was accustomed to the Manhattan rush hour, diesel fumes, and Fifth Avenue fashions. Had he misread her as badly as he'd done Ellen, thinking that Deanna was actually warming to his lifestyle?

Behind Shep, a horn blew loudly, startling him from his dirge of introspection. The crowd erupted into a rousing cheer for the winners of the roofing contest, the purse-snatching incident already forgotten. The world went on, he thought, too dour to bother with looking back to see who won. He was better company for the folks in the cemetery on the other side of the chain-link fence.

"Hey, handsome, you look like you just lost your best friend."

Just ahead, Maisy winked at him from the remuda of horses tethered next to the graveyard. With her were Esther, Ruth Lawrence, and Ty McCain.

"Is Deanna in trouble?" Esther promptly covered her mouth, as if she had no right to ask. "You don't have to tell us anything secret," she added hastily. "We're just concerned."

"Yeah, she looked like she'd been dragged behind a horse when those fellas put her in the car," Ty observed. "Kinda like somebody else I know."

Shep *felt* as if he'd been dragged behind a horse and kicked to boot. "I think it will all straighten itself out in time," he said uncertainly. At least Deanna would be cleared of criminal charges. Then she'd be free to go back to New York.

"You're not going to let her go, are you?" Maisy exclaimed. "Honey, she put more twinkle in your eye than a night full of stars in July."

Not to mention fireworks. Deanna made him feel like a new man…when she didn't have him twisted in knots. Or squirming in misery in front of his friends. He forced brightness into his voice. "What brings you four hanging out here anyway, when the celebration's back there?"

"Because we're all of *the same loaf,* Shepard," Esther told him. "That's what the Holy Book says."

"And you look like you're about to crumble." Maisy gave Shep a big hug.

"Besides, what's to celebrate?" Ty grumbled. "The farm boys beat us by no more than a shingle's worth of time."

"You'll take them on the riding relays," Shep assured his friend.

"And you'll get Deanna out of this mess and into that church," Maisy finished with a the-deal-is-sealed nod.

"Dragging feet win no race, Shepard," Esther reminded him, every bit the schoolmarm challenging her student. "And I fully anticipate this cowboy will win this one. So off with you."

Ty extended his hand. "Give 'em thunder."

"Thunder my foot," Maisy derided. "Give 'em—"

"Come along, Maisy," Esther cut in, herding the outspoken waitress like one of her prodigal students back toward the church. "Our prayers are with you, Shepard," she called over her shoulder.

"Me and the boys are coming out this fall to get that stallion. Mark it down," Tyler promised before heading back to the relay field.

Of the same loaf. Warmed by the support of his friends, Shep picked up his pace, thanking God for every slice and crumb.

The Jeep was intact, save a sprung handle on the back window where Majors had broken in. Shep slipped into the driver's seat with renewed determination. How could he fail, when he had the loaf and the Baker behind him? As he inserted the key Deanna left on the table in the community hall, an electronic beep sounded from under his seat. Raising a puzzled brow, Shep reached for the cell phone he kept there.

The message-waiting feature blinked on its face. Shep acti-
vated the caller ID, tensing as he recognized the number of Will
Addison's private line in D.C.

Of the same loaf. Esther's gentle reminder served as a balm.
After initializing the hands free option, he pushed recall.
Electronic fingers amplified by the Jeep speakers dialed a snappy,
if unmelodic, tune above the roar of the vehicle's reversing engine.

Lord, he prayed when the line started ringing, *I'm counting on
this being the icing on the loaf.*

The call was answered on the second ring. "Addison here."

"Shep back at you, Will," he replied crisply, bracing himself.
"What have you got for me?

Deanna brooded in silence on the ride back to Hopewell, while
Jon Kessler grilled C. R. on the extent of her involvement. C. R.
was doing the right thing, but for the wrong reason. The more he
cooperated with the authorities, the more consideration he'd
receive when charged. Singing like a songbird was how the crime
shows characterized his confession, but it was hardly music to her
ears. The more he said, the angrier she became—angry at herself
for being so gullible, angry at C. R. for his total lack of contrition,
and angry at Shep because…just because. She needed time to sort
out the information being revealed bit by bit.

"You have to admit, Deanna, you were the perfect choice." C.
R. announced, adding insult to injury. "Ambitious, which meant
you'd grab at the chance to manage your own team, with a nonexistent social life, which made you susceptible to charm from
unexpected quarters, like the boardroom. New to the job, which
made you the perfect patsy. People in-house would have questioned the deposits. Of course the fact that you're a looker made
it more pleasant for me."

Jon looked at the man in disbelief. "I don't think there's enough
room in here for your stupidity, much less your ego, Majors."

"He's right though." Deanna's flat-line admission capped a tumult of emotions, gnawing at her insides and clawing to be released. "I was an easy mark."

"But it was fun while it lasted, doll. That's why I'm clearing you."

"Ignore the jerk." Jon placed a restraining grip on her arm. "You can get even on the witness stand."

"That's all well and good, Majors," Agent Voorhees spoke up from the driver's seat, "but if she's so innocent, why did you tail her? She hide the money or what?"

"You figure it out, Mr. DEA man…or wait till my attorney cuts a deal with the prosecution."

How could she have ever fallen for such a slimeball? Uncertain if she was going to blow up with rage or implode with anguish, Deanna rested her head against the window as the car turned into the long dirt lane leading up to Hopewell. *Hopewell.* Two ramshackle rows of buildings of what used to be…or what could have been.

Either way they were in ruins.

As they pulled up at the shiny travel trailer, the third geologist, or rather agent, met them. "I've called for a chopper to transport the suspects to Great Falls. Should be here in an hour or so."

"What's wrong with the car?" Voorhees asked.

"It's all over the news that Majors' body was not found in the car, so headquarters didn't want to take any chances. Dusault will have his men all over this."

"Blasted reporters!" Voorhees swore under his breath. "Okay. Let's pack up this show." He turned to Jon as he shifted into gear again. "We'll take the suspects to the house. More room to wait there."

"Who is Dusault?" Deanna asked Jon. She hadn't heard that name before.

"He's the kingpin of the syndicate Majors double-crossed."

"You two help us nail him, and we'll go easy on you."

At least the younger agent acknowledged she could be innocent. In Voorhees's eyes, she was guilty until proven innocent.

"Don't judge me guilty until you hear me out." But how could she believe what Shep had to say? Granted, she'd told a few lies herself, but—

"Of course we'll have to keep you in protective custody until the trial," Voorhees explained. "Witnesses against people like Dusault have a way of disappearing or coming to a suspicious end before they make it to the court."

Protective custody? The words banished one quandary for another. "Do you mean jail?"

"I hope not," C. R. declared. "That's a death sentence, doll."

She pulled her arm from Jon's restraining hand and raised her purse in threat. "Call me doll one more time and it'll take more than this agent to keep me from busting your upper lip."

"Okay, I get it." C. R. threw up his cuffed hands in front of his face. "I never saw this side of you. Must be PMS or something."

Exactly what happened next was unclear. Someone who looked and sounded like her leaped across the car and Agent Kessler, digging for blood, a pound of flesh, a handful of hair, it didn't matter, just so it came from C. R. Majors. Like a cat gone wild, her evil twin called C. R. words that brought the taste of Ivory soap to her mouth. Then the white-hot fury of arms and feet dissolved into the bright light of the western sun as Deanna was hauled outside. The thunder in her ears gave way to heavy breathing and a fierce barking.

"What in tarnation is goin' on?" Ticker Deerfield scrambled over the corral fence and ran after Smoky toward the car Deanna was pinned to, her cheek crushed on the warm hood.

Before she could even guess, the man holding her down cried out in pain and started to thrash about in a bizarre dance. "Call off the dog or I'll shoot him," Voorhees shouted, digging in his coat for his gun and hopping about on one leg while trying to shake Smoky's snarling grip off his ankle.

Ticker had to pry the dog's mouth apart with his fingers before Smoky would give up the agent's leg. Voorhees pulled down his sock to examine the damage. "I ought to—"

Seeing the man reach inside his jacket, Deanna stepped in front of the still growling mongrel. "It's my fault, not his. Smoky thought you were hurting me. It's only a scratch—"

The agent produced a handkerchief and smirked. "Do you mind?"

"Does Shep know about all this?" Ticker asked, sparing her from blabbering some sort of reply.

"The marshal's cooperated all along," Voorhees said, pulling his sock up over the makeshift pad, "in detaining and apprehending the suspects. He should be right behind us."

"Ex-marshal, you mean," Ticker corrected. "You of all folks ought to know Shep ain't been in the service since you caused him to take a hit in the knee."

"Comes with the job, Pop." Voorhees flexed his foot. Determining it was okay, he stood up.

Shep's old war wound, Deanna realized. It also explained his buddies in the service. It wasn't the armed services, as she'd assumed; it was law enforcement. Of all the ranches in Montana, she'd picked a ghost town owned by an ex-U.S. Marshal. It was almost laughable…almost.

"I'll take the suspects into the house," Jon spoke up from the other side of the car. To Deanna's horror, a trickle of blood ran down from C. R.'s nose. Heavenly Father, had she done that?

"I'm so sorry," she gasped. "I…I don't know what happened, I just…"

"Looks to me like you went Western on 'em and gave 'em what for." The admiration in Ticker's observation did little to assuage Deanna's horror. Despite college and the finishing school she'd attended at nights, she behaved like Tony Triglia, the neighborhood bad boy.

"He deserved it," Jon assured her, hauling C. R. upright.

"She broke my nose!" the latter whined through the two fingers he clamped on it.

Deanna felt ill. *Lord, I don't know what happened. I just...*

The younger agent gave C. R. a shove toward the house. "How do you know it wasn't me? There was a lot going on at the time." He winked at Deanna. "Have you got any towels inside?"

At least she had one champion. No, two. Still... "Look," she said to C. R., "for what it's worth, if I did do it—" Like Jon Kessler had the nails to scratch C. R.'s face. "—I'm sorry. Come on in and I'll get you some ice."

Numb from her emotional overload, Deanna led the way.

"I'll put the dog up," she heard Ticker volunteer behind her. "Looks like we got enough trouble."

"Has that dog had his shots?"

Deanna sighed as she climbed the step to the porch. No better than she'd acted, maybe *she* was the one he ought to be asking about.

Once Jon was finished cleaning C. R. up, as best he could, his nose was packed in ice, and Deanna left them. Retrieving her silk blouse and slacks, thoughtfully taken to the cleaners by her host, she hurried to take a shower before the helicopter arrived. With luck, she might slip and break her neck, putting an end to this misery once and for all.

As she hung the garments on the back of the door, Deanna pulled off the cleaning tag, her thoughts going back to the man who'd paid for it. Had he taken her to the cleaners too? Even as the thought processed, another rebelled against it. Or could he have been really like her—innocent, in the wrong place at the wrong time, trapped by circumstances beyond her control? Ticker had confirmed, Shep was an ex-marshal.

Yet, he'd not trusted her enough to accept her on her word, her mind seesawed down. He'd called to check on her story the next day. On the upswing, she didn't trust him enough to tell him the whole truth. But—down again—she hadn't preached trust to him or toyed with his affections to win it. Deanna's feelings had been real. She'd done it all over again, fallen head over heels on the heel of her first betrayal. And this time, for some reason, it hurt worse.

Sheesh, Pavlov's dogs were smarter! Ripping the plastic off, Deanna wadded it in a ball and slam-dunked it into the waste-basket. She knew the reason. With C. R. she'd hoped he was real and took the risk, knowing she'd have the executive position with or without the romance. The revelation somehow took the edge off her initial betrayal. C. R. was a weasel who'd used her, but she wasn't exactly the lily-white innocent she'd worked herself up to be. He'd crossed the line of law and morality for his ambition. Her ambition led her to take a calculated risk and she'd lost.

But there'd been no calculation with Shep. It just happened. He was the real McCoy she'd hoped C. R. was—a straight shooter, gallant, shy but not too much so, and a good man. His friends were testimony to that. He might have fooled her, but he couldn't fool an entire town. And he hadn't faked that inner glow she'd seen when he sang in the church. No one could fake what Deanna saw.

God, how can I separate this hurt from the ruins of my hope when I can't even think straight?

Emotion collided with reason, feelings with knowledge. Yet above the confused clamor, there was one voice that, like Shep's plea, would not be lost in the fray.

"I will never leave you, nor forsake you."

Deanna seized at it like a lifeline. "Then hold me, Lord. Help me to see what is right." She squeezed her temples with her palms, relieving the throb of the pulse there. "Give me strength and courage to do what You'd have me do. You alone are the Rock that will not shift beneath my feet. You are all that I have left."

"God is enough." Shep's reassuring words came back to her, words of truth.

"Amen."

Taking a fortifying breath, Deanna turned on the shower to give the hot water time to reach it from the other side of the house. If she was going to step out on the water, she'd at least be warm. A mischievous giggle erupted from out of nowhere, followed by immediate contrition. *God, I hope You're at least smiling up there. Gram said You gave me my sense of humor.*

Deanna felt as though that silly, spontaneous pop of amusement had relieved a considerable weight from her chest. As she shed her soiled clothes, she imagined them her fears and doubts. What would be would be, she decided, testing the water. It was just right. God *was* enough.

Twenty-nine

The Jeep radio crackled with the hourly news brief, confirming what Will Addison told Shep.

"After an extensive manhunt involving federal and state law enforcement agencies, the fugitive was apprehended with his female accomplice earlier today at a social event in Buffalo Butte. Majors and Manetti face charges for embezzlement of 3 million dollars from a Great Falls business called Amtron Enterprises. An additional count of alleged money laundering by the firm is pending further investigation. More on this story as it develops." The announcer shifted to a brighter note. "And now, in the sports arena—"

Shep turned the button, silencing the speakers. Gripping the wheel as though it were Jay Voorhees's throat, he turned into Hopewell. Shep knew exactly what the man was up to. Voorhees called in the arrest, counting on Dusault's henchmen being on their way to Buffalo Butte the instant the news hit the airwaves, which had to have been a little over an hour ago. Addison said that wiretaps picked up the informant's call to Dusault, but the tech team couldn't trace it to the source before the caller disconnected.

So Voorhees was playing with a wild card. The informant could be on the agency's end or right here at Hopewell—which was why Shep came prepared to take no chances. Dusault was a new player to Shep, but by all accounts, he was a deadly one.

Leaving a trail of dust in his wake, Shep accelerated past the travel trailer when he spied Ticker rushing out of his home in the alley, waving like a wild man. The Jeep skidding to a stop, Shep leaned across the seat and opened the passenger door. Ticker poked his head in, breathless.

"Boy, all kinds of tarnation and surprise is broke loose since you left—"

"I know," Shep cut him off. "Just listen. There's no time for questions."

"But—"

"Saddle up the horses, take your guns and radio, and suit up. I'll meet you in the barn."

"About the barn, that's what—"

"Tick! We don't have much time. I need to get Deanna out of here and quick."

It had taken some doing, but Addison secured clearance for Shep to take Deanna and—if Voorhees was smart enough to cooperate—C. R. Majors up to the cabin in the high country. If not, let the man risk losing his witness and possibly his life. As for Deanna, she was going with him, like it or not.

"Suit up?" His partner repeated Shep's instructions as if he hadn't heard right.

"We're dealing with gun carrying critters this time."

Snapping to, Tick nodded and backed away.

Pulling off as Tick gave the door a sling, Shep raced straight down the narrow dirt street and pulled up to the house.

While he got a head start with Deanna, Tick would carry Majors and the agents over to the Double M for extra horses. They'd rendezvous at the cabin below the tree line and hole up until the authorities came up with a plan Dusault *wasn't* privy to.

"Hey, buddy, where's the fire?" Jay called from the porch as Shep vaulted out of the vehicle before the engine stopped.

"I'm taking Deanna out of here before she winds up another victim of your ambition."

"I'll be—"

Shep spun on his heel and grabbed the agent by the jacket. "Come with us or stay and shoot it out. Don't like it, call your supervisor. My friends in high places have already cleared it."

Letting Voorhees go as if he'd dirtied his hands, Shep ducked inside, the agent following him.

Kessler and Majors sat in the living area watching the news. Kessler jumped to his feet. "Something wrong?"

"You mean aside from you guys airing my death warrant on the evening news?" Majors sneered. "Like I'm going to live to testify."

Shep took up short. "What the devil happened to you?" C. R.'s face looked as if the barn cat had used it as a scratching post. Not that Shep really gave a hoot. "Never mind," he said, leaving Majors sheepish and fumbling for words. All he cared about was Deanna. She was the only one who mattered.

Deanna struggled with the delicate buttons of her silk blouse as Shep barged into the room like a steamroller. Her startled shriek blended with the bang of bedroom door against the wall.

"What…have you ever heard of knocking?" she sputtered, the same heat that flushed her face tripped her tongue, but her fingers were frozen on the last button.

"Hurry up and get dressed."

"Why? What are you doing—" she exclaimed as Shep began shoving the hem of her blouse into her waistband when she didn't move fast enough to suit him. "Is the chopper here?"

He stopped abruptly. "What chopper?"

"There's a chopper on its way to pick us up, Jones," Voorhees said from the open doorway, "so we don't need your Lone Ranger act."

"There's no chopper coming for you, none with clearance from Great Falls anyway." At Voorhees skeptical expression, Shep challenged him. "Call and see for yourself. I just finished talking to the agency less than five minutes ago."

"You can bet on it, buddy." Voorhees dug in his jacket for a cell phone.

"Shoes."

Shoes? Before Deanna realized Shep was speaking to her, he put his shoulder into her side and hoisted her foot like she'd seen him do to clean Patch's hooves. "Hey—" She hopped sideways as he shoved one of her slippers on. Frantic, she tried to hold up the trousers she'd yet to fasten with one hand and catch herself on the bed with the other. "I'm not a horse."

The bed slid under the weight of her impact as Shep dropped to his knees and reached for the slipper's mate.

"Don't I know it," he grumbled. "Horses are a lot easier to deal with."

"What is the matter with you?" Deanna jumped to her feet and hauled up the zipper of her trousers, only to have it snag on the tail of her blouse. "Jiminy blue Christmas!"

"Here." Shep stepped up to help, but she dodged the maniac. "I can dress myself, thank you very much."

"Jon, go get that tech head Gretsky and find out where in static land he got his information," Voorhees shouted from the kitchen. "This is one messed up…"

Deanna winced at the string of expletives the agent in charge—or rather, out of charge—used to describe the infectious mania that had assailed them. At the slam of the porch door, Shep hastened to the window to watch Jon Kessler leave.

God, You have just gotten me calmed down and everyone else is going nuts.

The silk material of her blouse wouldn't budge from her zipper, no matter how she tugged on it. Deanna rolled her eyes toward the ceiling. "What difference does it make if we go to jail in a chopper or a car?"

"Because bad guys are coming in the chopper and they can take out the car." Shep spun away from the window. "Let me get that."

Her eyes widened as he brandished a knife from his boot big enough to skin Old Bull with one fell slice. "Oh no you don't." Turning her back to him, she wrestled with the zipper.

Shep grabbed her arm. "Just hold still—"

"This blouse sells for ninety bucks at Saks," she grunted, "not that I paid that much, but—"

"I don't care if it cost nine hundred dollars, just—"

"Put that knife away or your head's gonna be up there with Old Bull's!" Deanna stomped her foot, glaring at the man glaring back at her in what had to be the most ridiculous standoff in the history of time.

"I think you would." The electronic tick of the Neanderthal radio alarm on the nightstand marked off the passing seconds as he considered his next move in silence. *One, two, three, four…*

Unable to stand it any longer, Deanna confessed in a tiny whisper. "You're scaring me, Shep…and I was just beginning to see your side of things."

The half-crazed look on his face gave way to surprise. "You were?"

She nodded.

"What changed your mind?"

"I decided to go with what I believed instead of how I felt." A sheepish smile licked at one corner of her mouth. "I realized that I was like the pot calling the kettle black. If I want God to forgive me for the lies I told, I'd better forgive you."

He answered with a corresponding twitch that accented a charming dimple she'd not noticed before. "I love you, Slick—"

She was in his arms, her eager lips meeting his.

"Me, too—" she groaned, burying her fingers in the thick of his hair. Apology sounded with every beat of her heart only to be echoed by his. Joining as one in a love song that traveled from pulse point to pulse point, they spread the word of surrender. It felt as though her senses waved white flags of passion, while fireworks popped in her ear…or was it firework?

Whatever it was, Shep jerked away from Deanna at the sound. Before she could think, he dragged her to the floor. "Stay down!"

"You bet," she managed, alarm snaking its way up her spine as he crawled to the front window. "Is it the bad guys already?"

Waving her to be quiet, Shep ventured a cautious peek over the ledge. He winced as two more pops sounded. "Aw, no—"

Without thinking, Deanna looked in time to see Jon Kessler stumble away from the tech trailer as though drunk. He reached behind him with awkward gestures as though he had an itch he couldn't quite reach when, knees buckling, he went down on his face.

"Omigosh—" Belated, Deanna covered her mouth.

"Stay down," Shep said, ducking her head below the window level. "And listen close. Ticker is saddling the horses." He paused as if thinking his plan through. "He'll take you to the safety of Double M and—"

"On a horse? Why don't you just shoot me?"

"I thought you were getting comfortable with Molly and Patch."

"Hey, I'm comfortable with a lot of things," she told him, "but that doesn't mean I'm going to hop up on their backs and hi-ho-Silver away."

"Everyone okay in there?" Voorhees called out from the kitchen.

"Secure." Shep's reply was mechanical, but his mind spun wheels behind the gaze he fixed on Deanna. It didn't take a genius to see that he was trying to figure out what to do with her.

"And I'm not leaving you," she declared. Anticipating objection, she stood defiant as a black gum tree in a lightning storm. "I got you into this mess."

"All right then. There's no time for me to argue, so you do exactly as I say, got it?"

"Got it."

"Crawl to the bathroom and stay there. It's the safest place."

"What are you—"

"Just move it," he said, shoving her forward with his shoulder. "I have a plan."

With Shep right behind her, Deanna met Jay Voorhees dragging C. R. into the central hall.

"Well, now you know who your friends are, *buddy.*"

Voorhees ignored Shep's dour observation. Phone in hand, he punched out a number by memory and touch, because there certainly wasn't any light.

"I have plenty of firepower in the gun cabinet, and Ticker's armed and got enough sense to lay low. I think we can take—"

The agent swore, throwing the phone down. "Either I have the worst luck in history and my battery's acting up, or that murderous tech wit out there has done something. I can't get through for backup."

"Think you and I can take him?"

"If we can flush him out of the trailer. Otherwise, all he has to do is—"

"What about Jon?" Deanna interrupted.

"Hey, best worry about us," C. R. reminded her. "Your golden boy's toast."

Voorhees gave the self-serving prisoner a sling into the bathroom. "Keep it up, Majors, and I'll turn the girl loose on you again."

Shame burning her face, Deanna looked away from the startled glance Shep cast her way.

"You're not going to take these cuffs off?" C. R. exclaimed as Voorhees pushed him into the bathroom.

"Why," the agent derided, "so you can cover your eyes?"

"I know how to use a gun. It's my life on the line here. Besides, someone needs to protect the girl."

"Oh, puh-leez," Deanna said, shoving her ex's face back into the room.

"We can slip out the back and circle round from both sides," Shep said to Voorhees, all business. "Or, we can make a run for it in the Jeep and leave the son-of-a-gun and his buddies for another time."

Voorhees shook his head. "No, I think between us, we can take them in. There can't be more than four in the chopper."

Shep thought a moment, his face darkening with each passing second. "Not worth the risk. You cover me while I—"

A shot rang out, simultaneous with a thunderous pop. Three more successive sets sounded as Shep hurried, hunkered down, to the kitchen window and peered out. Exhaling heavily, he dropped and leaned against the front of the sink cabinet.

"Who'd have thought that computer-addicted twerp was a marksman?" he said to no one in particular, before rallying. "Okay, the Jeep and sedan are out of commission. That leaves Ticker's truck and the horses." He scratched his chin, studying the floor as if looking for directions.

"Jay, if you can get the truck and drive behind the buildings, I'll cover you while you cross the open land, then I'll come up behind the house for Deanna and Majors."

"I'm not leaving," Voorhees said.

"Let him stay if he wants to play Wyatt Earp," C. R. told Shep, "I vote for your—"

"You're not going anywhere, punk."

"We don't have time to waste arguing, Voorhees." The quiet thunder in Shep's voice forecasted a fierce impending storm. Grim as the gathering darkness on his face, he dismissed the stubborn agent and motioned to Deanna.

"You can ride with me on Patch. Ticker can take Molly. As for you," he said over his shoulder to Voorhees, "help yourself to my gun cabinet, but I'd recommend you give one to Majors. You're going to need every gun you can get."

Shep ushered Deanna toward the back window. This déjà vu from her childhood cowboy games had come to life, except the bullets were real and she wasn't a deadeye shot, much less bullet-proof. Even the ghost town was the genuine article.

I was just a kid, God. I promise I'll be careful with what I wish for from now on. Remember, I also played with dolls.

Shep kicked out the screen panel, breaking the painted seal on the outside, and turned to help Deanna through. "We're going out here and around to the livery," he said, grim as their situation. "When I say go, you—"

"Hold it!" Jay seconded his command for silence with a cutting motion. Shep looked at the ceiling, intent on listening.

All Deanna could hear was the ka-thump, ka-thump of alarm echoing in her ears…and a faint belly growl. Bemused, she pressed against her abdomen, but the steadily churning rumbles had come from the outside, not from within, prompting her own stomach to roll in sympathy.

Standing in the doorway, head cocked smugly, the senior agent mimicked Shep's drawl. "Well, cowboy, can your horses out-run a chopper?"

Thirty

Shep grabbed Deanna, clasping her face between his hands. "Crawl, and I mean *crawl* into the kitchen and call in a May Day."

Call? Amid the mental picture Shep's order conjured of her yelling out the kitchen window, the word clicked. "The radio!"

"Someone's always listening." He sealed his assurance with a quick, hard kiss. "Then—"

"I know, *crawl* into the bathroom with Wimpy."

"And take this." He folded a small pistol in her hand. "Slide this back…" he instructed, moving the tiny button from the front of its small slot to the back, "…and the safety is off. Just aim and pull the trigger."

Deanna looked at the cold, lethal steel in her hand. Real steel. The only guns she'd ever handled were toys or those in an arcade. She fought the weak shrivel of her stomach with a stab at humor. "And to think—" hands trembling, she put the safety back on before she fired the gun accidentally—"I waited all my life for this."

"I sent Ticker to the house, so make sure you see who you're shooting at."

"Tell him to identify himself before he opens the bathroom door."

Shep gave her one more quick kiss and winked. "I'm glad you're on my side, Slick. Now go."

A warm flush staggering the fear mounting its attack upon

her spine, Deanna called after him, "Never do that to a woman with a loaded gun."

While Shep and Voorhees gathered all the firepower they could carry, she scrambled on her knees to the radio desk, reinforced by Shep's confidence in her. She could do this. God promised He'd never leave nor forsake her. If necessary, He'd give her the nerve to shoot someone—or at least scare the daylights out of him.

Deanna picked up the mike and pushed the button down like a professional. "May Day, May Day. This is an emergency. Nine-one-one. Repeat, Nine-one-one, is anyone out there? Hello?"

"Let up the button," Shep snapped from the other room.

She forgot! Deanna let up the button, as if it were on fire. From the back, she heard the shuffle of the two men slipping through the back window while she waited for a response.

"This is Kilo-seven-echo-charlie-foxtrot," the radio crackled, "what's the emergency, missy?"

Deanna knew that voice. "Charlie, is that you?"

"…Shep's city gal?"

Relief flooded through her as she machine-gunned the mike with her explanation of their predicament. "Yes, and there is a gunman, and one man is shot, and Shep and the government agent are trying to get him before more bad guys come in a helicopter to kill us all…and I can hear the chopper now."

After a shocked silence, Charlie's uncertain reply crackled over the airwaves. "Come again?"

The roar of the approaching helicopter forced Deanna to shout. She repeated the situation, slower this time.

Charlie said something about switching channels, but the racket of the helicopter coming down behind the shiny travel trailer drowned it out. The rotating blades kicked up a dust storm all around the far edge of the town.

"I'm a dead man," C. R. said from the cover of the hall. Morose was an understatement for his expression. "For what it's worth, I'm sorry for dragging you into all this, but someone caught on to what I was doing. I was being followed."

"So you got me to do your dirty work?" Deanna threw up her hands in exasperation. Then, remembering Shep's order, dropped on all fours. "Okay, I understand that part, but why follow me? What have I got that was worth the risk of getting caught for?"

"The key to the safety deposit box where I hid the money."

"What, are you blind? There is no key in my purse. I never saw a key in it." Deanna crawled to the kitchen table and retrieved the handbag from where she'd abandoned it earlier. Upending it, she opened the clasp. The contents scattered on the floor, the same ones that had been in there earlier. "See?" she said, shaking it. "No key."

"It's in your lipstick."

Stunned, Deanna grabbed the lipstick and pulled off the case lid. "You stuck a key in my twenty-five-dollar all natural La Belle Monde?" With a grudging glare at him, she dug the key out with her fingernails.

"I knew I was being followed, so I put it in there at the wedding reception."

Deanna made a mental note never to leave her bag in someone else's care again. At last, she got a grasp on the head of the key and drew it out, along with a creamy chunk of La Belle Monde. So this was what the whole shebang was over; she wiped it clean with a dishtowel.

"Maybe if we give this to these bozos—no pun intended," she apologized, "they'll leave us alone."

"That's a great idea," he mocked her with his fake enthusiasm. "Except for one thing…they'll leave us dead."

Gunshots punctuated C. R.'s prediction. Torn between wanting to look and keeping low, Deanna opted for the latter. Shoving the key in her pocket, she scurried across the kitchen floor on her knees. Just as she reached the bathroom door, a horrendous explosion shook the entire house, rattling the glass in the windows.

"Jiminy Blue Christmas, what was that?" She scooted into the small room next to C. R.

"That was your cowboy and his buddy making certain our assassins don't escape by air."

Deanna felt the blood drain from her face. "The chopper?"

At his nod, she leaned back against the wall, knocking down a pair of stranded pantyhose she'd left behind after her shower. Did that mean that Shep and Agent Voorhees stood a chance?

"Let's just hope Dusault's men were still in it."

The rapid fire of an automatic weapon rent the still aftermath, and with it, Deanna's brief reprieve. *God stay with Shep. Help him—*

Two single shots prompted what seemed like fifty times as many in rat-a-tat succession. The uneven trade of gunfire didn't bode well. With that many bullets to Shep's one...

"We've got to do something." Frantic, Deanna reached for the gun Shep had given her, digging first in one trouser pocket, then the other. In all the excitement, she'd left the gun in the kitchen, next to the radio.

"Oh yeah," C. R. said as she frantically patted her trouser pockets. "We'll be a big help."

Ignoring his sarcasm, Deanna started after the gun when something fell in the bedroom, sending her into reverse. *Ticker?* She froze, afraid to call out his name.

"Get in the tub and get down."

Having little alternative to offer against Deanna's urgent order, C. R. stepped into the enclosure. With a swish of vinyl, she closed the curtain and turned on the shower. Ignoring his startled oath, she grabbed the lid off the toilet tank.

There was no time to read the inspiration of the day from the book on the tank. She stepped on the devotional, which had fallen on the floor along with a box of tissues, and backed against the closed door. Ear pressed against it, she tried to determine above the patter of the shower where the intruder was, for if it had been Ticker, he'd have said something by now.

God, this worked before. Please let it work again if it's not Shep's friend.

The knob rattled, drawing her attention to the pantyhose half in and half out the door she'd hidden behind. At gentle pressure from the other side, the door opened a crack. The hose disappeared.

Deanna prayed the intruder would think someone was in the shower rather than behind the door…and that the sound of the running water would muffle her fear-strangled breath. Her forearms ached with the burden of the heavy porcelain, but she dared not give in to its weight. She needed to—

The door eased open enough for the black muzzle of a gun to show itself. Suspended with caution, it stilled Deanna's heart as well. Should she slam the door on the weapon or—

The door opened a little more. She could see the man's hands on the gun now, hear the slide of his elbow on the other side as he ventured in farther. The profile of his face followed—a beaklike nose protruding over a receding chin sent Deanna into action. She swung the lid at it for all she was worth, knocking a wild spray of bullets from the gun and into the shower curtain and ceiling.

C. R.! Her scream wedged in her throat. An eternity passed and still it would not release. The toilet lid clanged against the doorjamb, crashing to the floor. The gun lay next to a foot sporting good leather hiking shoes, both still. Suddenly, the shower curtain whipped to one side and her scream found its voice.

A dripping wet C. R. reached up from the floor of the bathtub to turn off the spray. "Way to go, doll." The grin he gave Deanna had once made her heart do a cartwheel. Now, numb with shock, it felt like her feet were nailed in place. She was still alive. C. R., his wet wavy hair parted down the middle by the shower, was still alive…and he had the thug's gun.

"Now get the cuff keys off the jerk's belt and help me with the cuffs."

"He's a policeman?" It couldn't be, but who else would carry handcuff keys around?

"No, he's a thug, Deanna." Shoving the door open with the gun barrel, C. R. exposed the sprawled intruder to Deanna. "Now get the keys from his belt. Maybe they'll fit these."

"Which belt?" Except in the movies, Deanna had never seen such a getup. An ammunition belt was strung across the man's sweatshirt and all manner of martial arts-looking stuff was attached to one around the waist of his jersey pants. He looked like a cross between a terrorist and jogger. But it was his face that gave her pause, not to mention a queasy feeling in her throat just beyond swallowing. It was a mess, just like Tyler McCain's had been. No, it was worse. His nose looked like it had been pinned on crooked.

"Get the blasted keys!"

Reluctant, Deanna started to kneel beside the unconscious man—*God, please just let him be in la-la land*—when she came to herself. "Wait a minute," she said, straightening, hands on hips. "How dare you point that thing at me and boss me around. I just saved your lily-livered, wet, behonkus."

"Look, doll, you and I have a chance of going out the back and getting away…with the money."

"You and me…*with the money?*" She heard right, but she still couldn't believe the nerve of this guy. "So," she said, feigning interest as she broke away the plastic band holding the keys to the cuffs, "how do I know you won't double-cross me, too?"

"Because I owe you my *behonkus*. I owe ulcers and prospective time in jail to Dusault."

Deanna straightened in disbelief. His brains were in his behonkus if he thought she'd fall for his line again. "All I want is out of this and away from you."

And five pounds of flesh, she fumed behind a façade of weary resignation. Or something that would hurt even more. Stepping over the prone hoodlum, she removed the safety deposit box key from her pocket and dangled it along with the cuff keys before her ex's face.

"Are you saying these are the keys to *our* future?"

"Three million dollars worth of future, if we hurry up and get out of here before either side wins."

The man had more gall than a Thanksgiving turkey and half the wit. "All right, get over here by the sink so I can see what I'm doing. You can put the gun on the tub for a minute—on your side, where you can reach it real quick if you need to," she said, hastening to assuage the guarded look that grazed his face.

Turning her back to him, she walked to the sink and waited for the man to put the gun on the ledge. As he leaned down, Deanna kicked him soundly in the hip and dropped to the floor as C. R. sprawled sideways into the bathtub. The gun spat once before he let it go, screaming. Moving quickly, she dropped the keys in the toilet and lunged for the gun. Snagging it by the butt, she leaped out of his reach and flushed the toilet.

Something like "Have you lost your mind?" came out between C. R.'s profanities and whines of pain.

"No, *that's* what I think of *our* future," Deanna announced in breathless triumph. "You lost your mind when you thought I'd run off with you for a measly 3 mil—or any amount, for that matter."

"You're nuts, la—" he broke off, staring through the open door.

Deanna followed his stricken look. In the dim light of the central hall stood a man about Shep's height but older. Impeccably attired in a tailored silk weave suit, he had the look of a gentleman of means. He also held a gun like the one in her hands.

"Well, Majors," he said, eyes cold as the dagger of ice impaling Deanna's chest. "Aren't you going to introduce me to your lady friend?"

"Am…am I glad to see you," C. R. stammered. He looked as

if he meant the opposite. "This is the woman who's been black-mailing me."

The absurdity of his statement prodded Deanna's fixation away from the gun aimed at her. "What?" Agape, she glanced at the iceman and threw up her shoulders. "He must have hit his head real hard."

"It's true, Victor, I swear. She found out what I was doing for you and insisted on a cut to keep her mouth shut. I tagged her all the way here to get it back."

"Do I look like an idiot?" Deanna asked the stranger. "If I had 3 million dollars, would I escape to Buffalo Butte, Montana?"

Victor smiled at her, but she'd seen corpses at funerals look warmer. His dark hair was even frosted at the temples. On some men, it was distinguished. On this guy, it was creepy. All he needed was a cape and fangs.

"Put the gun down, Miss Manetti. Thanks to your companions, I have no transportation and only two colleagues left. And from what I see here—" he gave C. R. a disdainful look—"I need you on my side."

Thirty-one

J ay Voorhees lay bleeding and exhausted in the tall pasture grass, just ten yards from the the old building that had been converted into a corncrib. "I can't do it, buddy."

Buddy. Shep assessed the situation from the building, his mouth a grim, bloodless line. The air was laden with the smell of burning fuel, electronics, and sage and mesquite that drifted north from the rubble of the helicopter the wounded man had destroyed It assailed Shep's nostrils with every breath as he wrestled with his conscience—risk getting shot himself to help Voorhees to safety or let the man lie in the bed of his own making.

So unnecessary, he fumed in anger and frustration. Taking out the chopper and its pilot had not been a priority. With Majors' testimony, the government had all they needed to extradite and charge Victor Dusault for his criminal acts. All Shep, Tick, and Voorhees had to do was protect Majors and Deanna until the authorities Charlie contacted arrived.

A burst of bullets whizzed through the tall winter-burned grass, blindly searching out the fallen agent for revenge. Shep fired a few rounds around the corner to stave them off. Four gunmen scattered when the chopper had touched down. Under the persuasion of Ticker's and Shep's rifles, the men took up positions on the east side of town, now at a disadvantage in the blinding light of the sinking sun.

"Leave me, Jones. Protect Majors and the girl," the agent called out.

That was mighty noble since it was the only alternative Voorhees's spectacular heroics left them. Now, with the assassins' transportation cut off, they became cornered animals, far more dangerous than before. And Shep was one man down.

The man never learned. Rage clamored, leave the jerk and back Ticker up, keeping the thugs away from the house. Logic dictated it, but conscience argued louder.

Shep watched as Voorhees struggled to pull off his belt and make a tourniquet around his leg. He deserved to lie there...but it wasn't up to Shep to judge and sentence. Deep down, he knew that that right belonged to a higher power. Walk away from the least of these and he might as well walk away from God, a quiet voice reminded him. Judge him and be judged likewise. Refuse to forgive and be refused forgiveness. If Shep honestly had forgiven Voorhees, then he'd do the right thing.

All right, Lord, I get the point. Just watch my back for me.

Shep's concession barely formed before a solution to the problem came to him. His back needn't be exposed at all.

"Hang tight, partner!" He should have thought of it before, but he'd been too set on rationalizing what was wrong instead of yielding to what was right. "I'll be right back."

An exchange of gunfire from up the street where Ticker was stationed speeding him even faster, Shep returned a few minutes later with a length of rope. There should be two men standing guard—one on the house and one on the trailer at the other end of the street. Instead, Tick kept an eye on both while Shep played rescue.

"Grab this and loop it around your arm," he shouted to Voorhees working the lariat bigger and bigger. When it felt right, he let it go. The circle of rope shrank as it sailed through a hail of bullets, falling short. With an oath of frustration, Shep reined it in.

The next time he tossed it, it was weighted with a chunk of brick from the crumbling foundation. It landed just short of Voorhees's reach, but the wounded man dragged himself to it.

After fastening it to his arm and then a couple of twists around his wrist, he gave Shep a go-ahead nod. Shep hauled on the rope, hand over hand, dragging Jay to him. The waving grass parted like water, tall enough to hide what they were up to because the shooters were still peppering the spot where the agent had been.

"Looks pretty bad," Shep said as he helped his comrade out of the rope. "Think you can hold the fort down here?" The agent's trousers had been torn, exposing what looked like a slice of raw veins where the bullet had torn into the thigh. The cinch of the belt had slowed the seepage a lot, judging from the blood-soaked material surrounding it.

"Yeah, thanks." Sitting against the building for back support, Voorhees put a fresh clip in the automatic weapon he'd dragged with him.

Shep hitched the tourniquet tighter, in case his suspicion of a nicked artery was right, then rose. "Got enough ammo to make them think twice about sneaking up behind you?" Maybe he should ask if the wounded man thought he could maintain consciousness.

Another exchange erupted, a single shot followed by a hail of bullets. Then came a single shot, a calculated pause, then another.

"I got this end. Now get out of here," Voorhees said.

"Right," Shep said. "Plan B—hold them off until the cavalry comes."

Leaving the wounded agent behind, Shep hurried toward the hotel, pausing only to be certain the coast was clear in each alley between the buildings, before moving to the next. Plan A—taking the horses to the safety of the Double M—fell through when the helicopter touched down.

Even though Voorhees had taken out the chopper, the horses did no good when Shep couldn't get Deanna to them. They'd be like sitting ducks in a shooting gallery between the house and the livery. Using the horses as cover, which Shep would consider only as a last resort to save Deanna, defeated their purpose. Big cover equals big target equals no transportation.

"Coming up," he warned as he entered the back of the hotel lobby and ran around the desk to the wide steps leading to the second floor.

There was nothing to do but wait for the police and make certain Dusault's men didn't cross the open area between the house and the buildings opposite the stables. At least they had plenty of ammunition. It was made for big game hunting, but it would stop a man as quick as Old Bull. Deanna was safe as long as she listened to what he'd told her and stayed put.

"Where's Mr. Secret Agent man?" Ticker asked over his shoulder as Shep emerged from the staircase.

"Watching our rear I hope. He took one in the leg. Pretty nasty."

Another report of gunfire came from the general store across the street. From the direction of the livery a few doors away from the hotel, a horse screamed amid the splintering sound of wood.

"Good thing you closed the barn doors. That mare is raising thunder."

"Heh," Ticker snorted. "She helped me get one of them guntotin' buzzards. He took a notion to make a break to this side o' the street. 'Bout halfway across, she musta kicked off that door you just fixed. Mr. Buzzard flew back to his cover. I blew that fancy bullet spitter right out of his hand."

The older man pointed with no small amount of delight to where the weapon lay in the street. "Winged him in the foot before he reached the store." Lost in triumphant review of the moment, Ticker savored the taste of his ever-present wad of tobacco and swallowed. "What with Charlie sending the police, I didn't see no need of killin' less I had to."

The seasoned hunter had the eye of an eagle and an aim just as sharp. Shep could envision the grizzled old man firing one unhurried shot, shifting his tobacco from one cheek to the other, taking aim, then firing another.

"What about Gretsky, the tech guy in the trailer?"

Ticker chuckled. "Every time that four-eyed cuckoo tried to pop his head out, I put another hole in his clock."

Shep gave in to a wry smile. "Well, try not to enjoy yourself too much."

When being in the Marshals was all new, Shep had been the same way. Problem was, he'd survived long enough to grow weary of it. There was a connection between time served and enjoyment. As time went up, the other went down. Of course, as in Voorhees's case, ambition threw off the curve.

Another sharp crack of splintering wood echoed down the empty street from the livery. Alarm stiffened Shep's spine. Patch would be nervous but fine. Molly probably had shivered out of her saddle by now. But the mare from the Double M was just broken and not at all accustomed to gunfire.

"I'd better go down and see what I can do with that mare before she hurts herself."

Ticker held up his hand, signaling Shep to wait. Cocking the gun as he raised it to his shoulder, he pulled the trigger and grinned. "The cuckoo again."

"Hold your fire!"

Ticker's head pivoted toward the man's voice at the opposite end of the street from the trailer. "What in tarnation…?"

Despite the command, an automatic hiccoughed two rounds, then stopped. The bullets tearing into the age-hardened siding around the balcony door dug out chunks but failed to penetrate it.

"I said hold your fire, idiot!"

Tick glanced at Shep and back to the house at the head of the street. "He ain't talkin' to us."

Shep hardly heard him. His stomach knotted at the sight of Deanna walking onto the porch swinging a white pillowcase from side to side. Behind her was C. R. Majors, but the voice of authority belonged to a man behind them and not yet visible.

But how? Shep leaned his head against the wooden doorframe.

How didn't matter. What he did about it was all that counted. *God, help me.* It was a lame plea, but it was all he could do while fighting to keep his fear for Deanna's life from making jelly of mind and muscle. *For her sake, Lord, not mine. Just show us what to do.*

"Agent Voorhees, I have your witnesses," the gunman shouted into the empty street.

Ticker sucked a breath through his teeth and gave Shep an apologetic look. "Maybe I'm an idjit after all," he fretted. "I swear, I never seen a soul slip by to the house. Maybe when I stopped to reload—"

"You couldn't cover both ends of the street at once." Voorhees's heroics had actually helped the other side.

"Voorhees?"

Keep the man talking. Find out what he wants. "Voorhees is hit bad," Shep shouted down in answer. "Who am I talking to?" Reassess the situation. Four men got out of the chopper before Voorhees played Rambo.

"Victor Dusault. Are you Jones?"

The boss man himself. Jay Voorhees could take some satisfaction in that, if he lived long enough. "I'm Jones," Shep answered, calculating on another track. Voorhees got one. Tick crippled one. "What have you got in mind, Mr. Dusault?"

"Simple. Throw out your guns and step into the street."

That left two, counting Dusault.

"Voorhees can't walk," Shep told him.

"Then you'll have to bring him out. Mr. Jones."

Shep grimaced. With Deanna in the formula, the overwhelming odds were in Dusault's favor now—even if the authorities did come up on them. "Look, Jones," Dusault shouted. "I don't care about you and your ranch hand or the girl. I want Majors, Voorhees, and the pickup."

Deanna was Dusault's passport back to Canada…which meant, shooting her would be a last resort.

Ticker said something in a tobacco-thick mumble.

Shep glanced at his partner, unable to help his annoyance. "What?" Surely Tick wasn't complaining about his truck?

Tick spit the whole wad of his tobacco out. "I said wait till they ask, then tell 'em I was headed for the barn and you don't know what happened to me." The older man slung his other rifle over his shoulder. "I'm hurt...in the barn."

At least one of them could think. If negotiation and compliance didn't work, there would be backup. "I owe you, partner."

"I expect to be best man," Tick told him. "And I ain't wearing no tuxedo neither."

"So what do you say, Jones?" Dusault shouted. "I think I'm being more than fair."

Tick's smirk of distrust reflected Shep's. His throat too tight to express either apology or gratitude, Shep clapped Tick on the shoulder. As Tick slipped into the hall, quiet as a shadow, Shep looked up at the cobweb draped ceiling. *Lord, I feel about as worthless as a colicky calf, but I'm going with what I know. You sent Deanna to me to protect. What work You have begun in me, You will see finished...somehow. My heart and my hands are Yours to command.*

"Okay, Dusault. But I'll need a few minutes to get Voorhees." Armed with faith and determination, he started down the steps.

Deanna stepped off the porch and into the street. Things hadn't changed much in the last hundred or so years. Hopewell was a ghostly witness to the gold fever that infected men with greed and criminal conscience. Now the weather-bleached buildings watched through indifferent dusty glass eyes of their windows, as twenty-first century counterparts faced off in the empty dirt ribbon of street. It felt as if she'd slipped into a "Twilight Zone" version of the O.K. Corral as she waited for Shep, Ticker, and Agent Voorhees to surrender their guns and show themselves—except one of the gunslingers looked like Dracula in Armani and the other a battered clown.

If she weren't so scared that Victor Dusault would notice the weapon she packed in her baggy trousers' pocket, she'd laugh at the picture they must present. Only God gave her the presence of mind to slip the pistol from the radio desk and into her pocket while the conscienceless man beat the exact whereabouts of the money out of C. R. Majors.

Since Dusault had just shot his own man with an indifferent, "He's been incompetent one time too many," it hadn't taken too long to convince C. R. to give up his blackmail story and admit where the money was. Then Dusault had turned his attention to Deanna, as incredulous as C. R. had been when she'd flushed the key down the john.

"So what would you do if some jerk set you up and then had the nerve to ask you to run away with him?" she'd retorted in indignation.

Instead, he laughed. "Hell hath no fury," he quipped to no one in particular. "Which is why," he added for C. R.'s benefit, "I don't let females in my inner circle…can't separate emotion from reason."

Deanna had the urge to shove her gun in the pig's face with a "Reason this," but she couldn't find the blooming safety with her finger. Besides, his gun was bigger. As for C. R., much as she'd like to throttle him for what he'd done to her, she'd cringed when Dusault struck his face with the butt of the pistol. It would take stitches and plastic surgery before he'd charm another unsuspecting heart.

"Mr. Dusault," she asked, "do you have a handkerchief?"

"Why?"

"Because if someone doesn't bandage that gash over C. R.'s eye, he's going to bleed all over you and anyone else in that truck."

Victor reached in his jacket and withdrew a handkerchief. "Women," he said to C. R.

"Hey, I hate to clean up messes. It's a woman thing," Deanna protested. "I read in *Home Digest* how suicidal men will blow their brains out anywhere—the recliner in the living room, wherever. But a woman will take pills and lie down in the bedroom, no mess."

Not the least interested in her chatty dissertation, Dusault looked at his watch.

"But if she does use a gun, she does it in the bathtub where no one will have to clean it up."

"I'll keep that in mind."

Deanna didn't know which was colder, his gaze or his voice.

"You said you weren't interested in me or the others," she reminded him. "We'd probably slow you down anyway."

"Miss Manetti, enough."

"Sorry." Deanna heaved her shoulders. "When I have a gun at my back, I get chatty. Not that I've ever really *had* a gun at my—"

She halted at a slight waver of her captor's attention. Looking ahead, she saw Shep bring out some rifles and a couple of hand-guns, tossing them out into the street at the far end.

"I'm going back to help Voorhees," he called out, before focusing on Deanna. "You okay?"

"For having a gun at my back, sure." If she could somehow get the pistol to Shep—

"Where's Deerfield?" Agent Gretsky called from the door of the trailer.

Like a creepy little mole, it was the first time Deanna had seen him come out since the men arrived. He'd been too busy eaves-dropping and feeding information to his real boss.

"He's not come out?" Shep appeared puzzled. "He left me to cover the house from the livery."

Had Ticker been shot? Catching up with the conversation, Deanna closed her eyes. *Lord, no, please.*

"Mr. Deerfield," Dusault hollered, voice echoing through the channel of the street. "If I so much as hear one shot, Miss Manetti will get the second."

The cold poke of the gun at her back hastened the end of her prayer. *God, I'm holding You to that never leave or forsake me bit. Amen.*

"Toss your weapon out first, then show yourself."

The crime lord received no answer aside from the horses' nervous snorting and pacing, stopping at one end of the stalls as though listening, then pacing back.

As though a heavenly finger had let the button up, a sense of reassurance released her panic-seized breath and pulse.

"I'll get Voorhees, then go look for him," Shep offered. "Ticker's an old man…could have fallen or taken a stray bullet."

"Just bring Voorhees out," Dusault ordered. "My men can look for your pal."

On cue, two gunmen left the cover of the general store, one helping the other. The latter dragged his right foot, which had been wrapped up in a piece of burlap.

"Gretsky!"

Deanna nearly jumped out of her skin at Dusault's outburst at her ear.

"Get the truck. Hotwire it if you have to. This won't take long."

Thirty-two

He was going to kill them all. Deanna could see it in Dusault's eyes as he watched Shep all but carry Jay Voorhees up the street. She had to do something. They wouldn't have given in so easily if not for her. It was her fault Shep and Ticker, wherever he was, were going to die. And all because they'd taken her in and tried to protect her.

"Lean him up against the barn door," Dusault instructed, halting them a few yards away. He jerked his head toward the prisoners. "Gris, Berman, pat them down, then slip around back and see if you can find the old man."

"I can't walk on this foot. I need to wait for the truck," the wounded gunman protested.

Dusault exhaled his impatience. "Berman, there's not enough room on my team for a whiner."

Although she watched Dusault swing the gun toward his henchman and pull the trigger, Deanna yelped in concert with the single shot he fired. The crippled man covered the hole the bullet plowed into his chest with both hands, all the while staring at his employer in disbelief…until he slumped over.

Then the muzzle of the gun, warm with the kill, returned to Deanna's back. "Hold it, Jones."

Shep abandoned his charge in midlaunch. As he straightened, the other man shoved him against the paint-roughened planks of the livery. Next to him, Voorhees witnessed the progression of events, but his impassive stare suggested he wasn't really seeing what happened. Pale as the chipped paint sprinkled in his thinning hair, he was in shock from blood loss—unconscious with his eyes open.

"Look at this pig sticker," the man searching Shep exclaimed as he removed the hunting knife Shep had hidden in his boot. With a sling, he buried it in the stump of an old hitching post a few yards away.

Neither Deanna nor Shep bothered to look. Her eyes locked upon his, she mouthed, *I love you.*

Shep answered, his eyes saying it all. Anger, frustration, and concern tossed on the bottomless sea of his emotions, anchored by steadfast love.

This couldn't be the last time she delved into their dark amber depths. *I have a gun,* she mouthed, praying Dusault was too engrossed in watching the search to pay any heed to an emotional, reasonless woman. She wriggled the hand she wrapped around its rough, nonslip grip in her pocket.

If Shep understood, he gave no indication.

"Clean as a whistle," the gunman announced as he finished searching Jay.

Deanna froze her attempt to manipulate the weapon that kept hanging in her pocket lining. At the moment, she'd shoot off a toe.

"But if you intend to kill him," the man added, "you'd best do it quick." Wiping Jay's blood on his trousers, Gris reached for the handle of the sliding barn door next to the men, but the sound of an anxious horse huffing and pawing on the other side gave him pause to reconsider.

"I wouldn't be surprised if all that shooting didn't cause them to kick down their stalls," Shep drawled, mouth curling without humor. "That's the main reason Tick split from me, to see to the horses before they hurt themselves. They just go berserk."

"Maybe I should try the back, huh?" Gris asked his employer.

From the alley that housed Ticker's trailer, the truck engine gave a faint cough and sputtered out, distracting the man.

Something gave on the gun. The safety? *Dear heavenly Father, help.*

"That could be just what the old man wants you to do." Dusault motioned the man away, reaching around Deanna with the automatic. "But there's more than one way to handle a horse." He aimed the gun at the closed door.

Realizing what Dusault intended, Shep seized Gris by surprise and slung him into the line of fire. His desperate no! was drowned by the thunderous rat-a-tat of the gun beside her. In horror, she saw the spray of bullets cut across the barn door and the two men in its path.

Time moved into slow motion as Shep recoiled, losing his grasp on the crumbling figure of the startled gunman. The bullets that tore into his shirt slammed him against the door behind him. Desperation strengthened Deanna's grip on the pistol. Wrenching it from her pocket, lining and all, she heard its thunderous report and waited for the bullet to plunge somewhere in her flesh, but before it could happen, she was body slammed by Victor Dusault.

As his weight carried her to the ground, her pistol and his coughing automatic took flight like a pair of deadly birds, lighting in the dirt a few feet away. Deanna struck the ground much harder, the wind knocked from her by her captor. Clawing her way out of the ensuing scramble of arms and legs, she crawled without regard away from where C. R. and Dusault grunted and swore at each other, toward the place where Shep lay, still as—

No, she wouldn't think it. *God, it can't be. Please, it can't be.*

"Shep!" His name tore from her throat as she shook him with all her strength. "Shep, darn your picture, I just blew a hole through a hundred dollar pair of pants for you, so you better wake up now, do you hear me?"

A gunshot drew her attention to where C. R. staggered away

from a sprawling Victor Dusault. It didn't matter to Deanna who shot whom, not when she was losing her heart and soul.

With both fists, she struck the unconscious Shep full in the chest—once, twice, three times.

"Shoot, Deanna, you're going to kill him," C. R. said. She could see his feet in front of her but couldn't make out what he was saying, the sirens ringing in her ears.

"What do you know?" she shrieked at him. Tilting Shep's head back like she'd seen on medical shows, she pinched his nose and inhaled.

"Look, I gotta leave."

"So go!" Deanna inhaled again. Beneath her knees the ground shook with rolling thunder. *God, I hope that's You coming to help*.

As she started to share her breath with Shep, it was stolen by the bizarre Wild West scenario unfolding domino fashion in the street. Either she was hallucinating or maybe she had been shot after all and this was either a neurological phenomenon or a parting glance at what she left behind.

By magic, the red stallion of Shep's dreams materialized out of thin air with a hair-raising whinny. It bolted, mane and tail unfurled, as it had been the first time she'd seen it, toward a shock-riveted clown. His feet appeared to be set into motion by the pistol that fell to the dirt from his hand. With an abrupt pivot, the bozo ran over Dusault, who struggled to his feet, one hand clutched to his abdomen. Both men sprawled before the magnificent horse.

Its coppery coat glowing surreal in the fiery blaze of the setting sun, the stallion leaped over them and raced before an Ozlike wind down the street and out of the proverbial Dodge. The dust swirled and kicked up in its wake sounded like the beating of a thousand pairs of angel wings. An aged figure emerged from the open door of the barn in worn Levis and flannel, not a white robe. A rifle rested over his arm instead of an avenging sword. Instead

of taking over with a powerful voice of omniscience, the slight figure cackled, shattering Deanna's shell shock.

"If that ain't a pair of wallerin' snakes, I'll quit. It took old
Charlie long enough," Ticker grunted, nodding at the line of
police cars driving single file up the street, sirens and lights flashing. Two ambulances rolled around from the backside of the
town, stopping in the yard. People in uniform scattered with a
purpose to the wounded.

It wasn't a heavenly vision after all, but it was heaven sent.

"You all right, Shep?"

Or was it? Dreading to look and more afraid not to, Deanna
glanced down to see brown eyes, beautiful, beautiful brown eyes,
looking up at her.

"You pack quite a wallop, Slick."

And those lips, now tugging in a grin that made her toenails
curl. Just inches from hers, they broke the chain of fear that held
her body in a relentless grip. But she'd seen him get hit. She saw
the bullets plowing into his chest. His shirt was ripped and...

Hard and bloodless.

"Bulletproof vest," Shep explained, hopping to his feet.
"Knocked the wind out of me, and I cracked my head on the
wood, but I'll take bruises over bullets any day."

Reluctant to let Shep out of her sight, Deanna stuck to his side
until the last of the police cars and the ambulance with the body
bags pulled away. Jay Voorhees was on his way to a trauma center by helicopter. Much to Deanna's relief, Jon Kessler, thanks to
another bulletproof vest, accompanied him with bruises and a
nonfatal head injury where a bullet grazed his skull.

Dusault and C. R. traveled by ambulance to Taylorville
Medical Center in police custody, where the crime boss was to
have two slugs removed. Not only had C. R. shot him in the
stomach during the struggle, but the shot that went off when
Deanna yanked the gun free of her trousers came close to making the man a soprano. As for Agent Gretsky, he was about to

enjoy the hospitality of the Taylorville jail.

In his glory, Ticker Deerfield regaled Charlie Long and Sheriff Barrett with the whole tale, starting with how he'd corralled the renegade Romeo that afternoon, shutting the stallion up before he could get away. Then things started happening so fast, he didn't have time to tell Shep about it.

"I was runnin' around like a skunked hound suitin' up in this fancy vest and gatherin' my guns. Like as not, I'll not sleep a wink for a month."

Deanna thought the same thing as she rubbed liniment on Shep's ribs later. For her sake, he insisted they stay over at Esther Lawson's bed-and-breakfast until the house was cleaned up. After showing them to their respective rooms, Esther went downstairs to call Maisy with the latest tidbits she'd gleaned from her guests. Drifting up in the breaks of her conversation, a hall radio played oldies but goodies.

When Deanna finished, Shep picked up the discarded vest that had saved his life and laid it on a chair.

"God is enough, but," he stipulated with a wince, "the Good Book also said there's no need to tempt Him."

God couldn't get enough credit for what she felt, nor was she ashamed of the joy and gratitude that had glazed her eyes and made her chin tremble all evening. Shep caught one of the sparkling tears with a kiss, just as he had every chance he'd gotten since they left Hopewell.

The bits and pieces of the incident replayed in Deanna's mind. The bloodshed and grim reality of a world she'd never seen except on TV, drove home again and again just how close she had been to losing Shep.

"You sure you're not hurt?" He'd asked her the same thing dozens of times, as if to convince himself that it was all over, that she was safe, and to convince her that she was the most important thing in his life.

Deanna shook her head. "Nah, it's just a joy leak." In the arms of her Shepard, she was light enough to float, ready to step out on the proverbial water of life at his side, no matter the storms that lay ahead.

"I'm not afraid anymore." She pressed her cheek to Shep's chest. "The bad guys can tie me to a railroad track and I'd just laugh."

Shep shook her with his chuckle. "What if they turned on the buzzsaw?" he asked in a sinister tone.

"I'd yawn."

"And what if they li..it," he drew out the word in a dastardly laugh, "the fuse to the *dyn...omite*?" He swung her around in his arms, almost dropping her as his injuries reminded him of his condition.

Deanna dropped instead onto an overstuffed ottoman done in the same material as the drapes and chair, giggling, "I'd sing 'Happy Birthday to Me.'"

"That's not what I want to hear." With a scowl, Shep reached for his hat. "Guess again."

Enchanted by his half-boy, all-man mischief, Deanna pretended to think. "'My Hope Is Built on Nothing Less?'"

He set the beat-up Stetson on his head. "Try again."

"'Rag Time Cowboy Joe?'"

Growling, Shep drew her to her feet and put his hands at her waist. "I'm only going to teach you this once."

"Just once?"

"Just once." He cleared his throat and pressed his forehead to hers, knocking his hat back. "And then…"

Deanna swayed to the left, following his lead.

"'And then…'" he said, voice going up a few notches. He swung her to the right and, moving up another octave, he squeaked out, "'And then…'"

The space between them vanished. Pressed against him, Deanna felt his deep-throated chuckle, the warmth of his breath upon her cheek. "'And then…'" Shep dipped her backward. As he pulled her back up, he launched into a soulful rendition of the chorus. "'Along came Jo-o-ones.'"

The wacky lyrics were enough to make a grown woman swoon; Shep's clumsy dance around the furniture-crowded room enough to shame the most romantic Viennese waltz. And that hat... Well, what could a gal say? It was a crowning touch.

Epilogue

I declare, I think our church bell sounds even clearer with our new roof!"

Esther Lawson counted off twelve strikes and, with her characteristic schoolmarm nod of approval, resumed her last minute check of the table decorations in the community hall. The ladies circle had turned the homey but nondescript decor into an extravaganza of wedding bells, doves, blue-and-silver ribbons, and coordinating plates, napkins, and table linens.

Shep and Deanna had planned to elope to Las Vegas, while the house was being remodeled and rewired to accommodate twenty-first century life, including a phone, fax, and internet for Deanna to work out of the house.

The church ladies would not hear of it. Deanna had no immediate family? Just what did she think they were? She would have a decent church wedding, just like her mother would have wanted for her, not some drive-through paper-signing with the price tag hanging over the door.

Deanna teared up every time she thought about the love and acceptance of the little community. She'd once thought it the backside of the world, but she couldn't have been more wrong. Buffalo Butte was the heart of the world. Before she knew it, the wedding was planned and all but a done deal. Four weeks had flown by. Shep moved back to the ranch so that Esther's second bedroom could be filled with shower gifts from *sisters* she hadn't even met.

Caught in a whirlwind of plans and activities, Deanna discovered the slower pace her city friends used to joke about was a choice. When the chips were down, these folks made Wall Street look tame.

Hands damp with perspiration, she wiped them on a tea towel rather than risk ruining the beautiful brocade of her wedding dress. It and the veil of Spanish lace had belonged to Maisy's grandmother. "I wore it forty pounds ago," the diner owner told Deanna as she removed the special bag it had been preserved in. "Last time I ever dressed up," she reflected with an unladylike snort of humor. "Been wearin' an apron ever since, so that just goes to show ya, don't it?"

Seeing Deanna had no clue what she was getting at, unless she was trying to discourage the bride, Maisy explained. "Love is love, no matter how you dress it up or down. In fact, I might even love my Chuck more since I took up the apron than I did when I wore that dress."

"More blue flowers!" The minister's wife hurried in with a large white box. "Juanita is putting the carnations on the men. Praise the Lord, they're white with just a smidgeon of blue."

The church ladies insisted the groom have some say in the wedding plans, even though he deferred without exception to whatever Deanna wanted. Trapped at the shower by a passel of mother hens, Shep picked the color blue, "To match Deanna's eyes."

Deanna thought Juanita Everett would swoon then and there in the hall kitchen, but the mayor's wife was made of sterner stuff. The president of the flower club, which she named the Buffalo Butte Bouquettes, managed to find more blue flowers than Deanna ever knew existed. And if they weren't blue, she spray-painted them.

"Oh my," Ruth said in a something-isn't-quite-right voice after opening the box and pulling back the tissue.

"Hey, Slick, is everything a go in here?" Shep called through the door.

The ladies set upon the groom the instant he walked in.

"Shepard," Esther chided in a tone that had kept children in their places for years. "It's bad luck to see the bride before the wedding."

"Now how am I going to cart her down the aisle without seeing her?"

With no one from her family to give her away, they'd decided to break with tradition. Shep was going to usher Deanna down the aisle and the entire congregation would answer "I do" when the time came to give her away.

Shep smiled over Esther's and Maisy's heads at Deanna.

"Besides, ladies, if that's bad luck, I can't imagine what good is."

Neither could Deanna. She'd heard of love light in songs and always thought it was some silly metaphor...until now. Deanna basked in it, her body tingling in its warm glow. It just didn't get any better than this.

"Well, just in case..." Maisy emptied salt from a nearby table and tossed it over Shep's shoulder.

"Maisy," Esther huffed, brushing it off his shoulders. "You'll mess up his tux."

His shoulders looked half again as wide, pronouncing the taper to his trim waist and hips.

"It's the man that makes the tux, not the other way around," Maisy argued. "It'd take more'n salt to mess up a handsome dude like Shep."

His embarrassed grin faded as Ruth pulled out the wedding bouquet. "You're not going to carry that, are you?"

No more impressed than Shep, the minister's wife just stared in disbelief at the massive collection of blue flowers.

"I've seen smaller sprays on casket lids!"

"The mayor's wife said she wanted something different just for me. They came all the way from Hawaii." Deanna felt compelled to come to Juanita's defense. "Anthuriums, I think she said. She had to keep them overnight in the bathtub."

Shep scowled. "They look obscene to me."

"They're used in large arrangements," Esther informed them, dubious as she fingered the large waxy petal that made up the flower. "But I've never seen them in blue."

Maisy snorted. "Anything that's stood still long enough for Juanita to fetch her can of paint is blue. She ain't been right since she got back from those islands."

"What are we going to do?" Ruth asked.

"Thoughtfulness is thoughtfulness, no matter how you dress it up or down," Deanna paraphrased Maisy. "*I'm* going to carry the bouquet down the aisle." She looked at her husband-to-be. "Unless you object."

"That's one of the reasons I love you, Deanna Rose Manetti." Shep leaned through the barrier of ladies and kissed Deanna on the cheek.

One more blast of that love light and she'd be too weak to carry it.

"Oh my goodness, look at the time," Ruth Lawrence exclaimed. "I have to start playing the organ."

She brushed past Shep in a rush.

Esther and Maisy gave the hall one last perusal and then turned to Deanna.

"You're pretty as a picture," Esther said, bussing Deanna on the cheek. "I'm going to miss my favorite boarder."

Maisy stepped up and gave Deanna a bear hug. "Just strut right up that aisle with that hunk of man on your arm and remind us all what love is."

Deanna groaned as a tear slipped out the corner of her eye. "Aw, sheesh, there go the waterworks again."

With the flourish of a magician, Shep produced a handkerchief. "Not waterworks," he corrected. "Joy leaks."

Maisy and Esther exchanged smiles and slipped out of the hall as he dabbed Deanna's cheek with a tender touch.

"Everybody has been so nice. I m—mean, I have as much family here as I had in Brooklyn with Pop's Italians and Mama's clan." She sniffed. "I'm drowning in love here. My m-makeup's gonna run, and it'll look like you're marrying a raccoon."

"I love raccoons with those little black rings around their eyes."

"Well, *that* really makes me feel better," Deanna wisecracked. "Now I gotta worry about being stuffed and put on the mantel next to Old Bull."

Shep laughed so hard that Deanna had to wipe the *joy leaks* from the corners of his eyes. Reverend Lawrence poked his head in to see the two of them sharing tears, laughs, and a wet handkerchief.

"Are you two ready? Mr. Deerfield said, and I quote, 'I'm sweatin' buckets in this here monkey suit.'"

"Ready, able, and willing." Grinning, Shep folded the handkerchief in his left pocket so that Deanna could reach it. "Do you think you can get through this without cracking me up?" He folded her hand over his arm.

Her knight in denim. Her best friend. Her hero. Her love light. When all was lost, he found her. When she was sinking, he lifted her up so that she could see.

"Only if the reverend adds 'excluding taxidermy' after the 'for better or worse' part."

"Never mind," Shep said, at Reverend Lawrence's bewildered look. "We'll just take our chances and jump in feet first."

As Shep escorted Deanna across the small parking lot, the steeple of the church gleamed white, a beacon of unity in one God afloat in an endless stretch of Montana sky. It drew her back into the church family and to the man with whom she would soon be one, in faith, hope, and love. Spirit dancing to the time-tried herald of the organ, she stepped over the threshold of her future with the Shepard God had sent her.

Walking with her husband-to-be down the aisle through a sea of familiar, loving faces, Deanna's heart sang what her emotion-choked voice could not. *Look at me, God. I'm stepping out on the water.*

Dear Reader,

Along Came Jones reaches beyond the heart and funny bone, not just to entertain, but also to illustrate how God's Word speaks to every person's doubts and struggles. In my years of affliction with chemical/biological depression, I have personally faced both Deanna's and Shep's dilemmas—feeling abandoned by God and reluctant to offer help to another depressed soul in need when I was barely recovered myself. Through these experiences, I've learned that things of this world—depression and dire circumstances—are temporal, while those of God—like His love and grace—are everlasting.

By that grace, I found the hope, the direction, and the strength to meet these challenges head on in God's Word, just as my characters did within these pages. With that hope in mind for others in similar situations, I've prepared a few questions, to be used for either personal reflection or group discussion, in the hope that you will be uplifted and reassured by the power of everlasting love and grace in God's Word.

Blessings always,

Linda Windsor

Questions for Reflection or Discussion

1. Have you ever felt like Deanna—desperate with no one to turn to, abandoned even by God? Describe how you felt then. Read Job 7:1–11 and Psalm 22:1–2. How was your sense of despair like that of Job and David?

2. Has stress or depression in a moment of desperation made you feel at odds with what you knew to be true, just as it did for Deanna? Consider David's cry in Psalm 22:3–11. Read Matthew 5:38–45 and think about how our feelings and natural impulses often conflict with God's way of doing things.

3. What roadblocks sustained Deanna's sense of hopelessness and caused her to maintain her distance from Shep—and from God and His love? Think of a time when you created obstacles that kept you from becoming close with someone you cared for. Read Psalm 127:1–2, Proverbs 3:7 and 28:26. What does the Bible say about trusting in our own wisdom?

4. Read Romans 5:8, Ephesians 2:5, and 1 John 1:9. How do Shep's efforts to reach out to Deanna reflect God's attempts to reach out to us?

5. Read Psalm 27, a favorite of mine in times of despair. Name some of the tangible and spiritual means of reassurance and comfort Deanna received throughout the story. Can you now offer comfort and encouragement to someone in your life who is suffering from the same feelings?

6. Read Matthew 25:35–40 and then Philippians 4:13. What personal reservations and doubts did Shep have regarding

helping Deanna? Think of a time when you were reluctant to help someone in need. Why were you reticent, and what did you finally do?

7. Read Psalm 18:33 and 63:1. For Deanna, is the wilderness a refuge or a danger? What example does Shep, as a hunter, use to explain his point of view on this? How does the wilderness work as a metaphor in the story?

8. Why is Shep so reluctant to help Jay Voorhees and the authorities? Read Matthew 18:21–35. Have you ever had to accept or work with someone who has betrayed or hurt you? How did you handle it? Have you really forgiven him or her?

9. Stories of obstacles in relationships may present solutions of the heart (romantic) and/or solutions of the soul (spiritual). What are the similarities between the two? What are the differences?

10. Of the bonds between man and woman, which one or which combination do you think is the most lasting: mutual physical attraction, social attraction, or spiritual oneness (closeness to God)? Why?

Multnomah Publishers®

The publisher and author would love to hear your comments about this book. *Please contact us at:*
www.multnomah.net/alongcame

> ## "LINDA WINDSOR NEVER FAILS TO DELIVER AN INSIGHTFUL, WONDERFULLY FUNNY STORY!"
> —**Lori Copeland,** author of *The Island of Heavenly Daze*

It Had to Be You

Dan Jarrett thinks shipboard romances are shams until he's forced into a family cruise and meets a nurse with a penchant for disaster—and a heart big enough for them both.

ISBN 1-57673-765-9

Not Exactly Eden

Returning a mysterious wedding gift leads a disillusioned socialite on a healing journey to a father she's never known and unexpected love in a savage jungle paradise.

ISBN 1-57673-445-5

Hi Honey, I'm Home

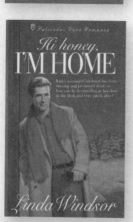

Kate finds herself face-to-face with her supposedly deceased husband! An obsessive journalist, Nick was reportedly killed in a terrorist attack five years ago, but there he stands, ready to take up where they left off. Well, she's not interested, but Nick and their precocious boys are determined to prove to her that God has truly changed Nick's heart.

ISBN 1-57673-556-7

The Fires of Gleannmara series

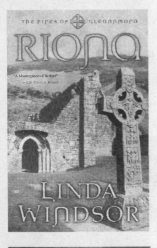

Maire ~ BOOK ONE

A romantic tale of passion and faith that invites readers to the "God-graced mountains and plains" of Ireland. Maire, Gleannmara's warrior queen, finds her fierce heart is gentled when she takes a reformed mercenary—a Christian, no less—as hostage during a raid. At first she wonders what kind of God would make a fine warrior like Rowan of Emerys such a coward. But as she comes to know Rowan and witnesses the force of his beliefs, she learns that meekness and humility to the one true God are stronger than any blade of steel. And in the process, Maire discovers the transforming power of love and faith.

ISBN 1-57673-625-3

Riona ~ BOOK TWO

Riona, a gentlewoman of faith, discovers that her plan to help the disadvantaged includes not only the plague orphans in her charge, but the arrogant, handsome adventurer who feels honor-bound to save her and her lands by marrying her—with or without her consent. Lord Kieran of Gleannmara depends on nothing and no one save his wit and skill with steel, but soon a deadly twist of fate forces him to acknowledge his need not only for the lady Riona and her worrisome entourage, but for her Lord as well.

ISBN 1-57673-752-7

Deirdre ~ BOOK THREE

A Saxon pirate prince, loyal to neither God nor country, is skeptical of his Christian mother's predictions about his birthright...until he captures a devout princess with the key to both heavenly and earthly kingdoms. What his mother said about his true birthright seems possible after all, even when his newfound faith is battered by storms of betrayal that wash him and his half-drowned bride upon the seaswept shores of Gleannmara. Deirdre, the third heroine in the Fires of Gleannmara series, is an Irish princess wed to a heathen thief. Although she is a reluctant heroine, compassion becomes her shield, prayer her sword, and God's Word her direction.

ISBN 1-57673-891-4

www.letstalkfiction.com

Let's Talk Fiction is a free, four-color mini-magazine created to give readers a "behind the scenes" look at Multnomah Publishers' favorite fiction authors. *Let's Talk Fiction* allows our authors to share a bit about themselves, giving readers an inside peek into their latest releases. Published in the fall, spring, and summer seasons, *Let's Talk Fiction* is filled with interactive contests, author contact information, and fun! To receive your free copy of *Let's Talk Fiction* get on-line at www.letstalkfiction.com. We'd love to hear from you!